Abandoned

Jeanette McCarthy

British Library Cataloguing-in-Publication Data:
A catalogue record for this book is available from
The British Library

All the characters in this book are fictitious, and any resemblance to actual persons living or dead is purely coincidental

Cover design by *www.briarcal.com*

ISBN: 978-0-9556911-0-2

Acknowledgements

I am deeply grateful to the following people:

John Craggs and Nadine Laman for their honest criticism, unstinting help, advice and encouragement

Tim Dunkley, ace reporter!

DI Martyn Ball of Leicestershire Constabulary and DC Stephen Beattie (retired) for giving me their time, detailed help, and friendly advice on police matters.

Andy at www.ptsd.org.uk for his moving and thought-provoking website, and his compassion and commitment to helping those suffering from PTSD

This is for Jed, Seth, Briar, Cahal and Tife
without whom…

then - in my childhood, in the dawn
of a most stormy life - was drawn
from every depth of good and ill
the mystery which binds me still

Edgar Allan Poe, *Alone*

Prologue

When Tess woke up on the first day, she was so cold she thought the bedroom window must be broken. She reached for the covers, blearily opening her eyes when she didn't find them. She should have been looking at the ceiling, but someone had taken it away in the night.

She sat up quickly, and a wave of nausea brought the contents of her stomach hurtling for the outside world. When at last the spasms passed, she stumbled to her feet, panic driving tears into her eyes.
She was in a wood of young trees. The ozone smell of the sea was sharp in the air, the sound of the waves barely discernable over the thudding of her heart. A thin drizzle began to fall. She had no idea where she was.

Mike, she thought.

She'd thought at the time that he'd taken it well. He stood on the doorstep as they exchanged the CDs and books each had borrowed, giving back the little pieces of themselves that they'd shared for a time. She'd asked him in, just to be polite.

No.

If she was honest, and she may as well be now, she asked him in because she was too pathetic to tell him to leave. That was the story of her life.

On that first day, Tess stood and looked around at the hard, unknown landscape, crying like a lost child, fear sizzling in her veins. She pushed freezing fingers into the pocket of her jeans and found a scrap of paper there. As she read it, dread closed a fist round her heart, and she fell to her knees, the hacking sobs making it hard to draw breath. The words on the paper smeared in the rain and ran together like hieroglyphics. It didn't matter, because she wasn't going to forget those words for a long time.

You said you could look after yourself, they said.
Go ahead and try.

ONE

December 1989

'Lewis, this tea is shite.'

Lewis grinned as if this was the greatest compliment. And what a grin it was. He had a mouth that seemed to fill up half his young face, and teeth that seemed far too many even for such a mouth. 'I thought you liked my brew,' he said.

'Donno's right,' Billy said. 'It's fucking crap. Tastes like nothing.'

'Anyone want any more?' Lewis said, picking up the bivvy tin.

Mike held out his cup. 'I'll have some.'

Donno and Billy laughed, and the sound echoed, breaking the silence of the woods. Donno pulled out his tobacco pouch and began to roll up a cigarette.

Billy pushed a stick into the fire. 'This is such a doddle,' he said. 'How many times have we done this now?'

'Five,' Donno said, drinking his so-called tea.

Lewis picked at a ripe spot on his chin. 'This island's new, though.'

'Yeah, it's bigger. There might even be deer.'

'Yeah, Donno, like you're going to kill a deer.' Billy sniggered.

'I never mentioned anything about *killing* one,' Donno said, his voice hesitant. 'I've never even seen a deer.'

No one replied. None of them had.

'Well, anyway,' Billy went on, wrapping his jacket around him against the December cold. 'Survival training? It's a fucking doddle.'

'You're complaining?' Lewis said. 'Like, you joined the army to get shot at, rather than sit around with your mates drinking tea?'

'Think I'd rather get shot at than drink *this* tea,' Donno said.

Mike grinned, leaning on his kit bag. He was the youngest of the four, although none of them knew it, they thought he was eighteen, same as them.

They fell into a companionable silence, as the woods around them began to fill up with dusk. Their tents had already been set up, but no one was in a hurry to sleep. Donno drew hard on his skinny cigarette, just as a twig snapped in the trees to their left.

All four froze, slowly turning their heads to the source of the sound. This island was uninhabited, or so they had been told. Mike gently released the catch on his belt holster and pulled out a darkened blade. In the silence, another twig snapped, and he heard Billy take a surprised breath.

Through the pale trees, dark shapes moved, lithe and swift and cautious. Billy let his breath out slowly, as they watched the deer move quickly through the birch woods. Even when the animals had long gone, the four friends stayed rooted to the spot, staring silently into the trees.

And then it began to snow.

Mike looked up at the thick flakes drifting through the silence, and knew deep in his soul that this was the happiest moment of his life.

'Did you see their eyes?' Donno whispered, his own eyes gleaming. 'They were huge!'

'I can't believe that just happened. We were just talking about - they weren't fifty feet away!' Billy shook his head, the snowflakes sticking fast to his cropped hair.

Lewis's grin had not moved.

'You know,' he said quietly, looking up at the falling snow, holding out his empty hands to catch the flakes. 'There's nothing like this, is there? I mean, all joking aside and that. This is what it's all about, isn't it? Just us, our wits, and the wild.'

The others looked at him. Normally such a personal admission would have been greeted with derisive hoots and laughter, but not tonight, when the deer and the snow had felt like the work of magic.

'Just us, looking after ourselves. Not needing anyone else.'

Despite his grin, Mike heard the bitterness in Lewis's voice. His friends nodded. None of them were here because they wanted to be. They were here because they didn't want to be somewhere else.

The snow began to pile up around them, but it didn't feel cold.

'I can't wait for tomorrow to go and explore,' Billy said.

Donno grinned. 'Let's see if we can track those deer.'

'Not to kill one-' Billy protested.

'No,' Donno said. 'Not to kill, just to look.'

Mike smiled, pulling up a sprig of heather. He raised it to his face and breathed in the faint woody aroma. The deer had seemed both delicate and perfect, like something from a fairy tale, too wonderful to be real. He looked round at his friends, the only ones he had, and knew that Lewis was right. This was what was important, this and little else.

TWO

Mike shoved his old kit bag hard into the locker. He really didn't need all its contents, not for this job, but he had been taught to expect the unexpected at all times, and once something was learned, it stayed with him like another layer of skin. He could hear the two men behind him whispering, and knew they were talking about him. This didn't bother him. He knew they thought he was different from them, and he was. He was better.

He straightened his tie, gazing at his pale features in the rust-spotted mirror. His thin lips looked lost in the square, clean-shaven jaw. His dark brown hair was close cropped, as it had been for the last twenty-odd years. He leaned forward, looking carefully into his own eyes, as he did every day.

'Hey Mike, you see that Lisa from *Next* this morning? Skirt the size of a belt!'

'Nah, Joe, Mike's into the quiet ones, isn't that right?' said Louie, cracking his knuckles.

Mike turned round and stared into the security guard's eyes. Louie swallowed and looked away, a pink stain invading his cheeks.
Mike's lips widened into a smile that never reached the rest of his face. He walked past his colleagues and into the early morning silence of the mall.

This was not quite the job he had in mind for himself when he left the mob, but it was strangely satisfying. The long hours walking the air conditioned corridors, so mind-numbingly tedious to the other security men, he spent staring intently at the shoppers, picking out potential shoplifters by the way their eyes shifted away from him. The kids were the easiest. He could almost smell their guilt, the thrill-sweat on their skin as they made off with their prizes. The terror in their eyes as they looked up into his made him feel good; in control. He obeyed orders, took the miscreants to the basement where the police were called, although if he had his own way, it would be very different. Oh yes.

He walked along the corridors of the mall, following his daily routine, as the early morning shoppers browsed and bought, ignoring him. He listened to the litany of footfalls on the cool tiles, the mingling of muzak from the various shops, the giggling gossip of the shop girls, more alive now than they would be after a whole day working here. It was comfortable, reassuring.

At exactly six minutes to ten he reached the top of the second floor stairs. Up here in the dim light the shops had a sad, tired feel about them. Not many people bothered to come up here these days, the prime sites were all down below. Mike came as usual to the china shop: *City of Glass*, and here he stopped, looked slowly and carefully around, and checked his intuition for anything untoward in the air. Then he looked into the window at the brightly lit crystal and china, all of it delicate and vulnerable. His particular favourite was a unicorn made of clear glass, its single horn the colour of clear water flowing over pebbles. He knew if he were ever to hold that unicorn, it would break into a million deadly shards. His hands shook at the thought of touching something so fragile, of it belonging to him.

He tore his eyes away from the figure and looked through the window to the counter within, where Tess was gift wrapping a box for an old woman. He watched their lips move as they exchanged pleasantries, Tess, smiling as she always did, a strand of her rich dark hair escaping from its clasp to fall across her pale cheek. He waited until the woman left the shop, then carried out his surveillance again before finally going in.

'Oh, hello Mike,' Tess said, still smiling. She had eyes as gentle and trusting as a doe's. She was the human version of the unicorn, only this one he could hold without breaking.

'Are you coming round tonight?' She asked, looking at him shyly. He loved the way she seemed embarrassed by the suggestion. He smiled, and this time it reached his eyes.

'Sure,' he said. His first word that day.

*

Tess sat at her dining room table, watching Mike eat.

'This is really good,' he said, between mouthfuls. Tess smiled.

'Glad you like it.'

He looked up at her, eyes as fathomless as ever. Even when he smiled, he held most of himself back.

'You wore my favourite dress.'

Tess looked down at her lap, touching the pale blue fabric. She always wore the dress. Wearing anything else wasn't worth the silent disapproval that ensued. She struggled to think of something to say.

'The men came to replace the glass yesterday.'

'Yes, I saw.'

She sighed. Of course he had.

'Mrs Dennis went on for ages about the cost. I don't know why, it must have been covered by insurance.'

A week or so ago, vandals had broken into the mall and thrown concrete rubbish bins at random shop windows. The toughened glass didn't smash, but instead shattered into a huge spider web of light. Tess's boss, who had a permanent padlock on her purse, had been furious.

Mike said nothing, and Tess stifled another sigh.

'So, did you have a quiet day?'

He shrugged. 'I didn't catch anyone stealing.'

'The shoplifters must have all stayed home,' she said with a bright smile.

'I doubt it.'

She turned away from his hard blue eyes, and began to clear the dishes. As she reached for his empty plate, his hand snaked out and touched her arm. She looked at him, and saw he was staring at his own fingers stroking her skin, his mouth open, his eyes now wide and curious, like a child's. As if aware of her gaze, he looked up into her face, and tried a smile. She smiled back, as he stood up and put his arms around her.

He was always gentle, but she never felt reassured. She knew he would never hurt her, but there were worse things. Every morning Tess looked at her thirty-one year old face and told herself it was time to move on, and every night she went to bed without having had the guts to do it.

She took his hand and they walked upstairs to her bedroom, where he banished the colony of teddy bears from her bed with one sweep of his arm. She lay down, pulling him with her, kissing him and reaching under his T shirt to touch his skin. He sighed, his fingers reaching to pull up the dress. For a moment she thought he was going to tear it, and an excited thrill ran through her, but instead, he let it go, and left her alone while he took off his own clothes. She sighed, doing the same. In the dark, she felt him come inside her, and heard him gasp as if he had never done this before. It was all over very quickly, and she lay there afterwards, looking at the streetlight outside, listening to his breathing becoming regular again.

'You are wonderful,' he whispered, after she had thought he was asleep. The words filled her with dread.

'Mike?' She leaned on her elbow, facing him. When he looked at her, she hesitated, but in the dim light, she couldn't see his eyes, and that gave her strength.

'Have you had many girlfriends?'

There was a long silence. 'Why are you asking me that?'

'I don't know. I just wondered. We don't know very much about each other, you know.'

He moved away from her.

'I know you were in the army, but that's all-'

'You don't want to know more about me,' he said. He reached for her hand and squeezed it so tightly she winced.

*

Next day, Tess woke up to find Mike had left early, as he always did. She replaced her soft toys on her bed, feeling bad about herself. She should have told him she wanted to finish it. As usual, whenever the moment came, she chickened out.

It wasn't that he was crazy, just a bit strange. She assumed being so long in the army had caused that, but if he wouldn't talk about the past, how could she understand? All he had ever mentioned were some of his training expeditions, gangs of young soldiers on Scottish islands learning survival skills. Nothing about war, although she knew he had been involved. She wondered absently if he had killed people. The thought excited her, and that itself made her startle with guilt. Something had happened to him, something bad, to make him as obsessed with her as he was. But she couldn't cope with it, she had to leave him. She had promised herself that she would tell him after New Year, but now here they were in February. Come the weekend, she told herself, looking at her reflection in the mirror. She was definitely going to do it. Definitely.

THREE

Cal Fisher couldn't sleep. He lay tossing and turning for a while, before giving in and getting up, walking into the kitchen in his T shirt and boxers, and heading for the cupboard. He poured himself a neat black label vodka, and took a sip of the clear liquid. It burned pleasantly in his throat, and he carried it through to the living room, where he slumped on the sofa and stared blankly at the dead TV.

Another sleepless night. What was the matter with him?

It wasn't the job. Hell, that was the only thing keeping him sane, the only thing that mattered. Cal had been a policeman for twenty years, and he was still only thirty eight. He could retire soon, as if. He knew he was obsessive and pedantic, but he preferred to think of it as *passionate*. That's what his mother had always called him.

A sharp spike of guilt made him sigh. He rolled the glass between his hands, warming the alcohol, as if that might make it go down easier. Mother didn't know his name, most days, but on those times she did, her eyes were filled with disappointment and regret.

Cal finished the vodka and lay back on the settee, gazing out of the wide windows at the dark city sky. His flat was on the top floor of a converted factory. He had a great view of streetlights, abandoned lots and the murky canal. Leicester wasn't the prettiest town in the world, but it was still home.

Maybe if he and Lynne had made it through things would have been different. But she was long gone, and never coming back. Thinking about his ex-wife brought on the familiar dull ache in his chest. He glanced at his reflection in the mirror over the fireplace. In the dim light from the kitchen, he looked as cold as stone, pretty much how he felt. Brown eyes, crooked nose, light brown hair heading gradually for the hills. The sort of face that wouldn't merit a second glance. Not from a woman, anyway. Hell, was that it, was he just lonely?

Thirty eight years old, he thought gloomily. Sitting here feeling sorry for myself.

He took the glass back to the kitchen and dumped it in the sink before wandering back to bed. Things were pretty quiet at work at the moment. He was sure that if they heated up a little, he'd sleep all right.

But not tonight, he thought sadly. Not tonight.

*

When Tess got home from work that night, there was a car in her parking place, and she sighed as she recognised it. She wiped at her tired eyes. Mother. Just what she needed.

'Is that you, Tessa?'

Who else would it be, she thought, dumping her bag on the kitchen table and walking through to the living room.

'You know, you ought to get these windows sorted. They're in a terrible state.'

Tess tried to smile. Her mother was peering at the windowsill, her blonde hair tightly fastened in a tortoiseshell clasp. She looked round.

'You should get them done now. The weather will be turning warmer soon. It'll be cheaper.'

'Yes mum. Do you want tea?'

'No, dear, you know I don't drink tea. Well, how are things?'

Tess sat on the sofa, picking up a velvet cushion and absently toying with the fringes.

'Fine, mum. You look nice tonight.'

Sheila Harrison smoothed her pencil skirt, her eyes fixed on her daughter. 'I'm on my way to bridge with Gilly and Rich. Just thought I'd pop in and see you-' she hesitated.

'So are you still seeing the weirdo?'

Tess sighed. 'Mum, he's not weird, just quiet.'

'Oh right. You know nothing about him, he never smiles or laughs, follows you round like a lost puppy, turning up when you least expect him, and that's not weird? Listen Tess, you'd do better just to get rid-'

Tess stood up, heading for the kitchen. The last thing she wanted to do was discuss Mike with her mother. She eyed the open bottle of wine on the windowsill, but hearing Sheila's footsteps, she filled the kettle instead.

Tess felt her mother standing behind her like a thundercloud about to strike. *Naff off and leave me alone!* Biting her lip, she busied herself with tea bags and milk.

'Have you thought any more about that job over at Taylor's?'

Tess concentrated hard on the bottom of her empty mug.

'You know Rich said he'd be happy to put in a word for you, and you'd have great prospects there. You could be managerial staff in no time.'

'Mum, I'm happy with the job I've got.'

'What, a shop girl? And look what than that old skinflint pays you. Look Tess, you're a clever girl. You can do much better. I hate to see you settling for second best.'

Tess turned round, looking at her mother in her ivory jacket and skirt, her perfect apricot silk blouse; better clothes than she herself

18

owned, and Sheila was only going to a bridge game. She didn't look at her own flouncy skirt and embroidered blouse. That would only draw attention to them, and Sheila would no doubt find some comment to make about her 'hippy' clothes. Second best. Was that what she was doing? She glanced again at the wine bottle, and this time her mother saw her and picked it up.

'Sauvignon,' she said, peering at the label. 'I prefer Chardonnay, myself. I hope you're not sitting here by yourself at night drinking, my girl.'

Tess shrugged, pouring hot water into the mug. 'It's nice sometimes to have a glass of wine when I come home from work.'

There was a lecture brewing, she could almost taste it. What time was the damn bridge match? Why couldn't she just go. In the awkward silence, Tess heard something scraping at the lock, and turned in time to see Mike opening the door. She let out a gasp, her mouth falling open.

'Mike!'

Mike looked from Tess to Sheila, his eyes carefully blank.

'You gave me a start,' Tess said, trying to sound light hearted. Her heart was pounding with panic. She had not given Mike a key, but there was no way she was going to have a scene in front of Sheila. Her mother's lips had pulled into the usual thin disapproving line.

'You have company,' Mike said quietly. 'Sorry. I'll leave you to it. See you tomorrow.'

Tess began to say thanks, but the door had already closed behind him. Sheila looked at Tess, her face hard. Tess waited gloomily for the tirade.

'Well. I hope you know what you're doing,' Sheila said, picking up her handbag.

'Oh mother, don't go off in a huff.'

Sheila gave her an angry look. 'As if I would! I must go or I'll be late, that's all.'

Tess walked her to the door, reluctant now for her to leave. She was sure Mike was simply waiting somewhere close, hoping she would go so he could come round.

'I saw dad at the weekend,' she said, desperate for something to say. Sheila looked at her, uninterested. 'Oh yes? What did he have to say for himself?'

'He's got a new job. Not plumbing any more, it's contract management.'

'At his age? Well good luck to him. Pity he didn't sort his life out long ago, when it mattered.'

Tess winced. Of course, it had been a mistake to bring up the subject of her father.

'Goodbye, love. And please, think about the job at Taylor's, will you?'

Tess nodded as her mother kissed her on the cheek. *Not a chance.* When Sheila left, she put the catch on the door and went to the kitchen, pouring herself a large glass of wine. How on earth had Mike got hold of her key? He must have taken hers out of her bag at the shop. Her heart pounding, she finally felt galvanised into telling him it was over. She gulped the wine, not daring to look out in case she saw him. She went upstairs and turned on the bathroom light, in the hope he'd think she was running a bath. Tess was scared now, but whether of Mike or of the inevitable confrontation, she didn't know.

*

Mike spent most of the night crouched in the ornamental shrubs surrounding the turning circle. He was good at staying still for long periods, after all, he'd had plenty of experience. He watched as the hard-faced woman left and the bathroom light clicked on. He toyed with the idea of going in and surprising Tess in the bath. The thought of her shy embarrassment at his intrusion filled him with the familiar emotion; a mixture of raw sadness and desperate love. The emotion suffused his whole body, making his muscles weak and his vision blurred. It didn't come to him often, but when it did, he was helpless. Now he crouched, the ache in his leg muscles nicely balanced by those wonderful feelings. He didn't want to move and lose them.

After a while he stretched out first one leg, then the other, flexing each muscle to bring the oxygen back. He watched cars come and go, Tess's neighbour getting off the bus and walking into the close. She'd had a drink, he could smell it, and she dropped her keys twice as she tried to work the lock, giggling to herself. He turned away, revolted.

He waited until he saw the bedroom light go off, and then he stood up. Perhaps he would surprise her now, slip upstairs and put his arms around her gently, and she would turn to him and sigh.

He padded over to the door, removing the Yale key from his pocket and slipping it soundlessly in the lock. It turned, but the door didn't open, and he realised she had bolted the door. He felt heat rush to his face. He hadn't expected this. How dare she lock him out! He padded back to his bushes, crouching down again to think.

Orange lights were flashing at the back of his eyes. He shut them tightly, taking deep breaths.

He had told her he would see her tomorrow, after all. And didn't all decent girls lock their doors at night? He began to relax. The simple explanation was obviously the right one. His heart began to slow down.

He checked his watch and saw that it was after midnight, but he wasn't ready to go just yet. He sat carefully in the leaf mould, imagining Tess in her bed dressed in her pink nightie with her soft toys on the pillow, her slippers shaped like hedgehogs, the walls covered with her prints of dolphins and flowers. She was as soft and gentle as a summer breeze. He closed his eyes. He couldn't get enough of her.

Eventually he dozed. He dreamed.

The door slammed with a dull thud, and the only light then came from the strip at the base, beyond which he could hear the radio playing, and a man's low laughter. It was the sort of laughter he recognised well, laughter that wasn't really funny, it meant something else, something he didn't fully understand. He crouched in his cupboard and listened until the only sound was the radio. He listened out for Sandy, but she knew better now than to make a sound. After a while the laughter started up again, and then he heard his name mentioned. They were coming for him, and his heart began to pound in terror. He cringed into the back of the cupboard, trying to hide behind the clothes hung there, smelling the familiar cheap perfume scent of his mother. Any second now the door would open and they would drag him out, and he would cry, but it wouldn't matter. No one would listen. The footsteps were coming closer, and suddenly the door opened and the light was blinding. Mike woke with a gasp, eyes wide, heart smacking at the walls of his chest as the car circled in front of the bushes and drove off.

He took deep breaths, just as he'd been taught to do, and after a long while, the dream receded. He crept out quietly and walked home.

FOUR

Tess was in the shower the next morning when the telephone rang. She rushed from the bathroom, dripping wet, catching it just as the ringing stopped. 'Bugger,' she hissed, as the drips from her soaking hair turned the pink carpet dark as blood. It looked horrible, and she hurriedly wrapped the towel round her hair before dialling 1471 and getting her father's number. She sat on the bed. Dad was sure to want to go out somewhere, and she wasn't in the mood, but nevertheless she dialled the number and waited for Roy Hardy to answer.

'Hello dad.'

'Hello sweetheart. Did I get you out of the shower?'

'Yes.'

He laughed. 'I'm sorry. I have a talent for that, don't I? Are you all right, love?'

'Yes, I'm fine. Are you?'

'Yes, love, you know me.'

The conversation was virtually identical every time. It made Tess smile.

'So do you fancy coming out for a drink with an old man?'

'Of course. And you're not old. Where do you want to go?'

Roy chuckled. 'Anywhere you like.'

'You decide,' Tess said, as firmly as she could. Dad could be worse than her. 'I'll meet you at the usual place. Seven o'clock.'

As she sat ironing her wavy hair straight, she decided that tonight it would be The Highcross. They'd not been there for a while, and Tess had inherited Roy's thought processes. She smiled to herself. At least the food was good.

*

Lights were going on all over the mall as Tess opened the front door of the shop. She caught sight of a few early shoppers hanging around with their children, waiting for opening time. Down on the ground floor, there was Mike, pacing slowly in his dark blue suit, like a shark in a paddling pool. Tess shivered. Something was going to have to be said about the key, but her heart began to race at the thought of the confrontation. She went back behind her counter.

It was a quiet day, and she had plenty of time to daydream. Tess had watched a Harrison Ford film the previous weekend, about a man and woman stranded on a Caribbean island. They had started off hating each other, but it inevitably turned out all right in the end. She was still imagining living beside the perfect beach, the sun in her hair, when there was a loud rap on the counter.

She jumped, startled. Mike looked torn between embarrassment and annoyance.

'You were miles away,' he said.

'I was,' she agreed, smiling uneasily. 'Are you all right?'

'Yes.'

The shop was empty, and she prayed for a few customers, just for some vestige of moral support. It was now or never. She took a deep breath.

'Mike, how did you get my door key?'

There it was out. She smiled, to ease the accusation in her voice.

'You gave it to me,' he said, staring calmly at her. 'Don't you remember?'

Did I? She thought, panic arriving. She didn't remember giving him a key, but she was so scatty. Could she have given him the key and forgotten?

No. She couldn't. She knew she hadn't given him the key.

'No,' she shook her head, 'I don't.'

'Well, you did. How else would I have got it?'

She looked up, but his eyes were as cold and relentless as ever. When he looked like that, his lips seemed to disappear into his face, making his jaw seem like an immovable mass. Her heart was racing, making her light-headed.

'Oh well, if I did, I did,' she said lightly, as if it were nothing.

'You can have it back, if you want.'

Now was the time. She should tell him the truth, get the key back, call it a day.

But, in a sudden moment of terrible clarity, she saw that there was no point in getting the key back. He probably had another one somewhere. And if she told him she no longer wanted to see him, he was not going to simply shake hands and say goodbye.

She smiled as brightly as she could. 'No, no. It's all right.'

At long last a customer came into the shop, and Tess let out a breath she didn't know she had been holding.

'Can I come over and see you tonight?' Mike asked, the small smile back on his face.

'Not tonight,' she replied. 'I'm going out for a meal with my dad.'

'Oh, that's nice,' Mike said, the tension lines round his eyes deepening.

'Where are you going?'

'I don't know yet,' she replied, suddenly glad that she'd made Roy decide. 'It's my dad's turn to pick the venue.'

'I see.'

Tess swallowed, turning to smile at the customer approaching.

'I'd better get on,' she said apologetically. Mike nodded.

'Bye, then.'

She served the lady and sat back at the counter, taking a deep breath to still her heart. This couldn't go on, she was becoming terrified of him.

What's more, her mother was right, he *was* following her. It wasn't normal. Yet there was nothing she could do. She was too scared to dump him, too scared to go out with him.

She would get the locks changed, that's what to do. But even as she thought it, she realised how angry that would make him.

Oh God, she thought. *I'm really in trouble.*

*

Mike walked down to the security room and gently closed the door behind him. Then he sat down at his desk and put his head in his hands. Blood was pounding in his head, coursing like acid in his veins. He took a series of deep breaths to try to still the pain. He clenched his shaking fists, cursing under his breath. *How dare she. How dare she!*

And the fear. He had seen it in her eyes, clear as sunlight. She was afraid of him, and he knew what happened when people were afraid; they lashed out. He was losing control. The pain pulsed in his head until he thought his skull would explode. Without control, he was nothing. And abruptly, a memory came stinging into his mind, the fierce heat of the humiliation bringing colour to his cheeks and tears to his eyes.

Get away from me! I don't need your help, you little shit. Just get lost!

Control. He had to get control. He screwed his eyes tightly shut. *Breathe deeply. Think of the calm place.*

But he had, after all, hadn't he? In the end, they had come full circle. In the end, he had taken charge. She had backed down. He had been the one in control.

The pain gradually waned, and after a while he opened his eyes and slowly unclenched his fists. He did his breathing exercises until his heart rate returned to normal, and only then did he stand up and go to the locker room, where he looked at himself in the rust spotted mirror.

He looked just the same. This always surprised him.

*

Tess was certain Mike had followed her to the clock tower. Just because she couldn't see him meant nothing. She decided to tell her father about Mike. Not that Roy would be much help, but at least it would be good to talk about it.

Of course, she could always put the whole problem into mother's lap. Sheila would delight in telling Mike where to go.

Roy was late, as usual. She watched him; a short, overweight man in a badly fitting suit and a silly grin, jogging unsteadily up Belgrave Gate towards her. She smiled.

'Hello, my sweet. You look gorgeous. I'm sorry I'm late.'

'Forget it.' She linked her arm into his. 'Where are we going?'

'I thought, the Highcross? If you like?'

Tess laughed. 'Great idea, dad.'

She ordered steak with all the trimmings. Though she spent most of her life struggling to avoid becoming the same shape as her father, somehow being with him eroded what little will power she had. She tucked in, listening to Roy's funny stories, watching his bright blue eyes grinning at her.

'This is better than last time, eh?'

'God, yeah. That seafood place.'

Roy chuckled, shaking his head. 'All these years, and I didn't know my little girl hated shellfish.'

Tess grinned. 'I had scallops once and they made me really ill. It put me off. It was my fault, I should have told you. You weren't to know.'

Roy grinned back at her through a mouthful of chips.

'So how's the new job?'

'Oh Tess, love, it's great. I should have done this years ago. The lads are a great bunch, and we've got more work than we can handle. I get my driving license back next month as well, you know.' He shook his head. 'I'm never going to be as stupid as that ever again.'

Tess reached over and patted her father's hand.

'Hey, I might even manage a holiday this year, how about that?'

She laughed. 'Well, it's about time.'

'I might need a companion to come with me, though,' he winked. 'Someone to keep me out of trouble.'

Tess shook her head. 'Dad, I'd bore you rigid.'

'You don't fancy it then, some exotic island in the sun?'

She took another bite of steak. 'Do I ever-'

Out of the corner of her eye, she caught sight of a man standing at the bar. She turned quickly, but he had gone. Abruptly her good mood vanished. She had almost forgotten about Mike, until then.

'What's up, love, you've gone all quiet?'

She looked into Roy's concerned face. Remembering all his good news tonight, the fact that at last things seemed to be going well for him, she hadn't the heart to spoil it with her own problems.

'Indigestion,' she grinned, making him laugh.

'It's good to see you tucking into your grub. Most of these lasses you see today, they eat like birds.'

'So, you going to get a car then?'

Roy shrugged. 'I'll have to see what the insurance will cost, what with the DD conviction.'

Later, as they stood waiting at the bus stop, Tess glanced around at the people wandering through town, heading for pubs and clubs. Couples, groups of lads and girls. She and her father. And, she thought bitterly, somewhere in the shadows, there was Mike. Roy's bus turned up first.

'I'll phone you tomorrow,' he shouted as he climbed aboard. Tess waved, knowing that he wouldn't. She leaned against the plastic wall of the shelter and looked down at the clock tower, at the office lights still gleaming in the buildings beyond.

'Hello.'

She jumped, looking up into Mike's face.

'Mike, you startled me!'

He smiled. 'You're easy to startle.'

'What are you doing here?'

There were six other people waiting for buses. Tess took a step backwards towards them.

'I came into town for a drink.'

'Mike, were you in the Highcross?'

He nodded, and now she could see the ice returning to his eyes, his lips vanishing into a thin line.

'Were you following me?'

He gave a quiet little laugh. 'You're paranoid.'

'Am I?' she said, sudden anger surging through her. 'This morning I was absent minded, now I'm paranoid. What's tomorrow's special; schizophrenic?'

Mike seemed to draw himself in, to become taller and stiller. Behind the anger, Tess felt her heart fluttering in terror, but knew if she didn't speak up now, she never would.

'Mike, I think we're getting too claustrophobic. I think we need to back off. See a bit less of each other.'

He said nothing, just stared at her, standing rigid under the streetlight. She sensed the people behind her, listening, and resisted the urge to run and hide behind them. A bus arrived, and she didn't care if it was hers. She turned to climb aboard, and felt his hand on her arm.

'I'll see you in the morning. We can talk about this.'

She pulled away urgently. 'No,' she said. 'I'm sorry.'

The bus drove off, and without looking, she knew he would still be standing there, looking after the departing bus. Despite her pounding heart, she felt exhilarated. She had done it at last!

But by the time the bus reached Kirby Muxloe, she was once again gripped with fear. What if he'd driven, and was waiting for her at home? On an impulse she got off well before her stop and called into the Royal Oak pub, where she phoned a taxi and self-consciously gulped back a glass of wine until it arrived. When it drew up at her house, she asked the bemused driver to wait until she signalled him to go, and put the key in the lock with trembling fingers.

The house was in darkness, as she'd left it. She stood in the hall, listening, ignoring the voice inside that told her that she'd never hear him anyway. She turned on the living room light, the kitchen, the stairs. The bathroom door lay open, and she ran past to check her bedroom, even looking in the wardrobe. No one. With a sigh, she turned and headed back down stairs.

And stopped dead halfway down.

Through the slats in the stairs, she could see the bottom half of a man, waiting for her. Gripped with terror, she looked back, but there was nowhere to hide. Looking down, she realised her only chance was to run, and try to get past him. She let out a shriek and ran downstairs, straight into the arms of the taxi driver.

'Hey hey, love, take it easy. I just came in to see you were all right.'

Tess could hardly draw breath to cry. The driver sat her down and made her tea, by which time she was sobbing into one of her best cushions.

'Drink this, me duck.'

She took the tea with shaking hands.

'Now, you're worried about someone being in your house? I think we'd better call the police, don't you?'

'N-n-no. It's all-ll-right.' She tried to take a deep breath.

'I was just being paranoid,' she said, giggling hysterically.

The driver took some convincing, but left eventually, after checking all the windows and insisting she put the chain on the door. Tess sank onto her sofa, her hands still shaking, feeling utterly drained. First thing tomorrow she would get the locks changed, then she'd take a taxi to work, and to hell with the expense. She glanced out at a chink in the curtains, remembering her mother telling her to get new windows. *Maybe I should start with a new backbone.*

Tess climbed the stairs to bed, kicked off her shoes and climbed under the covers fully clothed. She cried for a little while, hugging one of her soft toys, before reason began to shuffle back in, looking embarrassed.

Thirty one years old, she thought sadly. *And here I am crying into my pillow and cuddling a fluffy toy dog. No wonder mother is embarrassed by me. I'm pathetic.*

Eventually she fell into an exhausted sleep, and Mike came out from behind the bathroom door and stood in the dark at the foot of her bed. He stood there for a long time, before slowly turning and walking back into the bathroom, where he climbed back out of the window and disappeared into the night.

*

Mike awoke to the sound of screaming, and lay there, unmoving, his heart thudding in his chest. He wanted to get up and go to her, try to help, to at least protest, but another part of him said no; stay here, while they are hurting her, you are safe. That thought made him feel sick, even as he turned his head into the pillow. She needs you, said his heart. She needs you to help her, to take care of her.

You can't help her, said his head. You're too small. You can't do anything, and they will only hurt you too.

And as Sandy cried his name over and over again, he pressed one of her soft teddy bears to his skinny chest and made a promise; *I will help you. Somehow, I will find a way. I will take care of you. I will.*

FIVE

Tess woke up with her eyes stuck together, and gloomily surveyed the new day. She dragged herself out of bed, realising she was still wearing last night's clothes, and her face flushed hot with embarrassment as she remembered last night's events. What must that poor taxi driver have thought! What a fool she was. Of course Mike hadn't been here. Hell, maybe she really was paranoid.

But downstairs, she still dug out the yellow pages and arranged for a locksmith to come and renew the locks, before catching the bus to work.

Tess saw Mike often during the day, doing his rounds, and the sight of him made her heart pound. She alternated between tears and anger as she busied herself cleaning all the shelves, replacing the ornaments carefully and admiring their delicacy. But even that reminded her of Mike. He had always liked the unicorn, the one with the strangely coloured horn, though he would never hold it, never even touch it.

Somewhere around three o'clock, a spider dropped on her hand, and panic exploded from her in a scream. She was dimly aware of the other shop workers exchanging rolled eyes and grins as she ran out of the shop, waving her arms frantically. *Great,* she thought glumly. *Now* everyone *thinks I'm a nut case.*

She had arranged to leave an hour early to meet the locksmith, and as she walked downstairs to the ground floor, she saw Mike coming towards her. It was just as always; he didn't look as if he was deliberately coming to see her, but he was.

'Tess. How are you? Are you all right?'

She took a deep breath. 'I'm fine, Mike.'

'Can we talk?'

She shook her head, looking away from the cold eyes. 'I'm sorry Mike. I- it's just- it's not you, you're a lovely guy. I just don't think we're right for each other. I'm sorry.'

'I was worried about you last night, you didn't seem-'

'I'm all right,' she snapped, staring at the floor. 'Sorry. Look Mike, you don't need to keep checking up on me. And please don't follow me any more. I'm, sorry, but it's over.'

In the ensuing silence, Tess wondered if he could hear her heart pounding.

'I just wanted to look after you,' he said solemnly.

She looked up. For perhaps the first time, he looked sad, and a wave of guilt threatened to change her mind.

'I know, but you don't have to.'

She smiled. 'I can take care of myself, you know.'

Mike's head jerked suddenly, his eyes snapping open wide, and she stared at him, surprised. He opened his mouth, but didn't speak, and his skin suddenly turned pale.

'Mike, are you feeling all right-?'

But he had turned and stumbled quickly away. She watched him go, wondering what had happened, going over the conversation in her head. She thought about the number of times she had said sorry. She wondered what it was she had to apologise for.

Later that night, Tess sat in her living room and drank white wine alone and watched a soppy movie, and safe inside her new locks, she felt content.

Until the phone rang. She looked at it, as if that would help tell her who was calling. Eventually she picked it up.

'Tessa. What were you doing, having a bath?'

'Oh, hello mother.' She sighed. She should just have let it ring.

'Listen, just to let you know, I'm going down to Cambridge for the weekend with Gilly. There's a bridge tournament, and I won't be back until Monday.'

'That's nice,' Tess said. She knew mother was only phoning to point out that she was off somewhere else interesting, while her underachieving daughter sat at home watching crap on TV. 'I hope you win.'

'Oh, I shan't win,' Sheila said archly. Some of the best players in the world will be there.'

'Well, have a good time.'

'What are you doing this weekend?'

Tess hesitated. Her usual answer was: 'I haven't decided yet', meaning *nothing*. But this time she rebelled. She thought quickly for something to say, and remembered dad talking about his drink-driving ban being almost over.

'Actually, I'm going to take some driving lessons. I want to learn to drive.'

There was a long pause, during which Tess hoped Sheila wouldn't ask anything awkward, like which firm was she using.

'Well good for you,' she said grudgingly. 'It's about time. What's brought this on?'

'Oh, I just thought it'd be nice to be able to get up and go places.'

'Hmm.'

Tess felt her face burning. She knew mother was picturing Tess not daring to drive further than Wigston in case she broke down.

'Well, good luck, and I'll see you next week.' Tess sat back down, wondering why she had made up that story. Now she would have to book some lessons so she wouldn't be caught in the lie. Hell, she didn't want to learn to drive. Life was troublesome enough as it was.

*

Mike opened his eyes, and saw the light at the bottom of the door. He shuffled into the darkness, hiding among the perfume-smelling clothes, listening. There was the usual low laughter, then a lot of banging and groaning, and finally a man's voice: *'Christ!'* That made him jump. Then there was some more laughter, louder this time, and the smell of cigarettes, and then he heard his mother's voice.

'I'll fetch her.'

He closed his eyes.

'Sandy, Sandy, get in here.'

He huddled further back into the closet, keeping his eyes tightly shut. Once, a long time ago, he had looked through the keyhole to see what it was they wanted Sandy for, what it was that hurt her so much. He had seen what the man had done to her. Had seen the look of horror and misery on her young face, and he had done nothing. Shame filled him like hot acid.

Long ago, although the memory was still vivid as fresh blood on the snow. He drew his knees up to his skinny chest and wished one of them were dead, either he or Sandy, it didn't matter, then they wouldn't both have to suffer like this.

He could hear Sandy's voice now. She was talking quietly, and mother was laughing, drunk. The man spoke in a low voice, then mother laughed again, and the man swore and told her to shut up. He heard the front door bang, and then there was silence.

Had they all gone out? He waited a moment before shuffling up to the keyhole. The man was still there, but he couldn't see his mother or Sandy. He looked away, and then he heard his sister scream. It was a strange sort of scream, and after a while it became a groan. He hid amongst the clothes and tried not to listen, but after a while he heard another sound, the sound of flesh hitting flesh. Hard. Sandy screamed again, and finally all the horror and pain and impotent fury rose up in him and exploded. He pulled open the door and rushed into the smoky room.

The man had Sandy pinned against the wall, his trousers round his ankles. His fist was ready to slam into her face once more, and Mike lowered his head and slammed it into the man's back. The man fell heavily, taking a chair with him. Sandy screamed again, as the man tried to get up. Clenching his teeth, heart pounding against his ribs, Mike ran to the kitchen and pulled open the knife drawer. The man looked at the blade in Mike's shaking fist and slowly held out a hand, palm up. With the other hand he pulled up his trousers, then he backed away to the door. As it slammed behind him, the knife fell to the floor.

He looked down at Sandy clutching at her pink dressing gown, the one with the rabbit embroidered on a pocket. A livid bruise was forming over one eye, and she was staring at the door, her eyes desperate.

'Sandy-' he said.

'Don't you touch me!' She yelled. 'Get away from me, you little *insect!* What did you think you were doing! You stupid, stupid idiot! Get back in the closet and stay there. Go on. I hate you!'

He retreated under the force of her blows, stunned by her anger. Although he towered over her now, he didn't move as she struck him, but let her vent her rage on him. He reached the closet, but she was still hitting him, and he couldn't get the door open. He held his arms over his face until at last she ran out of strength and, with one final blow, swung away and threw herself down on the grotty sofa.

He stood for a long moment, staring at her, astonished.

'I only wanted to help,' he said.

'Help!' She screamed at him. 'I don't need your help, you little shit. Just get lost! Jesus Christ, he never paid me! You chased him away before he could pay.'

He stared at her. She was crying now, and the black stuff that she put on her eyelashes began to run down her face. She had pulled her knees up, just as he had done, clutching a teddy bear to her chest. Once again she was Sandy, his little sister. His chest ached with love for her. He desperately wanted to put it right.

'I'll make it up to you,' he said, 'I'm sorry.'

She shook her head. 'You don't understand. Go back in your closet.'

Her words stung him hard. He turned away so she would not see his tears. 'I only wanted to take care of you,' he muttered.

She stared up at him, her eyes as cold as a knife blade.

'Yeah? Well, I can take care of myself, Mike. I can take care of myself.'

He woke with a gasp, the bedclothes twisted round his feet. He got up, rubbing at his face with shaking hands, and opened a window, letting the cool wind dry the tears on his cheeks and the sweat on his skin.

The dreams were like wild animals, puma or cougar or lynx, let loose in the quiet English countryside where they appeared now and then to upset the natives. And try as he might, he couldn't catch them, couldn't shoot them down. They remained there, elusive but threatening, waiting until he was feeling vulnerable before striking hard, then disappearing again into the dark woods.

But there was one thing he could do to reassert control; one thing that would send those wild cats scurrying to their holes, at least for a while. Mike felt the cool spring air on his bare skin and breathed deeply.

The decision was not really his, not on any level that he could understand. It simply was. He knew what had to be done, and he slowly closed the window and sat cross-legged on the floor, waiting for morning.

SIX

Mike went home from work at the normal time, crying off from an offer of drinks in the pub with Joe and Louie, although he wished he had time to go. It would be useful later.

There was little time, however, and he needed to work fast.

Tomorrow was his turn for a Saturday off, and if he missed this chance, he would have to wait another three weeks until the rota came round again.

He didn't think he could wait that long.

He had hoped that the nightmares had been vanquished, but no. All he had done was restrain them for a while, and they had lain dormant, building their strength before edging their way back into his head. He didn't stop to think about what he was doing. There was no time, and anyway, no point. It had to be done, that was all. From the moment she had hurled those words at him, the future was set in stone. He opened his kit bag and checked its contents, then went to his wardrobe compartment for supplies.

It took three trips to the car before everything he needed was packed away properly, and then he checked the oil, tyres and water, and drove down Narborough Road to the filling station. When everything was ready, he looked at his watch. Ten to eight. Time to move.

He made a point of pulling into the turning circle anti-clockwise, so the headlights would shine on the windows and alert her. Then he slowly got out of the car and walked to the house. He rang the bell, smiling to himself at the new locks.

Tess opened the door, keeping the chain on. 'Hello Mike.' She sounded wary.

'Hello Tess. I'm just returning your CDs, and this DVD.' He held them up.

'I thought it best to get it over with now.'

He tried to smile, holding out the disks at arms length. Tess took them slowly. He reached into his pocket.

'Also your key, but I see that it doesn't matter now.'

He watched the emotions cross her face as she looked at the key dangling in his hands: regret, guilt, compassion. She was almost there. It just needed one little push.

'I'm sorry it all went pear-shaped. It's my fault. I understand why you don't want to see me any more. It's a problem I have. Since the army- I – well. I find it hard to open up.'

He smiled his best sad smile. Tess smiled back, and he looked down and turned to go.

'Wait, Mike,' she said, and then she closed the door and took the chain off.

Bingo.

'Let's not leave it like this. At least come in and have a drink.'

He remained on the step, not moving. 'Are you sure?'

'Yes I'm sure. Come in.'

And she turned and walked into the kitchen, leaving the door open.

He watched her open a bottle of white wine and hunt around for glasses. 'A mug will be fine,' he said, laughing softly at her lack of organisation. Tess turned to him, smiling happily. He realised that his laughter was making her smile, and felt a sudden sharp pain of loss. He did love her so very much.

'Here, then. Come on through.'

They sat in the living room, and yet again he was entranced by the softness of the place; the silk and velvet cushions, the flowing curtains, the flower paintings. Everything was lace and frills. It had always fascinated him.

She leaned forward in her chair. 'Was it really awful for you, in the army?'

He swallowed back the sudden anger. He would have to talk to her about it, at least for a while.

'It was pretty bad. Out in the Gulf. Mates of mine – well, they had a bad time. They never came back.'

Tess winced, and he concentrated on her fingers clasped round the mug. She was nervous, drinking too quickly, her eyes full of haunting shadows that he dare not meet.

'Somehow, coming back from that into the normal world, it's like a whole other planet.'

She nodded for him to continue. 'Normal things; going to work and fixing the car; stuff like that seems meaningless.'

'What about you?' she asked, finishing her wine. 'Did anything happen to you?'

He shook his head. 'No, but I saw some terrible things. Things I still can't talk about-'

A flash in his mind. The silent terror of the children, the hopelessness in the woman's eyes, the shots, ringing out. Memories that were never far away. He shook his head to clear it and tipped up the mug, finishing the wine.

She stood up. 'Here, I'll fetch some more.'

'No,' he said, 'I will.' And he looked at her so she could see the tears standing in his eyes. He took the mug from her and walked into the kitchen. Let her think him weak, it didn't matter. He was in control. It felt good.

He reached into his pocket and flipped the plastic tube open with his thumb. He swirled the wine carefully, before closing the phial and putting it away in one smooth movement. He picked up both mugs and the wine bottle and carried them through.

'Here. I brought the bottle.'

She laughed brightly, taking her mug and clicking it against his. 'Cheers.'

And looking at her he felt another surge of regret. If he wanted to, he could forget all his plans now. He knew he would have her back, and he did want her. She was perfect, everything he had always loved, and as he smiled at her, he wished things could be different.

But the words were like a wall between them, and even as he felt his heart soften at the sound of her voice, he could feel the cold solid weight of the words pressing down on him. The lightning was there, waiting behind his eyes, ready to strike him down again if he was weak. He sighed, listening to her chatter and pretending to drink the wine until at last she fell asleep. Then he opened the curtains and stood looking at her for a long time before taking her keys and leaving. He made sure he spun the wheels when he left, grinning as he saw the nearby curtains twitching. Tess's neighbour, the one who drank, was just arriving, and he saw her look through the window to where Tess sat, apparently watching TV. The smile was still on his face by the time he reached his flat, and he made plenty of noise for the benefit of his neighbours.

And then he sat silently in the darkness, taking himself away as he had been taught, as the hours quietly passed.

Just after one, he drove carefully, lights off, to the access lane behind Tess's tiny house and parked. He let himself in, went upstairs and packed a suitcase. He washed up and wiped down everything he had touched, then he carried out first the case, and then Tess, down the garden and through the door in the fence, and into the car in the dark street beyond.

SEVEN

Tess ran headlong through the spindly wood, tripping over rocks and bumps in the uneven ground, her hands squelching in the marshy grass as she pushed herself back to her feet. Finally reaching the edge of the trees she stopped, looking out at the expanse of sea like a slate table under the heavy clouds. The freezing air sandpapered her throat, and a little moan escaped her, fresh tears rushing to her eyes. There was nothing to be seen apart from the cold sea and the pebbly beach and the empty sky.

Heart pounding, she stepped onto the shingle, heading for the water's edge. The beach sloped sharply downward, and as she walked, a tiny jetty came into view, just a series of planks strung together, disappearing into the waves. The planks were held to the shore by a pair of uprights, and there was a plastic bag hanging from one of them. Tess began to run again, her feet twisting and sliding in the wet stones.

She tore the bag away from the post. Inside was a yellow nylon jacket which she quickly pulled on over her thin cardigan. In the left jacket pocket she found a small, battered tobacco tin, the name on the front so worn it was no longer legible. In the other pocket her fingers touched something sharp, and she yelped, dropping the tin. Carefully she pulled out the fierce looking knife, staring at her distorted reflection in the shining blade.

The edge of panic began to creep in.

Is this all? What have I missed? Frantically she turned the bag inside out, then tore it into pieces before collapsing on to the beach, tears blinding her, dry knots in her throat. She cried herself out under the uninterested sky, her fingers grasping at the material of the cagoule as if it held the answer.

After a while, the frozen air crept into her bones, making her shiver uncontrollably, and she staggered to her feet and headed slowly back to the trees. Now that the tears had gone, she could try to think clearly again, and she realised that this was just some horrible trick of Mike's. He was almost certainly here somewhere, watching. He'd just wait a while to make her suffer, and then come and get her.

Laying the knife on the post she let go the remains of the plastic bag, watching the wind collect up the pieces and carry them away.

And I thought he'd taken it well, she sighed. Details of their last conversation were coming back to her now; all his talk about the army, about his friends being hurt. Was that was he was doing to her? She pulled the note out of her jeans pocket and read it over again, but it hadn't changed: *You said you could look after yourself.*

Then she remembered that was the last thing she had said to him in the mall, that day. She remembered it had hurt him, as much as anything could burst through that impervious exterior. Mother was right; she was a fool, and Mike had to be totally mad to pull a stunt like this.

Where the hell am I?

Tess had been to the beach at Scarborough before, but it was nothing like this empty place, with the sea rolling in like a malevolent force, the sky darkening almost by the second. Did that mean rain, or was night falling? Her head still felt groggy from whatever Mike must have drugged her with. Well, if it was getting dark, he was bound to come and find her soon. Hell, he was probably laughing at her right now. She sat on a rotting log at the edge of the trees, wrapped her arms around her stomach and rocked gently back and forwards. The trees provided some shelter, but she was still shivering, her fingers so cold it hurt. She scanned the horizon, searching for any sign of a boat, until finally she realised that it really was getting dark, and she stood up and began to walk along the treeline, careful to keep an eye on the sea.

But there was still no sign of Mike.

What should I do? she thought. *Wait here and hope he'll turn up, or go inland and search for help?*

The first choice was favourite, because she could not believe he would simply abandon her. But if he did not come, she would be left to spend the night in the freezing open. Tess had heard about people getting hypothermia going for a walk in Bradgate Park.

She pulled out the note again and read it, in case it might have changed.

Well, if he came back and she wasn't there, that would shake him! She stood up, but hesitated, scanning the waves one last time, before heading into the trees.

The ground rose sharply as she walked, and Tess, unused to exercise, was soon breathing hard. *At least I'm warm,* she thought bitterly. As the sky darkened, her training shoes began to trip over rocks and tufts of reedy grass, invisible in the gloom. She tried not to think too much, because thoughts brought tears, and if she started to cry again, she thought perhaps she would never stop.

The trees thinned out after a time, and she found herself almost at the top of a steep hill. The thick clouds had moved off to leave wispy strands behind which the moon's light gleamed like a pale coin, and she could see the hillside stretching away around her. She turned and stared in all directions, desperate for the sight of a light, of habitation, anything. Up here the wind gusted keenly, and despite her efforts, the cold was seeping back into her bones. Tears lurking in her throat, she plunged desperately on up the dark hill. At last the ground began to slope downwards again, and she could hear something, something low and rumbling, like the thrum of an engine. Hope flared like an unexpected match. She hurried into the gloomy valley, down into a stand of conifers, as the noise and her breathing grew louder. At last she stopped to get her breath back and listen, and the match was snuffed out. She recognised the sound now, and as she walked further, she came upon the waterfall, tumbling through rocks and mossy trees, the water as white as bone in the dark wood. The sobs rose painfully in her throat again, and she gave in to them, crying and wailing until the despair turned to screaming anger, and then back to despair again. The wood was pitch black, and, heart pounding, she wondered if Mike was even now scouring the beach for her. Not that it mattered, for she would never find her way back there in the dark.

Tess stood and watched the water pour down the hill as the cold tears dried on her face. She had absolutely no idea what to do.

*

Mike beached the dinghy south of the headland where he'd left the car, in a place easy to find because of the familiar pattern of rocks. He spent some time cleaning the boat, packing the outboard in its waterproof protective, and hiding both behind the rocky outcrop in a cave not visible from either sea or land. Then he set a fire below the tide line and methodically burned Tess's cheap suitcase and clothes, her purse and credit cards. He stripped naked, ignoring the bitter cold, and added his own clothes to the fire, waiting until everything was reduced to ashes before dispersing the remains. The tide would do the rest. Then he pulled the bag containing his fresh clothes from the cave, dressed, and hiked back the kilometre and a half uphill to the car.

Finally, he removed the plastic sheets from the car and carried them down to the sea. The tide was on the turn, and he tied the sheets loosely round small rocks, to be washed away in the tide. Then the only thing remaining was the journey south.

It was a ten hour drive, but Mike had no trouble staying awake. He kept to the speed limit, stopping only for petrol, and then only at small stations off the beaten track. He paid with cash, and he smiled and acted pleasant, and didn't draw attention to himself.

He got back after nine, left his car in the street outside his flat and went to the Huntsman pub, asking frequently for change for the fruit machine, and annoying the barmaid so she'd remember him.

Then he went home and stood in the shower, and let the water wash over him like a blessing. Tess could look after herself. He was purged of responsibility for her. His problems were behind him.

He closed his eyes and smiled, knowing that tonight, the wild creatures of his dreams would be far, far away.

EIGHT

Tessa Hardy lived in a tiny semi-detached house out in the suburbs. The quiet village of Kirby Muxloe on the other side of the motorway, on the edge of the countryside, and her house was identical to most of the others in the new estate; tidy, if soulless. Number 4 was in a cul-de-sac, the houses arranged on three sides of a turnaround, where an island of bushes had been formed to try and bring some life to the place. The bushes looked tired and grey from the constant exhaust fumes. Most of the drives were empty, the owners out at work. Ideal hunting ground for burglars, Cal Fisher thought as he parked in the turnaround and waited for the mother.

As if he didn't have enough to do. A suspicious missing person case was the sort of thing Cal should have let Rob handle on his own, but his partner wasn't up to much at the moment. Cal glanced across at one of the little houses where a young woman was coming out, holding the hand of a small child. The toddler was wearing a scarlet anorak, and Cal watched as she broke away and skipped to the car door, waiting for her mother to catch up. He felt an unaccustomed lump in his throat and looked away.

Sheila Harrison arrived only seconds later, and stormed out of her car towards him.

'Who are you? What's all this about? Has something turned up?'

Cal took a breath. The woman had her arms folded over her chocolate brown suit and cream blouse. She looked immaculate, perfectly made up, tasteful jewellery. Her hard eyes were angry.

'Mrs Harrison, I am DS Calum Fisher. I'll be in charge of the case from now on.'

'Well, at last you're taking it seriously. About time.'

Cal nodded. 'Let's go in, shall we?'

The woman with the child gave him a wary look as he followed the woman into the house, which still smelled new; plaster and paint. A dead air freshener had been left on the hall radiator. Cal looked round the tiny living room. Brown wool carpet, Magnolia walls, lots of candles, pretend flame fire. The room was clean and tidy, nothing out of place.

'Has anything been moved?' he asked

'Not by me. I can't speak for your colleagues.'

Ah, I see, Cal thought, gloomily. It's going to be like that. He moved into the kitchen, again noticing the sparse cleanliness, not a cup out of place.

'Is your daughter always so tidy?'

'Hah,' Sheila walked to the sink and stared out at the postage stamp garden. 'Not likely.'

Cal walked up the open-plan stairs, past framed drawings of flowers on the walls. He spotted the initials *TH* in the corners. So Tessa was an artist. In the bathroom he noticed there was no toothbrush in the holder, no shampoo by the shower. He checked in the medicine cabinet, and the cupboard under the sink, but all he found were unopened toilet rolls and a bottle of bleach.

'What are you doing?'

Cal sighed, but didn't answer. He walked into the bedroom, glancing over the soft toys, the dolphin pictures, the flowery curtains.

'What are you looking for?'

He looked at the woman. The young PC who had taken the initial report had warned him she was a nightmare, and he hadn't been wrong.

'Mrs Harrison, we need to try and find out what happened to your daughter, whether she has been abducted, or simply gone away by-'

'I've already told the other officer. There's no way she'd go anywhere on her own. My daughter's not capable of making decisions.'

Cal nodded. He'd heard that before.

'Have you noticed anything missing?'

Sheila shook her head. 'Nothing.'

'I noticed there's no toothbrush in the bathroom,' he said.

Sheila stared at him, then brushed past him to look for herself. 'One of you people must have moved it.'

Cal raised an eyebrow. 'That's not likely, Mrs Harrison. Are you sure there's nothing missing? Think carefully.'

A flicker of doubt crossed the perfect features. Sheila pushed back into the bedroom and opened the wardrobe door. She tried to hide it, but Cal saw the intake of breath when she looked at the top shelf. He looked past her. The shelf was empty.

'What used to be kept up there?'

'Her suitcase.'

Cal looked around the wardrobe, noticing the empty hangers. He nodded again.

'Why are you nodding? I'm telling you, she's been abducted, and that bastard has just tried to make it look like she's run away.'

The PC had warned him about this too. Sheila had the girl's boyfriend firmly in the frame.

'I can see you don't believe me,' Sheila's voice was calm, but there was a pulse beating in the vein on her temple. Cal wondered whether he might not have run away too, faced with a mother like this.

Don't think about mother! Cal quickly looked away. He had to keep focused.

'Why would she simply disappear, leave her house, her job? You don't understand. Tess is not one of life's copers. She drifts from day to day, blown by the wind. She's not a sudden decision person.'

'I see,' Cal said, writing in his notebook. 'So she couldn't simply have gone away for a few days?'

'Without telling me?'

Well, yeah.

'She has a job at the Sunningdale mall. She hasn't booked time off.'

'I'll be going to her workplace after this.'

'Look,' Sheila grasped Cal's arm. He was surprised at her strength. 'I know you're thinking that Tess will probably turn up in another day or two, but you're wrong. You must believe me. Please!'

Cal looked into the woman's eyes. Beneath the arrogant self assurance, he thought he could see a glimpse of fear.

'I promise I will look at every angle,' he said. 'Wherever it leads.'

Sheila released him. 'Good.'

'No problem. Now, can I have a recent photograph of Tess? And I'll need details of her friends. Her financial records would also help.'

'Whatever,' Sheila said.

*

Cal made it back to Mansfield House just as it was getting dark, and ignored the valiant band of smokers hanging round on the steps outside. Cal swallowed. He caught a whiff of smoke and slammed the door, ignoring the craving and taking the stairs to wake up his newly-clean lungs. In the CID room, Rob Matlock, erstwhile partner, was laughing into the phone. Rob winked as Cal walked past, but he didn't respond, glancing over to where DC Roslyn, the most junior member of the team, was tapping into her computer.

'At least someone's working,' he thought angrily.

Cal was well into the process of setting up his own case file by the time Rob decided to swing over.

'Whatya got, the missing girl?'

'Uh huh.'

'A runaway?'

Cal looked up. 'Are you interested?'

'Well, of course.' Rob held out his hands in the familiar gesture of what did I do wrong. Cal shook his head.

'If you were that interested, you could have turned up at the house. I can't keep covering for you, Rob.'

His partner sat down with a thud.

'Look, I'm sorry. It's not for long, okay? Just until I can get this thing with Leese sorted out.'

Suitcase and toothbrush missing Cal wrote. *Suspect some clothes missing too – empty hangers. House very clean. No sign of foul play. Boring job, few prospects. Boyfriend 'strange' Mother stifling*

'Please, Cal? You know I'd do the same for you.'

Rob's eyes were everywhere but on Cal's. A poor detective, and a worse liar, he thought. But looking at Rob's anguished face, he felt his heart lurch, and he bit back his sarcastic reply.

'You still having to pick the kids up from school?'

Rob nodded gloomily. 'And take them there. Jesus, Cal, I'm making their sandwiches, making their dinner. By the time she gets home from her 'self assertion' course, I'm done in.'

Neighbours – keeps to herself. Nothing unusual. Boyfriend round often, last seen Friday Night, left at 9pm. Neighbour saw Tess still at home.

Co-workers – Tess runs shop virtually single handed. Mall workers recall seeing her around. Shop owner drops in once a week. Nothing untoward, no requests for time off, no complaints.

Friends – very few. Financial records – no large withdrawals/transfers. No withdrawals since disappearance.

'I mean, how long is this going to take, this 'finding herself' malarkey? I tell you man, sometimes I feel like just walking out.'

'Why don't you?'

Rob ran his hands through his sparse grey curls. 'The kids, man, she said I'll never see them again if I do.'

Cal felt another strange surge of sadness.

'Oh come on, Rob, you know she can't do that.'

Rob gave him a hunted look, shaking his head. 'She's got me by the knackers, Cal. You better believe it.'

Cal looked at him, feeling his heart thudding, understanding the threat better than his partner could know. Rob shook his head and sighed, reaching for Cal's case file.

'Hell, forget my shit, let's see what you've got.'

Cal looked down at his notebook, where he had doodled a child's swing in the corner. He sighed.

'Why are we dealing with this?' Rob said. 'It looks like a straightforward runaway.'

Cal nodded absently. 'The parents are adamant that it's not. Young Jim Burdock took the report, and he thought there was something funny about it. He's a smart lad, good instincts. Anyway, things are quiet for the moment.'

The CID team had recently made a series of arrests in connection with a protection racket, a case which had seen Cal and the rest of the small team working flat out for three months. After that, something quiet like this was a welcome change.

'What about the boyfriend?' Rob said.

'Mother says he's a weirdo. Ex army man. Works as a security guard at the Sunningdale mall. Other guards I saw today say he's a loner who doesn't talk much. He wasn't on shift this afternoon, I'll interview him tomorrow.'

'That's if he's there; if they've not run off together.'

'Hmm,' Cal said. He picked up the photograph of Tess. Sheila told him she had taken the picture the day her daughter moved in to her house. Tess was standing at the door holding up her key, her long dark hair loose around her shoulders. Despite her smile, there was something in her eyes, something uneasy, as if she was looking for something that she suspected she'd never find.

Cal was with PC Burdock on this one. There was something funny about it. The facts looked cut and dried, but there was something there, under the surface, niggling at him.

*

It took three days for the shit to hit the fan, by which time Mike was sure Tess was already dead. This was a break, because he knew very well that she called her mother every day, and if Tess missed the call, bearing in mind what a soft touch she was, it would have been noticed right away.

But it turned out that mother had gone off to a bridge party for the weekend, so it was only when Tess didn't appear for work on Monday that it all began to fall apart. Nothing was said when she failed to turn up on Saturday, but when she still wasn't there on Monday, phone calls were made, and the police were finally called, and Mike steeled himself for the grilling that he knew would come his way.

Not that it mattered. He had done the job. Done it well. And he felt fine, happier than he had for a long time.

It was the next day at work when it came, which was good. At least it meant he didn't have to let them into his home. The policeman looked about his own age, with thinning fairish hair and a nose that had clearly been broken. He was steady eyed and calm, and Mike put on his best easy-going face for him.

'Just a few questions, Mr Dole, if you don't mind.'

'Not at all,' he replied, trying to keep a balance between friendly and concerned. The policeman took him into the security office and they sat on either side of Mike's own desk. The policeman glanced round his pristine room with quick and careful eyes, and Mike felt his heart beating in fearful excitement.

'My name is DS Fisher, Mr Dole-'

'Please, call me Mike.'

Fisher gave him a quick smile. 'All right, Mike. Now, I expect you know that Tessa Hardy has disappeared.'

He nodded sadly. 'I know, It's very worrying. It's not like her at all.'

Fisher nodded slowly. 'I understand that the two of you were an item for a while.'

Mike put on a wistful face. 'Yes, for a while. Not as long as I'd like, mind you.'

'What do you mean?'

Mike gave a sad little chuckle. 'I'm afraid she gave me the heave-ho. With hindsight, it was my fault.'

Fisher leaned back in his chair. 'Your fault?'

'Yes. You see, I – well. I think I moved too fast for her. I was too serious. She didn't want to settle down.'

'I see.' Fisher said nothing else, and Mike knew that was a technique used by all policemen; leave a silence in the hope that the accused would fill it. Mike simply smiled.

'If there is anything I can do to help, please ask me. I- I'm very fond of Tess. I want to see her safe.'

'Of course you do.'

They looked at each other, and Mike thought; *I could have been you, if I'd wanted it. I could have been you.*

Fisher took out his notebook and flipped through it.

'I understand that you were at Tess's house last Friday night.'

'That's right, I took back some CDs I'd borrowed.'

The policeman read from his notes.

'A neighbour saw you leaving at approximately nine fifteen.'

Mike shrugged. 'I suppose. I can't really remember what time I left.'

'And did you see her at all after that?'

'No. Saturday was my day off.'

Fisher looked blank.

'I'd have seen her at work,' Mike explained.

'Tess was a reliable sort of person, I'm told.'

'*Was?*' Mike said, his voice rising. 'What do you mean *was*'

Fisher smiled wryly. 'Sorry, Mike. A policeman's bad habit, that's all.'

Mike looked relieved, while inside his heart soared with triumph. *I am better than you!*

'Tess is as reliable as clockwork. If she says she'll meet you at eight, she'll be there on the dot. If she's going somewhere, she plans it like a military manoeuvre. To just go off without telling anyone- well, it's out of character. That's why it's so worrying.'

'Yes,' Fisher said. 'You were an army man yourself I hear, Mike.'

Mike pushed out his chest in pride. 'Yes. 2 Para. I did almost twelve years.'

'See any action?'

This was the hard bit. 'Yes. I was- I served in the Gulf. I-'
He swallowed, tried to smile bravely. It wasn't an act. 'It was not a good time.'

Fisher leaned forward, his brown eyes smiling for the first time.

'I'll bet. Well, thank you Mike. You've been very helpful.'

Mike put on a relieved face. 'If there's anything I can do-'

The policeman nodded as he left. As the door closed, Mike sat down gently and smiled to himself. He went over the conversation in his head, rehashing every word, every look. No, it had all gone fine, he was sure.

There was just the mother to contend with now. He had seen the contempt in her hard eyes. He knew she would put him well and truly in the hot seat. Well, he'd be ready. After all, what could she do? There was no body, no evidence. Mike had not harmed her. Tess had simply vanished in the night, never to return. Mike smiled. He had done the right thing. Now that Tess was out of his life, the words and dreams were gone. Everything was easy.

That night Mike dreamed about the one time his mother had taken him and his sister on a trip. It seemed as if they were in the country, but he could have been no more than seven or eight, and couldn't remember the details. What he did remember was he and Sandy rolling down a grassy hill, the fresh smell of cut grass, Sandy's delighted screaming loud in his ears. They had landed at the bottom in a heap of arms and legs, giggling uncontrollably. They had done this again and again until mother had called them to get the bus back to the city, and then Sandy had picked up her ubiquitous teddy bear and smiled at him, and her little hand was warm and comforting in his as they ran back down the hill.

Any observer of this scene might have thought they were a normal, happy family out for the day. They could not have known the truth, which lived now only in Mike's heart, like a coiled serpent with a thousand poisoned teeth.

NINE

Light filtered slowly into the sky, the pale yellow of dead grass. In the hollow made by an uprooted tree, Tess looked up through the surrounding branches and watched the wispy grey cloud-shreds passing over. It had been reasonably warm in the hollow, but she'd had little sleep. There were rustlings in the night, twigs breaking, strange cries. Once she thought she heard a human voice, but it was almost certainly a dream. She stood up slowly, legs cramped and sore, and looked sourly at the waterfall.

A beetle, disturbed from his rest by the movement, climbed out of the hood of her cagoule and fell off her shoulder. A strangled scream erupted from her as she flailed her arms crazily, eyes clamped desperately shut. The ubiquitous tears arrived as she clawed at her neck and shoulders, pulling the jacket off and shaking her head frantically. 'Bugs! Bugs!' she yelled, as if her screams would drive them away.

Sobbing, dragging the cagoule behind her with shaking hands, she climbed out of the glade back on to the grassy hillside. In daylight, it looked no better. She could still see no houses, not even a barn. The tears were cold on her cheeks as she surveyed the expanse of heather and gorse, a few stick-like birch trees and the occasional boggy pond reflecting the watery sunlight. The hillside rose to the stark mountain beyond.

'Please God,' she said, breath hitching. 'Get me out of here.'

Tess shivered, rubbing her arms against the cold. She had the same two options: go back to the beach and hope Mike was finally there, or carry on up the hill in search of other people. The beach was favourite, but now out in the light of day she felt stronger, and didn't want to give Mike the satisfaction of finding her there pathetically waiting. If she could find her own way home, that would show him!

But all the same...

She tucked the tail of the cagoule into her back pocket, just the tail, in case there were any more insects, and walked back down the hill to the beach.

There was no one there.

Anger burst like a firework in her chest. *The bastard! What the hell was he doing?*

'Well, sod him', she muttered, wishing she had been brave enough to take option two right away. She turned and walked quickly upward again, the anger giving her feet momentum. *I'll climb the hill*, she thought. Up there she was bound to see either a house, or at least a road out of here. It might also keep her warm, since she was already shivering in her cotton blouse, cardigan and jeans.

She climbed all morning, stopping regularly as her legs grew heavy and tired and her lungs rasped painfully at the unaccustomed work. Her feet and ankles were soaked and sore, and the rumbling of her empty stomach competed with the cries of the seabirds. She cried, on and off, her thoughts depressing: *What if I can't find a house or a road? How far will I have to walk to find civilisation? What will I eat on the way?* Tess had been an avid fan of those TV shows that castaway celebrities on desert islands and made them eat worms. The thought of doing it herself was just impossible. She put her head down and slogged on.

The sun was warm now on her back as she climbed, sweating and gasping as the incline grew steeper. Her long hair fell around her face in annoying, sweaty strands, but she had nothing to tie it back with. She had always been proud of her long dark waves. Now that vanity seemed absurd.

She reached a ridge of brick-red stone, beyond which the land fell sharply away into a huge crater where a bright, still lake reflected the fluffy clouds. Hope flared as she saw movement down there, but after a long moment she realised it was a herd of deer. Her shoulders slumped, but all the same she felt a surge of delight at the sight; never having seen a wild animal before. The wind was strong up here, swirling her hair irritatingly round her face as she climbed. At last the ridge levelled off, and she took the last few steps to the summit.

Tess took a moment to get her breath back before looking around and surveying the land beneath as it sloped away to the sea in all directions. Heart pounding, she turned and turned, praying the view might suddenly change. 'Oh no,' she gasped, clenching her fists and biting her lip, hard. She turned again, her hands going to her face, covering her mouth but not suppressing the anguished scream that burst from her aching lungs.

'NO!'

She fell to her knees, sobbing into her hands. 'Please. I want to go home,' she whimpered, as the icy wind investigated the collar of her blouse, making a shiver run through her.

Eventually there was no choice but to get up and do something. Her chest hitching, she looked miserably out at the sea.

It was a big island, but a lonely one. Apart from a couple of other tiny islands a few miles away, there was nothing, not even a smudge on the horizon. Well, that explained the lack of habitation and roads. It also meant that she was really in trouble. Her thoughts raged, searching for some solution, some way out. She decided to go back down. 'There must be a boat somewhere,' she said, 'there *must* be.'

But what if there was? She had no idea where she was, where *land* was. She might just row out to sea and be lost forever.

Tess realised that she had never really been afraid, not till now. The blood was roaring in her ears as she reached into her jeans and pulled out the note yet again, like a talisman. Then she took a deep breath and crunched it in her fist. Mike would have to come back for her. If he didn't, she would die here. She knew he was mental, but surely not *that* mental. Turning, she tucked her hair behind her ears and started to climb down the hill, biting her lip against the urge to cry. The sun was beginning to fall, and she went as fast as she dared, following a stream down the mountain and stopping once to drink and wash her cagoule, in case there were any more insects in it. On the way she stopped to look at a dead seabird: beautiful, perfect, as if it had simply fallen from the skies. She felt a pang of sadness for the poor creature, which was quickly superseded by the need for food. *Maybe I could eat it*, she thought, *but how can I cook it?* With a sigh, she hurried on, and as she stumbled down the mountain she began to feel certain that Mike would be there, waiting for her on the beach.

She wondered what he would say. Would he be smug? Would he look at her with those hidden eyes of his, eyes that couldn't be read? And what would she say?

Nothing, she thought, grimly. Not until they reached land, and then she'd get away from him as fast as she could.

The sun was low by the time she reached the beach again, which was seriously deficient in the Mike department. Tess stared helplessly at the jetty.

It wasn't possible. He had to have come back for her!

But he had not.

She didn't think she had any tears left. Her throat and lungs ached with crying and exertion. Her legs felt like rubber, and her skin was shivering with cold. There was no shelter, and she was starving. She was going to die here, alone.

'I can't bear it,' she whispered.

The sun fell, wrapped in curtains of orange and gold, like the trappings of a grand old cinema. It might have been beautiful, but Tess sat on a rock and stared at it in quiet horror. 'I'm going to die here, alone,' she said.

She was suddenly filled with stillness. All ideas, all sense and reason drifted away with the wind. She watched the sunset, the quiet waves shushing the shore, and there was only calm and quiet. She was going to die here, alone, but it was all right. Somehow, it was all right.

The last semicircle of sun lit up the base of the clouds, and the pebbles on the shore gleamed in reflection. One in particular caught her eye, and as she looked at it, it became not a pebble, but an object. A shiny thing.

As Tess picked up the tobacco tin, the feeling of calm fell away, and her heart began to race. She had thought this was rubbish, but why would Mike have left it? It was sealed around the edge with tape, and she peeled it back carefully, opening the lid.

There was cotton wool, and under it, a lot of things she did not recognise.

But there was a roll of matches.

Before the light could leave the sky, she closed the tin and scrambled up the beach back into the trees, her blood pounding in her veins. She followed the sound of the water until she found the place she'd spent the previous night. It didn't take long to gather twigs and thin sticks in the shadow of the fallen tree, even in the dim light. Then she shoved some of the cotton wool into the pile and struck a match.

The wind snatched at the tiny flame, and she sheltered it with her hand, holding her breath, then letting it out in a relieved gasp as the cotton wool smouldered and suddenly burst into flame, the little twigs beginning to crackle as they caught.

Once the fire was going strong, Tess sat back against the bank and sighed, a little smile playing round her lips. It was a small achievement, she knew, but certainly the best thing that had happened to her so far. She experimented with bits of tree moss, fern and lichen to see which would burn quickly, knowing the cotton wool wouldn't last long. Then she pulled the hood up on her cagoule and drew the strings tight round her face.

Mike had not come back today, and deep inside the realisation came that he wouldn't be back tomorrow, either. That was when she accepted that she was going to be on the island for some time. Perhaps a very long time indeed.

*

Mike put the last tallow candle in the pigeon hole and moved to the slot beneath it. He slowly cleared out the contents; tubes of butter, bars of chocolate, packs of dehydrated meat. He checked the dates on them as he carefully dusted them and put them to one side. Then he cleaned out the slot thoroughly and replaced them, stacking them in neat piles. He had just moved to the slot beneath when he heard the knock at the door, and reflexively he reached into the bottom-most slot. His fingers closed round the smooth wood of the knife handle, before his brain could kick in and tell him not to be so paranoid.

He moved to the door and looked through the peephole, heart sinking as he saw Tess's mother standing there. She looked angry, as always. He took a series of deep breaths, during which time she knocked again, harder this time. He opened the door.

'Oh, so you're here after all.'

'Mrs Hardy,' he said evenly, stepping back so she could come in.

'That's not my name,' she snapped. 'That's Tess's father's name. We're divorced.'

'Oh.'

She stood in the living room, her arms folded, staring at him with her hard cold eyes and her tart's lipstick and her folded arms. The sour taste of hate filled his mouth, but he could save that for another day.

'Well?' She said.

'Well what, Mrs, um-' he held out his arms at his sides, Mr Reasonable.

She unfolded her arms and pointed a painted fingernail at him.

'You know very well what I mean,' she hissed. 'Where is she? Where's Tess?'

He sighed, and sat down on his sofa, absently flattening a crease in the fabric. The smell of the woman's perfume was stifling.

'I don't know where she is. The police have already asked me.'

'Yes, and they'll be asking you again, you can count on it. I know Tess. She wouldn't dare go off on her own. So you must have had a hand in it.'

Mike looked up, an aggrieved look on his face.

'I know what you must think, but this has nothing to do with me. Tess told me days ago that she didn't want to see me any more.'

The woman stared at him for a long moment, and then she began to laugh.

'You expect me to believe that? Little 'oh I don't mind if you don't mind' Tess. My little girl who couldn't be assertive if her life depended on it? Tess has all the will power of a dead battery, we both know it, so don't try that nonsense with me.'

She stood up and walked to the window. 'I assume you won't mind if I search your flat?'

He sighed again. 'Be my guest.'

He sat immobile while she walked into the kitchen. He breathed deeply and kept control as he heard his wardrobe door opened and closed, the bathroom checked out. She came back into the room more angry than ever.

'All right, so she's not here. You've taken her somewhere.'

Mike stood up. 'Look, if you really think that, why don't you go to the police.'

'I've already been!' She said triumphantly. 'You don't think I'd come here without telling anyone first, you weirdo!' Abruptly her eyes filled with tears.

'My poor darling Tess. Please tell me where she is.'

She sat down heavily, and Mike sat beside her.

'Look, if I knew, I'd tell you. You won't believe it, but I loved Tess.'

The woman looked up, her helplessness over. Her eyes were hard again.

'You're right, I don't believe it.'

She stood up and stormed to the door, slamming it behind her.

Mike sat still for a long moment, and then he got up and went to the kitchen, where he pulled out a handled box filled with cleaning fluids and cloths. For the next two hours he cleaned his apartment from top to bottom, until the smell of the woman's perfume was at last eradicated.

TEN

Tess slept soundly in the hollow, not waking until the sun was well up the sky. Her fire was out, and she was so hungry she felt sick, but at least she was still alive.

She crawled over to the stream and cupped her hands in the freezing water. As she drank, her empty stomach cramped painfully, bringing tears to her eyes, but she forced them back. She had to stop crying all the time, or she might as well lie down and die.

She made her usual pilgrimage to the beach in case Mike had turned up, then returned to her hollow, bringing the knife with her. Then she sat on the now hard-packed earth and folded her arms, trying to think. Somehow, she had to find something to eat.

She pulled the tobacco tin closer and carefully tipped out its contents, taking a mental inventory:

Matches. Candle. Magnifying glass. Needles and thread. Compass. Condom. *(a condom?!)* Several bits of wire. Fish hooks and line. Lead weights. Small pieces of serrated metal. A plastic tube full of purple crystals. Aspirin. Scalpel blades in a foil wrapper.

Fish hooks. That had to be the best shot. Carefully she unwound one of the fine lines from its bag and tied on a hook. Then she put everything else back into the tin and closed it.

She walked down to the shore, and watched the empty horizon for a bit. The sun was bright and warm today, although a bitter wind snapped at her hair. 'What day is it?' she thought. If she assumed she woke up here on Saturday, this must be Monday. It felt like she had already been here for weeks. She took off the nylon jacket and tied it round her waist by the arms. Then, still holding the fishing line, she walked carefully along the edge of the shore.

That was when she discovered the mussels.

Whole rocks were covered with them, and she felt her pulse racing hopefully as she began to pull them off. She'd seen Rick Stein cook Moules Marinière on the telly before, so they couldn't taste that bad. Stuffing the line in her pocket, she grabbed a handful of the shiny blue shells and carried them back to her hollow. She got a fire lit, then carefully emptied the tin's contents into the pocket of her cagoule. Feeling hopeful, she filled the base of the tin with water from the stream.

Tess hesitated. She couldn't just dump the tin into the fire, all the water would spill out. Staring at the flames, she tried to think of a way round the problem. It didn't even occur to her to simply cook the mussels in the embers.

'Rocks,' she murmured. 'We need some rocks.'

She traipsed back to the beach, returning with an armful of stones which she placed around the fire to form a makeshift platform. Then she carefully balanced the tin and waited for it to boil.

It took ages, during which time Tess found her mind wandering. Once she had eaten the mussels, she would go and check along the coast, see if she could find a boat. Or a building of some sort, because the wood would make a pretty miserable campsite if it started to rain. She felt the start of a headache coming on, and smiled to herself.

This was the hardest her brain had had to work in the last fifteen years.

The water finally began to boil. Tess dropped the mussels into the tin and waited.

The shellfish began to open, revealing the yellowy mass of flesh inside. Looking at it, Tess felt suddenly queasy. She waited until all the shells had opened, and then she knocked the tin away from the fire with a stick.

She picked up one of the mussels and gingerly pulled the shell apart. Inside, the creature's body was a rubbery blob with purple fringes and strange looking flaps. She touched it, grimacing, and finally she pulled the flesh free of the shell. The thing smelled of the sea, and reminded her of the scallops that had made her so ill, long ago.

But she was starving, and there was nothing else.

'Here goes,' she said, putting the mussel in her mouth. It was smooth and leathery, filling her mouth with a strong salty tang. She tried to bite it, but her body rebelled and she gagged instead, spitting the flesh out onto the hot rocks, where it hissed.

'I can't eat it', she thought, 'it's too horrible.'

But if not that, then what?

She clutched at her stomach, which had contracted painfully, as if angry with her squeamishness. There had to be something else!

Then she remembered her original idea. Grabbing the cagoule, she retrieved the fishing line from her pocket. She pushed the mussel flesh onto the hook and carried both it and the tin back to the sea. Clambering out on the rocks, she threw the line into the water.

The hook, with its mussel bait attached, floated on the surface.

Surely that wasn't supposed to happen? She pulled it back in, remembering the lead weights. It took a while to get them threaded on, but eventually the mussel sank below the water. She just had to wait for a fish.

Long minutes passed, and there was no sign of life apart from the seabirds circling overhead. They could see the mussel, but were too wary of Tess to grab it. This is not going to work, she realised, heart sinking.

She pulled the line in, and this time attached all of the remaining weights. Then she went to the end of the jetty and threw it in. There was a tug almost immediately, and, excited, she pulled hard.

The mussel was gone, although the hook remained.

'Shit!' she yelled.

Hours later, with no fish, and no cooked mussels either, Tess was struggling not to cry, as she stood on the jetty and stared out at the sun falling low in the sky. Another day drawing to a close, and she still had no food. Angrily she pulled another mussel off a rock and stamped on it until the shell collapsed. She hooked the slimy flesh on to her hook and threw it in again.

This time when she got a tug and pulled back, there was resistance. Holding her breath, she pulled again, and felt the weight on the end of the line. She took a step forward towards the edge of the jetty, keeping up the pressure. 'Come on,' she muttered, 'Come on!' The weight grew heavier, and she felt her arms aching with the unexpected work. One more tug ought to do it. She pulled harder, and immediately the pressure was gone, and Tess flailed backwards, landing with a thump on the planks.

She sat up, pulling up the line. The mussel was gone again, the fish had got away. Tess lay back and let the tears trickle from her eyes down the side of her face.

Returning to her hollow, Tess fed the fire, too tired and depressed to do anything else. She pulled on her nylon jacket and secured the hood against insects, looking out at the small flames and feeling as if even moving a finger would require too much effort. Then she leaned back in the hollow and closed her eyes and tried to ignore the hunger gnawing at her like a living thing.

*

Rob Matlock was late again. Cal sat drinking cold coffee in the team room while he read through his messages, brooding on his partner's continuing marital mess. Cal was wondering how long he could put up with it when the phone rang. Hearing Sheila Harrison's shrewish voice, his heart sank even further.

'Mrs Harrison-'

'What's been happening? Have you arrested that man yet?'

Cal stifled a sigh. 'Mrs Harrison we are still investigating your daughter's disappearance, we-'

'I want him arrested! I know he's taken my Tess, I know he has! You've seen him, you've seen what a lunatic he is, why aren't you doing something about it?'

Cal waited until she had run out of steam.

'I promised you I would investigate every angle, and I am doing that.'

There was silence on the other end of the line, but Cal had the feeling the woman was crying. He felt a surge of pity.

'Mrs Harrison, this is not on the back burner. We are working on it. In fact, I have the file right in front of me now.'

'Well, get to work on it then!'

The phone was slammed down and Cal looked up to see Rob, still wearing the same suit he'd had on for the last two weeks, greasy hair uncombed, bags under his eyes.

'Sorry, Cal,' he muttered, heading for his desk.

Cal ignored him, knowing any conversation would only lead to an argument. Opening the file, he checked his notes.

No local travel agent records. Tess did not own a computer, internet booking unlikely.

Canvass of train and bus stations inconclusive. No car rental (does not drive)

Re boyfriend: spoke to officer at 2nd parachute regiment. Dole discharged in 2000. Commanding officer was Major James Peters. Human Resource Officer contacted was reticent and unhelpful.

Conclusion – continue to monitor boyfriend.

Nb: interview with Roy Hardy (father) Monday am.

That was this morning, and Cal was not looking forward to it. He glanced round at Rob, but he couldn't drop that on his partner's lap, the man was too far out of it. He glanced at the other files on his desk; the robbery at the Bosworth antique shop and the serious assault outside Simpkins nightclub cried out to him for attention, but there simply wasn't the time. He made a mental note to get DC Roslyn to look at them; she would relish the opportunity. Cal glanced at Rob again, biting back a sudden burst of anger. In a way he was glad he was no longer married. It was selfish, he supposed, not having to worry about anyone else, but it sure as hell made life easier. Thinking about Lynne, the familiar sense of gloom descended and he shook his head. He got himself another coffee, staring out at the rain while he waited for Roy Hardy to turn up. He knew Tess's father would be nothing like her mother. Cal had checked up on him and discovered his failed business, his drink driving conviction. Here was a man who did not cope well with life. Perhaps this was where Tess got her apparent ineffectualness from.

Roy was a small, rotund man, with what was probably a jolly face, usually. He had clearly been crying, his face was blotched and his eyes bloodshot. But perhaps that wasn't all down to his emotion. The reek of whisky nearly made Cal gag, and he took a quick swig of his coffee to stifle the reaction.

'Can I get you something, Mr Hardy? Coffee? Water?'

The man slumped in the chair and leaned his elbows on the desk, and his head in his hands.

'Just my daughter,' he said.

Cal sat down, waiting as Roy struggled to control the tears running down his fat cheeks.

'I'll get you some water,' he said, standing up.

'No, it's all right. I'm sorry.' Roy scrubbed his face with his hands, took a deep breath and looked up.

'Please tell me there's something I can do to help find her.'

'Can you tell me when you last saw Tess?'

Roy closed his eyes, biting his lip. 'Wednesday, I think. We went for something to eat at the Highcross.'

'And how did Tess seem that night?'

Roy looked up, surprised. 'Well, she was just the same as ever. We had a couple of drinks, cracked a few jokes. She was fine.'

'She didn't mention any holidays or anything?'

'We talked about going on holiday together. Well-'

He gave a wry chuckle. 'I wanted her to come abroad with me. Not sure she would have a lot of fun with an old duffer like me, but she's a lovely girl, my Tess.'

He lapsed into memory, and Cal cleared his throat. 'She didn't mention any problems at work?'

Roy shook his head. 'She liked that little job. Sheila, my ex, she's always trying to get her to do something more impressive, but Tess is happy selling her little ornaments.'

'Mrs Harrison believes Tess would never have run away.'

Roy shrugged. 'I don't think she would, either. She's a bit scatty, like me.'

Cal wrote in his notebook, and Roy sat back and heaved a sigh.

'Did she mention her boyfriend at all?'

'Not really. I don't think it was anything serious, or she'd have told me. We can talk about anything, Tess and me, you see.'

Maybe not quite anything, Cal thought. He still wasn't sure about the runaway angle. Roy leaned forward.

'Have you any leads? Any idea where she is?'

Cal looked away from the desperation in the man's eyes. 'We're looking into every possible alternative, Mr Hardy, I promise you.'

Roy sat back, and Cal read the body language. The man knew Cal had nothing, but unlike the mother, he wasn't the type to shout and scream.

'Have you any children, detective?'

Cal swallowed, feeling a dull ache arriving in his chest. He shook his head.

'I know you're doing your best,' Roy said, a sad smile on his ruddy face. 'You will tell me if anything happens?'

'Of course I will.'

Cal gave him a card with his number on it, and Roy shambled out of the interview room, no doubt to climb straight back into the bottle. Cal felt a twinge of unease. Something wasn't right about this case at all. The boyfriend was distinctly strange, Cal had picked up the vibe at the mall. The army officer he had spoken to had been tight lipped and uncooperative, but Cal had the feeling that the boyfriend was involved in some way. Maybe he had just helped the girl get away, but he knew he had to be careful. From what Cal had sensed, the man wasn't all there.

God, he wanted a cigarette.

He glanced down at his notebook, where he had unconsciously doodled a picture of a pair of hobnailed boots. With a sigh he shut the book and glanced at the clock, wondering if he could spare half an hour to nip over to the home, see how mum was doing. That's if she was speaking to him. Or if she even remembered who he was. As long as she didn't cry, he thought. That was the one thing he could hardly bear. Roy Hardy's tears for his missing daughter meant less to Cal than Maggie Fisher's tears for her failing mind.

ELEVEN

It surprised Mike how quickly things returned to normal. By the Monday after Tess's disappearance, it was as if she had never existed. The owner herself was now working at the glass shop, and the talk in the staff canteen had moved on to upcoming summer holidays. Mike felt sad in a way. He had loved Tess. It was too bad.

So it came as a further surprise when the police turned up to question him at home that night.

He recognised the man from before; Fisher. Mike looked at the visitor through his peephole and took his usual deep breath to prepare himself, although he felt fine; no panic, no fear. He put a smile on his face and opened the door.

'Sergeant Fisher, isn't it? Come in.'

The policeman hesitated, then nodded. 'Thanks, Mr Dole. I just have a few more questions.'

Mike led him into the living room, watching Fisher checking out his flat.

'Would you like some coffee?'

'No thanks.'

They sat down, and Mike leaned forward anxiously. 'Have you had any sight of her yet?'

Fisher looked at him levelly. 'No, not yet. Enquiries are ongoing.'

Mike could sense the man's hesitation.

'Mr Dole, I'm, sorry about the intrusion, but you may appreciate that in a disappearance case such as this, we have to look at all possible avenues.'

'Of course. And you can call me Mike.'

Fisher nodded. 'I understand that you left the army in 2000. Do you mind if I ask why?'

Mike had known this would come. He nodded.

'I was discharged,' he said softly. 'That's what you're asking, I take it?'

Fisher pulled out his notebook.

'On what grounds?'

'Health. I was stressed out.'

The policeman raised an eyebrow. 'It must have been bad for them to chuck you out.'

Mike's lips formed a wry smile. 'It wasn't good, no.'

Cal stared at him. 'Did you have any treatment?'

'Counselling. Supposed to see a civvy shrink, but it didn't work out.'

'Why not?'

'It wasn't working. No matter how much it was all talked out, it still didn't make the nightmares go away. I don't think anything ever will.'

And that was the truth, he thought to himself, bitterly.

'So you suffer from nightmares?'

'Yes. Occasionally, but when I have them, I can't sleep for days. I was prescribed sleeping tablets, however, I take Camomile tea instead, it helps. I don't like taking drugs.'

Fisher stared at him, and Mike's heart gave a lurch as he wondered what the policeman was seeing.

'I should tell you, Mr Dole, that certain allegations have been raised against you by Tess's family-'

'Her mother, yes, I know. She came to see me.'

'When was this?'

'Last Wednesday. She said she thought I had something to do with Tess's disappearance, and she was going to the police about it.'

'And what did you say?'

He shrugged. 'I told her to carry on, if it made her feel better.'

The policeman sat back, but Mike had no intention of giving him anything else.

'It appears you were the last person to see Tess.'

'I still don't know where she is,' he protested. 'Look, Sheila never liked me, and she must be distraught, so I'm not surprised she's gone to you. I also understand why you're looking at me as the culprit in all this. But believe me, if I knew where Tess is, I'd tell you.'

Just keep telling the truth, he thought, breathing evenly. *You can't go wrong.*

The policeman stood up. 'Thanks for your time, Mr Dole. If we need to, would you mind if we searched your flat?'

'You can do it now, if you like.'

Fisher gave him a faint smile. 'I'd prefer to do it by the book. Thanks again.'

When the policeman had gone, Mike sat on his sofa and breathed deeply. The policeman smelt of too many cups of coffee, and too long since the last shower. He went over the conversation again, and then he rehashed the trip north with Tess. No, he had done everything correctly. As the policeman had said; by the book.

But it was time to prepare for the next chapter. His supply cupboard would have to go. It was important that he give the appearance of being Mr Ordinary, as far as he could.

It had been ten days now. The birds would be tucking in to what was left of poor Tess on the island. It was an island Mike had been to before, many times. An island he loved, and thought very beautiful. However, he had never discovered its name.

Mike thought this was a good thing.

*

Daylight came slowly, as Tess lay in the dark of the wood and listened to her stomach crying at her, trying to hold the panic at bay. At intervals through the night she fed the fire, as much for comfort as for warmth. The hunger filled the whole world, clouding her thoughts. In the reasoned logic that came in the middle of the night, when decisions are made that will never see action in the light of day, she decided to eat the mussels after all. As soon as it got light.

The sky began to pale eventually, and Tess got up, shook herself hard, eyes tightly closed in case there were insects on her, and walked slowly down to the water's edge.

No Mike again, but then, she hadn't really expected it.

She looked at the mussel-encrusted rocks in the pale dawn light, and a deep sense of gloom enveloped her. Eating them was impossible, no matter how hungry she was. They were bound to make her sick, and she'd be in an even worse position than now.

The waves rolled gently in, and Tess scrubbed her face with her shaking hands, breathing in the sharp ozone smell. A seabird cried overhead, a sound that was almost human, and she looked up, a memory returning.

Turning away from the sea, she began to climb the hillside, trying to keep to the same path she'd taken days ago, when she climbed the mountain and discovered she was on an island.

Although exhausted and hungry, it was strange how *alive* she felt. She could smell the emerging wild flowers above the peaty scent of the gorse, and the strange seabird cries were extra loud in her ears. *Maybe your senses are enhanced when you're about to die,* she thought, sourly.

It took most of the morning to find what she was looking for. The dead seagull had been attacked by predators, but had dropped into a deep rock crevice high on the mountain ridge. The bird still looked perfect, as if it had just fallen from the sky. Tess had to lie flat and stretch her arm to the shoulder to grab hold of it.

'*Yes!*' she hissed, feeling the soft feather of the wing beneath her fingers. She pulled, scrambling to her knees as the carcass came out of the hole, and as she dropped it on the grass the wing fell over to reveal the bird's body, which was a ruined mess of bone and tissue, teeming with maggots.

Tess's heart lurched. She struggled away on her hands and knees, and vomited her morning drink of water on to the grass. Her stomach heaved over and over, until she was crying with the pain of it. She curled into a foetal crouch, clutching at her stomach and sobbing, her eyes clamped shut.

'I can't do this,' she cried. 'Please get me out of here. Please!'
The words were snatched away by the swirling wind, which caught at her hair and snapped inside her cagoule.

The pain eased as her sobs subsided, and Tess slowly got her breath back. Taking one deep breath, she looked back at the bird. The tiny demolition crew had crawled away from the light, and the poor creature looked like a specimen laid out for dissection. Tess sniffed hard, trying to stop crying. The bird had been her last hope, and now even that was gone.

She stood up and took another deep breath, gazing up at the pale blue sky. 'What am I going to do?'

A flood of tears blinded her, bringing with them a sudden gout of raw anger.

'I'm sick of this!' she shouted. 'I've had enough. Do you hear me? I've had enough!'

There was no one there to hear except a lone gull circling above, and the wind moaning in the rocky buttresses.

And deep in her heart, Tess felt something change, something fundamental, as if her very genes were rearranging themselves. There were things in life that were too horrible to think about, but you didn't have to think. Animals didn't think much, but they survived, and that was the important thing.

She picked up the bird by the tip of one wing, and carried it down the hillside to dump it in the shallow pool by her waterfall. Then she rekindled the fire and took up the knife, making a point of not looking at what was left behind in the pool as she pulled out the bird. Using the sharp knife and the last vestiges of her anger, it was easy to cut the bird's wing from its body. Tess threw the rest back into the stream to be carried away.

The wing was perfect, white and soft, like an angel's wing. Tess found this thought arriving from a long way away, as if it had come from someone else and she was just listening in. She tucked the wing into the edge of the fire, then sat watching as the delicate white turned to brown and then black. The feathers stank of burning hair, but before long the smell that met her desperately rumbling stomach was roasting meat.

The old Tess warned against not cooking meat for long enough, and this was good advice, but the new Tess was ravenous. Heart racing with anticipation, she stripped the burnt skin from the flesh and felt her mouth fill deliciously with saliva. The bird tasted better than anything she'd ever eaten before. She stuffed the meat into her mouth with grease-soaked fingers, moaning to herself with the pleasure of it. When at last the bones were sucked dry, she sat back against the bank and smiled.

I'm not going to die, she thought. *If I could eat that, I can eat mussels. I can do anything.*

She closed her eyes, still smiling. Her stomach felt immensely full, and she was suddenly exhausted. The gentle crackling of the fire was soothing and she drifted into sleep.

Tess dreamed.

She was six years old. Dad had taken her to Twycross zoo for her birthday, and she came home bursting with stories, clutching her balloon in the shape of a monkey's head. 'Mummy!' she cried, rushing into the house. 'Mummy I saw a chimp and a snake and a hyena-'

Mummy was standing in the door of the kitchen, arms crossed. Tess looked up into her angry face, her heart beginning to race in fear, but Sheila looked beyond her, her mouth twisting.

'I told you four o'clock.'

'Well, the little 'un was having such a good time. Weren't you Tess?'

Dad reached down and tickled her, and she laughed.

'Do you never think about anyone other than yourself? I told you I have plans for tonight, but oh no, you have to go your own way.'

'Sheila, we're only half an hour late-'

'Just get out, Roy. Just go, will you.'

Tess looked up at the adult faces, not understanding.

'Please don't shout,' she said, tears approaching.

Sheila bent down to her, unbuttoning her coat with tugging, angry fingers.

'You, young lady, mind your manners. Now get upstairs and have a wash before dinner.'

And she grabbed the balloon and made off with it into the kitchen.

Tess stood watching her go, chin tucked into her chest, her throat suddenly aching. She felt her father's hands on her shoulders, felt his head against hers.

'I love you, sweetheart,' he said.

She could hear mother clanging pots in the kitchen. She didn't want dad to go. Mummy would shout at her. She could smell their dinner. It smelled burnt.

Tess woke, her throat still aching, to find the hollow swathed in smoke. The fallen tree was on fire, and in panic she scrambled to her feet, coughing, eyes streaming. Tripping over a rock, she sprawled to the ground, the wind blowing painful sparks into her face and sending them rising into the air like angry spirits. She got back up, heart pounding, and as she noticed the bank behind her smouldering, she tripped again and fell into the leaf litter, a scream erupting from her aching throat as a woodlouse crawled across her hand. Struggling upright, Tess began to run, crying hard, the wind slapping her in the face as she made for the sea. At last she reached the shingle beach, her feet sliding on the wet stones and sending her crunching to the ground again. She scrambled up, breath coming in rasping gasps, and looked out into the darkness. There was little to be seen under the heavy cloud cover, but she could hear the waves crashing in, and the chill wind delighted in tugging at her nylon jacket.

What am I going to do now?

Looking back at the orange glow in the sky above the trees, guilt poured into her like sour wine. How could she have been so careless, falling asleep and letting the fire get out of hand. The waves roared in to crunch across the pebbles, dragging them into the sea with a sound like bones rubbing together. Tess folded her arms, shivering in the cold, just as heavy drops of rain began to splatter on her jacket like a penance. There was nowhere to shelter, so she crouched under the bank where the soil gave way to the sea, staring into the darkness, trying not to think. Thoughts brought logic, and logic brought reality, which was simply too hard to bear.

Even though she kept her head lowered, the rain found its way inside her hood to trickle down her neck, making her shiver and squirm. The storm was relentless, and after a while, soaked and shivering, legs aching with cramp and cold, she stood and looked back at the trees. The orange light had left the sky now, and she slowly picked her way back to the hollow. The fallen tree had not burned through; the rain dousing the fire before too much damage could be done, but the young trees hanging on to life above the hollow were destroyed, and some had fallen into the gap. Tess stood staring at the still glowing mess.

Well, if there was one fallen tree, there might be others, she thought, trying to inject some hope into the situation. All her proud thoughts of survival, of being able to do anything, had turned out to be so much bullshit after all. Shoulders slumped, she bit back the tears. She was useless. She couldn't even start a fire without burning down the forest.

Tess hunted around in the faint light until she found the precious knife and tobacco tin, and then she walked away from the hollow, keeping the wind at her back. She kept walking through the dark, because there was simply nothing else to do. Somewhere in her hindbrain danced the insidious thought: if she stopped now, she would stop forever.

As she walked, she thought about Mike.

Why has he done this to me?

She remembered the two of them sitting in MacDonald's one day. She always had trouble with the burgers, the lettuce and gherkins kept falling out of the side, but Mike supplied his own answer to the problem. He had eaten the top bun, then the burger, then the rest, licking his fingers afterwards rather than wiping them on a napkin. She had laughed, and his face flushed, his eyes wary.

'What's so funny?'

'You! Eating your burger like that. As if you can't bear to waste any of it.'

He shrugged then, looking away. 'You should never waste food,' he said. 'You don't know when you'll get your next meal.'

Well, that had turned out to be good advice, she thought sourly.

The sky began to grow lighter, and after a while she stopped and watched as the eastern clouds turned pale pink and orange. There was a line on the horizon now that she thought might be land, although it looked so far away. The sun rose, darkening the horizon line, lighting up the clouds as if they, too were on fire. With a full stomach, she was better able to appreciate the beauty of it, but only for a moment.

She had walked north, not that there had been any thought involved in that choice. Her trainers coped badly with the rocky ground, and as soon as the sun was up and the chill wind began to ease, she sat down on a boulder to rest.

It's all so ludicrous! she thought. *I'm a shop girl, for God's sake.*

The nearest she'd come to the wilderness was a school geology trip to Charnwood Forest. Tess felt the tears sneaking up on her again, and tried to ignore them. It didn't matter what had happened to her in the past. This was now. She had to keep going.

But why? What was the point? She didn't even know where she was, what day it was, what *month* it was! She could be here for years.

No, a small voice insisted. No, you won't live that long.

The tears dried on her face, making the tiny spark burns smart.

'I don't want to die,' she said, staring down the hillside at the trees below. The sound of her own voice was loud in the still silence of the dawn.

Then she stood up, the sun warming her back, and carried on walking.

TWELVE

It was funny how his feet always led him to the same place. No matter how long he put it off, Mike always ended up at the shop with the window full of crystal ornaments. He told himself it was part of his job, to patrol every area, but deep down, he knew he was drawn to that window, and the tiny glass animal that transfixed him with its perfection.

He always felt calmer after he had been there.

But today was different. Since Tess's disappearance, the glass shop owner had been forced to work there herself. She was a fat woman who liked tight, bright coloured clothes, which did little to flatter her bulges. She wore a pair of spectacles on a chain round her neck, and when Mike looked into the shop, she raised them and peered through them without ever putting them on. Mike was disgusted by her lack of self-control. He could tell she was suspicious of him, but that didn't bother him.

Today, there was another girl working behind the counter. It appeared that every last person had given up on Tess now, which didn't surprise him. He walked into the shop, looking at the girl, who was punching numbers into a mobile phone and frowning. She looked up, and Mike smiled.

'Hello,' he said. 'I'm Mike Dole, security.'

'Oh, hello. I'm Marian. I can't get my phone to work.'

'It's this end of the mall,' Mike said. 'You can never get a signal here.'

'Oh. Right,' she smiled. Mike noticed a dimple appear on the left side of her face. He felt his heart beating faster.

'Is this your first day?'

'Yes.' She was still smiling. 'I wasn't sure about taking the job, after that poor girl disappeared, but I need the cash-'

She bit down on her lip, and Mike stared at the white of her teeth, the dark pink of her lipstick.

'Feeling sorry doesn't pay the bills,' he said.

'Do you know, have they found her yet?'

'Found her? It's more likely that she's simply run off.'

'Oh,' said Marian, brightening up. 'That's good. I thought she might have been, you know, abducted. There's a lot of weirdos about.'

'Yes,' said Mike.

'How do they know she's run away?'

'She took a suitcase with her.'

Marian tucked a strand of streaked brown hair behind her ear. 'Oh. So. Have you worked here long?'

Mike smiled, feeling a sense almost of elation, the feeling of being in control was better than any drug.

'Not very long. You've got some lipstick on your front tooth, you know.'

'Oh! Have I?' She produced a small mirror from her handbag and rubbed at the tooth with her finger. 'I'm such a bird brain,' she giggled.

Mike laughed too. 'There's a reasonable canteen here. I could show you at lunchtime, if you like.'

Marian looked up at him through her eyebrows, and Mike was pretty sure that was something she'd rehearsed. He felt a delicious tingle in his stomach. He had done right to take Tess away. She had clearly been the cause of all his problems.

*

It had rained all morning, insistent, grey rain that seemed to fall in lumps rather than drops. Tess lay on the floor of the cave, watching the heavy sky, not moving.

Finding the cave had been wonderful, but the brief excitement wore off quickly. After all, she'd have preferred a boat, or a house, and there was still nothing to eat.

As the morning sun climbed higher, casting shadows, she had spotted the fissures in the rock above the cliffs. The caves were all shallow, some no more than two or three feet deep, but this one was close to twelve feet deep and fifteen high, with just enough room for a fire and for her. She lay still, listening to her blood slogging through her veins and waiting for the rain to stop.

Perhaps it never will, she thought absently, imagining herself lying here forever, until the rest of the world left her behind.

Exhausted and starving, she dozed on and off as the day wore on, her sleep filled with fractured bits of dreams, most of them involving food. It was three days now since the barbecued seagull, but she was not as hungry this time. She felt more and more distanced from her self, as if the real Tess had shed her skin and left it behind in the woods.

Eventually the fire grew so low that the cold forced her out of her stupor. Trudging down the hill looking for wood, she noticed the rabbit holes pock-marking the hillside. *Maybe I could make a trap,* she thought, having absolutely no inclination even to try. The rain had stopped by the time she'd found enough wood, the emerging sun comfortably warm on her back as she climbed again.

The sun's about the only hopeful thing, she thought, aware that if the weather had been rougher, she would no longer be here to notice it.

From the cave mouth, she watched the sun move across the sky, gleaming on hanging raindrops, turning them into tiny, secret worlds. They reminded her of her old life, the shop where glass ornaments surrounded her, both fragile and potentially lethal. She had broken a glass bird once, and it had cut her deeply, lashing out in what she imagined as its dying throes.

'That's what I have to be,' she said aloud, just to be hearing her own voice. 'I'm easy to break. I have to be hard and sharp.'

She sighed. It was foolish, talking to herself. *But it's true*, her thoughts added. *It might be foolish, but it's still true.*

She glanced back down at the rabbit holes, taking a deep breath.

Reaching for the tobacco tin, she drew out the roll of wire. It had a loop at one end, and she threaded the other end through, putting the noose over her wrist and loosening the wire hastily as it cut sharply into her.

Yeah, but how to get a rabbit to run into it?

She hurried back down the hillside, looking at the rabbit holes. The earth around the holes was worn down and grassless, with nowhere to camouflage the wire. However, after the rain, the banks were slippery, and she could easily press it into a circle around one of the smaller holes. She smeared mud over the wire and looked around for somewhere to secure the end. There was nothing nearby apart from some stunted heather. She tugged morosely at a large clump, expecting to pull it out of the ground, but the woody plant was strong, and wouldn't give.

It has to be worth a try, she thought, twisting the wire round the bark and tying it as best she could. She stepped back to check her handiwork, then smeared more mud on the exposed wire. At last all that could be seen of the trap was the wire wrapped round the heather bark. With a sigh, Tess climbed back up the hillside. It was growing dark, and she hoped rabbits came out at night.

In the firelight, her cave felt almost cozy, but Tess was restless, unable to sleep because of the dull pounding ache of hunger, and the need to listen for the noise of a trapped rabbit. It never occurred to her that the animal wouldn't make a sound.

*

Cal spent a fruitless fifteen minutes on the phone trying to trace the whereabouts of Major James Peters. Whether the Army were being deliberately unhelpful, or just plain stupid, he couldn't tell. First they told him the major was in Canada, then his whereabouts were 'classified', then he was on a training trip to Botswana. Eventually Cal was put through to a training camp in Thetford, where he had to assume the telephone operator was a civilian.

'Major Peters?' He asked. 'Oh yes, he's overlooking the mortar exercises this morning. We're very busy, you know, what with the upcoming orders.'

Cal hesitated. 'Orders?'

'We're being deployed to Iraq.'

'Really? When?'

'Oh, I can't tell you that, you're a civilian!' the man laughed, and Cal thought, you can't tell me when, but you just told me who and where.

'Is there any chance I might speak with him?'

'I don't know when he'll be back. Would you like to leave a message?'

Cal chewed his lip. The chances were his call would never be returned. He was thinking about just driving down there.

'Can you tell me where -'

'Hey! I think you're in luck, I can see the major now. If you hold the line I'll see if he's got time to talk to you. What was your name again?'

'Fisher, Cal said, '*Detective Sergeant* Cal Fisher.'

'Right you are.'

Cal waited, thumbing through his notes while he waited to see if the great man had a few minutes to spare with the lowly copper. He glanced through the glass to the main incident room, where there wasn't a spare space to be had.

'Hello, Sergeant Fisher?'

'Hello Major. Thanks for talking to me.' Cal found himself sitting up straight in his chair. Peters had that sort of accent.

'Not at all. How can I help?'

The man had a confident, straightforward voice, used to command without appearing arrogant. Cal felt a twinge of hope.

'I'm investigating a missing person case, which I regret is looking more and more like a kidnapping. I think one of your former people might be involved.'

'Really? Well, that would surprise me.'

Cal glanced over the papers again. 'Corporal Michael Dole. I believe you signed his discharge papers in 2000.'

'I see.'

All hope was fading fast. Peters was as tight lipped as everyone else.

'Look, Major, I'm not trying to bad mouth your people. I'm trying to trace a missing woman, and this man might know where she is or what's happened to her. Now will you help me?'

'I'm sorry, sergeant, I didn't mean to sound dismissive. I will help you all I can. What is it you want to know?'

Cal could hear the sound of a door being slammed on the other end of the phone.

'Did you know Dole personally?'

There was a long and eloquent silence. 'Yes I did.'

'Can you tell me a bit about him?'

A deep sigh. 'Mike was a superb soldier: He loved the army. He excelled in survival training, and never hesitated to help others. He was loyal, dedicated, brave, and compassionate.'

'But you discharged him.'

Another sigh. 'He had personal problems. You must realise, Mike saw a lot of action. He was part of Desert Storm. He lost good friends there, it affected him deeply.'

'What sort of problems?'

'He had flashbacks, trouble sleeping, emotional disturbances. He went through counselling here, but it didn't seem to help him.'

Cal scribbled in his notebook.

'If a crime has been committed by this man, I will co-operate in any way necessary to bring him to justice.' Peters' voice was clipped now. 'But from what you have told me, he is only a suspect in a missing person case. No one is dead.'

'As far as we know.'

'Have you spoken to Mike? Asked him about this?'

'Of course. He denies all knowledge.'

Cal thought quickly about how to phrase the next question. 'Obviously Dole was trained to be a soldier, to survive, to kill.'

'Obviously.'

Cal bit his lip.

'In battle, that's his job, but what about in civilian life? Do you consider that Mike Dole is capable of committing a serious crime? A kidnapping, for example?'

'Detective, I can't possibly comment on his mental state since he left the army.'

'How about while he was still there? Is it possible, was he so disturbed?'

Cal read the ensuing silence well. He drew two black lines under the question.

'I'm sorry to trouble you Major, I'm just trying to find out the truth.'

'The truth. Yes.' Peters fell silent for a moment. 'Of course, sergeant. If I can help you further, please let me know.'

'I'll do that, thank you.'

Cal put the phone down and stared at the black lines. Then he went back a page and drew a line under the word *capable?*

He thought about the man, his tight thin lips in a stubborn jaw, his wary stormcloud eyes. It was nothing obvious, but Cal knew that behind those eyes, all was not well.

'What happened to you, Mike?' he murmured, pencilling the question mark into a shadowy face.

A moment later he looked up as the Chief walked into his office. Cal got up to follow, and was caught in the plume of cigarette smoke Colin Jarvis was tailing. He stifled a cough, raising his hand to knock, but his boss saw him and waved him in.

'Hey, Cal. What's up. Any sign of that waste of space Matlock?'

Cal ignored the jibe. Jarvis wiped ash from the lapel of his grey suit and gave Cal a rueful smile.

'You still off the fags?'

Cal nodded. 'I'm fed up of fighting the system, sir,' he said. 'You can't smoke anywhere these days, I may as well give up.'

'Well, bollocks,' Colin said. 'I'm not giving up.'

Wait for winter, Cal thought. *Standing outside in the freezing rain. Maybe then you'll think again.*

DI Jarvis reached into the drawer of his desk and pulled out a packet of mints. Cal had known the team leader on and off for years, and up till a month ago had never seen him without a cigarette in his hand.

'Are you and the team coping okay? What's Matlock saying about his problems?'

'His wife's having some sort of mid-life crisis.'

'Jesus. I'd better speak to him-'

Cal shook his head. 'Inspector, can I run something past you? This missing person?'

Jarvis raised an eyebrow at the interruption, but didn't comment. 'Fire away.'

He was a big man, well over six foot, which only served to highlight his thinness. Cal hoped that his boss might substitute sweets for cigs, and finally put on some weight. Right now Jarvis was obviously nicotined up and feeling expansive, exactly what Cal was relying on. He ran down the events to date, ending with his conversation with the major. Colin listened in silence until he had finished.

'So what do you want to do next?'

'I'd like to requisition his army records, sir. I think they might tell us more about the man.'

Colin sat back and folded his thin hands behind his head.

'That won't be easy,' he said. 'You know the RMP. To them, information is power. It'll be like pulling teeth.'

Cal knew the Royal Military Police would be the first port of call, and he was ready for this. 'Remember that case about 18 months ago, the one Rob handled? The off duty soldier who attacked the girl in *Liquid*?'

Colin nodded. 'That bloody student joint. The army wanted to take the whole thing away from us, and they did, as I recall.'

'Yes, I think he was court martialled or whatever they do to their own, But Rob built up a working relation ship with one of the MPs. I bet he could give him a ring.'

Colin shook his head. 'You need Special Investigation Branch if you want to requisition records. They'll never go for it.'

'This man might put a word in for us with SIB. It's worth a try, sir.'

Colin sighed and glanced out at the rain.

'All right, I'll bite. But it still sounds like a straightforward runaway to me.' He looked at Cal and smiled.

'But you've got good instincts, Cal. I'll go along with them.'

'Thanks, sir.' He hesitated. 'I suppose a search warrant would be out of the question?'

The chief chuckled. 'On what you have to date? You already know the answer to that.'

'Yes sir.'

He stood up to leave, the smell of cigarettes making him feel dizzy.

'And Cal, if Matlock doesn't sort this out soon, I'll have to do something about it. What does he think this is, a garden party?'

'Sir,' Cal said as he left. The DI was a decent bloke, but even he had only so much patience.

*

The little creature's eyes bulged, its tongue sticking obscenely through its teeth. It reminded her of the goldfish bowl full of fishermen's maggots that used to be in the pet shop window when she was a child, and how she would stand and stare at it in horrified fascination. 'Look what I have done,' Tess whispered, her mouth dry. She reached out to untie the wire from the heather, and the rabbit gave a lunge. A scream rang out, and Tess realised she had made the sound herself. *Oh my God it's not dead!* She stood up, backing off, her heart pounding with horror and guilt. 'I never wanted to hurt you!'

Tess crouched down, trying to get her fingers under the wire, but the rabbit's last lunge had drawn it even tighter round its neck, and Tess felt the lifeless body grow heavy in her hands. Tears filled her eyes and rolled down her cheeks to stain the brown fur. She pulled the wire free of the stump and carried both snare and animal back up the hill.

The fire is the only hopeful thing I have, she thought, as she sat cross-legged in front of it. She dumped the wire by the entrance, where it coiled itself into a circle, almost like a roll of barbed wire protecting her cave from the drizzling rain. She gazed at the dead rabbit lying on the stone floor, clasping her shaking hands together. The fur had been so soft, so very soft. Far softer than her cuddly toy rabbit back home. A jolt of reality hit her like a shovel in the face. *What the hell am I doing?* She stared out at the rain.

Here I am on some lost island, with no food and no hope, and I'm still thinking about soft toys.

She picked up the little creature, feeling how much colder it had become as death moved through its small frame. All at once her stomach growled, as her subconscious reminded her why the rabbit was here.

How can I do it? She thought. How could she break that perfect skin, rip apart what was a whole, perfect little body? *I can't.*

Then you're doomed, came the deeper thought. *How many days has it been without food? How many more do you think you can survive? This little animal has died so that you can go on, and you're being squeamish?*

She had no idea where the inner voice had come from, it didn't sound like her at all. She glanced up as the rain began to fall harder, and she watched raindrops bouncing back from the grass. She could see the edge of a rainbow, just the violet and blue, against the steely sky.

She took a deep breath, a sudden shiver running through her.
Reaching into the tin, she lifted the scalpel blade, pulling it from its foil wrapper.

The skin was drawn tight across the rabbit's white belly, the hairs fine and smooth. She could feel the ribs, other bones, *inside* things. She turned the creature over, her hands shaking, heart thumping. Despite the cold, beads of sweat were popping out on her forehead. The skin round the rabbit's neck was loose, and it was easy to grab a handful of it. Without any further thought she stabbed the blade in between her fingers, wincing, waiting for the blood to spurt out and splash her. But there was no blood.

This is the soft toy dad brought you back from Skegness. You need the stuffing for something else, so you're just removing the synthetic filling. Polyester, that's all it is.

Tess had her eyes closed as the blade completed its round. She could feel wetness on her hands, and she dropped the blade, opening one eye to see what she had done. Her hands were really shaking now, and she breathed hard as she grasped the torn skin, knowing she had to do this now, or it would never be done. She closed her eyes again, and pulled.

It's just a chicken. Just a chicken skin. You're pulling it off because it's not good for you; too fattening.

It took more effort than she had expected, and the air was suffused with an odd smell, not unpleasant, just strange. Tess felt filled with a detached horror, as if she was watching someone else do this. She put the animal back on the stone floor and sat up.

The rabbit now lay exposed from the head down, with the flaps of skin still attached to the feet, as if the carcass had been placed on a fur blanket. Outside, the rain was hammering the ground, and Tess looked out at it, her breath catching in her throat, wishing she could run out into the rain and not come back.

'Get it over with!' she told herself, picking up the rabbit.

The skin would not pull off over the feet. They would have to be cut off.

Tess picked up the knife. How ironic, she thought, that there was so much moisture outside, but none at all in her mouth.

'Look for the joints,' she said aloud.

The sound of the knife going through the tendons was something she knew she would have to learn to live with. The tearing, the crunching, the hideous sensation of the bones moving beneath their slimy protecting ligaments, the finality of the resistance ending as the bones parted. She bit back on the urge to retch and looked down at the fluffy bunny, now a butcher's carcass, the colour of cinnamon. The head, still attached, still normal, looked obscene, but there was no way she could remove it. Not yet. Not with the cold empty eyes staring at her.

She sat back against the wall, letting the cold of the stone sear through her and make her shiver. Outside, the rain was easing, the afternoon growing brighter. Not that it mattered. Tess felt as if she had taken something out of herself and given it away, and in return, something else had filled that empty place. Something hard and cold and knowing and angry. Something that even now was telling her to hurry up and finish the job and get the damn rabbit cooked. And something whose presence she acknowledged with deep regret, and knew she had no choice but to accept.

THIRTEEN

Mike took a deep breath of the clean-smelling air. After the recent rain, the air smelled good. He stood under the sign that said SUNNINGDALE CE TRE – EVERYTHING YOU NEED UN   ER ONE ROOF. The letters had been missing since he'd taken the job at the mall. No one would ever fix them.

He people-watched as he waited for Marian to turn up. A few feet away a young man was also waiting for someone. Small and skinny, with a floppy fringe of black hair over his eyes and cheeks angry with acne scars, he glanced over as he felt Mike's gaze upon him. He wore new, cheap clothes; black trousers that were too long, and a jade polyester jacket from which his thin wrists protruded like pale sticks. Mike gazed into the street, trying to guess who was coming to meet the boy; perhaps the young girl in the tight purple dress, no coat despite the cold air, her brown hair streaked with the same purple as the dress. She had a purposeful look on her face, and he dismissed her immediately. Behind her, he could see Marian. She was wearing a coat. A nice *sensible* coat. Mike smiled.

'Hi,' she said. 'Have you been waiting long?'

Mike shook his head. *All my life,* he thought. As they turned to go, the young man gave Mike a quick smile, as if they were co-conspirators. Mike didn't smile back.

'What shall we do?' breezed Marian. 'There's the new Matt Damon film over at the Meridien?'

Marian ended every sentence with an uplift in her voice, which Mike found very endearing.

'I'm not a fan of Matt Damon,' Mike said, having no idea who the man was. 'But we can go if you like.'

'Fabulous! Thanks Mike!' She looped her arm in his, grinning up at him in obvious pleasure. Her hand on his bicep was warm and soft, fragile against the strength of his muscle. Mike took a deep breath and felt his heart soar.

The film was about the feuding of shipwreck survivors on a small tropical island. The hero was all stubble and muscle, but Mike could tell it was all superficial. Not for Mr Damon the five mile run each dawn, the hundred press ups, fifty on each hand. It had been the routine of Mike's life for so long he could not imagine being without it.

Watching the characters trying their best to survive inevitably brought him back to Tess.

It was five weeks today since he had introduced her to the island. She was long dead. He looked into his heart for some vestige of regret over her passing, but there was nothing there at all, not even a space where something might once have been. It was as if he had sewn up the crack that her words had made in his life, and it had healed without leaving a scar.

At least, no scar that he could recognise. On the screen, the hero and his leading lady were having a *from here to eternity* moment in the surf, and Mike noticed a man two rows across snuggle up to his girlfriend. He put an arm round Marian's shoulders and felt warmth leach into his chest as she reached up to touch his hand.

As they left the cinema, Mike tuned out Marian's chatter about the beautiful island in the film, and some friend of hers who had been there, looking up at the brittle stars with the chill wind on his face. He imagined the wind ruffling Tess's hair as it blew across her prone body, frost forming on her open, dead eyes. That's if the gulls hadn't already made off with them.

'Shall we go for a drink? It's freezing!' Marian shivered theatrically.

'There's the Observatory across the road.'

Mike smiled. 'Okay.'

The pub was noisy and hot, and Mike immediately felt uneasy as someone jostled him heavily. 'Oops, sorry mate.'

The man was too drunk to see the sudden darkness in Mike's eyes, and Marian was oblivious. They managed to grab a small table just as another couple were leaving, and Marian settled in, taking her coat off and making a big deal out of crossing her legs. Fair enough, Mike thought, they were nice legs, but he was disturbed by her showing them off. *Tess would never have done that,* he thought, and at that, a tiny pang of pain seeped into his heart.

'You must tell me *all* about yourself, Mike,' Marian said, drinking her wine spritzer through a straw like a child. Mike thought she did that on purpose too, but if other men found it endearing, he certainly did not.

'Not much to tell,' he said, speaking as quietly as he could and still be heard above the din. 'I am your friendly neighbourhood security man.'

Marian seemed to find this funny. 'Have you always been in security?'

'Pretty much,' he said.

'Well, where were you born? Do you come from Leicester?'

He shook his head. 'London.'

'Oh, I'd love to live in London. It must be so vibrant and exciting.'

Mike recalled their filthy flat, the stairs stinking of piss and vomit, the druggies on the corner, his sister-

He took a deep drink of his pint. Some things needed to be put away for ever.

'Mike?'

'You can't hear yourself think in here,' he snapped. Marian recoiled as if he had struck her. He leaned forward, annoyed with himself at the lapse, and forced a smile.

'Sorry,' he said putting his head on one side in the conciliatory manner he had often practised. 'It's been a long day.'

'Oh, I get them all the time,' Marian breathed, relieved. She picked up her glass, continuing to drink through the pink straw, eyes strafing the room. Mike breathed deeply, twice, three times, until he was calm again. Strange, where had that anger come from?

He walked Marian to her bus stop and waited as she climbed aboard and sat down, waving manically at him. After the bus had gone, he headed home. It was a two mile walk back to his flat, but despite sidestepping bouncers throwing someone out of a pub, and having to avoid a couple of teenagers gunning their stolen car round a roundabout, he felt peace steal into his soul. The night was cold and clear, and he breathed deeply as he walked, letting the icy air fill his lungs.

*

The sun was painting the clouds in shades of chocolate and plum when Tess put the last branch on the pyre and stood back to examine her handiwork. The pile of wood was big enough. If she could get it lit in time, it would be visible a long way out to sea. Satisfied, she smiled to herself and looked out to the west. The weather had been even milder today, gentle enough for her to forego the waterproof. She sat on a rock and watched the sunset.

There were no boats to be seen, but she could make out the shapes of seals on the rocks below, and wished she had binoculars to watch them with. She noticed that they looked back at her, sometimes, which filled her with an odd delight. *At least I'm not completely alone*, she thought.

When at last the sun left the sky, and the clouds turned to wisps of grey, she made her way home to the cave. The fire had burned low, but soon flared up again when she added wood from her stockpile. She sat cross-legged in front of the flames and let her mind drift.

Three rabbit skins now lay on the jagged rocks at the back of the cave, drying out. Next to them was a makeshift net made of scraps of multicoloured rope, retrieved from the tide. It looked quite jolly.

Tess, stomach full of rabbit meat, feeling more hopeful than she had since arriving here, had been galvanised into some serious exploring. In the days that followed, she trawled the eastern beach as the tide receded, collecting whatever washed up on the shingle. Sometimes there was nothing but old plastic bottles and broken bits of wood, but often she found nylon rope, or an intact box, or a plastic bag. She gathered these things and brought them back, using them to store her leftover food, or collect mussels from the rocks. She was developing quite a taste for them.

The second time she set the trap over the rabbit hole, she didn't return to the cave, but instead climbed down into the woods below. It was too far away to tell if anything was caught, but she waited until nearly all the light left the sky before hurrying back up. If nothing was there, she would remove the wire and try again tomorrow. She wasn't going to be responsible for another slow agonising death.

The rabbit had not been caught for long. He was still struggling gamely when Tess grabbed him and pulled the wire taut. She heard a dull snick as the neck was broken, and the little creature's body went limp. The old Tess felt something cold stab her in the heart.

The new Tess felt nothing at all.

She had learned to distance herself from her actions, to separate her logical mind from her emotional self. The old Tess was still there. Sometimes she found herself in tears, for no particular reason, but she could control it. She knew she had to.

She climbed down the south-eastern side of the mountain, where the land looked flatter and greener, and there she had found a ruined house. It was no more than three rickety walls, the roof long gone, but inside she found the remains of a fireplace and a stone slab that might have once been a bed. The hope that had filled her was completely misplaced, for there had been no one here for tens, perhaps hundreds of years. Looking round the flat land surrounding the stones, she noticed something unusual.

The remains of a wall surrounded a patch of tall plants. They looked like nothing else on the island, and there was something about them that she vaguely recognised. Her heart stepped up its pace as she grabbed at the nearest plant and pulled it out by the root, wiping the heavy earth from the small tuber. Potatoes!

Tess laughed, holding the plant up in triumph. It was nothing short of a miracle.

It will save my rabbits, she thought, gathering a few of the plants and heading home.

Now she felt her eyelids drooping as she stared into the fire. An odd contentment had arrived in her heart. It was not something she could quantify, and it was not something the old Tess could understand. The new Tess didn't do much in the way of thinking, she just got on with it, but the contented feeling was part of the new her, she was certain.

She made plans for the morning; she would go further south, the only direction left to travel, and see what was there. The island was far bigger than she had first thought, and walking took so long across the rough and boggy terrain.

'Maybe at last I'll find a boat, and can escape,' she said, smiling wryly to herself, zipping up her cagoule. She lay down, pulling up the makeshift pillow she had made from a carrier bag filled with heather. Sleep took her seconds after she closed her eyes.

She dreamed. She was sitting at the table in her mother's house, reading a magazine. Mother was cooking something that smelled wonderful. Tess walked across the pristine kitchen floor towards her, her feet echoing.

'Can I have some of that?' she asked, looking over Sheila's shoulder. Sheila was stirring a pot, but the cooker was not switched on. The pot was full of maggots. Sheila pulled a plate over and tipped the pot out on to it. Tess watched as the squirming creatures moved with unnatural speed to spread all over the work surfaces.

'What have you done!' Sheila shouted.

Tess, heart pounding, backed towards the door.

'Tess, you're just like your father, totally useless! You can't even look after yourself.'

She said nothing as her mother ranted, drops of her spittle flying off to hit Tess on the cheek.

She woke up with the rain pelting her in the face, and in a surreal moment thought she was underwater. Blinking and gasping, she got up, stepping into the fire and sending orange sparks soaring into the darkness. The rain was coming straight into the shallow cave, and there was nowhere to hide. Tess looked out at the stormy night, her eyes adjusting slowly to the dark. The stormclouds were pale and heavy, coming straight out of the west. There was no escape. Tess pulled up the hood and drew the strings tight against the freezing rain, then dropped to her knees to find wood. The wind whistled and wheezed in the lost corners of her cave, rain sizzling in the remains of her fire as she pushed a few thin sticks into the embers, blowing on them. A sad wisp of smoke appeared, only to be seized by the wind.

Tess stood up and looked out again. There was nowhere to go to get out of the weather, and she took a deep breath and sighed. *I'll just have to make the best of it.* She walked to the very back of her cave and sat with her back to the opening, groping in the dark for her rabbit skins which she pulled into her pockets, tucking her hands in after them for warmth.

Tess closed her eyes. There were no tears, no sighs, no cursing. She simply closed down all her thoughts, all the anger and hopeless emotion, and waited for morning.

FOURTEEN

It was 10 am in the station, and for once Cal had the place virtually to himself. The Hardy case was beginning to eat at him, because there was absolutely no sign of the woman, and because he was intrigued by the boyfriend. The case file was open in front of him and was reading it again, hoping something might jump out.

Michael Dole, 37 years old. Discharged from the army on health grounds 2000. No records received yet.

Rob Matlock had phoned the MP he knew from the old case, a man named Johnson, but Cal read between the lines and figured that the army cop had either been promoted and was not interested, or was simply embarrassed by the past association. Rob's perpetual gloomy demeanour clearly hadn't helped. Nevertheless, Johnson had agreed to contact SIB and request their help.

Flat very neat - army discipline? Very jumpy, tight control. Volunteered search. Warrant?

2 years at present address. 'Good tenant.' No financial irregularities. No criminal record. Vehicle clean.

No family: 'lost touch'. Co-workers wary of him. A loner, very quiet. Extremely good record of apprehending miscreants.

Continue to monitor. Wait for RMP records.

What the report didn't state was: gut feeling - this is a bad, bad boy.

Cal stared out of the window. Until he got the MOD records, he had nothing to go on except his hunch. There was no way he'd get a warrant to search Mike's flat and car, not on the evidence to hand. He pulled up the file and dialled the number Rob had left for the RMP. He was shunted around three times before he reached someone from SIB, and he tried to keep his voice light as he stated his request for the fourth time.

'Yes, Detective Sergeant. We have your request. It is in the queue and will be handled as soon as we can.'

Cal took a deep breath. 'Is there any way you could give it priority? I'm working on a –'

'I'm sorry, I can't do that,'

The woman didn't sound sorry at all. Cal gritted his teeth.

'I'm working on the case of a missing person, and these records could be vital in saving a life.'

'I appreciate that, sir, but there's nothing I can do.'

Jesus Christ! 'If the queen was missing, I bet I'd get those records the same day.'

'I can't say, sir.'

He slammed down the phone, just as DC Roslyn walked in.

'Problems, sir?'

Cal shook his head. 'Bureaucracy,' he said. Roslyn gave him a wan smile and walked on. Cal caught the whiff of cigarette smoke from her clothes, and a sharp pang of craving hit him hard. He took a deep breath. It had been three weeks now, he had no intention of giving in to the craving. He was about to go for coffee when the phone rang. He entertained a silly thought that perhaps the soldier had had a change of heart, but no, it was Sheila Harrison.

'Sergeant Fisher, can I have an up to date report, please.'

Cal leaned back and closed his eyes.

'Mrs Harrison, I'm glad you've called,' he said.

'You are?'

'I wonder if I could take another look at Tess's house.'

'Why?'

Why indeed, he thought. *Just to be doing something positive.*

'In case anything has been missed. Can I-'

'I can meet you there in half an hour, otherwise it'll have to be tomorrow.'

'Half an hour is fine,' he said, but the line had already been disconnected.

What are you doing, Cal? He wondered, as he left the station.

*

Sheila was waiting for him outside the house, tapping her fingers on the steering wheel. He smiled at her as she got out, walking to the door, keys in hand. She didn't smile back, but opened the door and walked in, not waiting for him. Cal followed hesitantly, but she was standing inside the door, and shut it impatiently as he walked through.

'What's this all about?' she demanded.

'I just want to take another look. Sometimes things just don't appear significant first time round.'

'You mean you might have made a mistake.'

Cal raised an eyebrow. 'Everyone makes mistakes. It's how they remedy them that's important.'

Sheila said nothing. Cal thought she looked even more bitter than usual. Her smart dove-grey pinstriped suit had been mismatched with a harsh gunmetal coloured blouse. The dark shade did not suit her at all, and made her fair complexion look washed out. She folded her arms and sighed.

'Right, let's get it over with.'

Cal followed her upstairs to Tess's bedroom, where he walked in and just looked round. *Is there anything I've missed?* He thought. He was sure there wasn't, but he opened the wardrobe anyway. He noticed a shoe rack, with a gap where a pair might have been removed.

'You still don't think Tess might just have gone away alone? Perhaps if her boyfriend was pressuring her, she may have wanted to get away-'

'No. I don't.' Sheila gave an impatient sigh. 'I've told you over and over, it would never occur to her to do something like that.'

Cal nodded, closing the door and opening the top drawer of the dresser. It was filled with the sort of detritus that top drawers always fill with: receipts, old pens, forgotten make up, a roll of sellotape, small coins. He pulled out a tatty leaflet.

'A driving school. Was she taking lessons?'

Sheila's brow furrowed. 'Oh, well. The Friday I spoke to her she said she was going to start having lessons that weekend.'

Cal put the leaflet in his pocket. He didn't know if it might mean anything or not, but at least it was a lead. 'She didn't mention anything else about the weekend?'

'No. And look, would she have booked a driving lesson, then gone away somewhere?'

'Good point.'

Sheila scrubbed her face with her right hand. 'Oh for God's sake, this is a waste of time!' She took a step towards him. 'You don't care at all about what's happened to my daughter.'

Cal felt a painful jolt deep inside. 'That's not true, Mrs Harri-'

'You haven't a clue what's happened to her, and you're just trying to placate me so I'll go away and stop harassing you. Go on, then. Tell me I'm wrong.'

Cal felt his heart thudding and tried to stay calm.

'You're wrong. For what it's worth, I do think something strange has happened to her.'

'Something strange? Like what?'

Cal shrugged. 'Let me check up on the driving lesson angle.'

Sheila's lips drew into a thin burgundy line.

'If you had arrested that man she was seeing, she might be back here by now. You do know he's going out with Tess's replacement at the shop, don't you?'

Cal felt another jolt. No, he hadn't known. A warning bell went off in his head.

'We can't just arrest the man on the basis that he was Tess's boyfriend. We have no evidence-'

'Evidence! I'm sick of these excuses. You're all convinced she's run off somewhere, while he goes Scot free.'

She turned to the window, suddenly calm. 'Let me tell you about my daughter, Mr Fisher. My daughter still expects Prince Charming to come along and sweep her off her feet. She cries at soppy films, is scared of spiders and heights, and sometimes she still sleeps with the light on. This is a woman who won't eat prawns because she thinks they look like maggots, but she'll open a window to let a fly escape instead of just squashing it.'

She turned to face him, her face flushed now, where she had wiped her makeup away.

'Tess doesn't even have a passport, and when I wanted to take her on holiday to the Isle of Man she wouldn't come because she was afraid the ferry might sink. You're suggesting she's done something reckless and confident, when the truth is she's fearful and utterly pathetic.'

Sheila was breathing hard, but Cal had become very calm.

'You don't like your daughter very much, do you?'

'*What!*'

'You want me to arrest Mike Dole even though there's no evidence against him. But you've just given me plenty of evidence to suggest you and your daughter don't get on. Maybe I should arrest you instead.'

Sheila's mouth was gaping like a landed fish. Her cheeks were blotchy now, and the look in her eyes was pure fury. Cal held up both hands.

'I believe you care about Tess, Sheila,' he said quietly. 'Despite the fact that maybe she didn't turn out to be your ideal daughter.'

He held her eyes, holding his breath and waiting for the response. His hunch was right. The fire went out of the woman's eyes and her shoulders sagged. Sheila sat down heavily on the bed. It took a long moment, but eventually she spoke.

'I never wanted children,' she said.

Cal felt a flush of relief. She was just like Lynne, his ex-wife; full of secrets that were ripping her apart. Secrets that he might have been able to live with, if he'd known them up front, but that destroyed everything when they finally came out. He pushed away the bitter memory and sat down beside Sheila on the bed.

'Roy, well, he wanted lots, but he was so in love with me, I figured I could talk him out of it. And then, when I fell pregnant-'

She looked down at her scarlet nails. Her fingers were shaking.

'I was so angry! How could I have been so stupid! Roy was over the moon, of course. When Tessa was born, I hated her. This was the seventies, and I was twenty two. I wanted to be out night clubbing, having fun, not tied to a screaming brat. The accountant I worked for was forward thinking, and willing to put me through the accountancy exams. I would have had a great career. Tess spoiled it all.'

Cal waited while she looked into the middle distance, seeing the past.

'When she went to school, I went back to the accountant and asked if he'd take me back, He was reluctant at first, but I talked him round. When I told Roy, it was the only time I ever saw him lose his temper.'

Cal made a mental note that Sheila was used to 'talking people round.'

'He wanted us to move to the country, more room for kids. He wanted lots of them. He said I didn't need to work, his plumbing business was doing great. I told him it wasn't going to happen, I was going back to work. We had a blazing row.'

She hesitated, and Cal waited again.

'That was it, really. He left a couple of weeks later, we got divorced. He started drinking too much and lost the business. He turned into a wreck. If you'd known him back then, you wouldn't recognise him now. Tess, well, she grew up just like him, pathetic, devoid of ambition or drive. She was clever, a great artist, but she never wanted to do anything with it.'

Cal remembered the pictures on the stairs; the flowers signed *TH.* Sheila stared off into the distance and seemed lost in her memories.

'You wanted Tess to be like you,' he prompted.

'Hmm? Yes, I suppose I did. She's nothing like me. Doesn't even look like me.'

She looked at Cal, and suddenly stood up, smoothing back her hair needlessly.

'Why am I telling you all this ancient history-'

'It helps to talk, doesn't it?'

She looked down at her hands, and this time she managed a faint smile. 'Yes, I suppose it does.'

'I'm going back to the station now, and I'll check out that driving school.'

Sheila nodded, then looked away. Cal guessed she was beginning to feel embarrassed by her story. He followed her out, and she went straight to her car without looking back.

Back in his car, Cal pulled out his notebook and wrote quickly:
No passport
Dole dating Tess's replacement!
Cal dialled Rob on his mobile.

'Hi Rob, can you look into something for me? Check if the Hardy girl had a passport issued recently. Oh, and check out the Pass First Driving School in Hinckley Road. They may have had a booking for her.'

'Hell, Cal, what did your last slave die of?'

Cal felt colour rush to his cheeks.

'Jesus Christ, Rob, just do it, will you? It's not as if you don't owe me.'

He slammed the phone shut. What the hell was wrong with the man now?

The phone rang again instantly.

'Mr Fisher? It's Annie Flower. I'm matron of Lake Pastures?'

Cal's heart skipped. 'What's wrong?'

'Your mum's all right. She's just had a little fall and she's a bit upset.'

'A fall?' Cal had the sudden image of his mother, her leg angled out of shape, her face twisted in pain-

'She's all right, nothing broken. She was having a walk in the garden and tripped. I think she just got a fright.'

'Nothing broken? Are you sure?'

'Absolutely. Just a little bruise, but she's asking for you.'

'I-' Cal hesitated. What about Dole, the shopping mall? Damn!

'I'll be there as soon as I can.'

He clicked off the phone. Mum had always been independent, self sufficient. Now, just when she needed him, he had so little time to give her.

If he could nip over to the mall now, he'd avoid the rush hour traffic, and he could be at the home by four. Mum was all right, she just wanted reassurance, and he'd be there soon.

But all the logical reasoning did nothing to assuage the toxic guilt seeping through him.

He pulled the car out of the cul-de-sac, cutting up a BMW driver on the junction. The driver honked and gave him the finger, and for a moment Cal felt a cold rage and almost stopped. He imagined the man's face growing pale as he saw the police ID. No, no time. He raised a hand in a conciliatory wave. He had to be calm.

Cal parked in the roof car park and took the lift down to the second floor of the mall. The china shop was near the far end, and Cal wondered how it managed to keep going, so far from the main concourse. Few people came up here, and the other shops had a cheap, hungry look to them. Two or three were already closed down and boarded up. He pulled out his phone to ask Rob to chase up the army records, but the phone showed *no network*. It seemed even the signal had abandoned this place.

He glanced into the window at the china and ornaments and suddenly felt a prickling on his neck. He looked through the glass to the shop interior, and there was Mike Dole, standing very still at the counter, while a young brown haired girl leaned on one elbow and grinned up at him. Cal took a step back into the dimly lit corridor, just as Mike turned sharply to stare out. Cal felt his heart lurch. The man couldn't have seen him, it was too bright in the glass shop, but all the same he hurried back down the corridor and ducked into the doorway of an 'everything's £1' shop. Seconds later, Mike Dole appeared in the corridor, where he stood very still and slowly looked around 180 degrees. As he turned towards Cal, the detective noticed a twitch jumping in the man's neck. Mike stood unmoving for a couple of minutes before he finally walked away.

Cal let out a breath he hadn't realised he'd been holding. And yet, why was he hiding? He had every right to be here. There it was again, that *something* in the back of his mind telling him to be careful.

He waited until Mike was out of sight and then walked into the shop, pulling out his ID.

'Hello,' he said, putting on a bright smile. 'I'm DS Fisher.'

'Oh!' she exclaimed. Was he imagining it, or did the girl's eyes just light up? She was pretty, in a slightly synthetic way. She had put her index finger in her mouth as he spoke and was looking at him from under her eyebrows. Cal could tell this was designed to have the men falling over themselves, and hell, he wasn't completely immune.

'I'm Marian,' she said. 'I've never met a detective before.'

Cal raised an eyebrow.

'I'm investigating the disappearance of the girl who used to work here, Tessa Hardy.'

'Oh yes, the girl who ran away.'

'Why do you say that?'

'Well, she took stuff with her, a suitcase, didn't she?'

Cal felt his mouth go dry. 'How do you know that?'

Marian looked down, pushing her lips into a little-girl pout. 'Someone told me.'

Cal was already sick of the flirting. 'Please try and remember who it was.'

'I think it was Mike, the security guard. But it might not have been. Everyone was talking about it at the time.'

Cal's heart rate notched up a few beats. 'Mike Dole?'

Marian smiled. 'Yes. He was just here. He's nice, Mike is.'

Is he, now? Cal smiled back. 'Is he your boyfriend?'

Marian did the thing with the eyes again. 'Yes. Sort of.'

Cal was pretty sure she would drop Mike like a hot brick if he, Cal, were to ask her out. She was obviously a sucker for authority figures. 'Has Mike ever talked to you about his previous girlfriends?'

'What? No. Why would he do that?'

Cal shrugged. 'Do you know any of his old girlfriends?'

Marian shook her head, a frown across her forehead. 'What has this to do with the missing girl?'

Cal put on his best smile. 'Sorry, I'm being a nosey copper.'

She looked at him for a few seconds, and then giggled. Cal laughed along.

'Well, thanks, Marian. I'll be off.'

'Come along any time. It gets boring up here,' she called after him.

Cal went straight back to the car park. He had to think about this.

Maybe Mike had helped Tess escape. There were the clothes and toothbrush. That would explain how he knew about the suitcase. With his army connections, maybe he could have got her away without leaving a trace. Given her clinging father and stifling mother, he could quite understand why Tess would like to go away and start again.

And there was Marian's thing about authority types. Cal had no illusions about his looks. He knew it was the badge that she had been attracted to. Perhaps that explained their relationship. After all, Mike was an ex army man, now a security guard.

Was his instinct wrong? Was he being unreasonable? This man was a war hero, after all.

He pulled out of the car park and headed for Lake Pastures. Cal was convinced that there were no real coincidences. He had to get those records. He was certain they held the answer to all of this.

FIFTEEN

The storm had blown itself out by the time the first light reached the sky, the wind tearing the clouds apart to reveal glances of blue beneath. Getting stiffly to her feet, Tess walked to the cave mouth, ignoring the ruin of her fire. Everything was wet through, but then 'everything' didn't really amount to much. She chewed half-heartedly on some rabbit meat and checked her precious potatoes, safe in their Tesco bag, before picking up the wet pieces of rope and heading out into the morning.

Her shoes sank to the ankles in the boggy ground as she walked, and last night's resolve to explore south was soon shelved at the sight of the marshy land ahead. Her feet were now raw and constantly itching, the skin between the toes painfully split so that every step made her wince. Tess had taken to wearing her socks only at night, in an effort to keep her feet warm and dry while she slept. But during the day, her leaky trainers ensured her feet stayed soaked and cold. Comfortable feet was a luxury she thought she might never know again.

Tess walked north instead, where the ground was mostly rock covered in a thin layer of soil, and later that morning she came upon the remains of a boat abandoned at the far end of the beach.

It lay upside down, the few remaining wooden slats worn thin by wind and tide. Her heart sank as she stared at it, for it was well beyond repair. Looking east, she could see the far mainland. In the pale early light, she thought she could see faint details there, tiny dots that might be houses. *Is that England over there?*

'Perhaps it's not as far as it looks,' she murmured.

She looked away. Without a boat, it might as well be a thousand miles.

The wood was salt-eaten and brittle, the ends crumbling under her fingers as she pried the spars loose, flakes of ancient white paint dropping to the shingle like confetti. She gathered as many planks as she could, tying them together with the nylon rope. Then, tying another rope to the first, she hauled it over her shoulder and began to drag the wood back up the hillside.

She counted steps. There was no use wondering how many miles it was, how long it was going to take; that way lay despair. One step after another and don't think, that was the only way. The sun rose, the last of the night's wind moving away towards the east, and Tess felt the sweat trickling down her face and back and between her breasts. The salty rope bit into her skin, and her hands were soon achingly sore. She stopped now and then to get her breath back and rest her complaining muscles, and it was late afternoon by the time she reached the little wood west of the caves. Tess stopped and took a deep breath, ready for the final steep climb, and that's when she saw it.

Out to the west, the sun was gleaming on something in the water. A boat! Letting out a gasp, she dropped the rope, running up the steep slope as fast as her tired legs could carry her, using her hands to pull herself up. She reached her cave and ran past it, higher, her heart hammering, breath rasping in her throat.

My beacon! She touched her back pocket to make sure the precious tin was there. The beacon was built on the edge of the ridge, but she had no time to head for the ridge now, it would take too long to go round the mountain to reach it. And yet she could see the beacon, way up ahead, perched atop the steep western side of the mountain. The shortest path would involve crossing the scree, something even she knew was dangerous. She looked out to sea again. The sail was almost golden in the sunlight as the boat turned, and she couldn't tell if it was coming towards her, or heading away.

There's nothing else for it, she thought.

Taking a deep breath, she ran into the mess of sharp stones, her sore feet immediately beginning to slip. She reached out with her hands, wincing as the stones cut her skin. Her toes dug into the scree, but the more she pushed down, the more it gave way. Grabbing at the loose rocks, Tess felt her shirt tear, and a roar of anger erupted from her throat. The scree slid suddenly, carrying her ten feet down the mountain towards the boulders littered below. Breathing hard, she dug her feet back in, biting back the pain and forcing her exhausted legs onwards. The pyre was right there, no more than fifty, sixty feet. If only the ground would stop moving, she could run there in seconds. 'Come on!' she screamed, reaching up again. She spotted a rock up ahead that looked as if it were actually attached to the mountain, and grabbed at it. But she was wrong. The rock came away in her hand and brought with it a torrent of smaller stones, which turned into a rumbling storm of rocks, raining down on her. A burst of rage exploded like a light bulb inside her as a stone hit her forehead, then the ground beneath her feet gave way altogether, carrying her down the mountain. The stones seemed to have a life of their own, moving faster and faster amidst a hail of dust and rock. There was nothing to grab, no way to stop, and Tess was rolled over on to her back as she headed for the boulders below. The air burst from her lungs as she slammed stomach-first into the first rock, somersaulting over it to smack the next one head on. Vision blurring, she slid further down the mountain, her limbs growing numb. Then something brushed her right hand, a tree branch, and she grabbed reflexively at it. The whipping branches of the straggly birch tree slashed at her face and hands as she was driven into them, but the sudden sharp pain brought her back to her senses, and she hung on grimly to the thin branches as the stones continued to rain past her.

After what seemed like hours, the torrent became a trickle, and in the ensuing quiet all she could hear was the pounding of her blood in her veins. Tess opened her eyes and looked back. The scrubby gorse and thin trees continued to the edge of the cliff, thirty feet away. She tightened her grip on the tree, wincing at her painful hands. The little tree had saved her, although its roots were all but out of the ground. Tess looked out to sea, but there was no sign of the boat. It was gone.

She closed her eyes. Another couple of seconds and she would have been over the cliff and dead. And yet that seemed irrelevant compared to the lost ship, the forlorn chance of rescue. Slowly she stood up, swaying, her hand snaking round to check for the tobacco tin. *At least I haven't lost it.* Time for a deep breath.

She felt something trickling on her forehead and touched it. Blood. No surprise. She looked back out to sea, where the sun gleamed hazily on the empty water. She shook her head to clear it, but her vision stayed blurred.

Maybe the boat has sailed into the eastern jetty, she thought, trying for some vestige of hope. Sweat trickled into her hair and stung her cuts as she slowly made her way down, sidetracking the shale and keeping to the grass. As the adrenalin faded, the pain from all the other cuts and bruises arrived, her torn and blistered hands, her knees skinned through the torn jeans. Her trainers were finished, the left sole separated from the upper. Her feet hurt so much she daren't even think about them.

She made it down to the beach eventually. There was no boat. She felt no real disappointment; she had not really expected it to be there. Crouching by the edge of the sea Tess washed her aching hands and face, splashed water into her eyes. She pulled out her tobacco tin and looked at her blurred yellow reflection in the lid. Her head didn't look too bad, just a cut. She was lucky. Very lucky.

Yeah, she thought, looking out at the empty sea. *Lucky. Right.*

*

The Mall was quiet as Mike patrolled the ground floor. It was March now, and he put the lack of customers down to upcoming summer holidays. He heard people discussing their vacation plans, and decided that people always had to have something to look forward to: Christmas or bank holidays or summer. They were always talking about tomorrow, never today. He tried hard, but still couldn't understand it.

The lack of crowds did nothing to alter either his vigilance or his routine, and by ten o'clock he had made it to his usual spot outside the china shop. He looked around at the passers-by, checking their faces for guilt or threat, before turning his attention to the window display. He searched for the little unicorn. There it was, standing on a revolving glass shelf, its foreleg raised in defiance, head arched, pointing the horn like a spear. He felt the hairs prickling on his neck and looked up to see Marian watching him, her head on one side, smiling. He had another quick look round before going in.

'Were you spying on me, sir?' she asked, twirling a lock of hair in her fingers. Mike was entranced by the motion of the shining strand.

'Certainly not,' he replied, pasting on a smile.

Marian laughed. 'Caught any shoplifters this morning?'

He shook his head. 'It's very quiet.'

She bent down, resting her elbows on the desk to give Mike a view of her cleavage which he examined without much interest.

'What are you doing tonight?' she asked, looking up at him from under her eyebrows. Mike's heart took a little jolt.

'I don't have anything planned.'

'Well, would you like to go somewhere? Your choice, since I dragged you along to see Matt Damon last time.'

Mike felt his pulse kick up a notch, his eyelid twitch. This was almost more than he could have hoped for.

'Could we go somewhere nearer your home?' he said, swallowing in an imitation of nerves. 'I felt very guilty leaving you at the bus stop. I should have walked you home.'

'Oh Mike, that's so gallant,' she said, and he thought he saw a spring of moisture hit her eyes.

'You know what? My parents are still away, so we could go for a drink at the Marquis of Wellington and then you could come home with me. We could have pizza.'

'Great!' he said. *Pizza.* Christ.

'It's a date. The pub is on the corner-'

'Don't worry, I'll find it,' Mike said, suddenly consumed by the urge to leave, to be alone to think about tonight and all its potential consequences.

The Marquis of Wellington had a message above the ornate black façade that read "a taste of Victorian England". Mike had no idea what Victorian drinkers had been like, but he was pretty sure they hadn't been subjected to Spandau Ballet on the jukebox. He stood at the bar and sipped from his pint, feeling exposed and uncomfortable and wishing Marian would hurry up.

Nevertheless he was optimistic. Sex with Tess had been great; she was so compliant, full of secret sighs and gentle touches. He expected no less from Marian. And here she was, dressed in a low cut rose-pink dress under her sensible coat. A frown started on his forehead, but he quickly wiped it away.

'Hello!' she breathed, reaching up to kiss his cheek. He got a whiff of pungent perfume and briefly held his breath as she pulled off her coat. 'Have you been waiting long?'

'No,' he said. 'What do you want to drink?'

They carried their drinks to one of the dainty tables, Marian already rabbiting on about her day, awkward customers, the size of the spiders in the stock room. All rubbish that Mike happily drowned out, smiling at her absently and biding his time.

'You are coming home with me tonight, aren't you?'

'If you want me to,' he said, raising an eyebrow. Marian looked down, smiling to herself.

'That would be nice.'

He felt his heart lift at her quiet words. Tonight there would be no cold bed and unquiet dreams. He'd thought he'd seen the end of those, but no. The monsters were back. Not quite as bad, but-

Marian began to tell him a story about the last time she had had a drink in this pub, and Mike glanced surreptitiously around. It was all so safe and ordinary, middle England at its most parochial. He knew he would never be comfortable in places like this, no matter what.

'Let's go, then,' Marian finished her drink. 'We can collect a pizza on the way home.'

The night was freezing again, and Marian grabbed at his arm as they walked past Victoria Park. 'You're the quietest man I've ever known,' she said.

He laughed. 'Am I?'

'Yes you are!' she laughed too, Mike shaking his head at her inanity. It didn't matter. He was still in control.

Marion lived in Clarendon Park, in a street lined with large impressive properties, most of which had been converted to flats. Marion led him to a big house with a black and white timber façade, and Mike was surprised and impressed. He had put Marian down as a working class girl. She opened the door and turned on lights, showing him into a large flowery living room with a pretend coal fire and good, if old fashioned, furniture. There were ornamental plates hanging from the walls, and photos on the mantelpiece, jostling for position with china ornaments and trinkets. He stared absently at the TV which she had turned on before taking the pizza to the kitchen. It was some reality show, the contestants having to perform tasks before they could eat. Mike didn't own a TV, but he knew enough about this show from the conversation of the other security men.

'Oh, that's my very favourite programme!' Marian handed him a plate. The pizza looked as if it had been eaten already. He felt his throat closing up just at the sight of it. Nevertheless, it was food, and Mike remembered rule number one: always eat when you can.

Anchovies, he thought. Who invented anchovies? He slid them to the edge of the plate, watching Marian as she opened a bottle of wine and poured out two glasses. 'Last week, that bloke there had to eat this maggot, and it was at least an inch long and still wriggling about!'

Mike looked at the TV. Maggot man had a curious tint to his skin.

'Is that what turned his face orange?'

Marian threw back her head and laughed. Mike was amazed. He didn't realise he'd made a joke.

'Oh, you're such a bitch!' she said.

Mike raised an eyebrow, but said nothing. He finished his pizza and took a tiny sip of the wine. Marian lay back on the sofa and stretched her hands above her head.

'Oh, I'm stuffed.'

Mike cast his eye over her tight pink dress. Her breasts were too big for the rest of her body, and he wondered absently if she'd had them augmented. Checking out her affluent home, he thought it was likely. He knew that the stretch was entirely for his benefit, and Marian backed it up with a lean forward to give him an eyeful of cleavage.

'What would you like to do now?' she asked.

Mike slid across the sofa and put his arms around her. She hugged him tightly, and he kissed her, tasting wine and anchovies, feeling about as aroused as a wet sausage. She began to make little moaning sounds as he trailed his fingers up the soft cotton of her dress, and then suddenly she broke away and stood up, holding out one hand.

'Let's carry this on upstairs.'

He took her hand and followed her up to a room that softened his heart. The duvet was pink with white hearts, and as she drew the matching curtains, he noticed the bed was densely populated by fluffy toys. Thick white carpet covered the floor, and there was a picture on the wall of a bare-chested young man holding a baby. All at once, he was ready, and he took her in his arms and kissed her, his hands reaching under her dress and touching soft, yielding skin. Marian pulled away again, grinning this time, sucking at her index finger as she kicked off her shoes. Mike began to strip off his clothes, unable to stop himself folding his trousers neatly before laying them on the floor. Marian was down to her bra and pants, a matching set made of ivory silk.

'Like what you see?' she whispered.

Mike nodded, as she knelt on the bed and beckoned to him with a finger. His heart was racing now, and he didn't know how much longer he could hold on. She undid her bra, and as her breasts fell out, she began to fondle them, raking the nipples with long pink nails, then, leaning back, she slid one hand inside her panties.

Mike could not move. He felt his erection fade away. Marian didn't seem to need him, in fact he wondered if she had forgotten he was there. She closed her eyes and little moaning noises came from her open lips. Every fibre of Mike's being told him to get out, just run away, but he couldn't move. At last she opened her eyes and smiled at him.

'Come on, then,' she said. 'Come over here.'

He stepped towards the bed, and she reached out and grabbed his balls. Mike gasped, trying to back away, but Marian was laughing. 'Are you shy? I don't think so.'

A sudden flash, rushing in from school to find his mother, kneeling on the floor in front of a man, a stranger, who simply looked up at him and winked.

His head jerked back. Marian had her arms round his waist and was pulling him down. He was falling, in a moment he would disappear. He reached out, grabbing her shoulders, shoving her hard on the bed. She squealed, and with one jerk he tore the panties away. He forced himself inside her, thrusting at her with all the anger and pain and despair, as if he could expel it from his body. Marian screamed once, then she was quiet, and he held her tightly until at last the release came. There was no pleasure in it, no relief. It felt like the impotent slap of a punch drunk boxer. His head dropped on his chest and in a moment of complete clarity he felt tears arriving in his tightly shut eyes.

The monster is me, he thought.

He opened his eyes and looked at Marian. She was looking back, smiling. *Smiling?*

'I'm sorry,' he said, getting up.

'Wait, where are you going?'

He found the bathroom, and leaned over the sink. His head was spinning, lightning flashes going off behind his eyes.

'Mike?'

She came up behind him and put her arms round him. 'Did you think you were too rough?'

He closed his eyes again.

'You weren't, you know. It was great.'

'Great?' he said, turning to look at her. Was she serious?

'Yeah. I like it a bit rough. Hell, you can be even rougher next time, if you like.'

Mike stared at her, and suddenly felt the pizza making a bid for freedom. He pushed her out of the bathroom and slammed the door, turning for the toilet just in time. He went on retching long after his stomach was empty. He felt as if every cell of his body was screaming in revulsion.

'Mike? Are you all right? Oh I knew I shouldn't have ordered the anchovies.'

'I'll be fine. Just give me a minute.'

'Sure. I'll be downstairs. I'll make you some tea.'

He cleaned up, splashing cold water on his face with shaking hands. Looking down at his flaccid penis, he wondered how much it would hurt to cut it off. He dressed and looked at his face in her mirror. His skin was like parchment, his thin lips almost white, but his eyes were red rimmed and filled with a dark anger. He stared at his reflection until the anger faded, then went downstairs to tell Marian he couldn't see her again.

'Is that you, Mike, are you all right?'

Marian stood at the bottom of the stairs, looking up. She was biting her lip and holding her hands in fists against her chest. She looked small and fragile and soft again, and Mike had to swallow hard to maintain his resolve. When he reached her, he managed a smile.

'I better go,' he said.

'Please don't.'

Mike twitched as he heard another sound, behind her. He took a step back as a man appeared. Mike felt the sweat coating his skin turn to ice.

'Marian, bring your friend in. 'The big man smiled at him. 'Come on in and have a drink.'

Mike's heart seemed to be vibrating like a hummingbird's wings. There was something about the man, something from the past that made him feel both comforted and afraid. Marian's father was lean and looked fit, although age was taking its toll. A flap of useless skin dangled under his chin, and his eyes were surrounded by a roadmap of wrinkles. The eyes themselves, however, were sharp and intelligent, and curious.

Marian grabbed his hand and he followed her into the flowery room, where another woman was sitting drinking tea from a cup and saucer. Mike saw the family resemblance right away.

'Hello there, you must be Mike,' she said. 'I'm Brenda, Marian's mum.'

Mike shook her hand, knowing his palms must feel clammy and sick.

'And I'm Bill. I must say, we've heard lots about you,' he said, in time-honoured fashion.

As Mike shook Bill's hand, the connection clicked. He realised what it was that he had recognised. Bill seemed to sense it too, as his smile suddenly widened.

'I spy a past comrade in arms,' he laughed. 'What was your regiment?'

'2 Para,' Mike stammered. He felt as if every muscle was quivering. This officer would see into his heart and he would be lost.

I was with the Staffies,' Bill said, gazing curiously at him.

'I'd better go,' Mike said again.

Marian was staring at him, wide-eyed. 'You were in the army?' she asked. He picked up her surprise, the hurt in her voice.

Brenda laughed. 'We owe you an apology. We did tell Marian we'd be back tomorrow, but, well, the weather was poor, and we just felt like coming home.'

Mike just stared at her.

'Mum and dad have been in France,' Marian explained her face now one big question mark. 'They have a gite there.'

Mike nodded. 'That's nice,' was all he could manage.

'Well, it was nice to meet you, Mike,' Bill said, slapping him on the shoulder. Mike leapt from the touch as if he had just been shocked. 'I hope we'll see you again, and you and I can discuss old campaigns, eh?'

He laughed again, and Mike's smile froze on his face. *Breathe!* He told himself. *Breathe and remain calm*. Marian took his hand and walked him to the door, where he turned to say goodbye.

'Sorry about them turning up like that,' she whispered, 'maybe we can go to your place next time?'

'Not – next time,' he said. It was not what he wanted to say, but it was all that would come out. Marian looked concerned now. He had to get away.

'What?'

'I'll speak to you soon,' he said, turning and hurrying away.

He made it to the end of the road and broke into a run, his heart thrumming. Crossing the ring road, he made it to the park, heading for the trees and letting the cold air into his lungs, breathing hard. But the orange lights were there behind his eyes, and he could hear the screams: eyes wide, terrified, resigned. The girls, silent, stiff with fear, Wilkins shouting, his mate laughing. *Have to protect* – His fist in Wilkins' face, arms pulling him, everything falling, the shots: one, two, three, deafening, then the silence-

Mike fell to his knees on the wet grass, trying to shut out the pain, repeating his mantra:

I am alone. I am in control. I am safe. He remembered the major's words. He knew he could trust him, the major would not let him down. His words were true:

Breathe slowly, through your nose, count to six. Slowly, slowly. Now think of a place, a happy, calm place, somewhere you have always felt safe and content. Got it? Now listen to your heart, feel it. Feel your heart slowing down. Can you feel it? Yes. Slow, nice and slow.

Now breathe fast and shallow, one twice, again, again. Feel your heart speeding up, getting faster. You can feel it, can't you. Yes! Now, slowly again, through your nose, count slowly. Your heart slows. You can feel it. Slower, slower. There. You can control your heart. Think about it. You can control your heart! If you can control your heart, you can control anything.

Yes, he thought. *Anything.* Eventually his heartbeat did slow. He felt calm descend. He got to his feet.

Up ahead, he found a small dark pond, and he walked to the edge and looked into the still water. It reminded him of the lake he and Donno and Lewis had stumbled upon, back in the Gulf. Only that was a lake of gasoline, not water, and they had turned and ran like hell before the abandoned truck went up. He remembered the white-orange flares lighting the sky, the whudd of the explosion shaking the ground, thin coils of pale grey smoke spiralling into the dark. It had been very beautiful, all the more so for the fact that they were not in the middle of it.

He looked up, sighing. Reason had returned, and he was thinking of the problems he had walked into. Marian would have to be let down gently. He could hardly bear the thought of talking to her again, but care was needed. He wanted no trouble with her father, who could make plenty of trouble for him.

The Staffordshire Regiment, he'd said. Mike was willing to bet Bill had ended up at least a major. The Staffies had been to the Gulf as well, and to Kosovo. He winced at the thought, although from the look of him Bill would have retired by then. Mike knew Bill had seen what lurked behind his eyes. He had to get Marian out of his life as quickly as possible.

SIXTEEN

Tess spent the morning hauling the wood up from the base of the hill where she had abandoned it. To protect her desperately sore hands, she wrapped the rope round her waist and pulled, ignoring the other aches and bruises she had taken in the fall. Using the plentiful nylon rope, she tied the pieces of wood roughly together to make a haphazard door. It wasn't brilliant, but if the rain came from the west again, it would give her some protection.

She tugged at the remaining cuff of her once-pale blue cardigan, breaking off a loose strand. Most of the other sleeve had been lost in the fall from the mountain. Her shirt was filthy and frayed, offering little protection against the cold. But Tess thanked the god of islands for the fact that the sun was unseasonably warm again today, the sky winter blue with only a few cumulus clouds high above, the wind just teasing at her hair, tied up today with a strand of the ubiquitous nylon rope.

Her hair. How proud she had been of her thick dark waves. She recalled the delicious secret pleasure when other women commented on how beautiful it was, how they wished theirs was like it. Tess would sigh and say, oh, I don't like it. I do all I can to straighten it, all the time secretly agreeing with them. It was beautiful hair.

But not now. Now it was just a series of matted strands blown by the wind. She pushed her fingers into the tangles. For all she tied it back, she couldn't stop the onslaught of salt, wind and rain. There was nowhere in her cave to plug in a hairdryer, even if she had one. She had hoped she might find a comb on the beach, it being such a basic item, but nothing had washed up yet. If she ever got out of here, the whole lot would have to come off, it was unsavable. Strangely, that didn't fill her with the sort of tearful despondency she expected. Yet again, there was nothing could be done about it, there was no point even thinking about it.

The job done, Tess wandered down to the beach, following the shoreline north until the shingle became rocks, rising to cliffs. There were a lot of seabirds here, strange looking black and white creatures with brightly coloured beaks. They were alarmed by her at first, but soon learned to ignore her. Tess spent some time with them, for they were comical to watch, waddling along, their bright beaks full of silver fish.

They seemed to be using some old rabbit burrows to build their nests in, and she thought how easy it would be to catch one. But this time the old Tess resisted. Maybe a few eggs wouldn't be missed, but there was no need to kill. She still had rabbit meat, and mussels, and potatoes. *A veritable feast'* she thought, smiling to herself.

Around the headland, the cliffs grew rocky and fissured, teeming with wild birds, so many that the rocks themselves seemed alive. Tess watched as, again and again, the huge yellow-beaked birds folded their white wings and dived into the waves, returning with a shining fish which they gulped away.

She walked to the edge of the cliffs and wondered if she could get down there. The rocks extended out to sea, as if a careless giant had thrown a handful of stones. *Surely if I threw a line there, I would catch something.* Reaching into her back pocket, she touched the wonderful tobacco tin which she now carried everywhere, that and the knife; her treasured possessions.

It took a while to find a way down as the rocks were sheer in most places, the drop more than fifty or sixty feet. She had to backtrack almost to the beach before she found a place she could squeeze down through a rock split in two. Her feet crunched painfully on the shingle, the sound almost drowned out by the seabird cries. Prising a few mussels off the rocks, Tess used the hilt of the knife to smash them, hooking the flesh on to her weighted line. Then she climbed carefully across the rocks, the sea spray rising joyfully to splash her. Looking out at the diving birds, she took a deep breath and cast out her own line. Only a few seconds later she felt resistance, and as she pulled, the line came clear of the water, a shining silver fish attached.

A fountain of elation soared through her, a whoop of delight bursting from her mouth. Tess's eyes filled with delighted tears. Even though the fish was no bigger than her hand, there were plenty of them to be had.

Pulling the wriggling fish off the line, she baited it again and threw it back. Another fish took the bait a few moments later, and Tess started to laugh. She looked up at the white birds, some of them eyeing her catch, and felt a complete kinship with them. They were all in it together.

And this was joyous! And so easy! She had four fish in less than fifteen minutes, and she packed them in her carrier bag and stowed her line and hooks away carefully in their tin. Then she sat on the rock and watched the birds.

And inside herself she felt another change come about, nothing to do with cold hearted survival, but instead a curious sense of peace, a feeling that the sea and sky and rocks and birds were becoming part of her, and she part of them. A feeling that the sound of waves and wind and the cries of the many different birds were already echoing in her heart, and they always would.

*

Mike drove up to Beacon Hill and went running in the clear morning. The wind was still bitter cold, but the sun was bright and cheerful, the countryside lush green after the recent rain. He ran in his usual way, not too fast, his heartbeats synchronised with the padding of his feet on the ground. The air felt good in his lungs and on his bare arms. He was early this morning, and it was so pleasant he thought he might do more than his usual five miles.

After the debacle with Marian, he needed some peace in his soul, and this was just the thing.

The nightmares were back. They lay there in his room, silent in the dark, waiting for him to sleep so they could slide into his mind and rip it apart. Funny, he thought, how it was only in the midst of the horror that you truly appreciated its absence.

He crested the hill, not pausing to look over the panorama of the city, then dropped down to join the Loughborough Road. In the next field, a horse looked up as he ran past, its ears flickering back and forward. It watched him for a long moment before breaking into a long loping run. Mike picked up the pace as the horse ran alongside, still looking at him, delighting in its speed. For a moment they were kindred spirits, racing the wind. Then the horse drew ahead, and stopped eventually at the end of the field. It leaned over the fence and nodded its big brown head, as if telling Mike to hurry up.

Mike let out a laugh, the first real laugh for a very long time. The horse's ears flickered again at the sound, and Mike reached up and touched the velvet soft skin of the muzzle. The horse made a contented rumbling sound, and Mike felt as though he and the animal had shared a communication older than humanity. His heart filled up with an emotion so intense he felt as if he might burst with it. The horse's delicate ears flickered back, and Mike watched as it turned and galloped across the field to where its owner was banging a feed bucket.

He laughed again. 'Can't fault you, mate,' he said. 'Go get your grub.'

He picked up the pace again, feeling suddenly rather wonderful, and that was when the solution came to him. He didn't need to think about the Marian problem ever again. He could just get up and go. He'd done it before, plenty of times, it was no problem. He'd see the boss this morning and put in his notice. He could be out of here at the end of the week.

But where to go? Maybe north, to the wilderness, live with the animals. That solitude and self-sufficiency was something that had always eased his soul. Even the demons of his dreams were quieted there. Yes, he would go. Get in the car, and drive, see where it took him. It would be easy, after all, his cupboard had already been cleared out, its contents carefully wrapped and hidden in the boot. The more he thought about it, the more logical it seemed. He had been here too long, it was time to go. He turned, looking for the horse, thinking he should thank it for the insight, but it had gone.

*

Marian had spent most of her life surrounded by men. She knew exactly what most of them liked, and it was a happy coincidence that she liked it too.

When Mike left, she walked back into the living room, her thoughts confused. Why had he never told her he was in the army? At least it explained her attraction to him, but most men were happy to talk about their army exploits, not hide them away. She slumped into the armchair.

'Where did you pick that one up?' her father said.

Marian bristled. 'He's a security guard at the Mall. I think he's nice.'

'He's a bit strange,' her mother said. Marian gritted her teeth. Mother never approved of anyone she liked. Bill sat on the settee and leaned forward towards his daughter.

'Marian, I want you to leave that chap well alone,' he said. Marian stared at him, dismayed by her father's fixed stare. She knew perfectly well what that look meant.

'Why?' she asked.

'He's messed up. Believe me, I can tell. He's no good for you.'

'How can you say that after meeting him for two minutes! You just don't like me associating with army types-'

'But he's not an 'army type', is he? He didn't tell you he was in the army. Don't you think that's strange?'

She shrugged. 'Maybe he just doesn't want to talk about it.'

'You bet he doesn't.'

Bill sat back, sighing. 'I've seen it before. He's been somewhere or seen something that's damaged him. He's barely coping with life. He certainly can't look after anyone else.'

Marian folded her arms. 'Well I can look after myself,' she said. 'And maybe I can help him.'

Bill shook his head. 'You can't.'

Marian stared at her father, biting back her irritation.

'Bill, you're going about this the wrong way,' Brenda said. 'If you don't want her to see the man again, you should tell her you approve of him.'

Bill chuckled. 'Maybe so. Marian, have I ever warned you off anyone before?'

'There was that lieutenant in –'

'The married man,' Brenda sneered.

Bill nodded. 'You play by the rules. Married men are off limits. But hell, Marian, even when we were in Bremen and you took up with that crazy German, I never said anything. I just let you find out for yourself what a shit he was.'

'But this is not like that,' Marian said, wondering absently why she was sticking up for Mike so fervently. 'Mike's nice. He's quiet and kind and I like him.'

Brenda laughed. 'Show me the man you *don't* like.'

Marian felt the anger bubbling up inside her. Bill was still looking at her, calm and serious.

'I think this man needs help, and not the sort you or I can give. He needs counselling.'

'Well, why? What's wrong with him?'

Bill sat back. 'I saw it after the Gulf War. They used to call it 'the thousand yard stare'. Mike's looking at something only he can see, and he truly doesn't want to. Back then they called it shell shock, but now it's known as post traumatic stress.'

Marian felt the argument slipping away from her. 'Well, can't you help him?'

'How could I?' Bill said. 'I'm not a psychiatrist, and I guarantee you he won't want to talk about it, to me or anyone.'

'But you could put him in touch with someone-'

She leaned forward, putting on her best daddy's girl smile. Bill had never refused his only child anything, she couldn't imagine he'd start now, but Bill sighed and stood up.

'I'll get the number of a chap at my old regiment who might be able to help him. You can give Mike the number.'

Marian grinned, relieved. 'Thanks, dad.'

Bill put his hands on her shoulders. 'You can give him the number at the same time as you tell him goodbye.'

Her heart sank. She looked away, stifling the anger again. Acting like a spoilt brat would do no good at all. Bill stroked a finger down her cheek, making her look at him.

'Is that a deal?'

'I suppose so,' she said.

Brenda stood up, yawning. 'I'm off to bed,' she said, fixing Marian with a look as she walked past.

Bill smiled. 'Your mother's not as trusting as I am,' he said.

'I just wanted to help him, that's all.'

'What's so special about this one?' Bill said. 'Could my wayward daughter finally be calming down?'

Marian looked past him. 'I don't know.'

All she did know was that she really liked Mike, a lot more after tonight than she had before. And she could help him, she was sure of it. She wanted him, and there was no reason why she couldn't have him. So what if he had this post-stress thing? She'd talk to him and get him his counselling, and everything would be fine. Then her parents would see that she wasn't just the airy fairy little tart they believed her to be.

'I'll look the number out for you,' Bill said, ruffling her hair as if she were six years old. Marion smiled dutifully, her mind already busy thinking up a plan.

SEVENTEEN

The waves came grinding in, like tumbling shards of broken glass which the sun turned to liquid before her eyes. Tess waited until they began to recede, before beginning her daily trawl of the shoreline. She knew it was too much to ask that a box of clean dry socks would be washed up. With her toes now resembling brain tissue, her feet were, as it were, on her mind.

She had done her what she could with the needle and thread supplied by Mike's tin, but they were not strong enough to hold the shoes together. Then she had spent a long dull afternoon patiently threading strands of nylon rope through the soles and uppers, resulting in a pair of shoes that at least protected her against the stones. But they did nothing to keep her feet away from the sodden mossy grass, the damp shingle.

Tess fantasised about dipping her feet into a warm bath, how ecstatic that would feel, how much better than anything else she could ever want.

She sighed, imagining the hot water seeping gently into the raw sores, easing the split skin between her poor toes, soothing the burning pain. As she walked, she realised she had closed her eyes, and she shook her head.

Back at her cave, she built a fire and eased off her shoes, careful not to tear her stitching, or cause any more damage to her painful feet. Then she stretched out with her back against the rock and her feet facing the flames to let them dry. This was a slow process. If she got too close to the fire, her toes would heat up quickly, something she had discovered to be excruciatingly painful. As they dried, her feet took on the texture of rough stone. She pulled one foot towards her and examined it. The skin looked like the cracked glaze of an old terracotta pot. She carefully slipped her feet into the rabbit skins, which she had sewn together to make a rough pair of slippers.

'Quite handy with the old needle and thread,' she said aloud. Maybe one day in another lifetime she could take up sewing. She gave a soft chuckle at that idea. Another lifetime was right.

Through the cave entrance she watched torn wisps of cloud move slowly into the west. The day had been as grey and bland as the inside of a plastic box, but now the clouds had broken, and the first stars blinked shyly through them.

What's happening back in the word?' Tess thought. They might have built the new cinema in the town centre by now. Maybe Leicester City were out of the relegation zone.

'No, maybe not,' she chuckled to herself. 'I wonder if mother won her bridge tournament.'

A sharp sadness tugged at her heart. Was Sheila worried about her? Or did she just think her hapless daughter had just run away somewhere? Then a lump lodged in her throat.

Dad will be worried, she thought. *He'll be worried sick.*

But again, there was nothing she could do about it.

She sighed, shoulders slumped, and gazed into the fire. The burning wood gave off a sharp, acrid smell, the low flames flickering soundlessly.

'Maybe the whole world has gone to war and destroyed itself,' she whispered. 'And I'm the only one left.'

Even as she shook her head at the foolish thought, the hollow ache of loneliness filled her and brought unaccustomed tears to her eyes. She felt empty and cold, hope vanishing like the last light from the sky. She squeezed her eyes shut tight.

A strange rustling sound came from outside the cave. Something was moving outside. Her eyes snapped open, her heart lurching. Confusion and dread churned inside her as she concentrated, trying to decipher the sound. Had rescue come at last? Or was it Mike, come to finish her off properly?

She dropped to her belly and pulled herself across the stone, careful to stay silent. At the lip of the cave, she slowly raised her head and peered out.

A group of red deer were on the hillside, some with their heads lowered to the lush grass, others guardedly sniffing the air. Their antlers were covered in dark velvet, their eyes huge and liquid. Tess held her breath. The wind was moving west, away from the cave. They couldn't smell her.

The nearest doe was only a few feet away, contentedly cropping the grass, unaware of her presence. Tess could see each individual hair on the sleek russet coat. The powerful musky scent of the animals filled her nostrils, making her eyes water.

All at once the empty feeling dissipated, and she felt suffused with a rare and unquantifiable emotion, a quiet joy she had never known before. The deer moved slowly across the hillside, and she watched them until all the light was gone, all except the small glimmer of hope that had returned to her heart.

*

By the time Cal got back to the station, he was frazzled. Mother had been in one of her lucid phases, cursing him roundly for dumping her here with a bunch of senile old farts waiting to die, loudly proclaiming that she had no son; at least; 'not one worth ha'pence'. The other residents had watched in fascination. This was better then Coronation

Street. Cal had kept his mouth firmly shut and let Maggie rant herself dry. Then he had simply stood up, told her he hoped her bruised leg felt better soon, and left.

The matron had been waiting for him, a rueful smile on her face.

'It's not much fun, Cal, not knowing what to expect,' she said.

Cal smiled. 'No. You're right there. She is all right, though, isn't she?'

Annie nodded, smiling back. She had a quiet, easy smile, and Cal thought, not for the first time, how attractive she was, with her pale freckled skin, her wide clear blue eyes. She had been one of the main reasons he had decided on this place for mum. Annie Flowers seemed honest and genuinely kind.

'I need to get back to work,' he said.

'Of course. A policeman's lot and all that, eh?'

Cal smiled again. 'Thanks for the call.'

'No problem. We're looking after her, don't worry.'

But he did worry. He knew he always would.

Now, back in the team room, he ignored his messages, laying out the Hardy file and getting up to fetch a cup of coffee. He heard his name called, and turned to see Rob hurrying along the corridor.

Rob looked a bit better today, Cal thought. He was wearing a different suit, and his grey hair was clean and newly cut. Maybe his wife's problems had finally turned the corner.

'Got that information you asked for,' Rob said, a sheepish smile on his face. 'Sorry about earlier, Cal.'

Cal shook his head. 'Forget it.'

Rob had a big bundle of papers under one arm.

'Number one: Tessa Hardy has never had a passport. Number two: the driving school have never heard of her. Number three: -'

He pulled out a thick envelope from the papers.

'Mike Dole's records have finally turned up.'

Cal grinned, taking the package eagerly. 'Brilliant,' he said. 'Go get some coffee, Rob, we need to look at this carefully.'

'You betcha.'

Cal pulled his chair up to the desk. His heart was pumping and he couldn't bear to wait for Rob to come back. Spilling the contents of the envelope on to the table, he immediately flicked through to see if anything caught his eye. Then he stopped. This was stupid, he thought. The problem had to be approached logically. He put the papers back together again and took out his pen and notebook as Rob returned.

'Here, have a read of the file,' Cal said, pushing it across the table. 'Get yourself up to date. There've been some developments today.'

Cal started at the beginning. The first three pages were factual, simple chronological records of Dole's service. His date of birth was listed as the 12th April 1971. He had joined the army on the 10th May 1989, 28 days after his 18th birthday. Cal read reports of his training, much of it in army shorthand that he couldn't understand.

'I'm back with the programme,' Rob said. 'Need any help?'

Cal looked up. 'Yeah, you can help me trawl through this.' He handed over the pages he had already read, together with the next chunk.

The next page Cal looked at was to do with the Gulf conflict. He read down:

General patrol second watch ambushed, Pvts Donovan, Jameson, Dunn KIA. Pvt Dole treated minor injuries.

Cal made notes as he went along: *How many in a patrol? Was Mike the last man standing?*

Mike's career after that was dotted with frequent visits for counselling. He served in Ireland, Gibraltar, Germany. A recurring phrase was 'requested active duty'. Did that mean he was fond of killing? Or maybe he just needed something to keep the nightmares away.

Rob cleared his throat, and Cal looked up expectantly.

'Found something?'

'Just a wrinkle,' Rob said, frowning. 'This lad was obviously made for the army, he loved it. His training record, adapting to discipline and so on is exemplary. Says here he 'always wanted to be a soldier''

'So?'

'So how come he waited until a month after his 18th birthday to join up?'

Cal frowned. It was a minor point, but a valid one. There had to be some reason for it. He nodded to Rob and made a note in his book, before returning to the papers in hand.

He had reached 1999.

Peacekeeping force Kosovo. General duties.

Tour interrupted. Returned to base. Received counselling

January 2000 Discharged– medical grounds. Demobbed to Arcadia House, Shepherds Bush, London.

Cal felt his heart flutter. He looked up. That was the key, he was sure of it. He made another note before reading on, hoping for more clarification, but there was none. Rob glanced up.

'Our boy here is seriously fucked up,' he said.

'How do you mean?'

'All these medical reports,' he pulled one over and began to read: ''frequent bouts of depression, rage, insomnia. Symptoms of intrusion becoming uncontrollable. Hyperarousal. Resentful of counselling, hampering its effectiveness. Classic avoidance symptoms.' I don't know what half of that means, but I know it's not good.'

Cal nodded. 'Here, have a look at this.' He pushed over the last page he had read, waiting for his partner's response.

'So what happened in Kosovo?' Rob said.

Cal grinned. 'Bingo. That's what we need to find out.'

Rob sat back and folded his arms. 'So what are we thinking here, the girlfriend dumped him and he wasted her?'

Cal scrubbed his face with his hand, noting absently that he needed a shave. He could use a nicotine buzz as well, but that was still out of the question.

'I still don't know.' He told Rob about Mike knowing about Tess's missing suitcase, about him seeing Marian.

'It's all a bit weird,' Rob said.

Cal reviewed his notes:

Mike knows Tess took a suitcase. He is seeing the girl who took her job. He has mental problems from his army days, he experienced something terrible. He joined up after a gap of a month. Why?

Tess is weak and pathetic, overbearing mother, clinging father, no friends, dead end job. No passport.

No body. No sightings. Tess has vanished. What happened to her?

1.   Mike has killed her and stashed the body well

2.   Mike helped her escape

He looked up. 'I need you to look into the Shepherd's Bush angle. Where did he go when he left the army? What did he do? I'm going to track down the major I spoke to on the phone. The one who signed the discharge papers.'

Rob nodded. 'Okay. I'll try and find out what those medical terms mean too.'

'Yeah, good point,' Cal said, smiling. 'You look better, Rob, how are things?'

Rob shrugged, but his sheepish grin was back. 'Well, Leese is still doing these daft self-expression courses, but she's back to looking after the kids properly. I even had me dinner cooked for me last night.'

Cal laughed. 'That's great, Rob, maybe she just needed some time to work stuff out.'

Rob gave him a look. 'Yeah, well, we all have issues, we don't all make other people's lives a misery because of them.'
Then he grinned. 'But it's good to have the old Leese back.'

'Good to have you back, Rob,' Cal said. Rob stood up quickly, but not fast enough so Cal could miss his flushed face.

'Cheers, Partner. I'll phone you when I learn anything.'

Cal grabbed all the paperwork and went to see the chief. He wanted to meet this major face to face, where he couldn't be evasive.

*

Mike got into work early, and headed for the supervisor's office, eager to get the wheels in motion. Already he could almost taste the sweet air, and feel the chill mountain wind on his face.

The security guards had a locker room on the lower level, between the supervisor's office on one side, and the exit to the basement car park on the other. No one used that exit except for the guards themselves and the police when they had a shoplifter to arrest.

Mike knocked and walked in as usual. 'Morning Mr Sanders.'

'Oh, hi Mike,' Fred Sanders stood up, smiling. He was a small, thickset man who smiled a lot. Despite his height, he looked very strong, and gave the impression that he didn't mess about. Mike had a lot of respect for him.

'Mr Sanders, I wanted to talk to you. I need to hand in my notice.'

Fred's smile disappeared. 'Oh Mike, I'm sorry to hear that, you're my best guy.'

Mike gave an uncomfortable shrug.

'I was hoping to promote you, you know.' Fred gave him a wistful smile. 'But if you have to go-'

'I'm sorry,' Mike said. 'I'll work the week out, no problem, until you can get a replacement.'

'That's good of you, Mike, but I'm not going to get anyone as good as you.'

Mike felt his face flushing.

'If you've had a better offer, I can ask the boss about maybe matching it?'

'Thanks. But I really can't stay.'

Fred sighed and sat back down. 'All right, Mike, but if you need a job back here again, it's here for you.'

'I appreciate that, Mr Sanders.'

'Hell, Mike, call me Fred. I'll put the call in and have your papers ready come Friday night, is that okay?'

'Yes, thank you.'

Mike left the office feeling light as air. He didn't need the week's wages, but he didn't want to let the man down, and it was only five days. He'd done harder things. *Much* harder.

Mike spent an uneventful week, doing his job. He took simple pleasure in the routine, and the anticipation of being far away from everything that fed his nightmares. He waited until lunchtimes to patrol the west wing of the second floor, knowing the glass shop would be closed for lunch and he wouldn't have to see Marian. He also kept away from the guards' room, except to stow his bag in his locker every morning and collect it at night. He could no more leave his kit bag at home than he could stop his own heart.

Friday came, and dragged on and on, until at last six o'clock arrived, and Mike hurried to the locker room, smiling to himself in anticipation. He grabbed his bag and opened the door to leave.

Marian was standing there waiting for him.

He felt his mouth go dry. She had a hurt look on her face. No, he thought, not hurt, it was something else, something he couldn't quite figure out.

'Mike, I haven't seen you all week. I've been worried about you.'

'I'm fine,' he said, his voice hoarse.

'Look, can we go somewhere and talk?'

'I'm sorry, Marian, I can't. I can't see you any more. I have to go now.'

He pushed past her, but she grabbed his arm. Mike shuddered. Something flashed behind his left eye.

'Mike, I know all about it, I know what's wrong with you, and I want to help.'

He looked at her, sweat bursting out on his forehead. 'Please let me go.'

'No. I won't. My dad explained it all to me, it's post traumatic – something or other. Something that happened to you in the past. In the war. You just need to talk about it and it'll be fine.'

His heart was pounding now, the blood beating in his temples.

'Come with me,' she said, her voice pleading. 'I've told my folks I'm going down to their house in France for the weekend. Come with me and we can talk.'

'Please-' he said, pulling his arm away. Orange lightning was flashing behind both eyes now. 'Please leave me alone.'

'Mike, you need to trust me. I know you've seen terrible things. I want to help you.'

Terrible things.

'You can't', he whispered.

'Yes I can. Look at me, Mike.'

He recognised the look on her face now. Pity. It made his blood run cold.

'I want to look after you,' she said.

The words seemed to echo, not only in his mind, but all through his life. *Look after you.*

Amidst the lightning and the blood pounding in his temples, the horrors of the past danced and laughed, each one a wave of broken glass crashing into his head. He screwed his eyes shut, trying to keep them out, trying to find the calm place, but the monsters were in control now, brewing up a storm, and Mike was mere flotsam on the waves.

You don't need to leave, the monsters said. They felt like creatures of the deep, pulling him into the depths.

But I want to!

'Mike?'

You know what you need to do. Do it now, and you'll be at peace again. You know you must.

No!

Mike? Please? Let me take care of you.'

A zap of electricity rode up his spine and blasted pain into his brain. Mike threw his head back, waiting as the pain slowly subsided, taking with it the edge of all sensation, as if a glass wall had lowered between him and the world. He opened his eyes and looked at the woman. Grabbing her arm, he pulled her along the dim corridor towards the door.

'Mike, you're hurting me, let me go.'

He pushed through into the fluorescent-lit car park, footsteps echoing as they headed for his car.

'Mike, my car's over there, I've got my things in-'

He gripped her tighter, and she gasped at the pain. He heard the tears start, and the sound seemed a long way away as he opened the car door and shoved her inside, forcing her over the gearstick into the passenger seat. She was crying loudly now, and he could almost smell her fear. He hurled his kitbag in the back and got in, locking the doors and starting the engine.

'You didn't need to do that,' she sobbed, pouting. 'I wanted to go with you.'

Mike drove up into the evening streets, heading for the motorway. Marian continued to sob quietly beside him and he ignored her. He reached the junction and turned north.

'Mike,' Marian said in a small voice, 'You're going the wrong way.'

Mike kept his eyes on the road.

'No,' he said. 'I'm not.

EIGHTEEN

The night's rain gave way to a bright morning with silver fish-scale clouds populating a pale sky. Tess had fish for breakfast and decided at last to travel south. She had seen the rest of the big island now, and a few days keeping to the woods and the high rocky ground had allowed her feet to begin to heal. A watery sun appeared as she walked through the marshy grass towards the cliffs.

There were ships out there now. She saw them all the time, but they were a long way out, too far to see her little fire. These were huge commercial ships, sailing back and forward from some far off place, she couldn't guess where. 'Where the hell am I?' she asked often, though there was no one to answer.

The weather was turning warmer, and she knew that if one boat had come close, others would too. It was only a matter of time, and hope filled her heart like the little fish caught in the shallows when the tide went out.

Tess walked along the tall cliffs, looking down at the water, pale green and clear. A few days ago she had spotted what she could only imagine was a whale, moving slowly through the clear seas, giant mouth agape. It was a sight of such wonder that it had filled her eyes with sudden tears. She walked the cliffs and looked out for her fellow islanders, and a deep yet simple joy filled her. She wished she had something to paint with. She had given up drawing and painting years ago, for reasons she could no longer remember, but now the urge was back.

She followed the cliffs for miles, down behind the gentle slope of the mountain, where the landscape subtly changed. The tussocky heather and gorse gave way to mossy turf, spindly grasses. The land rose and fell in lumps and bumps, until she finally climbed a rise and looked down at the shore below.

A long thin finger of land stuck out into the sea like a giant grass covered toothbrush. Behind it, for what seemed like mile upon endless mile, stretched sand as white as flour. A gasp caught in her throat at the beauty of it.

She hurried down through the thin grass to the beach, stripping off her tattered shoes. The sand was firm and warm beneath her sore wet feet, a sensation so welcome that she let out a heartfelt sigh of relief. And then she began to run, the wind's cool edge in her face and the smell of the sea opening her lungs. The waves rolling into the sand were enormous, rearing out of the slick sea to collapse in a cascade of dirty old lace. The frothy remnants reached for her, the breaking air bubbles like gaping mouths reaching to swallow her up. A laugh began somewhere in her stomach and erupted from her throat in delight. Above, the seabirds wheeled, crying in surprise, as she turned and ran into the sea. The chill waves soaked her legs as she danced in the shallows, kicking the spray high into the air. Then finally she collapsed, still laughing, on the soft sand.

'All this time, and I never knew this was here,' she said. 'I could have had warm feet all along.'

She spied a small white bird above, its wings outstretched like an angel. It dived, leaving the water with a sliver of silver in its beak, and Tess looked past the bird to the horizon, in case here might be a boat there.

And, for the very first time, she hoped she would not see one.

Tess lay back and folded her arms behind her head. If she closed her eyes, she could imagine she was on holiday on some Mediterranean island, the sun warm on her face, the sound of the sea and the birds lulling her to sleep. But she didn't sleep. Her thoughts were full.

What has happened to me?

I am alone, and enjoying it. I have nothing, and don't really want anything.

Not even rescue.

She dug her feet into the sand, enjoying the blissful warmth. Opening her eyes, she sighed. The sky was the palest blue, almost translucent. It felt as if the universe were secretly looking in.

Not much to see down here, she thought, closing her eyes again. She dozed, contentment filling her heart like the incoming tide, which woke her a few minutes later with its first touch against her arm. She got up, laughing at her foolishness. She should have known the tide was turning.

But how? She thought again. *Yes, I knew. How?*

She put it down to the shape of her days, the fact that her beachcombing was governed by the self same tide. She had become aware of it without thinking.

She grabbed her shoes and walked across the beach towards rising dunes, making her way through the shifting sands where tough grasses waved in the breeze. The dunes gave way to gentle grassland on this, the flat side of the island. She spotted a few stone gatherings, perhaps other former homes, and was on her way to investigate when something shiny caught her eye.

She crouched and picked up the object, her heart immediately beginning to race. What she held was a piece of dark saw-edged metal with a hole at one end. A thin wire had been passed through the hole, fastening it to a serrated silver bar. She took hold of the bar and struck it across the edge of the flint, watching the sparks erupt. She knew what to do with the tool. After all, there was an identical one in the tobacco tin Mike had left her.

How did that get here? Looking up, she scanned the grassland for any sign of life. There was nothing but the usual gorse and broom, a couple of rocky outcrops, and a few groups of huddled stones. She hurried towards the first group, the remains of what might have once been a wall. The stones had long since fallen over, to be overgrown by grass and colonised by pale green lichens. She scoured the surrounding area, but saw nothing unusual. Climbing higher, she reached the first outcrop, where something was flapping in the breeze. She caught at the flimsy plastic and pulled it from its place between the rocks. The bright yellow had long since faded to washed out lemon, and the material tore as she pulled it out. A rainjacket and a flint. She felt a warning lump in her throat as she scrambled over the rocks and headed for the final group of stones. And there in the grass was another shiny object, this time reflecting the bright sky. A magnifying glass. Tess picked it up and slid it into her pocket with the flint. She broke into a run, scanning the ground for further objects, and so she didn't notice the bones until she was almost upon them.

She stopped, staring, her throat dry and tight. A few wisps of thin cloth, faded by time and wind, still clung to the ruined frame. One arm reached out, the bleached bones sandblasted into rough stalagmites, the fingers long since stolen away. Tess felt the wind steal into her heart and freeze her where she stood. She couldn't look away, and every sight was more horrible than the last: the leg bones, yards away, the foot still encased in a hopeless little flat slip-on; the strands of yellow hair still attached to the grey skull, fluttering merrily in the breeze. Beyond the corpse was a little circle of stones, a fire pit built in the shadow of the ruined wall, but Tess could see that no fire had ever had any success there. Beneath the wall, she could see the shiny lid of the tobacco tin, caught in the thick grass.

She walked slowly round the body, Aware of the silence but for the wind whipping in the grass and the thudding of her heart. *Who are you?* She wondered. *What did you do to piss Mike off?*

It took no more than five minutes to locate the rest of the tin, its contents tipped into the grass. Carefully she picked up the tiny fish hooks, the rusted saw wire. It appeared the unknown woman had no use for a condom either, but Tess took it just the same.

She walked back to the edge of the dunes, looked out at the waves. She tried to imagine what it must have been like for her predecessor, trying to survive. Her feelings were confused. It was a nightmare, being dumped here, struggling to stay alive. She had been lucky, the weather had been on her side. But behind that she struggled to hide an edge of contempt. How could she not survive?

Didn't she *try*? Jesus Christ! Tess was one of the most pathetic women on the planet. If she could do it, anyone could.

Beyond the golden semicircle of sun, setting in clouds of dark grey and purple, came the memory of the few strands of blonde hair clinging to the skull. It had been a young woman, perhaps no older than she was. Golden hair, thrashed by the wind, but the salt water had not dimmed its colour.

She thought again about Mike. A man she had really liked, seen something in, a decency, a kindness. The fact that it had got out of control was her fault. She should have let him down gently.

But, wait a minute, why was it her fault? The man, however nice, was desperately troubled. Why was he her responsibility?

Maybe she should have been sympathetic. But she wasn't. Why not? Did he tell her enough and she did not care? Did she know and did not care?

Her own memories of her past were strange as well: a woman devoid of decision, of ambition. Her mother: strong, brash and unemotional. Tess knew Sheila had never wanted her, yet now she was desperate for her daughter to make something of herself, and sneered at her dull, simple life. Her father, even more pathetic than she was, clingy and saccharine-sweet, but he had not always been like that, and he was still the best friend she had. And Mike, who had seemed attractive, the exotic tinge of the army, the life he would not speak of, and the steadfast knowledge that he would always be there for her.

Even if I didn't want him to be.

And there it was, in a nutshell. She had let him down. This was nothing to do with normal human manners, decorum, courtesy. This was real life. He had needed her, and she had thrown his need back in his face. What her wishes were didn't matter now. The man had brought her here, for reasons of his own, but they had also served her well, she thought. Her past life seemed like a distant event, like a long ago foreign trip. Nothing remained but broken fragments of memory, out of time and place.

She might have died here. She could easily have died here. He wanted her to, it was obvious.

But she couldn't find any hate in her heart for him.

Tess listened to the waves hushing her troubled thoughts. She thought it was ironic to be sitting here feeling sorry for her kidnapper. She was sure there was some fancy psychological term for it. When she got off the island, she would find him. She wasn't sure yet what she'd do, but she'd find him. And she would get off the island, she knew it. When the weather turned warmer, there would be sailboats, and yachts. One

116

would come close enough to see her beacon. Tess had no doubts that her days here were numbered, and perhaps that was why she was enjoying them. Unlike the poor woman in the dunes, whom it appeared had not stood a chance.

She stood up, pulling on her tattered shoes. It was a long way back to the cave, and the air was chill now, she would have to run to keep warm. She took the cliff path, the cool air feeling good in her lungs. The torn sole of her training shoe made a shlupping noise as she ran, keeping time with the beat of her heart. She looked up at the stars growing brighter. There was Venus, brightest of them all, the same star that looked down upon her now, every night. It was something she could rely on, one of the few things, but now she had one more.

If Mike had left two women to die on the island, he would do it again.

Even if a boat didn't turn up to rescue her, it didn't matter.

Mike would be back, sooner or later, and Tess would be ready for him

NINETEEN

The drive down to Colchester was miserable. The DI had still been sceptical when Cal had talked about getting a warrant to search Dole's flat and car, and he was probably right, but Jarvis had agreed that a trip down to talk with Major Peters might be worthwhile. As he drove, Cal tried to keep his mind on the way he intended to handle the interview, the questions he had. For once, it was proving difficult.

Last night, as he had opened the door to his dark and empty home, the telephone had been ringing, and he hurried to answer it, expecting it to be Rob Matlock.

'Fisher.'

'Hello Cal. It's me, Lynne.'

It had felt like a punch in the chest. Three years down the line, and she had finally picked up the phone. Cal stood in the dark, gazing out at the rain, feeling his heart beating hard.

'Cal? Can I speak to you? You're not going to be upset?'

He sat on the edge of the sofa. 'I'm not upset,' he said. His hands reached absently for the cigarette packet that until recently lived in his inside pocket. His fist clenched as it came away empty.

'I'm sorry it's taken me so long to do this, but I was really messed up, you know?'

Cal said nothing. He was remembering the good times, the times before Lynne's mood swings and sudden tears. Before the secrets.

'Cal, are you there?'

'Yes. What do you want, Lynne?' he said. He felt ashamed at the hope in his voice, even after all this time.

She sighed. 'I want to apologise. I never meant to hurt you, but I did. I should have said this before, but... anyway, I'm very sorry.'

He swallowed, his mouth suddenly dry. 'Is that it?'

'What? Oh. Yes, I suppose so.'

Cal felt the colour rushing to his cheeks. After all the shit she put him through, and all he was getting was a half baked apology, three years late.

'Well, thanks a lot,' he said. 'Goodbye.'

The sound of the handset crashing down on the phone had been oddly satisfying. He pulled the plug out of the wall as well, just in case. The cops could always ring his mobile. Then he poured himself a large black label vodka and sat on the sofa in the dark to drink and remember.

So this morning his mouth was dry and tasted bitter, and his head still felt woolly even after three mugs of coffee. He pulled into the slip lane, taking a deep breath. Back to the job, he told himself. The only thing he could rely on.

The garrison was in the centre of town, and Cal went through the usual security drill before being directed to Meeanee Barracks, a name he couldn't even pronounce. There was a lot of activity about, probably because the troops were supposed to be heading out. He held his old briefcase over his head as he hurried out of the rain. All the squaddies he saw looked at him with suspicion, and he wondered if it was because he was a cop or a civilian. Probably being both was even worse.

He was told to wait in a bland room, with only the rain to look out at. The walls were bare, and the chairs hard, and Cal had to smile. That was an old copper's trick, to make people uncomfortable, uneasy. He sat on a wooden chair and waited.

After a long fifteen minutes, he heard positive sounding footsteps and the door swept open.

'Sergeant Fisher. I am very sorry to have kept you waiting so long.'

'It's quite all right,' Cal replied, shaking the man's hand. Major Peters was a huge man, well over six feet, with shoulders and hands to match. Even his voice was big, He had bright blue eyes in a round cherubic face, very pink skin, and hair the colour of cut wheat. It looked like a child's head on a man's body, but the mouth was drawn into a careful smile, which didn't quite reach the shrewd and watchful eyes. Cal picked up his briefcase and followed the man along a short corridor to what was presumably his office. Peters immediately sat down behind his desk, and Cal took the seat opposite, glancing round at the regimental photos on the walls.

'I know you're busy,' he began, 'I understand you're off to the Middle East soon-'

'Who told you that?'

Cal hesitated, then shook his head. 'Just a rumour.'

'Rumours!' Peters said, leaning back and smiling his careful smile. 'What can you believe these days, eh?'

Cal put his briefcase on his lap and opened it.

'Thank you for seeing me, anyway,' he said.

Peters shrugged. 'I don't think I'll be able to help you, but fire away.'

'You might recall I'm investigating the disappearance of a woman-'

'Tessa Hardy,' Peters said, steepling his fingers. 'I checked it out after our last chat. I take it there's been no sign of her?'

'Not even an unconfirmed sighting. She's simply vanished.'

Peters nodded slowly, and Cal let the silence grow. Eventually the side of the major's mouth turned up and he leaned forward.

'So how can I help you, Sergeant?'

Cal looked down to hide his own smile. The major wasn't going to fall for any of his tricks, that was for sure. Maybe he should try another tack.

'I tell you what, Major, I'm going to give you what I've got. I don't have to, in fact I shouldn't, but I'm going to, and then I'd like you to tell me what you think.'

Peters sat back again, the smile still on his face. 'I'll help you if I can,' he said.

'Okay. Tess Hardy has been missing now for almost three months. She doesn't have what you might call model parents, and she has few friends, except for Mike Dole, with whom she had been having a relationship for several months before she disappeared. I interviewed Mike at his place of work and at his home, and although he seemed a little strange, he gave me no reason to suspect him of any wrongdoing.'

Cal paused. He had seen a change come over the major's face.

'There's something you want to tell me?' he prompted.

Peters shook his head, 'no, nothing yet.'

Cal made a mental note.

'Everyone who knows Tess has told me she is a timid, absent-minded character, who would never dream of doing something reckless or spur of the moment. Despite a suitcase and a few clothes being missing from her house, her bank accounts have not been touched, and, as I mentioned, there have been no sightings.

'Maybe she's gone abroad.'

'She doesn't have a passport.'

Cal held the major's eyes for a long moment, then looked back at his notes.

'The missing suitcase has been kept quiet until now. Mike Dole is now dating another woman, Marian, who works at the shopping mall where he is employed as a security guard. Mike told Marian that Tess – and I quote – "took a suitcase with her."'

He watched Peters carefully, but couldn't see any reaction.

'Couldn't that just have been a guess? I expect he was trying to impress her with a bit of gossip.'

Cal shook his head. 'Only the police and the girl's mother knew about the suitcase. It wouldn't have become gossip.'

Cal could see the man was unconvinced, and decided to throw one in from left field.

'Incidentally, this Marian took over Tess's job when she disappeared.'

There it was, a quick raise of a blond eyebrow, a sudden opening of the mouth. That got home.

'Have you any idea what that might mean?'

Peters looked down for the first time. 'Only that he is attracted to the same types.'

Cal waited, but there was nothing else coming. He wanted to yell: *why are you protecting him!* He reached into the briefcase and pulled out a folder which he threw on the desk.

'Then there's this,' he said.

Peters took the folder carefully and opened it. His shoulders slumped as he opened it and saw Dole's military records.

'Now I don't know much about the army, or the medical problems listed in there, but reading between the lines, it's clear Mike is not a well man.'

Peters closed the file and sat back.

'He's not a criminal,' he said.

Cal waited again, and this time it worked.

'I've known Dole for years. He's a good man. He would always go out of his way to help others weaker than himself. That's not the blueprint of an evil man.'

Cal shrugged. 'Evil? Perhaps not. But it doesn't mean he couldn't have abducted the girl. Maybe it all started out innocently and got out of hand?'

Peters' piercing eyes looked seriously uncomfortable now.

'Look, the two features that stand out about Dole are his intelligence and his compassion. I can't see him doing anything like this.'

Cal leaned forward. 'Let me tell you about intelligence, major. About three years ago I put away a university professor, a man who had written countless books on physics and astronomy, he was a leader in the field. A genius, almost. He was also married with a wife and daughter who were both wheelchair-bound after an accident twelve years before. When this man wasn't working, he was looking after his family. Yet he wasn't unhappy or depressed. As far as everyone knew, he coped well and was fine. Then one night he took his telescope out to the local park to view a lunar eclipse. There were lots of people there, lots of kids. One seven year old boy got over excited and tripped over the telescope, knocking it over. The professor strangled him with his bare hands.'

Peters winced.

'It doesn't matter what you see on the surface, Major, it's what's bubbling away underneath that counts, and I think our Mike has got lots bubbling under-' he hesitated, waiting until Peters met his eyes. '-and so do you.'

Cal noticed the sadness creeping into the soldier's eyes. Peters leaned both arms on the desk and clasped his hands together.

'Tell me about, Mike, major. Tell me what happened to him.'

Peters bit his lip.

'He had a bad childhood,' he said, the reluctance heavy in his voice. 'He never spoke to me about it, but it was known. He joined up at eighteen, probably to get away from home. The army became his family, his real family.'

Cal slipped his notebook out, not talking his eyes away from Peters.

'He was a quiet lad, never spoke much, but he looked out for the others, and they all liked him. He had three really close mates, and I think he was genuinely happy. He loved the survival training. In fact, he was so good at it he became one of the trainers. We used to send them up to a Scottish island with nothing but their packs, and leave them there. His teams always came back well fed.'

He paused, looking back at the photos on the wall behind him. 'That's Mike, second from the left.'

Cal stood up and peered at the photo.

'That was taken just before they went off to the Gulf. The three lads in front of him are gone now. They never made it back.'

Cal remembered the notes he had made.

'What happened?'

'Ambush. They came upon a pipeline that had been breached. There was a vehicle left there that was filled with explosives. The thing went up like a rocket. Mike got away with minor injuries, but the loss of his best mates hit him hard. He was despondent that he hadn't been able to look after them.'

Cal wrote quickly. 'Was that the start of his problems?'

Peters shook his head. 'He'd had moments of it before, depression, sometimes he would have nightmares. But he coped. He was-'

Cal's phone began to ring, and he gritted his teeth and swore to himself. He should have turned the damn thing off. Peters just stared at him.

'I'm sorry, sir,' he said, looking at the phone. It was Rob. Well, the moment was lost now, he may as well take the call. 'Would you excuse me for a moment?'

'Cal, where are you?'

'What's up?'

'There's another one gone missing.'

'What?'

'Another woman. It's worse. Dole's missing too.'

Cal stood up, feeling the colour draining from his face.

'You're not going to believe it. It's the shop girl. The one who replaced the first one.'

Cal stared at the photo on the wall. In it, Dole was grinning, looking as happy and normal as all the other young lads. The sour taste of guilt was in his mouth. He should have known, should have done something about it.

'You there, Cal?'

'Yes.'

'The woman's father is ex-army too. He's going apeshit.'

Cal looked back at Peters, who now had a concerned look on his face. And about bloody time too. Now Cal not only had to try and find a psychotic soldier gone awol, but deal with a family furious that no one had arrested him before now. And no doubt Sheila Harrison would have some special words, just for him. A deep bleakness filled his heart. He only had himself to blame. He should have pushed for a warrant.

'Speak to Chief Jarvis, get a warrant. The house and the car.' He said. 'I'll be back this afternoon,' Cal closed the phone.

'Problems?' Peters said.

Cal nodded. 'The second shop girl has gone missing. And so has your friend Mr Dole.'

Peters swallowed. 'What? Are they together, or-'

'We don't know,' Cal said, hearing the bitterness in his voice. He sat down heavily, looking at the major.

'I need you to tell me everything about Mike Dole. Everything you know.'

'Well, I-'

'Let's go back. The problems started after the Gulf war?'

'That's when he stopped being able to cope with whatever plagued him. He was diagnosed with PTSD. Classic symptoms, really. The nightmares got worse, he became jumpy, agitated, sometimes he would seem to be in another world. But through it all he never wanted to leave. He couldn't leave, I don't think. Like I said, we were his family.'

'Tell me about Kosovo,' Cal said.

Peters sighed. 'You worked that out from the records, I suppose.'

'It's clear that after that tour he was seriously messed up.'

'Yes. The army turfed him out. Told him to get help in civvy street. In short, we let him down.'

'Tell me what happened.'

Peters hesitated, and Cal leaned across the desk. 'Tell me, major. It might save someone's life.'

'I wasn't there. They were a peace keeping force only. They were not supposed to act in any hostile way. And nor did they. The locals were more scared than belligerent. They kept out of the way of the soldiers.'

Peters began to drum his fingers on the table.

'Inspector, what I am going to tell you is in strict confidence, between ourselves. I'll tell you because it might help, but if you repeat this to anyone, I'll deny all knowledge.'

'Understood.'

Peters took a breath and continued.

'Mike's battalion came upon another group. Not Paras, and you don't need to know who they were. While all the hellos were going on, Mike heard screaming coming from one of the Albanian refugee tents, and went to investigate. He discovered a woman being raped by three soldiers.'

Cal held his breath.

'Like I said, they were not soldiers from our regiment. Mike didn't know them, but he was furious and started fighting them, and somehow in the melee, the woman got hold of his gun.'

Peters looked down at his hands. There was a long pause.

'She shot the soldiers?' Cal asked.

The major shook his head.

'It turned out she had two little daughters in the tent with her. Just children. She must have thought they'd be next. She killed them and then herself.'

'With Dole's gun.' Cal said. He thought he was beginning to see it. Mike wanted to look after them, instead, he was the means to their end.

He closed his eyes. Where had he put Tess and Marian to look after them? Somewhere safe? Somewhere dark and lonely, and cold?

'That's a big help, major. Thank you for telling me.'

'You can understand why this has never-'

'Perfectly,' Cal said. The army, cleaning up its own dirty laundry, he thought. He bit back the anger and stood up, checking his watch.

'I'd better get back before all hell breaks loose.'

Peters stood and offered his big hand again. 'Please call me if I can help in any other way.'

Cal thought for a moment. 'Have you a photo of Mike that I can borrow?'

The major hesitated, then he turned and walked over to a table by the wall. He pulled open the top drawer and Cal saw that it was full of photographs. Peters caught his raised eyebrow.

'I'm a bit of an amateur photographer,' he explained. He fished about for a moment before pulling out a black and white 8x10. It showed two men, both dressed in fatigues, standing in front of the blurred door of a Chinook helicopter. One was fair haired, laughing, and the camera had clearly caught him in mid sentence. Mike was standing next to him, his face a blank mask, his eyes staring at the camera as if it might really steal his soul.

'Here,' Peters said, holding it out.

'Who's the other chap?'

'That's Henderson. He's one of the helicopter pilots. He's shouting to me to take his picture. That was taken just before Mike was discharged.'

Cal studied the photo for a long moment. Then he slipped it into his briefcase.

'Thanks, sir.'

As he opened the door, the major said his name.

'If it does turn out that Mike is involved, would you – I mean, could I see him? Whatever has happened to him, I feel I owe him something.'

'Let's not be premature,' Cal said. 'But if we find him, you might be able to help.'

Cal got back to the car, his emotions twisting. The information he now had made him feel buzzed, but the thought of the missing women was eating at him. Now he had to work fast to find Mike Dole before he had two dead women on his conscience. Marian's trail would still be fresh, there was hope. As for the first one, Tess, well, it was too late for her.

TWENTY

The garage attendant looked out of the window and smiled as Mike handed over his cash.

'Your missus is out for the count all right,' he said.

Mike followed his gaze to where Marian's head rested on the passenger window.

'Yes,' he said. 'You'd think she'd been knocked out.'

The attendant chuckled and scratched at his bald head. 'My wife sleeps like that. Snores like a drunken sailor an' all. You want a receipt?'

Mike forced his mouth into a smile. 'No thanks.'

He walked back to the car and made sure he gave Marian's unconscious form as fond a smile as he could manage before driving off.

The fact that it was becoming increasingly difficult to keep control made it all the more important that he try to appear normal.

Thank God he'd had the presence of mind to clear the flat. He had no doubt that the police would be swarming all over it by now, but they would find nothing. It was all in the boot of the car.

Marian had cried on and off for a while, in between pleading to know where he was taking her and trying to reassure him that she wasn't upset. He had simply taken himself away from her, until every sound she made sounded muffled and distant. After a couple of hours she had fallen asleep, and he had pulled off the motorway, stopped the car and retrieved some items from his kit bag. Then he woke her up and told her he was sorry.

She had looked at him uncertainly.

'It's all right,' he said quietly. 'Here.' He gave her a can of Coke and some chocolate. 'You must be hungry and thirsty. I'll take you home now.'

He took a pull from his own can and stared out at the dark.

'I want to help, Mike,' Marian said. 'Please let me.'

He nodded absently.

She put the chocolate on the dashboard, but drank deeply from the tin. 'You're really going to take me home?'

'Home it is,' he said, starting the car.

'Where are we?'

'Just off the M1.'

He drove off, and heard her sigh as a few minutes later they passed a signpost for the motorway. When they reached the junction, Mike took the southern turn and she sighed again. They drove in silence until finally her head lolled on to the passenger window, and Mike took the next exit, drove round the roundabout and headed north once more.

Once they were over the river Clyde and away from the cities, he felt his shoulders relax. There was still a long way to go, but this part would be easy, he could almost enjoy it. He drove along the shore of Loch Lomond and pulled into the car park of the Ardlui Hotel. It was gone eleven o'clock, but the car park was full. Mike knew the place attracted a lot of hillwalkers up from Glasgow for the weekend to climb the Cobbler.

It took no more than three minutes to remove the number plates from a Range Rover the same year as his Astra, and head off back on the loch road. He changed the plates over at a lay by, disposing of the old ones in the surrounding woods. Through it all, Marian never moved.

*

The journey back took almost three hours, the roadworks on the A14 slowing him down. Cal hoped Rob would have got the warrant sorted out by the time he got back. When he reached the A6 he dialled his partner's number.

'Matlock.'

'It's me. What's happening?'

'Where are you? We're ready to roll.'

Cal said nothing, taken aback. 'You've got the warrant already?'

''Course. The Chief stepped in as soon as he heard about it. There's no sign of the car, so we can take it the bastard's in it.'

'Look, I'm only twenty minutes away, I'll meet you at the flat.'

'Okay.'

Cal put his foot down, adrenalin racing his heart. He hoped they would find something at Dole's flat, but knowing the man's background, he had to doubt it. He joined the traffic crawling along Narborough Road in the drizzling rain, finally turning into the side street where Rob's unmarked car was parked. Rob got out as he pulled up outside the terraced row, wincing at the rain.

'You took your time,' Rob smiled.

'Roadworks.'

'Any joy from the Major?'

'I'll tell you in a bit.' Cal smiled absently at DC Roslyn as she got out of the car.

'I thought we could use another pair of hands,' Rob explained.

'Good thinking. Let's go.'

The street was deserted, it being mid-afternoon. The house was a typical terraced property which, like most of its neighbours, had been split into two flats to cater for the local student population. Dole had the first floor, and they climbed the steep stairs in silence. The place smelled of damp and takeaway food, and the wallpaper was filthy. Matlock knocked when they reached the top, doing it by the book, and then he produced a key.

'Landlord decided to be helpful,' he grinned.

Compared to the rest of the house, Dole's flat was a palace. His furniture was cheap and sparse, but, as Cal had noted before, spotlessly clean. There was nothing out of place, nothing personal, not even a picture on the walls, which smelt of fresh paint.

'No TV?' Rob said. 'What is this bloke, a monk?'

'I can't see us getting much joy here,' Cal said gloomily. 'Split up. 'I'll take the kitchen.'

The fridge still had a pint of milk and a carton of margarine in there, as well as some cheese and a half-full jar of jam. There was a loaf of bread in one of the cupboards, all of which were also recently painted, inside and out, and scrubbed clean. Cal wondered what had happened to drive him away so quickly. He felt sure Mike would not have left the food to spoil. He glanced round as Rob walked in.

'Anything?'

Rob shook his head.

'Not even a book. What did the guy do of an evening?'

Cal didn't want to think about that. 'Tell me about this latest girl.'

'The father came in. He's an army officer. Said his daughter was going down to their villa in Normandy on Friday. When she didn't call to say she'd arrived, he tried her phone. No answer, so he got a neighbour down there to go round. The girl never arrived. The uniform who took the report knew about the other missing girl, and gave it to me. I sent him round here, and there was no car and no one home.'

Cal bit his lip. 'So you checked out the mall?'

'This morning. Spoke to the supervisor. Dole wasn't there, but he wasn't meant to be, on account of handing in his notice last week.'

'Shit.'

'Yeah. And next thing, the girl's father is back. He's been to the mall and found out Dole's in the wind. Puts two and two together, and –'

Rob held his arms out.

Cal winced. He should have anticipated Mike doing a runner and kept a check on the man. He shook his head. This was not the time for recriminations.

Walking past Rob into the bedroom, he saw the young DC standing perfectly still.

'What is it?' Cal asked.

She hesitated. 'I'm not sure, sir. These old terraces - I was brought up in one. The main bedrooms, they're usually bigger than this. But I might be wrong.'

Cal looked around. The room had a double bed surrounded by an ugly fitted sixties-style wardrobe. She was right, it did seem like a very small room, but who knew what work the owners had done to make more living space out of the house. Cal opened the wardrobe doors and looked through the clothes hanging there. There was nothing out of the ordinary, everything was arranged as neatly as the rest of the flat.

The wardrobe had been built out from the wall, there was no back to it, and the wall still had a coating of ancient wallpaper. Cal felt a little sizzle of something not right.

'What is it?' Rob asked.

'He's such a perfectionist. Why leave this grotty wallpaper here?'

Cal pushed the coat hangers to the side and banged his fist against the wall. Instead of the solid dull sound of a thick wall, he heard the hollow ring of plasterboard.

'Here,' He began pulling the clothes out, piling them on top of his partner. 'Roslyn, see if you can find an edge anywhere.'

He ran his hands over the wall, but felt nothing other than the grainy paper.

'Here, sir!'

He crouched down to where the DC had her hand over a small indentation. Cal put his hand into the gap and pushed. The wall slid smoothly to the right, revealing a network of pigeon holes. Every one was empty.

'The bastard knew we were coming,' Rob said.

Cal took a deep breath. 'Get forensics up here, I want to know what he used this for. Roslyn, check the rest of the place for any other hidey holes.'

Rob threw the clothes on the bed, pulling out his phone. Cal tuned out his conversation. The fact that the wardrobe store was bare contradicted the food left in the kitchen. Cal was sure Dole had intended to go soon, but not this soon. He had been caught out. Why? What had been hidden in the cupboard? What the hell did it all mean?

He looked at Rob as his partner snapped his phone shut.

'Did you find out anything about Dole's past?'

'I've asked the locals to help. I know DS Warburton from Acton, and he's promised to get back to me tonight. Dole gets a disability pension, and I've asked them for their records of where that gets paid. And Roslyn looked up some gen on all those medical terms. She's put it in the file, but what it boils down to is that Dole feels detached from the real world, he's not part of it, and it might even be that he has no memory of what he's done.'

Cal sighed. 'We need to know what happened to set him off. When was he last seen?'

'At work on Friday. He never turned up to pick up his P45.'

That fit with Cal's theory. 'I'll get over to the mall. His trail's still fresh.'

Cal caught Rob's sceptical look, and took a deep breath.

'Rob, get forensics to work fast. And chase up your London DS. We have to be quick here.'

Rob raised an eyebrow. 'Why? What did the Major tell you?'

Cal shook his head impatiently. 'I haven't time to go through it right now, but I think Dole's been hanging on to the edge of sanity for a long time, but now he's lost his grip, and if we don't move fast, the woman hasn't got a chance.'

TWENTY ONE

The outboard motor was still secure in its waterproof wrapping, and burst into life at the first pull of the cord. Mike looked behind him at his car. He had driven it off the road into the croft land surrounding a small lochan, something only possible because the weather had clearly been very dry here recently. The car was not visible from the road, only from the sea, but he was still concerned about the supplies in the boot. There was no room for them on the dinghy, although he had his kit bag with him, of course.

The boat puttered out into the pre-dawn light, and the chill wind brought goosepimples to Mike's skin. The sensation made him shiver, not just with cold, but with anticipation. He was returning to his beloved island, the place where he had always felt at home. In a few hours, everything would be all right, and he could head off again. This time, he would stay away from the rest of humanity, return to the only time he felt truly happy. Maybe then, the nightmares and other waking horrors would grow tired of him and leave him alone. He looked at the hairs on his arms standing on end, feeling the cold as usual, from a distance. Mike felt that he lived much of his life behind an invisible screen which kept the intensity of existence away from him.

Or perhaps, he thought, in a moment of clarity, *it keeps the world away from me.* His cheek twitched as he considered it, and he felt a brief flutter of unexpected panic. A lone seagull soared over him, grey and silent in the lightening sky, and watching it, he felt calm return.

Maybe this time he could leave the past behind on the island with the woman. He looked down at the motionless figure in the prow, his lip curling in distaste. The woman had wet herself on the journey. His car would have to be disinfected when he got back.

The sky turned to pale gold as the little boat headed into the west. The sea was flat calm, and it felt to Mike as if it was watching, waiting to see what would happen next. Mike's cheek twitched again. He knew what was going to happen. After all, he was in control.

He beached the dinghy on the shingle, tying up to the jetty. Leaning over, he tapped the woman's cheek. There was no reaction, and he carefully lifted one eyelid. Nothing. The dose was perfect. He stood up, breathing deeply of the cold perfect air, and thought he heard the echo of a laugh, a seventeen year old laugh, the crunch of squaddie boots as they ran up the shingle. A smile came to his lips. It had been so long since those happy times here. He bent to lift the woman out of the boat, and something caught his eye on the jetty. He bent to pick it up.

A fish hook. He turned the tiny thing in his fingers, curious and surprised.

And then Mike remembered Tess. He looked up. Of course! How could he have forgotten? Well, she'd be bare bones by now. He tucked the hook into his shirt pocket, and reached down again. Then he felt a surge of curiosity. Tess must have used the hook, otherwise how could it have got there? He looked at Marian's still form, then glanced at the sky. It was no more than six o'clock, he had a little time, and it wouldn't take long to find the body. He climbed out of the boat and walked up the beach.

The scrubby wood was exactly as he remembered it. This was where he had left Tess, all those months ago, and it would not surprise him to find her body still there. However, all he found were footprints heading back to the sea, and he turned back along the grassy bank until he picked up tracks at the far end, leading away up the hillside. Mike hesitated. What was the point of looking for a dead body now? He was anxious to leave the Marian woman and just go.

But the tracks were well worn. Tess had not died immediately, and he was curious. He had liked Tess. No, scratch that, he had loved her, he really had. For a second he wondered if she had somehow managed to survive, but then he smiled. Not Tess, that was impossible. All the same –

He walked up the track until it wound downhill again into a thick coniferous wood that smelt of damp earth. Here in the dim light he struggled to follow the track, but eventually picked it up by a waterfall, where the land began to rise again, and then he stopped.

There's no time for this.

He had to maintain discipline, not wander off on some wild goose chase. He shook his head and turned to head back the way he had come.

The noise of the waterfall began to fade as Mike climbed toward an uprooted Scots Pine, and the sound jogged a long lost memory: daft Willie falling into the stream they were crossing, the other squaddies laughing fit to burst. He had not joined in the laughter, but it had been funny. Those had been great days, happy time-

There was a movement to the left. Mike turned and ducked at the same time, instinctively turning his weapon to face the enemy. Only he had no weapon, his hands were empty. His stomach knotted in fear, his left eye twitching as he scanned the wood, silent and still. Nothing moved, but he knew he had seen something. He took steady deep breaths, calming himself. *Think logically!* Tess was dead, the island had no inhabitants, and the Marian woman was still too drugged to move. It must be an animal. He waited for long moments, but saw nothing. At last he stood up and turned in a full circle, carefully scanning the woods.

Nothing.

He had always relied on his instincts, and they had served him well. Could they be failing him now? His left eye twitched again.

He began to walk slowly out of the wood again. Up ahead, the mossy bank was filled with rabbit holes, and he wondered if that was all he had seen. He had the urge to get his gun out of his kit bag, but resisted, reluctant to make unnecessary noise. The edge of the trees was only a few yards away, but the wood seemed suddenly oppressive and claustrophobic. The sound of the water was masking all other sounds except his feet crunching twigs as he walked. He imagined the trees watching him, and felt his heart fluttering.

Don't be such a fool, he thought. Once he was out of this damn wood, away from these gloomy conifers, he'd be fine.

Then something dropped on him from above.

Mike had no time to yell before something hard smacked him on the head and his knees buckled. He reached out his hands, vision swimming, as the thing hit him again and again. The sound of the waterfall was suddenly louder, and behind it he could hear something else, a frantic, breathless screaming. The earth was cold and damp between his fingers, and he stared hard at the forest floor, as the leaves and moss and pine needles slowly merged together in black and white and faded away. He tried to shake his head, but nothing was working any more. There was the dim echo of footsteps running, twigs breaking, then no sound at all except someone breathing hard – himself? He opened his eyes and found they were working again. He was alive.

Mike shook his head again, and this time it hurt. He winced, and the pain blossomed into anger. He staggered to his feet, blinking hard.

Everything was still blurred. Something was trickling down his face, and he knew it must be blood. He lurched uphill from tree to tree, the bag on his back knocking him off-balance. Out on the open hillside, he fell to his knees and crawled up to the hilltop, where he got up again and tried to run down the hill. His legs were still not obeying instructions and he fell, tumbling painfully down towards the beach.

He picked himself up, swaying as he hit the stones. Above the *shrunk* sound of his feet on the shingle he could hear something else – the sound of an engine bursting into life. He looked up and saw his dinghy.

Someone was in it. He took another step and the stones slid, dropping him on his face. He looked up in time to see Tess using his old knife to cut the line, then dropping into the water to turn the boat around.

'Wait!' He shouted, but it came out as no more than a whisper. As he got to his feet once more, Tess hauled herself into the boat and twisted the throttle. The boat ripped away from the jetty, and Mike pulled his kit bag round and reached inside. The little dinghy was well out now, and he raised the gun unsteadily and aimed it. He saw Tess looking back at him, saw her duck down as far as she could.

He dropped to his knees on the jetty. He could see a pine needle sticking out of his index finger. Absently he thought about how painful that would be to remove. When he looked up again, the boat was gone.

TWENTY TWO

Fred Sanders looked at Cal over the top of his steepled fingers.

'I told the other officer all this, you know.'

Cal nodded. 'Yes, sir, but that was before certain other developments came to light. Can you just tell me again, the last time you saw Mr Dole?'

Fred sighed and leaned back.

'Monday morning, about ten to nine. That's when he handed in his notice.'

'Can you tell me how he seemed?'

'What? Well. Just the same as usual, really.'

'And what's that?'

Fred smiled. 'He doesn't say a lot, Mike. My type of guy.'

Cal let that one pass. He was trying to stay calm despite the pounding of his blood.

'He didn't appear agitated, upset?'

Fred shook his head. 'He was polite and quiet. I said I was sorry to lose him, and I am. What is it he's supposed to have done? Kidnap someone?'

'And you didn't see him after that?'

'No. He was supposed to come down at quitting time on Friday for his papers, but he didn't show. Ask some of the other guys, they'll have seen him after me.'

'I will do, sir. Thank you. Can you tell me who was working the same shift as Mr Dole last week?'

Fred sighed, but stood up and looked at the wall chart behind him.

'You want Alan Rossiter and Louie Gibson. Alan's on earlies this week, but Louie will be about the mall, if you want to look for him.'

'Could you page him for me?'

Fred looked at him, chewing his lip.

'This is really serious, isn't it? All right, I'll put a call out for him. Wait here.'

Cal got his phone out as the man left the room.

'Matlock.'

'Rob, where are you? Anything to report?'

'Not yet, but Gareth Bailey's here. I've been having a quiet word, off the record.'

Cal held his breath. Gareth was a highly respected forensics man, an explosives expert.

'There're traces of accelerants, possibly some plastic explosive. He's not certain, but –'

Cal sighed. 'Anything else? Heard from your London sergeant yet?'

'Not yet, but-'

'What?'

'I've had a call from Della at the station. You're not going to like it.'

Cal felt his shoulders sag. What else could go wrong?

'The girl's parents are there, waiting for you. They won't go home until they see you.'

'Great. Look, Rob, chase the information, will you?'

Cal shut the phone. Just what he needed. He waited impatiently until at last Sanders returned with a security guard, a tall beefy man whose eyes slid away guiltily when they met Cal's.

'This is Louie Gibson,' Sanders said. 'I'll leave you to it.'

Cal pulled out his notebook. 'Mr Gibson, when was the last time you saw Mike Dole?'

Gibson looked down. 'Um, Friday night, I think. He was in the locker room getting his stuff.'

'And where were you?'

'I was there too. We didn't speak, he just got his stuff and went.'

Cal nodded. 'And how did he appear to you? Was he in a hurry, or upset-?'

Gibson shrugged. 'I didn't take much notice. Mike never says much anyway. I did hear him arguing with this girlfriend, though.'

Cal felt a thump in his chest.

'Really? When was this?'

'Right after. He went out, and a few minutes later I heard her shouting at him. I didn't eavesdrop, you know.'

'Of course not. But did you hear what she said?'

He shook his head, looking away again. 'If you must know, I was on the toilet. All I heard was something like 'I know all about it,' and then the voices went off down the corridor.

Cal bit his lip. Know all about what? 'Did you see him after that?'

'No. Well, he was driving out by the time I went out to my car.'

'Was he alone?'

Gibson screwed up his face. 'Please try and remember, Mr Gibson.'

'It's dark in the car park, you know, and he was going up the ramp. I couldn't really be sure, but no, I think there might have been someone in the passenger seat.'

Cal sat back. 'Thank you.'

'Can I go back to work now?'

'Yes, yes of course.'

The man couldn't get out of the room fast enough. One with a chequered past, Cal thought as he headed for his car. He imagined Mike and Marian coming out here, going off in his car. Why did they leave hers? Did he force her to go with him? Rob had posted notices looking for witnesses, but so far the guard was the only one.

He drove back to the station, dreading the meeting with the family, but anxious to be back where he could look through the file. He wanted to speak to the major again, and chase up the pension details he was sure Rob had forgotten. Right now his partner would find it hard to move fast even with a thousand volts up his arse.

*

The adrenalin had begun to wear off, but the blood was still fizzing in Tess's veins, her breath coming in urgent gasps. The mixture of terror and elation was like a drug. Tess had never taken any sort of drug except alcohol, but if this was what it was like, when she got back to the mainland she was sure as hell going to try it.

The mainland! Tess slowed the boat down. A thin morning mist had come down, and she had no idea where she was. She had just torn away from the island without a direction in mind.

Reaching into her pocket for the tobacco tin, she glanced at the woman in the prow, who was coming round. She was a very pretty girl, Tess thought. *Much prettier than me.* Mike's taste had obviously improved. She felt a sudden surge of panic and looked back, then shook her head at her stupidity. Mike was stuck on the island, just as she had been. The girl flailed her arms about, trying to sit up. Tess pulled out her compass and checked it. After so many long days of watching the empty western horizon, she knew she had to go east. The girl's eyes were open now and staring, her hands grasping the side of the boat. Then abruptly her face creased and she threw up.

At least she did it over the side, Tess thought, feeling strangely unmoved by the plight of Mike's next victim. Tess wrinkled her nose at the smell, turning the throttle. The girl lost her balance and fell back into the prow. She stayed there, staring at Tess, who checked the compass again and then looked straight ahead.

A warm bath, she thought. *Clean socks. A soft bed. A cup of tea...*

'Wh-who are you? What's going on?'

Tess looked down.

'I'm Tess,' she said, pulling the throttle full out. 'I was Mike's last victim.'

TWENTY THREE

Cal went in the back way, past the smokers who greeted him with conspiratorial looks. Cal was beginning to despise them. He felt better now without the fags, and despite the withdrawal, it was time to move on.

Cigarettes were as old hat as Zapata moustaches and Ford Capris. They belonged to another time. He was willing to bet Mike Dole had never smoked.

Now where did that thought come from? He shook his head. Dole was becoming an obsession.

He made it up to his office without seeing Rob, but the chief spotted him and waved him in.

'Fisher, this missing girl thing has turned to shit.'

Cal sighed. 'I should have pushed for a warrant earlier, sir.'

'You did. I ignored you.'

Cal said nothing. Jarvis smiled. 'I should have gone with your instincts, Cal. So where are we now?'

Cal brought him up to speed, leaving out the Kosovan incident, for now.

'I was just about to chase for the pension records. He's obviously a drifter. I need to find out where he's been. It might give me a clue to where he's taken the women.'

'He's a loner as well. No friends.'

Cal nodded. 'The public haven't helped. There have still been no sightings of the first girl at all.'

Jarvis met his eyes, and Cal sighed again. *Because she's probably buried somewhere,* he thought.

'The bad news is the second girl's family have been waiting to see you.'

'I know. Matlock told me.'

'If you want to leave it, tell Della you've had a lead and gone out.'

'No sir,' Cal said. 'I'll see them. I'll just chase those records first.'

He found Rob in the incident room, on the phone. Rob put his hand over the mouthpiece.

'I'm on to the Pensions people,' he said.

'Good. Any word from your friend?'

'I'll chase him soon as I come off. You going to see the folks?'

Cal nodded. Rob went back to his conversation, miming putting a rope round his neck and pulling it upwards.

'Thanks for that, Rob,' Cal said.

Another Major, Cal thought, as Bill Warren introduced himself. He was a fit looking man, with the same confident stare as Peters. His wife looked a lot younger than him, and her face was blotchy with crying.

Next to them sat Sheila Harrison, face almost devoid of make-up, wearing a shapeless beige raincoat. Cal looked into her hard eyes and could almost taste her fury. He ushered them into an interview room, where the major took charge immediately.

'Detective, Mrs Harrison here has told us that you suspected Mike Dole of involvement in her daughter's disappearance, but did nothing about it.'

Cal waited for them all to sit down, but remained standing.

'As Tess's boyfriend, of course we checked out Mr Dole. However, there were indications that Tess may simply have gone away of her own accord.'

'You just can't admit you were WRONG!' Sheila shouted, getting to her feet. 'I told you, over and over, Tess wasn't capable of 'going away of her own accord'. I told you to arrest that man, and you did nothing. Now these people have lost their daughter too.'

Bill stood up and put his arm round Sheila. She was shaking with rage, and ignored him.

'Detective,' Bill said, 'could you have arrested Mike Dole earlier?'

'Sir, if we were to arrest people because someone told us they were guilty, the cells would be packed full. Mike Dole had no criminal record, and he seemed genuinely concerned that Tess had vanished. We had no reason to suspect him of anything criminal.'

'Genuinely concerned?' Sheila sneered. 'How the hell would *you* know?'

Cal winced at the sting, but said nothing.

'And you have a warrant out for him now?' the major said.

Cal nodded. 'And we're looking into his past. Hopefully that will help us find where he's gone.'

'Ha, fat chance of that!'

Sheila slumped in the chair, arms folded, turning her bitter face away.

'You know this man is close to the edge.'

Cal looked at Warren. 'How do you mean, sir?'

'I mean, he's ex-army, and he's had a rough time of it. I could see it in his eyes. He's got problems.'

Cal nodded. 'I've spoken to his old army commander, who was very helpful.'

The major nodded. His eyes were bleak.

'I warned our Marian off him, but she never listens to me. She's always been attracted to the wrong sort.'

Brenda Warren gave a sob at this. Sheila shot her an unsympathetic look.

'We will find them,' Cal said, putting all his determination into his voice.

'Yeah, right.' Sheila scraped her chair back and stood up. 'When it's too late. Don't listen to him, Brenda,' she snapped. 'He doesn't care.'

She stalked out, and Brenda followed, blowing her nose.

'Major-'

Bill Warren looked round. Cal swallowed.

'I could be wrong here, but I don't think Dole's an evil man.'

Bill nodded slowly. 'Neither do I. But I don't think he knows what he's doing. Not any more.'

Cal went to the coffee machine, wishing for once that it would dispense vodka, and a large one at that. He took the cup back to his desk and opened the file. He read the latest reports from Rob and Roslyn, then went back to the beginning and read the whole file again, his notebook beside him to jot down his thoughts. He wrote:

Tess's suitcase. Mike packed it? Find?

Quiet. Edgy. Controlled.

No family

Great record for catching shoplifters

Need to 'look after people'

Store room – Explosives?

He read Roslyn's report again, the explanation of all the medical terms:

A major characteristic of PTSD is the invasion of the traumatic events into the patient's everyday life by flashbacks, nightmares and panic attacks. They may also exhibit a state of nervousness known as hyperarousal, or 'fight or flight', where the sufferer is too easily startled by high pitched sounds or quick movements.

These symptoms can become so disturbing that the individual does all he can to avoid contact with everything and everyone, even their own thoughts, which may trigger yet more painful memories. The sufferer isolates themselves and their ability to respond emotionally becomes restricted, even detached.

Sufferers can also experience dissociation; a disconnection between memory and affect, so that the person is "in another world". In extreme forms the person may have no memory of their actions at all.

Cal added:

Fight or flight

Flashbacks

Detachment

In another world

He looked up at the soft rap on the opposite table. Rob looked sheepish.

'How did it go?'

'As you'd expect,' Cal said. 'Anything new?'

Rob sat down. 'I've heard from Warburton now. Dole lived in the halfway house until 2002, after which he disappeared. We'll need the pension records to know where he went next, but he turned up in Leeds in 2005. He bought the car he's still driving, it was registered to an address in Headingley.'

Cal looked down at his notebook, where he had drawn a poor version of Munch's 'The Scream'. *Never mind Mike Dole,* he thought, *what's going on in my head?*

'He started the security job in February 2006,' Rob continued, 'Rented the Narborough flat the same month.'

Cal looked at him. 'Have you spoken to the Leeds landlady?'

'No. Why?'

Cal gritted his teeth. 'Because she might be able to tell us what he did, where he worked. He's stashed these women somewhere, Rob, and we need to find them.'

Rob looked down.

'I'll get on it,' he said, standing up.

*

'Mike? You mean Mike Dole? He was- I was in the car with-'

The girl's forehead creased and she looked down at her hands.

Tess peered through the mist, as the flank of another small island approached. She was watching the waves for signs of shoals. The boat had some kind of reinforced rubber hull, and the last thing she wanted was for it to get torn up on the rocks, for her to be stuck on yet another island. She steered out into open water, going slowly.

'He was trying to kidnap me.'

Tess looked at the girl. 'I would say he succeeded, wouldn't you?'

'Where are we?'

'Good question. We'll find out soon enough.'

Tess glanced back at the compass. She became aware that the girl was staring at her.

'What?'

'You're Tess Hardy, aren't you? You're the girl from City of Glass who went missing.'

City of Glass, Tess thought. How long ago that seemed, the shop, her stupid dreams.

'How do you know that? Did he tell you?'

The girl shook her head. 'I – After you had disappeared, I took your job.'

Tess felt a jolt of surprise, and somewhere under that, hurt. Life went on. Whatever had happened to Tess, no one really cared. She felt a wry smile come to her lips and chuckled softly.

'I'm sorry, but Mike said you'd run away. He said you took a suitcase.'

Tess nodded to herself. That figured. Mike must have planned it all well. And it didn't seem as though he moved too far from home to find his victims. The same shop! But then, maybe it was something about the shop itself. She remembered his fascination with the glass unicorn. She felt a twinge of something, some hint of what was in his troubled mind.

But why he had done this to her, she couldn't guess.

She steered round the end of the island, turning due east again, still watching the water.

'I'm Marian,' the woman said in a hesitant voice.

Tess looked at her. Marian's lower lip was trembling. She was about to cry. Tess was unmoved.

'Where was Mike taking me?'

Tess glanced back. 'An island. He left me there to die, and I assume he had the same idea for you.'

'But, but why?'

'You must have done something to piss him off.'

'I didn't!' Marian yelled. 'I didn't do anything. I was trying to help him. I wanted to look after him.'

Look after *him*? Tess thought, as a small light bulb came on somewhere in the back of her head. Instinctively she reached for the pocket of her jeans, where the note was carefully folded. Marian began to sob quietly, and Tess put both hands back on the rudder and looked sharp as another island, really just a big rock, loomed out of the grey. She steered carefully out to the north east, as the mist swirled round her, making her shiver.

'How long have I been gone?' Tess asked.

Marian shrugged and wiped at her nose. 'I've been working in the shop for three months.'

Three months!

'Where is he now? What happened? He must have given me something to knock me out, I don't-'

'He's back on the island,' Tess interrupted. 'You're safe from him. We'll find land soon, and you'll be fine.'

Marian heaved a sigh.

But what about me? Tess thought. *Will I be fine?* All the exhilaration of her escape, the excitement of being free, had been washed away by the hot rage coursing through her. The bitter taste of it was in her mouth, the tension of it in her arms. It would be sheer madness, but she longed to turn the boat around and go back to the island, find Mike, and beat seven shades of shit out of him. To think she had felt sorry for him! What the hell was she thinking of?

Something strange emerged from the fog. Tess squinted, trying to make out what it was, and then she saw the light on the top and realised it was a buoy. She looked round, but couldn't see any rocks.

'Lean over the prow and look out for rocks,' Tess said. Marian reluctantly moved to the front and looked over. Tess kept a close eye on each side, so close that she didn't notice what was in front of her.

'Look!' Marian shouted.

Tess looked. Just visible ahead in the thinning mist was the solid wall of a harbour, with a fishing boat moored alongside. The mainland!

Relief filled her and she resisted the urge to stand up and whoop for joy.

'Where is this?' Marian said.

They came alongside the fishing boat, and Tess noticed a man messing with his nets.

'Hello there,' Marian shouted, waving.

The man stared at them. 'Christ, lassie, where the hell did you come fae?'

Scotland, Tess thought, with quiet satisfaction. *I'll be home by tea time.*

TWENTY FOUR

Mike had investigated all the caves, and this was the best of them.

He examined the door Tess had built out of old boat timbers tied together with rope. Of course, he'd have used birch bark, or even better, sinew, but she wouldn't have had that knowledge, and in the circumstances she had done all right. He found her small cache of potatoes, two Puffin eggs, a couple of rabbit pelts, and was gripped by a cold unease that had nothing to do with her escape. He had misjudged her, and if his judgement was out, he was in trouble.

He had struggled to maintain consciousness as the boat headed out into the channel, but the blows to his head had been good ones. When he finally came round, the sun was high and the early mist had burned away. The boat was long gone.

The astonishment that Tess had survived, no, she had *thrived!* on *his* island quickly gave way to an utter fury that burst out of his mouth in a raging shriek, sending the seabirds wheeling away. She had outsmarted him. *No one* had ever outsmarted him. He shouldered his kit bag, ignoring the pain from his cut scalp, the throbbing headache, and begun to follow the woman's tracks. They were easy to find once he got out of the woods. Tess had been a girl with a routine, and had worn a path between her home and the beach. Mike imagined her standing on the shingle each morning, searching the horizon for a boat.

But she had survived. She had *looked after herself,* just as she said she could. He had been wrong.

He left the cave and searched for tracks, finding them climbing up to the ridge. He smiled when he saw the signal beacon. How the hell was she going to get that lit in time? The wood was damp and wouldn't fire, she'd need an accelerant. Way out to sea he could see three small sailboats, clearly heading for the Hebrides. Tess must have seen boats like this every day, but the wood showed no sign of having been lit. Why not? Had she tried and failed? Or had she realised the truth, that no one was watching, that the boats were way too far out to see a small fire?
There was a lot of wood here. She had spent a long time gathering and building it. All for nothing.

Then he tasted bitter bile in his mouth. *She hadn't needed it, had she?*

Everything was falling apart. Tess would reach the mainland, and alert the police. It wouldn't take them long to search the islands, find this one. They would come for him, take him back. They'd send him to jail, which was bad enough, but there would be counsellors. The nightmares loved counsellors. He didn't think he could survive that.

He took a deep breath. *Stay calm. Think straight.*

The island was no more than seven or eight miles offshore, but the currents in the channel were treacherous, and although Tess had worked out how to operate the boat's engine, she had no experience on water. The mist was low this morning, and she could head completely the wrong way, out to sea. Or she could steer the dinghy onto the rocks and rip it apart.

But that's if he was really lucky. If he was less so, she would find the mainland and drag the boat ashore somewhere, find a road and hope for a car. All in all, it would take her the best part of the day. Then she'd have to notify the police, and they'd start a search for him. Depending on where she came ashore, they could head north or south of here. There were many islands, few of them distinctive, and he didn't think they'd set out at night. Tess had seen the gun.

So he figured he probably had until tomorrow evening, if the worst came to the worst.

He would have to work fast.

*

Cal had to smile. Where to hang out if you didn't want to be noticed?

Somewhere with neighbours who were always either out, drunk, stoned, or in bed. The student area. Mike had done the same thing in Leeds as he had down in Leicester. The terraced street was deserted, most of the dingy curtains still drawn. The front doors opened straight on to the pavement, most of them old wood with cracked and blistering paint.

The houses looked tired and uncared for, but the students wouldn't give a damn, that was for sure. Cal made his way to the end of the row, thinking about what he was going to ask, and what he hoped to find.

When Rob managed to track down Dole's old landlady, she remembered Mike. Cal had decided to pay a visit in person. Not that he didn't trust Rob, but...

Well. He didn't trust Rob.

He could do without this. Annie at the home had called him again this morning to tell him his mother had had a bad night, and was asking for him again. Cal had gritted his teeth, wishing he had some way of stretching an extra couple of hours out of the day. He'd promised to come in that afternoon, after he got back. The chances were his mum would have forgotten about her bad dreams by then. Maybe she'd even have forgotten about his visit.

Cal stopped before number 68 and checked his notebook.

68 Chamberlain Street Headingley Leeds. Landlady lives at No. 70. Remembered Dole. Tenant from 2005 to January 2006. Quiet, no trouble.

Well, we'll see, he thought. Number 68 looked exactly like all the others. Cal knocked on the door of number 70. He heard the sound of shuffling feet and then a pause.

'Who is it?'

'DS Fisher, Mrs O'Hanlon. From Leicestershire Constabulary? I spoke to you on the phone earlier.'

The door opened a fraction to reveal a thin faced old woman with a tight white perm peering at him from behind the door chain.

'Can I see your identification.'

She split the word into six long syllables. Cal held his ID up to the woman's face.

'Calum,' she said. 'My grandson's called Calum,'

He smiled. 'May I come in?'

'Yes, yes.'

He tried to stifle his impatience as her frail shaking fingers grasped the chain and slid it off. Then he followed her inside to a dim living room filled with china ornaments and photographs. He was reminded of the shop in the mall, the one where the missing women had worked.

'Can I get you a cup of tea?'

'No thank you, Mrs O'Hanlon. I just-'

'It's no trouble.'

He swallowed, trying to be patient. 'Thanks, but no. I need to ask you a few questions about an old tenant of yours.'

'Yes, Mr Dole. The other gentleman told me. Please sit down.'

Cal nodded, and sat on an armchair that sagged, and kept on sagging as he sat. He felt as if the seat of the chair was headed straight for hell. When at last it stopped, he was left with his knees opposite his chest. Mrs O'Hanlon nodded her approval.

'It's a lovely comfy chair that one. Now what was it you wanted to ask me?'

Cal tried to ignore the embarrassment of his position.

'What can you remember about Mike Dole?'

The old lady looked up at the ceiling. Cal noticed that her chair didn't appear to have anything wrong with it, and felt a tug of irrational anger.

'Well, he kept to himself. He wasn't a student, like the other tenants I had, that's why I remember him. He was a working man, a very neat and tidy person. When he left, I hardly had to clean up before I could let the place again.'

Cal noticed the old woman's liver-spotted hands still shaking. He wondered how long it would take her to clean up a house.

'Do you still let it out?'

'Oh yes, but my daughter in law looks after it now. I can't be doing with it at my age.'

Cal nodded absently. 'Is there anything specifically about him that you remember?'

She shook her head. 'He really was very quiet. The perfect tenant, I would say. No trouble. Always paid his rent on the dot.'

Cal felt his back cramping up. This was turning into a wild goose chase.

'And no wild parties, not like those other students. The way some of them carry on, you'd think-'

'Did he have many visitors?'

Mrs O'Hanlon shook her head again. 'No, I don't think- wait, yes he did. Just once.'

She looked up, frowning.

'Yes?'

'It was a woman. A young woman. I must say, I didn't think she looked his type at all, but she only came the once, so-'

'Can you describe her?'

The old lady stuck out her bottom lip, her face a mask of distaste.

'To tell you the truth, young man, she looked ill. She looked as if she lived on the streets.'

'How do you mean?'

She folded her arms. 'She was *dirty.*'

Cal could almost hear the quotation marks clanging round the word.

'Do you mean you think she was a prostitute?'

'Well, I can't say. But she looked no better than she should be.'

Cal took a deep breath. 'Mrs O'Hanlon, can you describe her in detail? What colour hair she had, and so on?'

The old lady's face creased. 'It was all greasy, I remember that. Blonde hair, hanging round her shoulders. She was thin as a rake, with a long face, and she was all pale and spotty. I remember thinking, she looked to be in her thirties, why was she still as spotty as a teenager?'

'When was this, can you remember?'

'Yes, it wasn't long before he left. I think her visit upset him.'

'Did you catch her name?'

'Oh no. I didn't eavesdrop.'

'Of course not, but did you hear any of their conversation, say in passing?'

'Well, they did have an argument. Not that I was listening in, but these walls are paper thin you know.'

'An argument?' Cal felt his blood beginning to race. 'What about?'

'I don't know. But it was mostly her, ranting and raving at him. There was a lot of foul language. Disgusting, it was.'

Cal took another deep breath. 'Can you remember anything of what she said? Anything at all? It could be important.'

The old lady's eyebrows rose, and her dark eyes glinted as if he had offered her something precious.

'Important, you say? Well.' She put a hand up to her thin lips, staring off into space.

'I heard her laughing, and she said something about taking care of herself, and she didn't give a whatsit if it sent him to hell.'

Cal went to stand up, only to find he was trapped in the damn chair. He had to twist to one side and use both arms to push himself to his feet.

'Thank you, Mrs O'Hanlon, you've been very helpful.'

'Have I? Oh good. What is this about anyway, is Mr Dole is some kind of trouble?'

Cal looked at her. 'We're not sure yet.' Stock answer. Then something else occurred to him.

'You said this was just before he left? How long before?'

'Well, that's what I meant by her upsetting him. He left at the end of that week, and he'd paid his rent to the end of the month, as well. I don't know what their relationship was, but he was really upset. And no wonder, all that swearing and shouting. I don't know how he managed to get rid of her.'

Cal felt a cold thud in his chest.

'What happened after the argument. Did the woman just leave?'

'I never saw her leave. If I'd been him I'd have kicked her out the door, but he was such a nice, quiet chap, I couldn't imagine him hurting anyone.'

But I can, Cal thought. 'You're sure you didn't see her leave?'

'Yes.'

'Mrs O'Hanlon-' he hesitated. It was well over a year ago. Would there be anything left for forensics to find?

'I may have to bring some officers to examine your house next door.'

'Oh, really? Well, I suppose that's all right. The young couple who are staying there are out all day anyway.'

She looked quite happy at the prospect. Cal thought she was probably lonely, and that reminded him of his own mum. Another stab to the heart. His phone began to ring and he smiled.

'Thanks again. I'll be in touch.'

Out in the street, he opened the phone. Rob.

'Cal? You're not going to believe this!'

Cal sighed. Why, just once, couldn't Rob just tell him what it was without this bloody preamble.

'What?'

'Tess Hardy, the missing girl, she's showed up!'

Cal felt something begin to flutter in his chest. 'Is she all right?'

'Yeah, she's fine.'

Cal felt a surge of pure joy, followed quickly by confusion.

'And guess what?'

'Rob, just tell me, for God's sake!'

'All right, all right,' Rob sounded like a kicked puppy.

'She had the other missing girl with her. Marian something. They're in a police station up in Glasgow.'

Glasgow? Where the hell did that fit into the picture? What about Dole?

'What happened?'

'Seems Dole dumped the first girl on some Scottish island, and was going to do the same with the second when the first one jumped him. I guess he thought he'd killed her off, but there she was, alive and well.'

Well good for you, Tess, Cal thought, a smile coming to his lips. Both women alive!

'Where's Dole now?'

'Still on the island. The girl stole his boat and left him there. The police are trying to identify which island it is, seems there are hundreds and they all look the same. But they were slow off the mark. They didn't believe the Hardy woman at first, until the chief got on the phone to them. Now Jarvis wants to know if you can get up there? Since this is your investigation-'

'Yes, I'll go,' he said, the warm feeling dissipating. That meant leaving his mum for another day. But what else could he do?

'Tell me where she is.'

He wrote down the address of the station.

'Rob, I need you to have a trawl back through missing persons reported around January 2006. Check for a missing woman, around thirty. Possible prostitute or drug user.'

'Is this the same thing? You don't think there's another one?'

'I don't know. Just check. And get Roslyn working on it too.'

He didn't add what he was thinking: *she's more likely to find something than you are.*

'You think someone's going to report a missing pro or junkie?'

Cal bit his lip. 'Even whores have mothers, Rob,' he said.

TWENTY FIVE

Just what I need, Tess thought, as Sheila came hurtling towards her, already crying, with her arms wide and her bottom lip wobbling. Tess watched her impassively.

That is, the *new* Tess watched impassively. The old Tess was thinking, why am I not crying? Why am I so unmoved? I should be sobbing and wailing and hugging mother and telling her how terrible it was and how I thought I was going to die, and –

'Oh my Tessa, my darling Tessa. Thank God you're safe.'

Sheila's hug was stifling, but Tess said nothing, patting her mother on the back, noticing one of the officers raising an eyebrow at her. It was obvious he thought she was acting strange, and Tess looked away. Sheila seemed to sense something wrong and pulled back, touching Tess's tangled hair and shaking her head.

'My poor love,' she said. 'What must you have been through? Come on, let's go-'

'No, mum. Not right now.' Sheila had grabbed her daughter by the arm to march her out, but Tess pulled away easily, noticing too late that her action had left Sheila holding her arm and wincing. She pulled herself up short. What was wrong with her? There was no need to be rude.

'Sorry,' she said. 'But there's an officer coming up from Leicester, the one in charge of my case, apparently.'

Sheila's expression turned sour. 'Oh, *him*. He's useless, Tess. It's no thanks to him that you're safe.'

Tess just looked at her. What had happened to her dapper mother, the natty dresser, the consummate professional woman? Her roots needed doing, her face was pasty and blotched rather than the smooth fake tanned look she usually presented. And her clothes! That terrible beige suit did nothing for her awful complexion, and the chocolate brown blouse looked like it came from the Oxfam shop. Belatedly, Tess realised Sheila might genuinely have been worried about her, and offered a blank smile by way of apology.

'I want to speak to him,' she said.

'You can speak to him back home,' Sheila said, fixing her lips in a tight line that broached no argument.

'I'm staying,' Tess said, gazing calmly at her mother. Sheila's mouth opened, but nothing came out.

'Mrs Harrison?'

Sheila managed to pull her eyes away from Tess's long enough to glance at the policeman, who was beckoning her over.

'I'll just be a minute, dear,' Sheila said.

Tess didn't reply, and sat down as her mother walked away. Amazing how calm she felt, almost as if all her emotions had been purged.

The village where they had come ashore had no police station. In fact, it had nothing at all except for a few houses and a post office that doubled as a sell-everything shop. As soon as they left the boat, Marian had collapsed into uncontrollable tears, and nothing Tess could say would make them stop. She left her new friend sitting on the wall outside the post office, and walked inside. It was early, seven thirty, but there was already an elderly woman behind the counter.

'Hello,' Tess said, quite calmly. 'Do you have a telephone, please?'

The postmistress smiled warily at her. 'Och no, dear,' she said, taking in Tess's wild hair and torn, filthy clothes. 'We used to have a box, but it got taken away. Everyone has those mobile things these days.'

'Oh, I see.' Tess took a deep breath. 'But I assume you have a phone, I mean the post office has one?'

The woman began to look uncomfortable. 'Well, it's not for public use, you see-'

'Could you please do me a favour and make a call for me? It won't even cost you anything. I want to call the police.'

'The police? Why, whatever's the matter?'

Tess sighed. 'Long story.'

Of course it didn't take long for the police to check up and find that a missing person had reappeared. *Two* missing persons. They sent a car for them, which took almost two hours to arrive. By that time the story had gone around the tiny village, and Tess had had no less than four mugs of wonderful scalding tea, a huge bacon sandwich, and half a packet of chocolate biscuits. Possibly the finest meal in the world, ever.

The whole village turned out to see them off. The postmistress pressed a tea towel filled with warm shortbread into Tess's hands as they left. 'For the trip,' she told her. Everyone waved, and a few even clapped.

It felt surreal.

And through it all Marian cried and cried, until Tess wanted to strangle her.

Tess looked out at the wild and ruggedly beautiful countryside as they drove south. Her now expert eye could tell where there might be deer hiding, and she recognised the seabirds colonising the rocks of the coast as old friends. She snuggled into the blanket that the policeman had put round her shoulders, anticipating the comfort and relief of going home. Yet deep, deep inside, she was sorry to be leaving this lonely landscape, this place of strange light and barren beauty, a place that needed no people. Of survival at all costs.

She had been ferried south to Ullapool, to Dingwall, and then to Glasgow, by kind, cheerful policemen, all of whom brought flasks of tea. Tess shared her shortbread with them. The officers tried all they could to console Marian, but even after the tears eventually stopped, she just stared out of the window, her eyes red and miserable. They made Glasgow by six o'clock and the police took them into different rooms.

Tess had no idea where Marian was now. Perhaps her family had arrived to take her home.

Two Glaswegian detectives had brought her yet more tea and sandwiches, and asked if she was ready to give them a statement. One of them was an Asian woman who had an incongruous Glasgow accent. The gruff-looking man introduced himself as DS Cramond, smiled at her absently and asked if she was warm enough.

'Fine,' Tess said. The room was tiny and sparse, with only a few chairs, a desk and a phone, but it was centrally heated. It had been some time since she'd felt this warm, although her feet still felt like frozen blocks.

'Can you tell us what happened, as far back as you can remember?' the woman said.

Tess couldn't resist it.

'Well, I remember there was this teddy bear I was very fond of, and my mother-'

'Before you were *abducted*,' the detective said in a caustic voice.

Tess grinned, tucking into the sandwich. Tuna and mayo; maybe a day old, the bread slightly stale, but still wonderful. She told them all she could remember about her arrival on the island, the struggle to find food, try to survive. Cramond leaned forward.

'This island, you didn't recognise it?'

'I've never been to Scotland before this. I have no idea where it was.'

'But you came in near Scourie, so it must be one of the small isles off to the west.'

'I can take you there, if you like?'

Suddenly, it felt like a really good idea, but Cramond shook his head.

'You told the officers from Dingwall that this man, Mike Dole, returned to the island?'

Tess nodded, told them about her escape. The detectives both looked at her with thinly veiled disdain.

'You need to get up there and arrest him,' she said.

'We'll have a search team sent out.' Cramond said. He seemed in no particular hurry, and Tess felt a jolt of unease. She shifted awkwardly on her chair. Her survival stuff in her back pockets was uncomfortable.

'Mike Dole is still on the island,' she said, in case they had somehow missed it the first time. 'I did mention he's got a gun.'

The detectives looked at each other. She could tell they didn't believe her. Hell, perhaps they didn't believe any of it.

'You're certain you saw a weapon?'

'When someone's pointing a gun at you,' she said caustically, 'it tends to stick in the mind.'

They had left her, then, telling her they would notify her family, and now here she was, four hours later, about to have another argument with her mother. Some things, it seemed, never changed.

Her attention was drawn back to the whispered conversation in the corner. Sheila appeared to be crying again, and Tess concentrated to hear what the officer was telling her.

'-been through such an ordeal, it's no wonder she's not herself. She may even be suffering from post-traumatic stress. Feelings of dissociation are quite common-'

Dissociation, Tess thought, *what the hell does that mean? I don't feel stressed out. What do I feel?*

She looked down at the chipped formica of the table and thought about it.

Angry, she thought, *I feel angry. And – sad. How weird is that?*

Finally, Cramond had come back to tell her that DS Fisher from the Leicester force was on his way. He had been investigating her disappearance. Would she wait to speak to him? She readily agreed.

Fisher must know all about Mike. Tess wanted to talk to him, find out all she could about her friend Mr Dole. She still wasn't sure what she would do with the information, but she knew she needed it, all the same.

TWENTY SIX

It was just like old times. Mike settled into the rhythm of the run, the pack secure on his back, and everything right with the world for the moment. He headed away from the shingle bay, there was nothing useful there, and ran round past the offshore rocks teeming with birds. He recognised gannets, guillemots, kittiwakes, their feathers gleaming white in the sun, a predatory skua gliding above.

He rounded the clifftop, heading down towards the softer southern side. He knew that most of the debris brought in by Atlantic swells would be caught by the currents close to shore and carried south. He was hoping for some wood, plastic bottles, maybe even an old pallet to help him fashion a makeshift raft. If he was careful he should be able to make it the mile or so to the next island. At low tide, the current would be easier to navigate. The next island was tiny and barren. The police wouldn't even leave their boats to search it, but Mike knew of a hidden depression to the north, not visible from the sea, where he could hide out until they had moved on. From there, the next island was only another half-mile, and this one had a deep bay rising to a sandy shore, a favourite summer haunt of couples. It would be a no-brainer to steal a boat and return to the mainland.

He came over a rise and spotted a group of rocks above. The sight of them jolted some long lost memory and filled him with a sudden dread.

He came to a halt, feeling the sweat trickling down his face, the immediate pounding of his heart.

Up ahead among the fallen rocks were the remains of an old house, only part of a wall remaining. Something in the grass caught his eye, and he tried hard to look away. It was a piece of wire. Nothing terribly unusual, except that it was serrated like a saw, with a loop at each end.

Mike knew exactly what it was.

This was the place of nightmares. He had to turn back. He tore his eyes away. Nothing to see but rocks and skinny grass, pink sea thrift flowers, bright sunny blotches of gorse. And there, just to the right, the blank white of bone.

Mike couldn't help himself. He crouched by the body, looking at the scrap of fabric still clinging to the bones. It had been a pink blouse with tiny cream flowers, but now it was colourless, a flag without its colours, flapping hopelessly in the wind. Sadness landed on him like a giant bird whose wings blotted out the sun.

'I never meant for you to die,' he said, knowing that at the same time it was both the truth and a lie. The memories were at the edge of his sight, like a tiny movement that couldn't be ignored, for all he tried. He stood up, meaning to run away, but his legs wouldn't move. He closed his eyes, imagining the bones clasping his ankles, dragging him down.

'No!' he cried, staggering backwards, stumbling in the soft sand and landing on his back in the dunes.

And then Sandy was leaning over him, her sunken cheeks so wasted he could see the imprint of her teeth below them.

'Did you think you'd get away with it?' she said.

'Leave me!'

'What, like you did? Leave me here to die?'

'I didn't want you to die,' he sobbed. 'I never wanted to hurt you!'

He squeezed his eyes tight shut, as waves of pain and hopelessness made his heart race and his breath come in tiny gasps. Somewhere in the back of his mind he remembered the major's words: *stay calm. Breathe deep. It will pass.*

But not this time. This time he was falling into the abyss. His heart felt as if it was about to explode, and Sandy was giggling, laughing, her lank hair blotting out the light as she leaned over him.

'Told you, didn't I? I didn't need no little boy looking after me. I've done all right on my own.'

'No you haven't Sandy, look at you. What are those marks on your arms, drug tracks?'

The hard look in her shadowed eyes. 'What's that to you? I'm a big girl now. In fact, I've always been a big girl. You never liked that, did you?'

'You were a child!'

'And so were you! You know the difference between us, Mikey? I saw the big picture, and you never did.'

The words, always there, always waiting. *I wanted to look after you. I needed to look after you!*

He bit them back. She whirled away from him. They were in his house, in Headingley. She looked round at the empty walls of his empty home.

'You've got nothing, have you? Nothing. You're a fool. Mother used us, but I used her right back. You? You just ran away.'

Yes, I did. Tears sneaked out of his tightly shut eyes. 'I left you.'

'Damn straight you did. Left me to the life. Being sold for money, for drugs, hell, sometimes just for booze. But I got my own back, something you never did, and never will. How does it feel, Mikey, knowing your own mother sold you to strangers, and you never got your own back?'

A spike of pain, like a spear driven through his spine. He leaned back and screamed as fragments of long hidden memories snapped into his head, like reflections in a splintered mirror, each one more exquisitely horrible than the last. He felt his whole body begin to shake, and knew he was going to die.

'That's it, give up,' Sandy said. Abruptly she sat down on his faded armchair.

'Christ, Mikey, all I wanted was some money. Couldn't you have helped me out instead of this?'

She held her arm out and pulled a strand of machair from the dune. She began to shred it in her fingers.

'I didn't have any money,' he gasped. 'And you would have told everyone-'

She grinned. 'You must have money. You're a war veteran. A hero. And yes, you're right. I'd have told all your secrets, all the things you won't even tell yourself. Look at you, killing yourself over stuff that happened years ago. Stuff that doesn't matter any more. Life goes on, Mikey. Even for you.'

She stood up and came towards him. He tried to shuffle backwards, but barely moved. Lightning was flashing behind his eyes, a storm from which he couldn't hide.

'You should just have killed me when you had the chance.'

She leaned over him again and he could smell her breath, foul from cigarettes and booze. 'No!' he yelled, striking out hard with both fists, one after the other. Sandy fell back and tripped over the edge of the sofa. She landed on her back and lay still and Mike stared at her unconscious form.

What do I do now? I can't let her leave. Why did this have to happen! I loved her, I wanted to – Oh God, I wish the lads were here, they'd help me. Billy was always smart, he'd know what to do, and Donno would crack some terrible joke and Lewis would make some of his rubbish brew and –

Breathe deeply, the major had said. *Control your heart. Think of the calm place, the place you have always been happy...*

A sudden quiet descended, and Mike could feel a chill wind cooling his fevered skin. High above, a seabird let out a lonely cry. He knew what to do. He lifted the limp body and carried it out of the room and across the shingle and into the spindly wood. She sighed as he put her down, and he turned away from her noxious breath, revolted by the sweaty, druggy odour of her skin, and all at once he remembered how she used to smell. Like coconut.

Yes, coconut, he thought, and the memory threw a tiny lifebuoy into the sea of horror.

His mind grabbed at it. Her hair, it must have been the shampoo she used. He concentrated on the fresh sweet smell, until another memory appeared. Sandy, in her dressing gown, the teddy bear hanging out of the pocket, drying her hair before the electric fire. Why are you doing that, Sandy, why don't you use the hairdryer? Because it makes it go frizzy, stupid, like yours!

And she laughed. But this was a giggly, teasing, little girl laugh, and Mike laughed too. Did he have frizzy hair? He couldn't remember. Tears ran unchecked down his cheeks.

'You'll be happy here,' he said, taking the tin out of his pocket and leaving it beside her on the moss. 'I was happy here.'
He heard a sound, a sigh that was relief and regret, all at once. He dared to open his eyes.

The sand was blazing white in the sunlight, the sky beyond as blue as cornflowers. He sat up, breathing hard through his nose, concentrating on the beating of his heart until after long, long minutes it began to slow.

He had to get away from here, had to move. He blinked hard, trying to clear his thoughts.

The black terror still cast a shadow over this bright clear day, and he knew that the island was lost to him now. He had to get away, and quick. His cheek twitched as he dragged himself to his feet and into a stumbling run, lumbering awkwardly over the dunes and down to the beach. It stretched for almost a mile, he knew, having raced along it with the lads, and by himself. He pushed himself into a hard but steady pace, forcing reluctant eyes to dredge the shoreline for what he needed. The remains of the nightmare still had hold of him, and it was hard to concentrate. He longed to lie down somewhere in the dark.

But as he ran along the firm white sand, with the warm wind in his face and the sharp tang of the sea in his nostrils, a touch of peace began to steal into his heart. He scanned the tideline; plenty of plastic bottles, bits of rope, but not much in the way of anything else. A flash of sunlight out to sea caught his eye.

Not far out, maybe half a mile or so. A small yacht, her white sail catching the rays as she tacked into the wind. That meant she'd have to keep turning his way. What a chance! Mike picked up his pace and headed across the sand and up towards the grassy slopes, his heart pounding now with the work, as he tried to keep it steady. He'd need something in the tank to get him up to the ridge. He didn't look out to sea, it was a waste of energy, instead he did as he had been taught, and focussed on the job in hand.

He scrambled up the grassy bank using his hands to help him, and was unslinging his bag before he reached the pile of branches. Now at last he looked out to sea, breathing in through his mouth and out through his nose, staying calm and steady. The little ship was there, her hull gleaming in the sun. He reached into the bag and his fingers closed round the small shape. It fitted his hand neatly, and a grim smile came to his face as he pulled it out, fastening the bag and hauling it over his shoulder.

He waited until the little ship began its eastward tack towards him, and then he pulled out the pin and threw the grenade into the middle of the pyre. He hurtled down the ridge, huddling behind an erratic boulder as the explosion shook the ground beneath his feet. He crouched low as bits of wood and stone landed around him, until everything grew quiet again, not just still, but silent, as if the very earth was shocked at what he had done. Then he ran back up to the ridge and looked out to sea.

The boat seemed to have halted in the water. He reached for his binoculars and could see the people on board looking straight at him: two middle-aged men and a woman. No problem. Just to put the icing on the cake he pulled out a flare and set it off. As it shot into the sky, he watched the boat's crew shield their eyes to watch it burst. Then one of the men pointed to the rudder, and the other pulled it hard to the left.

Mike grinned, his confidence restored. He re-tied his kit bag and began to make his way down to the shore to wait for his rescuers to arrive.

TWENTY SEVEN

The Glasgow station had the usual complement of smokers hanging around outside in the rain, but Cal walked past them without comment.

At the reception desk, he flashed his ID and the pretty duty PC smiled at him and asked him to wait 'just a wee minute'. Cal sat down in the waiting room, expecting the usual cross border nonsense; keeping him waiting, withholding information, making him uncomfortable, and so on. He tried to ignore his impatience. He felt so close to getting a grip on Mike Dole, although what he was going to do with the knowledge, he had no idea. It seemed now that the man was merely crazy, not a murderer, and so probably out of his jurisdiction.

All the same, Cal wanted to know the whole story with this one. He was about to open his briefcase to look at the file when an Asian woman approached him, dressed smart casual in black trousers and a cream top under a grey wool jacket. Nice clothes. Her jet hair was cut short at the sides and longer on top, to compensate for her rather square jaw. She had a kind smile.

'Are you DS Fisher?' she asked, in broad Glasgow. Cal tried to hide his surprise. She smiled.

'Aye, I know, no one expects an Indian wi' a Glesga accent. I'm DC Chandra. Will you come wi' me, please?'

Cal followed the woman, embarrassed by his lapse, although she didn't seem fazed.

'We've got Miss Hardy in room 6,' she said. 'her mither wanted her to go home wi' her, but she wanted to wait an' see you first.'

'She did?' Cal was surprised again. 'Well, I'm pleased about that.'

'Aye, but my boss wants tae see you first, okay?'

The boss turned out to be DS Cramond, the archetypal dour Scot. He looked to be in his late forties, with thick curly brown hair cut in a side parting, a chunk hanging down over one scraggy eyebrow. His brown eyes looked sleepy, but Cal wasn't fooled.

'So you've been investigating this one,' he said. 'What have you got?'

Cal was expecting this. No one ever gave anything away for free. He gave Cramond the short version of the case, Tess's disappearance, her mother's insistence that Dole was to blame, his investigation into Mike's life, then Marian's disappearance. He left out a lot of stuff, including much about Mike's past. In the end Cramond nodded.

'So what, you think this guy Dole is firmly in the chair?'

Cal nodded. 'Too many coincidences.'

'Aye well, your SIO thinks the same.'

'What's Tess Hardy saying?'

'You can talk to her yourself, but between you and me, it all sounds a wee bitty far-fetched.'

Cal raised an eyebrow, and Cramond smiled. The smile changed his appearance totally, turning him from a grumpy bear into a big puppy.

'We'll have a wee chat afterwards, okay?'

'Sure,' Cal said, following the man along a narrow corridor painted a washed-out green. He stopped in front of room 6, a blank grey door with a peephole.

'She's all yours,' he said.

Cal opened the door and walked straight in. The young woman stood up and took a step forward.

'You're detective Fisher?'

He nodded.

'Good,' she said, holding out her hand to shake. 'Maybe you'll believe me.'

Tess Hardy was nothing like Cal had expected. Sheila Harrison had insisted that her daughter was a quiet, scared little mouse, with neither confidence nor independence, and from the photo she had given him, it looked as though Sheila was right. But this woman was none of those things.

She was dressed in jeans that could only really be described as rags. The hems were shredded, the knees torn out along with most of one calf.

A thin pale blue cardigan with only one sleeve covered a frayed white blouse, and her training shoes were no more than strips of rubber and plastic tied together with orange nylon rope. Everything was dirty, unsurprisingly, and yet she didn't look like a victim. In fact she couldn't look *less* like a victim. Tess oozed self reliance. She was lean and strong, and her grey eyes seemed like the colour itself; shrouded and secret, giving nothing away. Cal pulled out a chair to sit down, aware that he was staring and trying to hide the fact that he was wildly attracted to her.

'I'm sure I will,' he said, trying to sound brisk. 'I'm also sure you've told the story already, but would you oblige me?'

He smiled as warmly as he knew how, and she smiled back like a wary animal. Then she began to tell him about Mike, the returned CDs, waking up on the island. Discovering it *was* an island, waiting for Mike to come back for her, trying to survive. Cal made notes as she talked, and he found himself wondering how he would have coped given those circumstances. He had a sneaking suspicion that it wouldn't have been as well as Tess had.

'Do you believe me so far?' she asked.

Cal frowned. 'Of course,' he said. 'Why wouldn't I?'

She shrugged. 'I think the Scottish police think I went for some sort of jaunt and got lost.'

Cal looked at her. 'What about Mike?'

She grinned. 'They probably think I made him up. When I mentioned his gun, they-'

'Gun? He's got a gun?'

Cal wondered what he was saying. Why was this a surprise?

'Tell me the rest, Tess.'

He leaned forward, and Tess raised an eyebrow. She had a fresh scar running along the left of her forehead and down the edge of her brow. Cal found himself staring and hurriedly looked away.

'I had a routine every day, down through the woods to the beach, search the horizon. This day, I wasn't even near the beach yet when I heard the motor. I hid in the broom and saw a boat coming in with Mike driving it. As he pulled closer I saw he had someone in the boat with him. They were unconscious or asleep, and it didn't take a genius to work out what he was doing. He came out and noticed something on the dock, and then he looked around and started searching. I figured the thing he had found was one of my fish hooks, and he was looking for my body.'

Cal nodded for her to continue.

'I hid in the woods. I knew he'd find my tracks there. I hid up in a tree with a big rock in my hand and waited for a chance. He was like a dog, sniffing the air, looking around. He knew something was wrong. As he walked up out of the wood, I dropped out of the tree and hit him. He had that big kit bag on his back which helped knock him over. I hit him over and over, until at last he stopped moving, and then I ran for the boat.

Took me a while to work out how to start the motor, then I had to get the damn thing turned around, by which time he was lurching up the beach towards me. I finally got the boat moving away, and he pulled out a gun. I ducked, but he didn't shoot me.'

Cal's mouth was open. 'Why not? Was he badly hurt?'

She shook her head. 'No. Yes. Oh, I don't know. But it was – he didn't fire it. It seemed as though he didn't want to shoot me, rather than he couldn't. Doesn't make any sense, I know.'

Cal stood up and began to pace the room.

'You do believe me,' Tess said. 'In fact, you're not surprised.'

Cal looked at her. 'I've been doing a bit of research on our Mr Dole, so you could say I know a bit about him by now.'

'He didn't want to kill me,' Tess said, folding her arms.

Cal nodded. 'Abandoning you on a remote island was tantamount to the same thing.'

Tess reached into her pocket and pulled out a small tobacco tin and a scrap of paper which she handed to him. Cal unfolded the paper. The note was written in a neat careful hand:

You said you could look after yourself.
Go ahead and try

He sat down heavily. He put the tin on the table and carefully opened it. He noticed wire, hooks, a few broken matches, a scalpel blade.

'He left that for me. And this.'

She reached in her remaining pocket and pulled out a knife. It was about eight inches long with a worn wooden handle. The blade's business side was slightly curved, the other side scalloped at the top and deeply serrated at the base. Tess laid it gently on the table.

Cal looked at her, wondering about Mike's lost buddies, the Albanian woman and her children. All the people Mike had not been able to take care of. What had twisted in his mind to stop him trying to look after people, and instead put them where they had to fight to look after themselves?

'Does the note make sense to you?'

She nodded. 'I told Mike I didn't want to go out with him any more. He said he only wanted to look after me, and I told him I could look after myself. It seemed to shock him, hurt him in some way. Next thing he's taken me to the island and left that in my pocket.'

Call looked at the note again. It seemed petulant to him, the sort of thing an angry child would write. Maybe that was all Mike was, a disappointed child. One with a gun.

He glanced back up at Tess. Her wary eyes were calmly fixed on his, and again he felt a jolt of desire deep in the pit of his stomach. This was one brave, smart woman, and beautiful too. He wondered if-?

Cal shook his head. Stay on the damn case!

'You did well to survive,' he said.

'Someone else wasn't so lucky.'

Cal sighed. He had been dreading this.

'You found a body?'

Tess nodded. 'Nothing but bones. Been there a long time.'

Since January 2006, he thought. Who was she? He needed to ring Rob, find out what Roslyn had uncovered-

'So are you going to send someone after him?'

'Am I – what?'

Tess sighed. 'Mike is still on the island, with his gun, and whatever it is he keeps in that big bag of his. Shouldn't someone go and arrest him or something?'

'My boss has spoken to the local police,' he said. 'They're on it. But there are a lot of islands up there. You said you had no idea which one it is.'

Cal thought about the major. Peters had mentioned the soldiers' early training was on a Scottish island. Maybe he could help them. He glanced at his watch. It had gone ten o'clock, but it was worth a try. He opened his briefcase and pulled out the file, searching for the phone number of the garrison. The phone's battery died mid-dial. Damn. Fortunately there was a phone on the desk and he picked it up and dialled again.

The man on the other end said that Peters was 'unavailable at this time'. Cal hid a frustrated sigh.

'Will you tell him to call DS Fisher of-'

'Oh, wait a minute, sir. He said if you called to give you this number.'

Cal raised an eyebrow. So Peters was true to his word. He grabbed his notebook and pen and jotted the mobile number down. As he dialled he looked round and saw that Tess had pulled a photograph out of the file. It was the picture Peters had given him. Tess looked up at him and gave him a grim smile.

'Peters.'

'Major, it's Fisher here.'

'Detective? Any news?'

Cal waited until he had his questions straight.

'When we spoke before, you told me Dole was sent to a Scottish island for training.'

'Yes, that's right, but not just one island, there were many. Some were near Mull, I recall, others up by Oban.'

Cal felt his shoulders slump.

'Can you remember what they were called?'

'Not offhand, but I can let you know. Why?'

'It seems Mr Dole has been taking his victims there and leaving them to die.'

He caught sight of Tess's raised eyebrow, but she kept quiet.

A heavy intake of breath on the other end of the phone.

'How do you know this? Is Dole in custody?'

'One of his victims made it back.'

'Oh, thank God for that. But -'

'Can you get me the information quickly?'

'Yes, I'll get right on it tonight.'

He closed the phone and saw her looking at him.

'Tell me about Mike,' Tess said, putting the photo back on the desk.

Cal hesitated. 'What about him?'

'Tell me what you've discovered about him. I need to know.'

'Why?'

She laughed. 'How long do you think he's going to stay trapped on the island? I heard what you said, that he's been there before, probably lots of times. He'll know a way off. And when he gets off, what's he going to do?'

Cal felt his stomach lurch. 'You think he's going to come after you?'

She shrugged, looking at him carefully. 'Do you?'

Cal looked back at the knife on the table. Up till now Mike's pattern had been abandonment, not direct action. But what about his army career? He needed to speak to the major again. And the other girl, Marian. And he needed to charge up the damn phone. What if Rob had discovered something? He looked at Tess again.

'Can you stay around here for a while? I think I'm going to need to talk to you again, and anyway, you'll be safe here.'

Tess smiled. It was her turn to glance at the knife, and Cal felt a rush of colour to his cheeks. Tess had done pretty well at looking after herself, after all.

TWENTY EIGHT

When at last her parents arrived, all the pent-up fear and anxiety rushed out of Marian in a storm of tears.

'Oh daddy!' She hugged her father, leaning into the strong, lean reassurance of him, burying her face in his chest.

'It's all right now,' he said softly. 'We're here. You're safe.'

She screwed her eyes shut. Never again would she let herself be attracted by men who could harm her. That edge of danger had always been irresistible, but now, no way. She would stick to accountants and boring old bankers, leave the army lads alone.

'Are you hurt?' her mother asked, anxious tones in her voice. Marian reached out and the three of them held each other. Then her father took her by the shoulders and pushed her gently so he could look at her face.

'Now, love, you tell us what happened, will you?'

There was a discreet knock on the door. It opened to reveal Detective Fisher, an apologetic smile on his face. Marian remembered him from that day at the mall. She remembered she had been attracted by his badge, his attitude. She shuddered.

'Sorry to intrude, I just wanted to ask Marian a few questions. I can come back later.'

'No, come in, detective,' Warren said. He took Marian by the arm and sat her on one of the hard chairs, sitting next to her, keeping hold of her hand. Brenda Warren sat on the other side of her daughter. Marian noticed the detective looking at them carefully and wondered what he was thinking. He got out a notepad and pen and put them on the table next to the phone.

'Marian,' he said, smiling gently at her. 'Can you tell me what Mike Dole was like all the time you were seeing him?'

Marian opened her mouth, surprised. She had gone over the abduction with one of the other officers, and had expected to have to do it all again, not answer questions about the freak who had kidnapped her.

'I don't want to talk about him,' she said.

'Marian, love, the detective needs to know.'

'I don't care, mum. I – he frightened me!'

'I know,' Fisher said. 'But if you can tell me, hopefully we can stop him doing this again.'

'Tell the detective, Marian,' her father said. She looked up and saw he had that face on, the one where she knew she wouldn't win. She sighed and looked down at her hands, still dirty from the horrible boat.

'He was – quiet,' she said, thinking about how little Mike spoke. 'Never said much, never smiled much. He was sort of aloof.'

'Did he ever talk about his army days?'

She hesitated, glanced at her father again.

'Marian didn't know he was in the army, did you?'

He looked at her.

'He didn't tell me, I-' she paused. Even now she was surprised and a little hurt. Why hadn't he told her? Her father sighed.

'We came home early from a trip away and Mike was just leaving. I clocked him for an ex-squaddie right away. He couldn't wait to get out of the house.'

Fisher turned his attention to Warren. 'You told me already you thought he was troubled.'

Her father's lips curved in a tight smile. 'He didn't look good. If I had to guess, I'd say he's seen terrible things in his service, things that still keep him awake at nights. I told Marian not to see him any more.'

Fisher turned his gaze on her. Marian felt the tears starting again. Why couldn't they leave her alone? It wasn't her fault he turned out to be a maniac. She felt the detective's eyes boring into her. What did he want from her?

'Marian, can you remember when you met Mike at first? Can you describe that to me?'

She looked at her father again. Why was he asking her this?

'Answer the man, Marian.'

'I don't know!' she hunched her shoulders, rubbed her face with her hands.

'He came into the shop. We chatted about Tess, and he offered to show me the canteen.'

'I expect you had your little girl face on,' her mother said, spitefully.

Marian noticed the detective's head snap round to look at her.

'Little girl?'

'Yes, my daughter knows how to press all the right buttons where men are concerned.'

'Mother!' Marian stared at her. How could she say that, in front of the policeman!

'I bet he thought you were a soft, vulnerable woman,' the detective said softly. 'Someone he needed to look after.'

'Look after? He nearly killed me!' The tears slipped out and trickled down her cheek. Real tears, hot and uncomfortable.

'What happened when you went to see him at the mall, when he abducted you.'

She sniffed, and her mother dropped a tissue in her lap. It fell like a coin in a beggar's cup. Marian felt a fresh rush of tears, but her father put his arm round her shoulders and squeezed gently.

'I – well.' She glanced up at her father, but he was smiling at her.

'Dad gave me the number of someone who could help him with his PSD thingy. I was going to give it to him, but he went mad, grabbed me, put me in the car.'

It was the story she had told the other officers, but she could see the detective didn't buy it.

'What did you say to him, Marian?'

She stifled a sob.

'Tell him the truth, Marian,' her father said. 'I know you wanted to keep seeing him.'

It's all right. Just tell him.'

She looked down at her hands.

'I said I was going down to the gite for the weekend, and why didn't he come too.'

There, it was out. She felt a flush of relief at the confession, but the detective was still staring at her.

'What else?'

'I – I said I knew he had problems, and that he could talk to me about them. But he just ignored me and tried to walk away.'

Ignored her. She wasn't going to stand for that, was she? She looked up at her mother, whose face showed her thoughts quite clearly. Marian felt her own face flushing.

'What did you say then, Marian?'

'Nothing! I didn't provoke him, if that's what you think. Just the opposite.'

'I don't think you were trying to provoke him,' Fisher said, his eyes still on her.

'I was sorry for him,' she said. The truth felt strange in her mouth. 'I liked him. I told him I knew about the bad things he had seen. I wanted to look after him, take care of him. But when I told him that, he went mad.

His eyes went all cold and hard and he grabbed me by the arm. It hurt, and I was crying, but it was as if I wasn't there.'

The detective smiled. He had a nice smile, it lit up his face. It looked as though what she had told him had pleased him.

'Thank you, Marian. You'll be going home now?'

Her father nodded. 'If you don't need us here?'

He shook his head. 'Maybe later, back south. But for now, it's late. Go home.'

Her father shook the detective's hand. 'Thank you.'

Why was he thanking him? Fisher had done nothing. It was Tess that had saved them. Marian would have to look her up when they got back home, to thank her. She knew she had not been a lot of help on the journey back.

Why had he been asking those questions? It was strange. Almost as if Mike was the important one, the one in trouble, and not her.

*

Mike had no idea how to sail a yacht, but it didn't matter anyway. The boat had a decent motor. In fact it had just about everything he could want. GPS, complex sonar equipment, not to mention a well stocked galley and a bar. The fridge was fully of nibbly, picnic style food, and he ate some and tipped the rest into a carrier which he stored in his kit bag. Then he sailed the boat the seven miles in to the coast near the village of Clashnessie, dropped the anchor and climbed into the rubber inflatable, which had its very own little outboard.

What luck that he had waylaid a bunch of rich people. He looked back. The stolen yacht bobbed gently among the others moored there. It would not draw attention for a while. He steered for the familiar coast, the shallow waters beneath the cliffs that he knew so well.

There was plenty of room in the cave for the small boat, and he felt his muscles tense as he thought of Tess sailing off in his own one.

Tess. He would have to think about her, but not yet.

He wrapped the new outboard, stored it carefully, then lugged his kitbag up the hill and along to the lochan where he had left his car.

And dropped to the ground like a stone.

There were three men standing round the car, staring at it, talking. Two of them had collie dogs sitting at their masters' feet. Mike took deep breaths, staying calm. They were just looking. One of them tried the driver's door and found it locked, then all three shielded their eyes and looked out to sea. He let his breath out slowly. They were farmers, or shepherds. They thought some tourist had left his car here and gone for a walk or a sail, or something. One of the dogs rolled on to his back, feet in the air, pushing his shoulders into the hard ground.

Mike crawled backwards and then slid back down the hill. He tracked round until he could watch the men from behind a stand of gorse, then moved his shoulders, getting the bag comfortable on his back, and settled down for the wait.

TWENTY NINE

The local police offered to put Tess up in a hotel, but she decided to stay where she was. When Fisher left, DC Chandra came in carrying a bundle which she laid on the table. She gave Tess an uneasy smile.

'Now, I'm a good bit fatter than you, so ye'll likely need a belt, but they'll do for the now.'

She unfolded a pair of faded jeans, a black T shirt and a dark grey sweatshirt with *Heriot Watt* written across it. Tess felt a lump in her throat.

'I can't take your clothes!'

'Why no'?'

'No, I'm not saying there's anything wrong with them, there's not! But they're your clothes! You don't even know me.'

Chandra shrugged. 'Don't worry about it. They're old.'

Tess looked at her. She'd never had any real friends, and it had never bothered her. Suddenly she began to understand what she had been missing. Chandra looked embarrassed.

'Look, if you feel that bad about it, you can wash them and send them back, a'right?'

Tess smiled, already stripping off her ruined cardigan.

'Here, wait a minute, people can look in!' She stood in front of the peephole.

'And d'ye no' want to take a shower first?'

'A shower? Oh yes, yes please!'

Chandra grinned. 'I'll take you along.'

Tess groaned as the hot water engulfed her. The pleasure was almost orgasmic. Her brain-tissue feet were wonderfully warm, the permanent itch banished for the moment. She could have stayed there all night, but knew the detective was waiting for her, so she reluctantly turned off the spray and walked out, wrapping a towel around her.

The women's locker room was empty, and Chandra had laid out the clothes on one of the benches, along with a bag of toiletries, her own, presumably. Again, Tess felt that warm sense of delight at another person's generosity. She pulled on the clothes. The T shirt fit well, but the jeans were snug round the hips and baggy round the waist. She sat on the bench and pulled her right leg over her left knee, examining the mess of her foot. There was a tentative knock, and when she looked up, the detective was peering round the door.

'Everything all right?'

'Oh, thank you, yes.'

'I've been in the lost property. We're a bit low on the shoe front, but I found these – Jesus Christ!'

'What?'

'Your feet? What the hell happened?'

Tess looked back at the pale split and wrinkled skin. She shrugged.

'They've been wet for about three months. This is obviously what happens.'

'Is it painful?'

'Itchy.'

'Aye, I had athletes foot once, it was a nightmare, but-'

Tess shrugged. 'I'll get them seen to when I go home. For now-' she took the offered socks and tatty trainers. 'These will do just fine.'

She pulled the first sock on carefully, sensing the woman wincing at her side.

'It must have been terrible. What did ye find to eat?'

Tess looked up and sighed. 'Fish, mostly. Mussels, a few eggs.'
She could feel the woman's eyes on her. 'I bet you could use a good feed.'

Tess nodded, grinning. 'Char Siu pork and egg fried rice. I've been fantasising about it ever since I got to the mainland. It's my favourite.'
She put both feet on the ground, sighing at the sensation of warm cozy feet.

Chandra chuckled. 'I think we can bring that particular fantasy to life. C'mon, Fisher wants to see you again. Tell you the truth, I think he's got the hots for you.'

Tess laughed. 'I don't think so.'

But as she walked into the same little room and saw Fisher standing there, she wasn't so sure. He looked her over quickly, then drew his eyes away and smiled awkwardly.

'That's better,' he said, trying for brisk. 'Is there anything else you need?'

She shook her head. Fisher had an energy about him, he looked like a man with a mission. He was not particularly good looking, but he had dark eyes that seemed at once gentle and compelling.

'Can I ask you a few more questions?'

'Sure.'

He sat down, his notebook open in front of him. She spotted a little drawing in the corner, a beach with big waves rolling in. He was about to speak when the phone on the desk rang.

She saw his eyebrows make a rush for his hairline.

'He's come here? Really?' he said, then looked at her hard. 'Just a minute.'

He cupped the phone in his hand. 'I'm sorry, something's come up. I'm going to need to see someone.'

Who is he seeing? She thought. *Not Mike!*

Of course not. He was stuck on the island. She breathed a sigh and thought back to her previous conversation with Fisher, the talk about the island, his call to someone called Major Peters. *He's come here? Really?*

She smiled. 'Bring him in. We can both talk to him.'

Fisher stared at her, saying nothing.

'Listen, if this is your major, I can confirm what he tells you. About the island?'

One look at his face told her she was right. She felt her heart lift.

'Look, you want to find him, don't you? Let me help. Please.'

Fisher dropped his eyes. He uncupped the phone.

'Could you let him through?'

Tess was elated. At last she hoped she was going to get some answers.

*

Cal watched Peters as he came into the room, curious as to why the major had come all the way here so fast. To begin with he had wondered how the hell he knew where Cal was, but no doubt Peters' mobile phone would have recorded the incoming number with a Glasgow code, and he could have easily confirmed where he was with his own force.

Peters looked at Tess, raised an eyebrow, then turned to him, hand outstretched.

'Detective, I thought I'd come here to see if I could help.'

'A phone call would have been fine.'

He smiled.

'Better to chat face to face. And we had a colonel visiting from Lossiemouth. I hitched a lift back with him.'

Cal nodded. Peters might be telling the truth, but he doubted it, and to get here this fast would have taken a helicopter. Seemed that the major was more than a little concerned about his former soldier.

Cal motioned him to sit.

'This is Tess Hardy. The woman Dole abducted.'

Tess's smile was wary. 'Hello, Tess,' he said. 'I'm sorry you've been through an ordeal'

She raised an eyebrow. 'It wasn't your fault.'

She let her voice rise a little at the end, as if to add: was it? Cal could have kissed her. She wanted answers too. And Chandra had given her some fresh clothes to put on, a grey cut off sweatshirt that matched her fathomless eyes and showed off lean, athletic arms. He took a deep breath and shook his head.

'I have a list of the islands we went to, still go to, some of them.'
He handed a list to Cal, who read down it. The names were mostly unpronounceable.

'I've been on most,' he said. 'So if you could describe the island, I should be able to identify it.'

Tess looked at him. 'It's at least four miles long, north to south. Big sandy beach to the south, shingle to the east where there is a jetty. There's a tall hill with an exposed ridge, and towards the centre there's a mainly coniferous wood.'

Cal stared at her. He had been reluctant to let her in on this meeting, but now he knew he had made the right decision.

'That sounds like Toilichte,' he said. 'Very few islands that big and unpopulated. And that would fit,' he added.

Cal flicked through the list for something that resembled the word Peters had said. He was out of luck. 'Why?'

Peters hesitated. His eyes were dark in his big baby face, a combination that made him look quite scary. He glanced over at Tess, and Cal knew what he was thinking. He didn't want to talk in front of the girl. Normally, he wouldn't have wanted that either, but this time it was different.

'Go on, major.'

Peters licked his lips.

'I've told you Mike was terribly troubled by events in his past. He struggled to come to terms with them, and believe me, it was a hard task. He loved the survival training, he was always the first to volunteer.'

Cal waited, noticing Tess was leaning on the table, listening avidly.

'And?' he prompted.

Peters sighed. 'He once confided to me that when he had leave he often went up there by himself. Being all alone on a remote island was his idea of paradise.'

Cal checked the list again, to no avail. 'You mean this specific island?'

Peters nodded. 'It was his favourite.'

'Point it out to me.'

Peters pointed to a name that looked nothing like its pronunciation. Then he sat back and looked up.

'I wish you'd told us this earlier, sir.'

'How could I have known what he would do?'

'You had no idea? None?'

Peters shook his head. 'Mike cares for people. He wants, *needs* to look after them, to do the right thing. Why would he do this?'

'That's what we're trying to find out.'

'He needs to look after people?' Tess said. Peters gave a wary nod.

'So when I said I could take care of myself, that was like a slap in the face.'

Cal looked at her. 'Yes. You hurt him, albeit unknowingly, and he wanted to hurt you back.'

'No, no!' Peters said, bunching his fist on the table. 'It's not that simple.'

'Then why did he take me to this Tolly place and leave me there?'

Peters looked at her. He sighed.

'I don't know.'

'He wanted me to try to survive. He left me a knife and a tin full of things.'

Peters' eyebrows lifted, as if he had seen a glimmer of hope. 'A survival kit?'

He looked down at his closed fist and slowly opened it. Then he swallowed.

'Dole can't react the same way as the rest of us. If something reopens old wounds, he can't shrug them off. He needs to be in control. When he was discharged, I spent some time with him teaching him yoga techniques. Relaxation and meditation, things to help quell his nightmares. If something happened to set off his demons, he would not be able to control his environment. He might panic and do something rash.'

Cal nodded. 'Well, I can see that, but why not something instant? Why not lash out?'

Peters shook his head. 'That's not the way he's put together. He wouldn't deliberately hurt a woman. It's not in his wiring.'

So he turned his life ethic on its head, Cal thought. The need to help, to protect. He made them do it themselves.

'He hurt one,' Tess said. 'There's a woman on the island who never made it off.'

Peters stared at her. 'You mean – she's dead?'

She nodded.

'Yes, a woman who didn't manage to survive. So you see, major, this is no longer just a kidnapping.'

'But if he left you a survival kit-'

'Yes, he left her one too. But she still died.'

Cal leaned forward.

'We found a secret store cupboard in Dole's flat. It had been cleared out, but amongst other things forensics found traces of plastic explosive.'

Peters' eyebrows rose another inch, then Cal saw his eyes darken as he considered this.

'I don't think he'd use it.'

'Then why have it?'

Peters opened his hands. 'He has been taught to be prepared for all eventualities. Remember this is a man who has seen war. I think it's likely he stocked up on everything he thought might ever be useful.'

'Plastic explosive? He was a security guard for Christ's sake. What was he going to do, blow up shoplifters?'

The major just looked at him.

Tess leaned forward.

'What made you come all this way, major? Did you hope you might see him?'

He looked at her for a long minute, then dropped his eyes.

'Dole is one of the best soldiers I ever trained. Not only that, but as I got to know him, I realised he was a good man, the best of men, but that life had conspired against him. He looked on the army as his family, and they, like everyone else, turned him away. I just want to redress the balance. If he's arrested, I want him to see someone there who's on his side.'

Tess slowly nodded. She smiled.

Cal looked from the girl to the man. 'Let's find him then.'

He picked up the phone.

'Get me Cranmore.' He turned to Peters. 'How do you say that word again?'

THIRTY

Tess walked into the corridor, which was cold after the tiny heated room. She shivered, and it made her smile. She was back to feeling a slight chill, not freezing on a cold island. Normal service had been resumed. She grasped her bare arms, spied a drinks machine at the end of the corridor, and wondered if Cal Fisher might be up to lending her a couple of pounds. She had left him in the room when the major had gone, making phone calls and seemingly excited by the information.

Tess was getting the gist of Mike Dole, and the more she learned, the more her earlier reaction, the one she'd had on the island, came back to the fore. She was sorry for him, the poor guy was a wreck. Funny how soon the memories go, she thought. This time yesterday, she wanted to kill him. The memories of bitter cold, gnawing hunger, the cuts and bruises, her miserably painful feet, they had all diminished. She smiled to herself. She was just a little tired, but then, it was two in the morning. She spied Chandra up at the machine and waved at her.

'Hi, detective?'

Chandra smiled. 'Your jeans not fallen down yet?'

Tess laughed. 'I don't even know your name.'

'It's Yas. You want a Coke or somethin'?'

'Listen, can somebody lend me a couple of quid? It's embarrassing. I've got nothing.'

Chandra grinned. 'I can stand ye a Coke. Ask your boyfriend for a loan.'

Tess said nothing, but took the can gratefully. She opened it and took a sip of the syrupy sweet liquid as DS Cramond came out of a side room.

'Miss Hardy, your mother's here waiting for you.'

'Oh. Thanks.'

'I think she's been waiting some time.'

Tess nodded. The man was still giving her that look, the one that said he hadn't believed a word of her story, and he was just humouring his superior officers.

'She's in the waiting room.'

'Thanks.'

'I'll take you.'

She looked at him. 'Ok, but I have to come back here afterwards. DS Fisher will be speaking to me again.'

'Will he now?'

She nodded. He certainly would if she had anything to do with it.

She followed him out through a series of doors and into the waiting room. It was painted the same pale green as the rest of the place, with posters advising *don't drink and drive*, and *lock it or lose it*. There were hard chairs in three rows. Tess had expected it to be quiet this time in the morning, but the room was half-full. There was a teenage girl, blowing pink gum and staring at her with hard eyes, a couple of middle aged men wearing suits, an elderly woman with a small dog, two couples in their thirties, taking turns to throw daggers at each other, and, of course, her mother. Sheila stood up, her lip still quivering, and Tess hurriedly sat in the seat next to her.

'Mother, why are you still here? I told you you should go home.'

'What? And leave you here? How ever would you get back?'

'The police will take me. Look, they've not finished with me yet, it could be ages. You should just go.'

Sheila's eyes grew hard.

'It's ridiculous, keeping you here after all you've been through. Look at the time! I'm going to make a formal complaint.'

'No you're not,' Tess said, keeping her voice low. The other occupants had spied a bit of entertainment in the offing.

'We need to get hold of Mike, and I can help.'

Sheila's face softened again. 'Oh Tess, I'm so proud of you, coming through this against the odds.'

Tess felt a curious sense of sadness. Pride was the one thing Tess never expected to hear from Sheila.

'Mum, go home. I'll see you when I get back.'

'I'll check into a hotel.'

Tess stifled a sigh.

Does dad know I'm back?'

Sheila stiffened. 'I gave his details to the officer. He said he would phone him.'

A fountain of anger welled up inside her.

'What, you couldn't tell him yourself?'

'The police are perfectly capable of-'

'I can't believe you,' Tess said, standing up. 'You can't even get over your anger with him to tell him his daughter's safe. You know how upset he'll be. Why do you have to be so cold hearted?'

Sheila's mouth made a fine line.

'Don't you talk to me like that, young lady-'

'Mother, I'm thirty one. I'll talk to you however I want. Now go home.'

She walked back to the glass panel set in the wall. The officer there gave her a wry smile, which told her the audience had enjoyed every word.

'I'm to come back and see DS Fisher,' she said.

'Step over to the door.'

Tess walked back into the police building without looking back. All the years of saying yes, no, whatever you want, were over. If Sheila was disappointed in her daughter's behaviour, too bad. She wasn't going to apologise for herself again. She knocked on the door of room 6 and Fisher answered.

'Tess? I thought you had gone home.'

'Uh uh. Listen, can I use your phone a minute?'

Fisher stepped back to let her through. 'Tess, there's no need for you to stay now, it's just a –'

'I'm staying.'

She turned and stared at him.

'No offence, Cal, but this guy nearly killed me. Never mind what the major said, he's got some explaining to do, and I want to hear it.'

Fisher smiled.

'Tess, even if we do pick him up soon, you won't get anywhere near him. He'll be arrested-'

She picked up the phone, dialled her father's number.

'I have a feeling I'll be seeing him before you do,' she said.

'Hello?'

'Dad, it's me. I'm all right.'

She listened to the sound of uncontrollable sobbing, as Fisher raised an eyebrow and left the room.

*

Cal checked his mobile. He had three missed calls. One was an unknown number, the second was the nursing home, and the third was Rob. A pang of guilt swept through him. He should have been at Lake Pastures this afternoon to see his mother. Well, there was nothing he could do about it now. He couldn't ring in the middle of the night.

It was curious about the unknown caller. Who would have his number? He decided to leave it till last, and dialled Rob instead. The phone rang on and on until a sleepy voice finally answered.

'Rob, it's me.'

Cal, hey, what's happening? You caught the bad man yet?'

'How are you doing with the missing person angle?'

A sigh. 'I take it that means no. Cal, it's nearly three in the morning, can't this wait?'

'No it can't. What about the missing persons?'

Another sigh. 'Roslyn has made up a list of likely suspects. There are six of them. You want her to fax it up there?'

'Yes, soon as she can. Anything else I should know about?'

'You've got a big list of messages, but nothing that can't wait. Oh, and –'

He hesitated, and Cal waited.

'What?'

'You had a call from someone. I gave them your mobile number.'

Well, that explained the unknown call. Cal felt the hairs stand up on his neck. Rob was suddenly wide awake.

'Who is it, a witness?'

'Um,' Rob drew in his breath. 'I might have done the wrong thing here.'

Cal sighed. 'Rob, for God's sake, just tell me. Who called?'

'Lynne.'

A lump of lead landed in his belly. Not again. What did she want this time?

'Cal? I'm sorry if I did the wrong thing, I–'

'It's OK, Rob. Just fax me that list, will you?'

He snapped the phone shut, trying to ignore the small hope that had flared inside him. There was a knock on the door and Cramond came in.

'All right?' he said. Cal nodded.

'I've spoken to Dingwall. They're sending some guys up right away, a bunch of them, well briefed. It'll take them a couple of hours to get to the coast, another hour to get out to the island. They should get there by seven.'

Cal nodded. 'Good.'

'It's a place I've never been, the highlands,' Cramond said. Cal raised an eyebrow.

'Really? Why not?'

The older man frowned. 'Well, I like the sun, and there's not much of it up there.'

'Wait for global warming,' Cal said, 'It'll be fine then.'

'Ach, but then it'll be too busy.' Cramond smiled. 'It's late. If you're tired, you can bunk down in a cell.'

Cal grinned. 'I've done that before. It's not a lot of fun. Think I'll just have some more coffee and wait to hear from your men. What about the women, where are they?'

'The weepy one's gone home with her folks. The other one's in the back, drinking tea and keeping my PCs awake. We'll have a job to get rid of her, I reckon, but maybe you're not bothered about that.'

Cal spotted the man's lop sided grin, and had to grin back. No, he wasn't. Not bothered at all.

THIRTY ONE

He must have drifted off to sleep. Cal woke up with the taste of stale coffee in his mouth and a crick in his neck from the uncomfortable chair. He sat up and rolled his neck, yawning. Glancing at his watch he saw it was just after eight. He stood up and went to find Cramond.

The big man was on the phone, and he raised an eyebrow when Cal arrived. Tess was already there, sitting quietly by the wall, being unobtrusive in the hope they wouldn't notice her and send her away. Cal smiled at her absently as Cramond put the phone down.

'Any word yet?'

'Aye, they called when they got to Scourie bay, about an hour ago. Won't be long now.'

Cal ran his hand through his thinning hair. He could do with more sleep, but that wasn't going to happen.

'Did anyone send a fax up for me?'

One of the PCs waved a wad of paper, and Cal retrieved it. He pulled out his pen as he read down the pages, doodling in the margin as he checked through the names. None of them jumped out at him, but then, why would they? He found an empty seat at the back of the room and began to read the report. It was clear it was Roslyn's work. It was neat, succinct and to the point.

'Want a coffee?'

He looked up. Tess was holding two paper cups. He thought she looked a lot better than he did after a sleepless night. He took the cup, fighting an urge to replace it with his hand.

'Thanks,' he said.

'Nothing's happened,' she said softly. 'I've been paying attention, and you've not missed anything.'

He chuckled. 'You'd make a good copper, you know that?'

She looked at him, a strange little smile on her face. 'Would I?'

He nodded, curious at her reaction. But then he realised she couldn't go back to working in the china shop. He wondered what she would do. He glanced up and saw she was grinning.

'What?'

She sat beside him. 'Your drawings. They're really good.'

Cal looked down at the little boat he'd sketched, feeling the heat rush to his face.

'Just doodling,' he said gruffly.

'No, seriously. Do you like to paint too?'

He chuckled. 'No. To tell you the truth, I don't know I'm doing it.'

'Hey, Fisher.'

He stood up. Cramond was on the phone again, and Cal saw him press buttons on the table. A second later a voice came out of the phone speaker.

'- three people, two male one female. They were taking their boat over to Stornoway when they witnessed an explosion on Toilichte.'

'An explosion?' Cramond said, incredulous. 'Are they sure?'

'Aye, sir. Said they saw bits of wood and debris flying up, and there was a real boom. After that, a couple of flares went up, so they went in to investigate.'

Cal felt his heart in his throat, thinking about Mike's store cupboard, and what else he might have had in there.

'When was this?'

'Yesterday, sir, about four o'clock. They left the boat in the bay, went on to the island, and they were following a trail through the woods when they heard the sound of their boat engine. By the time they got back to the jetty, it was well out to sea.'

'They never saw the man?'

'No, not at all.'

'Are they all right?'

'A bit cold from spending the night here, but aye, they're fine. I sent a man up to where the explosion happened and a fire is still smouldering. We need someone up here to tell us what caused it.'

'Damn,' Cal murmured, turning away.

Tess let out a hollow chuckle, and Cal looked at her.

'Three months I was on that island,' she said. 'Three months. He's there less than a day and he escapes.'

Cal sighed. *You didn't have Mike's secret stores.*

'Any trace of the boat?' he asked.

Cramond relayed the question. 'Not yet. There's lots of little bays on the western coast. We'll check them out.

'Check the beach and the dunes,' Cramond said, the astonishment still in his voice. We have a report of a body there.'

'Affirmative.'

Cramond turned to Cal.

'Well, where's your man going now?'

Cal shook his head, looking at Tess.

'Don't look at me,' she said.

'He's got his car hidden up there. We'll find him as soon as he drives somewhere.'

Cramond nodded, but Cal sensed his reluctance. 'What?'

'Four o'clock yesterday,' he said. 'In a fast boat, an hour and a bit to get to shore. Fifteen hours have passed, with no reports of the car. He could be anywhere.'

Cal sat down heavily on the chair. Think positive, he told himself. You couldn't have helped the dead girl, you never knew about it, and the other two are safe. We'll pick Mike up sooner or later.

Then he glanced up at Tess, who had the same enigmatic look on her face. He remembered what she had said, that she had the feeling she'd see Mike first.

Well, stuff that. He'd protect her, make sure Mike couldn't harm her. He'd need the major's help, but he'd do it. He stood up.

'Well, I'd better get back home,' he said. 'There's nothing else I can do up here.'

Tess raised an eyebrow, and Cramond heaved a sigh.

'He'll turn up, don't worry, a man on his own will stand out. We'll keep a look out for the car, and all the local forces have his photo. We'll find him for you.'

'Thanks,' Cal said. 'You'll keep me informed?'

Cramond put his head on one side and let out a sigh.

'All right,' Cal said, holding up his hands. He turned to Tess.

'Mike's off the radar. I've got stuff waiting for me. We should go home.'

She nodded. 'I suppose.' She looked down at her broken fingernails.

'He might just go away,' she said.

'What?'

She looked at him. 'The major said he was never happier than when he was somewhere remote and alone. He might just stay up there.'

Cal shrugged, unconvinced.

'If he does, fine. If he doesn't, well,' he smiled at her.

'We'll be ready for him.'

*

Mike waited half an hour after the men left his car, until there was silence apart from the rush of the sea and a busy stream tumbling down the hillside. Then he hurried over, checked the boot, and got in. He closed his eyes, taking deep breaths, feeling calm.

Trundling out of the field, he drove along the single track road until it joined a larger one. There he pulled into a layby and spread a map over the bonnet, just another tourist finding his way. He knew there were very few wildernesses left in Britain, but that he was in the wildest of them; miles and endless miles of mountain and rock and loch and sea, the perfect place. Somewhere that people never came, where he could at last relax and be at peace.

He wondered absently why he had never thought of this before, why he had carried on trying to live a normal life in places where he couldn't belong, among people who didn't give a damn about him. Or about anything, so it seemed. Why hadn't he done what he knew eased his soul, and gone away alone long ago?

Well, he was doing it now.

He looked around him. Summer was coming, and the flanks of the mountains were already mottled with pale shades of green. There would be trout in the streams, salmon in the lochs, crabs and scallops in the sea, deer in the hills. He would live with them and be part of them, part of the landscape, the wild, his own world, and there would be no one to take care of except himself.

He pulled up a sprig of heather and smelled its comforting scent. Peace began to steal into the wilderness of his heart.

He found the side road above a river, and drove slowly up. The car bumped along the stony track, the sun gleaming silver on the rushing water below. Mike felt his shoulders relax. He breathed deeply of the clear, sweet smelling air. He smiled.

He felt a sudden change of pressure, and tensed.

Why are you driving north, Mikey? Sandy said.

We need to be going south.

THIRTY TWO

Cal felt guilty that he hadn't looked at the missing person report by the time he arrived back at Belgrave Gate, but the guilt was assuaged by the pleasure of spending the last four hours in Tess's company. The normally tedious motorway drive had been easy. She had told him about surviving on the island, describing the place in detail. It was clear that it was very beautiful.

In return, he had told her about his mother and her intermittent dementia, leaving out the ever-brewing guilt he felt for putting her in the home. Tess seemed to sense it, all the same.

'It's clear you love her very much,' she had said, to his surprise.

He took her home, where she retrieved a spare key from a neighbour and waved him goodbye. It had been on the tip of his tongue to ask her out, but every time the opportunity arose, Tess started up another conversation. He wondered now if she had done that on purpose. Still, he had her phone number. She had asked him to keep her informed, and Cal was happy to agree.

Rob was in with the DCI when he arrived, and Cal caught his eye. Rob said something and Jarvis motioned him in.

'He got away,' he said. Cal took a deep breath.

'Hell, I'm not blaming you, Cal, sit down. Give me the whole story.'

Cal laid it all out, all the time wondering if there was something else he could have done.

'The body on the island, has this been found yet?'

Cal shook his head. 'The Glasgow police promised to let me know.'

'So we don't know yet if there has been a murder, it's still just a kidnapping.'

'Sir, it all fits, the visitor the landlady never saw leave, the pattern of abduction and abandonment. And Tess Hardy was quite specific about what she saw, there's no reason she would lie.'

Jarvis nodded, rubbing the fingers of his right hand together. Still on the fags, Cal supposed.

'OK, but until we know for certain, Rob here can carry on with the missing person check. Keep me informed. And Cal, I think it's time you gave your other cases some time.'

Cal felt gloom descend, but it lifted quickly. The body was bound to be found soon, and then the case would be right back at the top of the agenda. He walked back to his room, Rob walking with him, saying nothing.

'Sorry he got away,' he said eventually.

'We'll get him,' Cal replied. 'Have you read these missing person reports?'

Rob nodded. 'Want me to run them down for you?'

Cal hesitated, then shook his head. 'No, Jarvis gave it to you. Let's not piss off the boss.'

He opened the door, but Rob was still standing there.

'What's up?'

Rob looked sheepish. 'Look, I'm sorry about giving out your number.'

He read Cal's blank expression. 'To Lynne.'

Cal had forgotten all about it, but the usual feeling of sadness associated with his ex-wife's name was strangely absent. Maybe at last he was getting over it.

'It's OK, Rob,' he smiled. 'Really.'

His partner left, looking relieved, and Cal walked to his desk to catch up on everything he had neglected over the last days.

*

What the hell was I doing? Tess thought, standing in the doorway of her bedroom. She felt like a woman returning to her parent's house after many years, to find they had kept her bedroom the way it was when she was seven. *Did I really like pink so much?*

She sat on the bed and picked up one of the soft toys. A rabbit made of fake beige fur, with big floppy ears and a red bow round its neck. She thought about the real thing; the pounding, tremulous heart, the wide panicked eyes. She had taken it in her arms and then killed it. There hadn't been a bow round its neck.

The fluffy bunny stared at her with its blank button eyes, and she felt a chill run through her. Why had she kept these things? She searched inside herself and found the answer: *because you couldn't bear to throw them out.*

She nodded to herself, an uneasy tension in her chest. She had thought like that. But not any more. Scooping up the toys she carried them downstairs, tossing them inside a black bin liner. Then she added the velvet cushions, the lacy curtains. There had to be a local charity shop that would have them. She would put up blinds, they were tidier and more efficient.

Somewhere in the middle of the clearout, she stopped and sat down. *What am I doing?* This time last week she was daydreaming about being home, safe and content in her sweet little house. Now, she was destroying everything she had so looked forward to. She stood up, feeling the stretch in her aching toes. The doctor had told her there was no long term damage, she just had to take care of her feet and they'd heal. Until then, she had comfy trainers and soft socks, and it wasn't so bad, really. At least her feet were dry and warm.

She looked around again, the uneasy feeling still with her. Outside, the houses opposite were silent and empty. Thursday afternoon in suburbia, and she was the only one home. She dumped the bin bags in the yard and looked at her postage stamp garden, a ten foot square of grass bordered by a six foot fence on three sides, an access gate to the dustbins set in the back panel. She could hear the faint traffic sounds from the main road, but there was something wrong. Something missing.

The sea. She couldn't hear the sea. Her heart gave a jolt.

She closed the door and walked down the road. Somewhere between the end of her cul de sac and the Lucky Dragon Chinese take away, the walk became a run. The pain in her feet eventually went away, though she knew it would be back. It didn't matter. As she ran, she felt the curious unease drift away, to be replaced by a quiet calm.

When she got home an hour and a half later, there were three messages on her answerphone. The first was from Mrs Dennis at the china shop.

'Hello Tess.' The voice was strained and falsely cheerful. 'I'm so happy to hear that you're back safe and sound, and I'm really sorry about it all. Could you pop into the shop sometime? I'd love to see you, and in any case, I, uh, have your last pay packet here. Hope to see you soon.'

Embarrassed, that's how she sounded. Because she'd given up on Tess. Given her job away. Last pay packet indeed. Pop into the shop! The bloody last place she wanted to go. Tess felt the edgy feeling returning, and erased the message quickly. She listened to the next.

'Hello Tess, this is George Seymour of *The Sun*. We're all delighted that you're back safe, and I'd like to come along and talk to you about your ordeal. I can-'

She cut the message off in mid flow. How the hell did the newspapers get to hear about her? Well, they could stuff it. She hesitated, looking at the blinking red light, was that another paper calling? She shook her head and pressed the button. It wasn't a newspaper, it was worse. Mother:

'Hello darling. I've got the morning off tomorrow and I'll pop round to see you. We'll go shopping over at the new mall in Derby. I'll call over about ten. See you then.'

What happened to asking, she thought bitterly. Old Tess would have sighed, resigned to the unwelcome trip, but new Tess was having none of it. She picked up the phone and dialled her mother's number.

'Hello?'

'Mother, it's me. I-'

'Oh, hello darling, are you all right?'

'I'm not coming shopping with you tomorrow.'

There was a pause. 'Oh, well if you have other plans, we can-'

'I don't. I just don't want to go. And please don't come round, I'm busy doing things in the house, all right? Bye.'

She hung up the phone, the tension back in her chest. She could feel a headache starting. She needed some time to thinks things through.

Tess went into the kitchen. Her half drunk bottle of chardonnay was still there on the windowsill. She didn't fancy a glass of three-month-old wine so she pulled out another bottle and opened it. She took a sip and felt the alcohol hit her empty stomach like a cold wave.

What was it that policeman had said she had? Post traumatic stress? Post *mother* stress, more like. But she sighed. She had not meant to be so harsh. She would never hurt anyone's feelings. Never! She should ring back and apologise. There was no excuse, just because Sheila felt comfortable being rude to people. Like that time in the travel agents when mother had booked her latest jaunt, dragging a reluctant Tess along as usual. Tess had looked at the poster of Bali on the wall, palm trees and white sand.

The travel agent had smiled. 'Beautiful isn't it?'

'Whereabouts is Bali?' she'd asked.

'Oh for God's sake, Tess,' Sheila had snapped. 'Don't you know anything?'

The travel agent's face had gone red, but not as red as Tess's. She felt her grip on the wine glass grow tighter.

I know something, she thought angrily. *I know I'm not bloody going to apologise.*

THIRTY THREE

The phone rang at midnight, just as Cal was drifting off to sleep. He checked the number, and saw it was a Glasgow code.

'Fisher,' he said.

'Hello there. It's Cramond here, from Glasgow'

'Hi. You got something for me.'

'I surely do. It took them a while, but the lads found the body. They're bringing it back now, but initial report says it's a woman, likely in her twenties or thirties. There's a lot of damage, wild animals and such. I'll let you know the results when we do.'

Cal stood up and opened the wardrobe door, pulling out a shirt.

'Thanks, mate. Appreciate it.'

'Not at all. We've started the search for Dole, but it's not going to be easy.'

Cal sighed. 'I know. I'll keep in touch.'

He dressed quickly and hurried out, driving to the station in record time through city streets quiet and shiny with rain. He was feeling jazzed. The Dole case was back on, and he was anxious to get to work. He found the file on Rob's desk and took it to his own, where he left it beside his notebook and fetched coffee from the machine.

He pulled out the missing person report. Rob had made a series of notes, but Cal set these to one side. He wanted to do this himself. Roslyn had made a comprehensive list of women reported missing in the whole of the UK between December 2005 and February 2006. Then she had narrowed it down to women aged between 25 and 40, which took it down to forty two.

Cal absently wondered what had happened to all these people, where were they? So many people in just three months, and that was just the women. Of that number, fifteen had turned up safe, eight had turned up dead. Of the nineteen remaining, eight had been known prostitutes, and Roslyn had prepared detailed schedules for each.

He checked his notebook. The woman he was looking for was thin, with blonde hair, a long face and bad skin.

Who are you, he thought, *how did you meet Mike? And what did you do to make him angry, so angry that he killed you?*

He laid out the photos of the missing women and immediately discounted two; one, a freckled redhead that made him think of Annie from his mother's care home, and the second, a lumpy overweight woman who looked older than forty. All of the other six were stick thin. Four were blonde, three had what might be regarded as long faces. Cal read down the first of their reports:

Alison Taylor, aged thirty. Disappeared from her home in Sheffield. Reported missing by her alleged boyfriend, more likely her pimp. He said he had no idea where she had gone. Everything was fine, she just didn't come home from work the previous night, and none of her friends had seen her.

Cal looked at the photo, trying to get a feel for the woman. The photo had been taken after an arrest six months before. The woman was staring at the camera with knowing, streetwise eyes.

The second woman was younger, in her twenties. Her blonde hair obviously dyed, the roots showing half an inch of black. Lindy Collier had disappeared from her home in Knaresborough, reported missing by worried parents who couldn't understand why their beautiful daughter had gone astray. The photo had again been from an arrest report, and in it the girl looked sullen and resigned.

Setting the first two photos aside, he pulled the third report. Sandra Noone, of Bermondsey, London. Reported missing by her mother, Jessie, also a known prostitute with a string of convictions. This photo showed a sick looking woman, with greasy blonde hair and eyes that were more angry than anything else. Cal read on.

Mother reports daughter was trying to trace missing brother who disappeared seventeen years previous. Had information on where he was. (Brother still reported missing – case No. 2278631)

Cal felt an alarm going off in his head, and sat back to think about it.

Seventeen years back Mike Dole was signing up for the army. He wondered where Mike was born. *Who can I ask?* Then he knew. Tess. He looked at his watch, it was gone one o'clock. He shouldn't disturb her.

But she had said he could call any time.

Cal had the urge to hear her voice, even if it was chewing him out. He pulled out his mobile and dialled her number. She picked up on the second ring, making him wonder if she had even been asleep.

'Tess? It's Cal Fisher. Sorry about the time.'

'Hello Cal. What's up?'

A warm feeling filled his chest. 'Did Mike ever tell you where he was born?'

'Um, London, I think. He wasn't specific.'

'Thanks, Tess. That's a help. I'm sorry to ring so late.'

'You're still working? What's the latest?'

He told her that the body had been found, that he was trying to identify it.

'So it looks like someone from near his home?'

'Could be.'

'Cal, can I come in and help you? I might be able to, you know, give you bits of info, like this tonight.'

She sounded sad and lonely, and Cal would like nothing better, but there were rules.

'Sorry, Tess, I wish you could, but no. This is a murder investigation now.'

He hesitated. Now was the time.

'But I could meet up with you, out of the station, if you like. We could talk about it then.'

There was a silence, and he felt his heart fluttering. Had she seen through him?

'Yeah, sure. When?'

The surge of joy was like a drug infusing his blood. 'How about tomorrow lunch?' Keep it casual, he thought.

'OK. Ring me in the morning.'

He closed the phone, a bright smile on his face. He wrote the name and address of Jessie Noone in his notebook. First thing in the morning, he'd be paying her a visit

*

The early rain had given way to broken cloud and warm sun, and a herd of cloud shadows moved slowly across the mountainside. Mike sat cross legged by the fire and looked over the Cromalt hills. Before him a cock pheasant was roasting on a spit, the juices hissing into the fire. The smell was making his mouth water.

From the north west side of this small hill, he could see across to the Coigach mountains, a place he thought he might travel next. He was wary of coming across climbers, not so much because they might recognise him, but because he just didn't want to see anyone. Few people ever came here to Rappach. There were no serious mountains to climb, and the scenery nearer the coast was richer. It suited Mike, with the forest at the base of the hill, the river a few feet away. Everything he needed.

Hungry, he tucked into the leaves of white mustard and primrose which he had intended to eat with the pheasant, but couldn't wait.

He had left the car in a small clearing beside a communication mast near the village of Lubcroy. It was unlikely that the mast would be checked often, and anyone doing so would assume someone had simply parked his car and gone for a walk. He had cleared it of all his belongings, many of which he had packed up and buried in the woods nearby, just in case. Then he had packed a rucksack and walked the few short miles to this hill, just like a regular hiker, bagging the pheasant and the salad on the way.

He leaned back against a rock, enjoying the warmth of the late afternoon sun on his face. He closed his eyes, content.

Wasting time, Mike'

He winced, sitting up quickly, but the voice had vanished. He felt the angry fearful beating of his heart. Why was this happening to him? He had done the right thing, hadn't he? Gone away from everyone. He didn't want to hurt anyone, just wanted to be left alone.

The sun slunk behind a cloud. Maybe it was too late. Maybe he had done too many wrong things. He walked to the stream and washed his face in the chill water, the tic in his cheek jumping under his hands. The gentle sound of the running stream slowly calmed him. Sandy's dead, he told himself. She's not talking to you, she can't.

Behind him, a pocket of pheasant fat exploded, and Mike threw himself to the ground. 'Donno!' he yelled. 'Get down!'

The stream continued down the mountain. Mike closed his eyes to stop the hot tears.

THIRTY FOUR

Cal glanced at DC Roslyn as he drove. She had her head in the file, engrossed, but some sixth sense told her Cal was watching her, and she glanced up.

He had not intended to bring Roslyn along, but she had come into the station just before six as he was leaving, and asked if there had been any progress. Cal had looked at her eager, anxious face and knew what she was thinking.

Emma Roslyn had a pretty heart-shaped face and wide set dark eyes. She rarely smiled, but when she did she was truly beautiful. Just 24, it was obvious she adored her job, and with her brains she was destined for great things.

'Good work with the missing person list,' he said.

Roslyn smiled absently. 'But has it thrown anything up?'

He told her about the Jessie Noone angle, told her he was on his way there.

'Sir, could I tag along?'

'What?'

'I just thought- well, I've taken a real interest in this case, sir.'

Cal was surprised. She was young, clever and ambitious, but this wasn't the sort of case that would make her name. Still, he knew if it hadn't been for her they wouldn't have discovered the secret store, and it was her work that had brought her to Noone.

'I'll be gone all morning. Don't you have other cases?'

'The SIO has assigned me to this investigation, sir, since I'm already CID. I've been working with DS Matlock.'

He looked at her carefully, but her pretty eyes were giving nothing away. Working with Rob meant she probably spent most of her time making tea and running errands, but she wasn't complaining. Cal smiled. Knowing her skills, she could be helpful, save him some time.

'Well, tell you what, you're good with the computers. Get a trace on this woman; home, work, whatever you can. If you can come up with that in the next twenty minutes, you're in.'

'Sir, no problem.'

She took the pages he offered and hurried off. Cal smiled again. His plan had been to drive down and hope to find Jessie at the same address where she'd filed the report. If she wasn't there, he'd ask around. Not a very good plan, he knew, but he felt he had to keep moving.

He returned to his room and opened the file, reading the work Rob had done on the missing person list. Rob hadn't come to the same conclusions as Cal. In fact, he hadn't come to any great conclusions at all. Cal sighed. His partner was on a downward spiral. He had never been the brightest cop, but he had always been hard working and conscientious. Whatever was happening in his personal life, Rob wasn't the copper he had once been. Cal was wondering what he should do about it when he saw Roslyn coming towards him.

'Got it, sir.'

He raised an eyebrow. She'd been gone less than fifteen minutes.

'Got what?' he asked warily.

'Jessie Noone, aged 59. lives at 15 Victoria Terraces Streatham. Doesn't work, in receipt of invalidity benefits. Rent paid by the council.'

Cal stood up. 'Let's get her out of bed then, shall we?'

He turned into Streatham High Street. He wanted to ask Roslyn how she had found the information so quickly, but that would give away how little he knew about the modern systems. He was aware that the young coppers thought of detectives like Rob and him as old farts who couldn't detect a bad smell in a bin lorry. No need to give them any more ammunition.

'It's the second right, then first left,' Roslyn said, looking up. She had even brought directions. Cal was secretly impressed, and couldn't help comparing her to his hopeless partner.

He turned into the street in question, a tidy little terraced street, not so different from the one Dole had lived in in Headingley. The doors were set back four feet from the pavement, and some of the houses had a dinky little brick wall at the boundary, or bright coloured gravel and grassy plants.

Number fifteen had a filthy dustbin surrounded by garbage. A stinking carpet was thrown carelessly on the ground next to a soggy cardboard box that had once contained a TV. Black bags filled with rubbish were piled up. One had been broken into by animals, and the food waste dragged out. Instead of clearing it up, the inhabitant had simply kicked it to one side.

'What a shithole,' Cal murmured, banging on the door.

Roslyn simply nodded. Cal could tell she was eager and excited, but hiding it well. Nothing happened, and Cal hammered on the door again, stopping when he finally heard a voice.

'All right, all fucking *right!*'

The door was dragged slowly open. The woman had trouble pulling it, and Cal noticed that was because there was a huge pile of junk mail inside.

'What do you want?'

The woman had long greasy hair the colour of a wet pavement, and hungry dark eyes surrounded by a ploughed field of wrinkles. She looked about seventy, the sort of mad old woman often seen shoving a shopping trolley through the streets, muttering to herself.

'Jessie Noone?' Cal said.

'What do you want, copper?'

'Well spotted, Jessie. Can we come in?'

She backed up, shaking her head. 'I've done nothing wrong. I've got none on me, you know. You won't find any.'

Roslyn raised an eyebrow, about to speak, but Cal caught her eye.

'We're not here for that,' he said, following her through the dim hall to a living room. The house smelled of mould and tired cooking fat. The wallpaper was peeling off, the carpet shiny with wear and covered in unknown stains. Grey towels were hung on the radiator, presumably to dry, although there was no heating, the house was chill. The bay window in the living room was full of newspapers, pizza boxes and tin cans. Cal looked up and saw the ceiling had detailed Victorian coving, an intricate ceiling rose. Jessie sat down on a sofa the same dreary colour as her hair.

'Well, what is it then?'

Cal sat gingerly on the edge of the sofa, trying to avoid a vivid mustard coloured stain.

'I'm DS Fisher, this is DC Roslyn.'

The woman looked Roslyn up and down, sneering. The detective stared straight back, her face impassive.

'Last year you reported your daughter Sandra missing.'

The woman's sneer fell away, and she sat forward, clenching her fists.

'What is it, have you found 'er? Where is she?'

Cal was curious. Her eagerness seemed almost predatory. There was no trace of the whispered hope he would have expected bringing news to a mother of her missing child.

'We're following up on your report,' he said.

Jessie sat back, deflated. 'So you aint found her.'

Cal shook his head. 'Can you tell us again the circumstances in which she disappeared?'

Jessie picked up a packet of cigarettes from the floor at her feet and lit one. She sucked hard on it, making a noise like steam escaping. Cal was suddenly grateful he had given up.

'I told them lot down the road already. Why do you want to know again?'

Cal tried a smile. 'New faces, new ideas, Mrs Noone. We're just trying to help.'

'Well, there's no point. She's not coming back now, is she? Someone's done her in.'

'Why do you say that?'

'Obvious, innit? People don't just vanish 'less they're dead. She was a pro. It's not a safe life.'

Cal pulled out his notebook and pen and pretended to write something in it.

'When was the last time you saw her?'

'I can't remember that!' Jessie laughed, blowing out smoke. 'A couple days before I reported it. You tell me.'

Cal just looked at her.

'She went out on the Saturday morning. In high spirits, she was. I asked her where she was going, and she said she was about to come into some money.'

'What did she mean?' Roslyn asked. Jessie gave her a hard look.

'If I knew that, sweetheart, I'd have gone meself.'

Cal looked at his empty notebook.

'You reported that she was trying to trace her brother?'

'Oh. Him. Yeah, she said so. Didn't believe her though.'

'Why not?'

Jessie shrugged. 'Same reason. He's been gone nearly twenty years.'

'Well, how was your daughter going to trace him?'

Jessie ground out her cigarette in an already overflowing ashtray, and pulled another out of the packet.

'You're thinking maybe he killed her, aint you?' she laughed again, and it turned into a hacking cough. Cal imagined her beleaguered lungs desperately trying to escape her raddled body.

'She said she saw him on the telly.'

Cal and Roslyn exchanged a glance. 'On TV? Doing what?'

She lit the new fag, took a more gentle toke this time.

'Coming out of a plane from somewhere foreign. She said he was a soldier.'

Cal felt something fluttering in his chest. He bit back the urge to smile.

So, Mike, now we know who you really are.

'I told her it was rubbish. As if the army'd have him.'

'Why wouldn't they, Mrs Noone?'

Jessie sneered at Roslyn again. 'Cos he was a cissy. Always hanging round Sandra, trying to look out for her. She was a big girl, and smart. She could take care of herself.'

'What happened to him?'

She shrugged. 'He went off one day, didn't come back.'

'Did you report him missing?'

'Oh yeah, yeah. 'Course.'

She looked away, wiping imaginary ash from her scummy polyester trousers. No you didn't, you old bitch, Cal thought.

'How old was he?'

'Sixteen. Old enough to look after hisself. If he didn't want to stick around, stuff him.'

Sixteen. How the hell did Mike get into the army at that age? They'd have wanted parental consent, and he wouldn't have –

But wait. He didn't, did he? Mike *Noone* didn't join the army. Mike *Dole* did.

Cal stared at the woman, her squalid clothes, her pinched, bitter face.

'You claim invalidity benefit, Mrs Noone?'

'Me back,' she said, putting her skinny arm behind her to touch the small of her back. 'Gives me terrible gyp. Some days I can't even get out of bed.'

She met his stare, daring him to make something of it, but Cal didn't care. He was picturing little Mike, trying to protect his baby sister from the reality of having a mother on the game. He was certain the woman on the island was Sandra. She had found her brother, gone to him looking for money, and Cal could guess how. She knew his true identity, she would blackmail him. But why would it have mattered to him then? After all, he was out of the army, and in any case, who would believe a junkie over a war hero?

But then, Mike didn't think like that, did he? Cal took a deep breath, smelling dirty wet towels and cigarettes. He stood up.

'Well, we'll keep the case open,' he said, trying to keep the distaste from his words.

Jessie shrugged. 'Like I said, she's dead.'

Roslyn stood up, and Cal could see the anger in her eyes.

'You don't seem very upset by the prospect.'

Jessie gave her a snide little smile.

'Upset that she won't be paying back the money she owes me,' Jessie grinned.

Cal turned and walked out. He couldn't stand being in the house any longer. He stalked back to the car, Roslyn jogging to keep up. Once inside, he put his hands on the steering wheel, but didn't start the car.

'Sir?' Roslyn said, her eyes cautious. He let out a little laugh.

'I don't know why,' he said, 'but I feel sorry for our Mike.'

Roslyn opened the file.

'Jessie Noone has seven separate convictions for prostitution. She did time, but managed to bargain the sentence down in exchange for information. After that, it appears the locals turned a blind eye as long as she was keeping them up to date. The daughter, Sandra, was arrested for soliciting aged eighteen.'

'The mother taught her everything she knew,' Cal said bitterly.

'That's the body, isn't it?' Roslyn said, 'Sandra.'

Cal nodded. 'Can't prove it, but I don't think Jessie cares what happened to her daughter.'

'Oh, I think we can prove it all right, sir,' Roslyn said. She held up a plastic baggie containing a long greasy grey hair.

Cal laughed. 'Roslyn, you deserve a medal for picking that up. I wouldn't have touched it.'

'When we get back, I'll run a check for the missing brother,' Roslyn's dark eyes were shining.

Cal nodded. 'Good work again,' he said, holding her gaze. She looked down, clearly embarrassed

'We're nearly there,' he said. 'We just have to find him now.'

THIRTY FIVE

Cal pulled into the station car park, wincing as he saw David Driscoll waiting in the rain for him. David was a reporter with the *Mercury*, a decent bloke that Cal had worked with before on a few cases. But Cal had hoped this story might stay quiet a little longer.

'Cal, how's it going?

'David, I've got nothing for you right now.'

Driscoll put his head on one side. The rain was bouncing off his bald head, but he didn't appear to notice. 'Come off it, Cal. I know you're the man in the 'body on the island' story.'

Cal sighed. 'That one didn't take long to get out.'

David shrugged. 'You know how it is. I have sources.'

'Well, then you better speak to them. You know this is out of our jurisdiction.'

David smiled. He had a wide friendly mouth and intense eyes that gave the impression that you were the most important thing in his life. A definite asset for a reporter. Cal felt Roslyn shifting uncomfortably beside him.

'I'll get on it,' she muttered, smoothing her short blonde hair as she walked inside. Driscoll gave her his best smile and Cal saw her face redden.

'Still a hit with the ladies, eh Dave?'

'I do my best,' he held his hands out. 'Come on, Cal. Give me something.'

Cal shook his head, and took a step past him.

'I know all about the two abducted women.'

Cal turned. 'So speak to them. What do you want me for?'

'Tell me about the suspect, the security guard.'

'Dave, you know the ropes by now.'

'Come on, Cal. The rest of the story's out there.'

'Yeah? Well, so's the murderer.'

'So it is true.'

Cal sighed. He should have known better. 'Listen, Dave-'

'I can help,' Dave interrupted. 'Give me all his details, his photo. We'll help you find him.'

'He could be dangerous,' Cal said in a quiet voice. 'We're hoping to apprehend him quick and clean.'

'Dangerous?'

Cal walked on, keeping his head down.

'Cal?'

He looked back. David was giving him his best kicked puppy look.

'This bloke, Mike. He doesn't appear to have a past.'

Cal felt a stab of something, some unnamed emotion. Driscoll was right and wrong, all at once. Mike had a hell of a past, one that he had almost managed to erase. Cal recognised the emotion as pity. No one had stood up for Mike, and it didn't look as though anyone ever would.

'You might want to check army records,' he said.

David's eyebrows rose an inch. His grin grew wider, and he licked his lips.

'It's a big army. Lots of different regiments.'

'I believe some of them wear red berets,' Cal said before the door closed behind him.

Cal's first stop was the coffee machine. Rob was already there, looking angry.

'What's up?' Cal asked.

'You took the file away. Jarvis told me to work on the missing person thing, and now I hear you've already gone and interviewed one of the parents.'

Cal looked at him. 'They found the body on the island. It's officially a murder now. You know what the chief said.'

'And you took the junior, that Roslyn girl. What's going on, Cal?'

'I don't know what you're on about,' Cal said, looking down to pick up his coffee. He knew perfectly well, but it was better to let Rob rant for a while, get it off his chest.

'You could have called, I'd have come with you.'

'At six in the morning?'

'Cal-'

Rob looked hurt now, and Cal felt a stab of regret. He liked his partner. He didn't want to hurt him.

'Chill, Rob. The lass asked to go. She's on our team, and she's ambitious. Where's the harm? If you'd been here, chances are we'd have gone together.'

But Rob wasn't listening. 'Just because I've had a bit of trouble the last couple of months, there's no need to freeze me out. I don't know, taking some wet behind the ears DC who doesn't know shit. We go back a long way, Cal, don't forget. I've helped you out times, and now you're being an arse.'

A blossom of anger burst in Cal's stomach.

'Yeah, right, Rob. I'm being an arse. Hell, if you feel that way, why don't you go see the chief and ask for another partner.'

The shock hit Rob like lightning.

'And Roslyn's good. Don't forget, it was you brought her into the case. She's keen and hard working, the way you used to be.'

And smart, Cal added mentally. 'Ah, sod it.'

He walked quickly back to the office, leaving Rob alone in the corridor. Hell, he thought, maybe it'll be good for him, shake him up a bit. His phone rang, and he recognised Cramond's Glasgow drawl.

'Is that DS Fisher?'

'Hello, Cramond. What have you got?'

A pause. 'A nice big yacht, is what. Anchored off of Clashnessie bay.'

Cal wrote in his book.

Cramond sighed. 'But it's not that easy.'

'Why not?'

'Most bays are too shallow for the yacht to sail into, so these folk had a rubber inflatable thing. They'd park the boat in the bay and take the wee boat in to shore.'

Cal knew where this was going.

'And there's no sign of the rubber boat.'

'Not a jot.'

'He could be anywhere.'

'Aye.'

Cal sighed. 'Well, it's not as if we weren't expecting it.'

'Any news your end?'

Cal thought about Jessie Noone.

'I'm pretty sure I know who the dead girl is. I'm sending something up for your forensics people, see if they can get a match.'

'Who is she?'

'Our man's sister.'

Cramond said nothing for a long minute.

'I've been a copper thirty years,' he said. 'And this is the weirdest bloody case I've ever come across.'

Cal chuckled. 'You and me both, Cramond.'

'I suppose you know the story's broken up here? We've got details of the murder all over the papers.'

'Have you released the photograph?'

'Not yet.'

Cal chewed on that. There was only one reason why not. Cramond was trying to keep it quiet.

'Not such good news for your tourist season, is it?'

'Don't be a smart arse, Fisher. It's got nothing to do with that.'

Cal said nothing.

'Look, we've got hikers and climbers all over the mountains. The last thing I want is some gung ho idiot spotting the bastard and having a go.'

'He won't go anywhere near other people, I can promise you.'

'I'm not taking chances. Listen, we've got coppers out asking questions, search teams with heat-seeking helicopters. Wherever he is, he can't hide forever.'

Cal hesitated. He wasn't so sure.

'Listen, keep me informed, yeah?'

'Aye, all right.'

Cal hung up the phone and glanced at the clock, dialled again.

Tess answered on the first ring.

'Hello Cal.'

Amazing how warm her voice made him feel. He smiled.

'Hi Tess. I've got some free time, how about that lunch?'

'All right.'

He arranged to meet her at the Red Cow. It was a bit out of town, but close to where she lived, and he knew the food was good. He left the station past the usual smokers, most of them complaining about the warmth of the day. On the drive he called the nursing home and spoke to Matron Annie, who told him his mother was fine today, playing whist with three old gentlemen and flirting with them outrageously. Annie had an infectious laugh, and as he hung up Cal realised he hadn't felt this good in a long while.

He got to the pub first and ordered a half of bitter, glancing at the menu specials on the blackboard.

'Hi.'

He turned. Tess was wearing a black 'v' necked T shirt with the Nike swoosh on the left breast. She had on pale blue jeans and tan ankle boots. Her hands were in the pockets of her jeans. She didn't have a bag.

And she had cut her hair. It fell to her jawline like a dark shining wing. Cal felt himself staring and blinked.

'Hi, Tess, what'll you have to drink?'

He ordered her white wine, unable to do anything about his pounding heart, the dryness of his mouth. They ordered food and sat at a table looking out to the garden.

'So, what's been happening?' she asked, resting her forearms on the table.

Cal hadn't meant to tell her, but now he couldn't stop. He told her about Jessie, about Mike's sister, about the boat. Tess watched him through it all, saying nothing until he was finished.

'So no one knows where he is?'

'He could be anywhere.'

'Like I said, he might just take off, live off the land. Has anyone checked the island? He might have gone back.'

Cal shook his head. 'I think the island's spoiled for him now.'

'Really? Why?'

He hesitated. 'It was his special place. Somewhere he was happy and felt safe, where he was the one in control. Last time he was there, you were the one in control.'

She smiled, but it looked sad. 'I'm sorry to have ruined it for him.'

'Not as if you had a choice.'

The food arrived. A baguette for him, steak and kidney pie for Tess. She tucked into it hungrily and Cal grinned. She caught him and chuckled.

'I've done nothing but eat since I got back.'

'But you must need it.'

She shook her head. 'Something Mike once told me. He said you should always eat when you can, because you never know how long it'll be until you get to eat again.'

Cal felt a shiver at her words. Again he felt a pang of sadness for the man, and had to remind himself that he was a murderer. The afternoon sun slanted in through the conservatory roof and lit up Tess's hair.

'You've cut your hair,' he blurted out.

She nodded. 'Wasn't much choice. The rest of it was a mess. Mike never left me a comb.'

He knew she had cut it herself, he could see the uneven edges. It's beautiful, he thought, but didn't say.

'So, what're you doing the rest of the day?'

She shrugged. 'Going into town. I need to think about work, there's the mortgage to pay.'

'What will you do?'

She smiled, looking at him. 'I might join the police.'

Another wild jolt in his chest. How was she doing this to him?

'Are you serious?'

She laughed. 'No, I'm joking. I'm not smart enough to be a detective.'

He frowned. 'Don't put yourself down. Of course you are. I said the other day-'

She shook her head to stop him. 'I don't know yet what I'll do.'

She looked past him, out to the garden, and he knew she wasn't looking at anything at all. Tess realised she had drifted off and looked back at him, smiling in apology.

'I'll think of something. Anyway-'

She stood up, and he scrambled to his feet.

'Thanks for lunch. I know you shouldn't be telling me things about Mike, but I appreciate it.'

'After what he did to you, I think you have a right to know.'

She smiled, and it turned into a sigh. 'You know, he did me a favour, in a way. Being on the island has made me stronger. I was pretty pathetic before.'

Cal couldn't think of anything to say. He just looked at her.

Outside in the pub garden, two small boys were wrestling on the grass. The fight got out of hand, as they always do, and one of them let out a shriek and started to wail. The moment broken, Tess raised an eyebrow and chuckled.

'I better go.'

'Tess-'

He hesitated. She looked at him, her calm eyes curious.

'How about dinner, some night? Would you like to, maybe?'

Damn! He thought.

She laughed softly. 'Sure, Cal. Whenever. Give us a ring.'

He followed her out of the pub into the heat of the afternoon, which was still not quite as warm as the emotions flooding his heart.

THIRTY SIX

A week later, Tess stood by the clock tower, arms folded and drumming her fingers against her bicep. A few feet away, an embarrassed looking teenager in a pair of brand new jeans scanned the Saturday crowds, head bowed, ready to walk away fast if he was stood up. Tess glanced at him, wishing she was the one being stood up, but alas no, as she spotted Sheila coming towards her, dressed immaculately as usual in a pair of cream slacks and a burnt orange blouse. Big sunglasses hid her eyes, but her mouth was split in a wide smile.

'Hello darling. How are you?'

Tess endured the stifling hug. 'Fine, mother. Where do you want to go?'

Sheila let out a breath and looked around her as if it was the first time she'd been here. 'Well, let's go to the Shires, hmm?'

Tess didn't reply, but started walking across the precinct towards the shopping centre. The teenager watched them go with bleak eyes.

'There's a lot of new shops opened on the second floor,' Sheila continued. 'Let's take a look. You could do with a new wardrobe.'

'Gee, thanks.'

'Oh, you know what I mean.' Sheila waved a hand in the air. Tess dug her fingers into the pockets of her jeans, sighing. She knew all right.

She followed her mother into an expensive looking shop, waiting patiently as Sheila browsed through rows of smart jackets. Tess thumbed listlessly through a rack of lacy pastel tops, not liking any of them.

Somewhere in the back of her head was the unwelcome thought that four months ago she would probably have bought one.

'What do you think?'

She turned to see Sheila holding a peach linen jacket in front of her.

'Very nice.'

'What about the colour?'

'It suits you. Goes with your hair.'

Sheila smiled. 'I'll try the trousers on.'

Tess left her to it, wandering through the store. She perked up at the jeans section, but these jeans were all designer made, with bits of embroidery or lace, or strategically placed rips and tears. A young girl came out of the changing room wearing a pair that managed to show off most of her candy pink knickers. Tess supposed that was the whole point.

Turning away, she spotted a normal jeans shop across the mall, and was about to go over when Sheila called her name.

'Voila!'

The suit did look nice, though it clashed horribly with her mother's blouse. Tess said all the right things and Sheila took the garments to the till. Tess was horrified at the cost, but said nothing, not wanting to provoke another argument.

'I'll just wander over to the jeans shop,' she said as Sheila's credit card was taken.

'Oh, Tess, not more jeans.'

Tess hurried away from the lecture. Two workmen were replacing the glass in the window, and one of them winked at her as she walked past. She smiled absently, and quickly scouted out a pair of jeans before mother could come over and cause the usual scene.

'Don't you want to try them?' the assistant asked.

Tess shook her head. 'They'll be fine.'

She looked round, and the assistant mistook her glance.

'Someone put the window in last night.'

'Oh,' Tess said, remembering the broken glass at her old shop in the Sunningdale centre.

'Kids, I suppose?'

The girl shrugged. 'Dunno.'

She took Tess's money and rang it up as Sheila came breezing in, ignoring the workmen.

'What have you been buying in here?'

Tess raised an eyebrow, looking deliberately round the store at the wall-to-wall denim. The assistant hid a grin.

'Come on, mum.'

Tess walked out of the store, and one of the glass fitters whistled at her. Sheila bristled.

'You know that's very rude.'

The man laughed. 'It's not meant to be, love. Just appreciative.'

'Come *on*, mother,'

'Why don't you just get on with your job.'

The other workman made an *oo* sound and put his hands on his hips. 'That's us told, eh?'

A furious Sheila stormed out. 'With any luck they'll fall through their own glass.'

'Can't do it, love,' the man shouted. 'It's toughened. Just like yourself!'

Tess felt her lips twisting in a disloyal grin and quickly looked down to hide it.

'People today have no courtesy whatsoever!' Sheila hissed. Tess looked round, anxious to change the subject.

'Let's go into the shoe shop.'

While Sheila poked about among the high heels and court shoes, Tess found a pair of fleece lined walking boots, which she eased her sore feet into. The sensation of the soft wool against her aching toes was wonderful, and she almost closed her eyes in pleasure.

'Oh, Tess, you're *not* buying those! They look like work boots.'

'They're incredibly comfortable.'

'There are lots of comfortable shoes that have a bit of style about them. They're awful.'

'I like them,' Tess said, keeping her voice calm, although her heart was thudding.

'No, Tess, come on.'

She turned to go, and Tess reached down and undid the laces, pulling on her old trainers again, and feeling the painful pressure return to her soles. She hesitated for a moment, then took the boots up to the till. The shop assistant smiled and took her bank card.

'Tess, what are you doing?'

'Buying some boots.'

'I told you not to.'

The shop assistant, who looked all of seventeen, glanced from Tess to Sheila, and back to Tess, who nodded pleasantly at her. Then she turned to Sheila calmly.

'The days of you telling me what to do are over.'

Sheila's mouth made a little round 'o', and her eyes widened as if she had been slapped. Tess turned back to enter her pin number, surprised to find that her hands were not shaking. She ignored the worried face of the shop girl, as she felt the volcano of her mother's rage boiling up behind her.

'Thanks a lot,' she said, smiling at the girl as she took her purchase.

As they walked out of the store, Sheila grasped Tess's arm urgently.

'Don't you ever, *ever* talk to me that way again, my girl.'

Tess pulled her arm away so hard that Sheila took an involuntary step forward and almost fell. Tess made no effort to help her.

'I'll talk to you however I please,' she said. 'You have no right to be rude to me, or try and control my life.'

Tess moved closer, so that their faces were very close, close enough for her to see the sudden fright in Sheila's eyes. A surge of adrenalin roared through her.

'I'm not a child, so quit telling me what to do. I'm not taking it any more. If you can't accept this, tell me now. Otherwise, change the damned record.'

Tess saw the tears starting in her mother's eyes and blinked. What on earth was she doing, talking to her mum like that, hurting her? In a moment of clarity she saw that apart from their blood connection, the two of them had nothing in common whatsoever. She felt a deep tug of sadness.

'It's nearly twelve,' she said. 'I'm meeting dad for lunch at half past. Do you want to come along?'

Sheila looked like she'd just learned she had ninety minutes to live, and the doctor should have told her an hour ago. Her eyes flickered from Tess's to the ground and back again, her perfectly lipsticked lips quivering.

'Come on,' Tess said. She wanted to take Sheila's arm, but thought that would just upset her more. Together they walked out of the mall into the afternoon sunlight. Neither spoke, and Tess felt emotions grumbling around inside her, anger, guilt, resentment, sadness. They walked into the Silver Street diner, and there was Roy, already waiting for her. His big smile froze as he saw his ex-wife, but Tess went up to him and hugged him quickly.

'Hi dad.'

'Hello darlin''

Tess took Sheila's hand. 'Do you mind if mum joins us?'

'Uh, no, of course not, uh, hello Sheila, will you sit down?'

The three of them sat, and Tess smiled. 'Let's have some wine. I've never had a drink with both of you together.'

Sheila seemed to have recovered a little. She picked up the menu and began to scan it, keeping her face blank while Tess glanced round the place. It was clean and bright, fresh flowers on the table and the smell of warm bread and garlic in the air.

'Good choice, dad,' she said. Roy smiled, but she could see he was pained. She felt a tug of disquiet for bringing mother, but hey, it was turning into one of those days. She reached over and squeezed his hand, smiling at him until at last he grinned back.

Tess looked up as the waiter arrived.

'A bottle of Chardonnay to start with, please,' she said. 'That's your favourite, mum, isn't it?'

Sheila stared at her as if she had grown another head. Tess laughed.

'Guess what,' Roy said, unable to hide his news despite the setback.

'What, tell me?'

'I've bought a car.'

'Really? What sort?'

'Oh, it's just an old Ford. It's all I can manage right now, what with the cost of insurance.'

Tess nodded. 'That's great, isn't it, mum?'

Sheila was staring at Roy with a sneer already forming on her lips, and Tess could almost taste her derision.

'ISN'T IT,' she said, in a voice loud enough to quieten the café.

Sheila started, looked at Tess, and dropped her eyes.

'Yes, I suppose it is.'

'Good. Now, what shall we have to eat? I wonder if they have any mussels.'

Roy raised his eyebrows. 'But love, I thought you didn't like shellfish?'

Tess laughed again.

'Things have changed, dad. Things have changed.'

THIRTY SEVEN

The path switched back for a long way up the mountain, making it a fairly easy, if slow climb. However Mike had abandoned the track in favour of a scramble up the scree-covered northern face. The mountain felt alive under his feet as he climbed, the stones shifting as he put his weight on them, threatening to start rolling and send him tumbling down a thousand feet. But he had climbed scree before, and knew what he was doing.

Sweat trickled down the side of his face as he concentrated, placing his feet carefully, distributing his weight. It was just another few feet to the summit, but a sudden rush could be deadly. He eased forward and tested a nearby boulder for stability. It was solid, and he pulled himself up, feeling firm ground beneath his feet again.

Mike looked around. The summit was a rough plateau, with a cairn of rocks at the far end. Mica in the surrounding rocks gleamed like crystal, and far below the loch was a perfect summer blue. He breathed hard, feeling his heart slowing, the sweat drying on his skin. It felt good. Very good. He unloaded his pack and sat on the boulder, taking off his beanie hat and letting the cold wind dry the sweat in his hair.

This truly was a wild place, miles from any road. According to his map, the only way in was along a track seven miles long, and he thought few people would relish the journey here and back combined with a hard climb.

But he was wrong. He sat very still as he heard the voices approaching, gloom settling over him. He took deep breaths, staying calm. Just a few walkers to deal with, nothing too stressful. The first one came over the edge, a young man, laughing. The second walker was older, leaning heavily on his ski poles, and looking very tired. They didn't notice him, and headed for the cairn where they stood with their backs to him and looked around at the view.

Mike wondered if he could sneak away without them noticing him, but didn't relish climbing back down the way he had come. He eased his pack back on, and got tentatively to his feet, heading swiftly for the edge of the track. He was almost there when he heard the shout.

'Hey, hello there. We didn't see you.'

Obviously, he thought. He was tempted to ignore them and walk on, but it would look strange. All climbers shared a camaraderie, and his rudeness would be remarked on and remembered.

Mike turned slowly.

'What a view, eh?' the man grinned, holding his arms out. He was no more than twenty, fresh faced, black curly hair escaping from his wool hat, wearing a scarlet North Face jacket and good boots. Expensive clothes, and Mike took him for a serious walker, despite his youth. He fixed a smile on his face and nodded as the older man approached. The resemblance between the two was obvious, they were father and son.

'Hi,' said dad. It looked about all that he could manage. His face was blotchy, sweating, angry red cheeks below a pasty forehead. He was still breathing hard, and holding a shaking hand up to his chest. Mike felt a warning knell as he saw the man suddenly wince.

A red bolt of panic started to beat in his chest. He couldn't get involved here. It was time to go. He turned and took a step down the path.

That's right! At last, you're learning!

Mike hesitated, the tic jumping in his cheek, his fists clenched. Abruptly he turned around. The two men were looking curiously at him.

He walked quickly back.

'I think you should sit down,' he said. He put a hand on the older man's shoulder and pushed him gently on to a boulder. He shrugged off his pack and retrieved his water bottle. The man took it gratefully.

'Hey, dad, I've got water here-'

'Sip it slowly,' Mike said, looking into the man's eyes and seeing the beginning of panic there.

'What's wrong?'

Mike glanced up at the young man, then looked back at the father.

He was remembering Ronnie Tipp, his old sergeant. They had been close to one of the bitter Irish parades, both soldiers depressed by the violently chanted songs, the angry drumming, the twisted faces as the marchers strode down the streets of their enemies. And then doors were opening, men were running, and falling, bloodied, in the road. The drums and whistles were abandoned or transformed into weapons. The banners lay like forgotten plans. The police moved in, and Ronnie caught Mike's eye. Mike knew the drill by now: *don't get involved.*

Only this time, the fighters looked up and saw the soldiers, and Mike saw the hatred on their faces. He clutched his gun, ready to use it as a bludgeon, when Ronnie nudged him.

'Let's go.'

They turned and moved away, avoiding the confrontation, but a group of a dozen men followed them, and soon they were running, the men behind them roaring, furious. Mike was not worried. There would be a patrol round the next bend, barriers to stop the violence, if not the anger. Ronnie roared at the soldiers, who quickly opened the barricade to let them through. The furious men stood and screamed abuse at them, but Mike no longer heard. He was looking at the sarge's pasty face, beads of sweat popping out on his forehead. Ronnie was pulling in air as if it were treacle.

'Sarge, you all right?'

'No I'm fucking not.' Ronnie sat down right there in the street, staring straight ahead, his arm closed across his chest, fist clenched. He was trying to get his breathing under control.

'Get a medic.'

Mike looked up and saw Billy, told him to hurry. The sergeant seemed to have taken himself away, somewhere deep inside himself, where he could concentrate on the problem. Mike said nothing, just watched and waited, hoping Ronnie was going to be all right. It took fifteen minutes before the medic arrived. The doctor knelt down, took one look at Ronnie and barked orders for an ambulance.

'You'll make it, Tipp,' the doctor said. 'Tough old bastard, aren't you?'

Mike saw the sarge's blue lips quiver. 'Fuck off, doc,' he said.

The sergeant had had a heart attack, but staying calm and focussing on his breathing had saved him. That and being bloody minded, Mike guessed. Now he was seeing the same symptoms in this man. He held the man's eyes.

'Breathe steadily.'

The man nodded. 'I –'

'Don't speak. Stay quiet, just breathe.'

'What's wrong dad?' the young man's voice was now filled with fear. 'What's wrong with him?'

'Stay calm,' Mike ordered. 'His heart's not too good, but he'll be fine if he just stays quiet and breathes. Won't you?'

The man gave an uncertain nod.

'What's your name?'

'Adam Guild. This is my dad, George.'

'Well, Adam, have you a phone?'

'Yes.' He pulled out a small handset.

'Call for help.'

Mike sighed. What was he doing? He couldn't wait for the authorities to turn up and find him. He should just leave now. But the man was sick, and likely to panic. If Mike left, he might die.

So what? came the little voice inside.

It's not as if you haven't done it before.

The tic jumped in his cheek.

'Phone 999. Do it now. Give them the grid ref. Can you do that?'

'What? Of course.'

Mike looked round. There was enough room for a helicopter to land here. He looked at George again. His lips were turning blue.

'Just keep breathing steadily,' he said, keeping his voice calm and listening to the phone conversation. It would be all right. He would hear the chopper coming, and then he could leave before it landed. No problem. And next time, he'd pick a mountain to climb that had no paths up it at all.

'They're coming,' he said.

Adam knelt next to his dad.

'I thought he'd be fine,' he said. 'He said he wanted to come, although it's a hard trek.'

Mike said nothing. George was looking at his son with a deep sadness in his eyes. Mike thought it was the sadness of wanting to be part of the young man's life, and knowing that he no longer could.

Mike looked away, trying to quash the bitter taste in his mouth, the cold knowledge that this was a sadness he would never experience.

George reached out a hand and clasped Mike's arm. In the older man's eyes, Mike saw something he faintly recognised: gratitude, approval. Unfamiliar emotions filled him, and he swallowed. His heart felt full, and he stood up, unsteady. He heard the unmistakable low rumbling sound of the chopper approaching, and crouched down again.

'The helicopter's coming, I hear it. You'll be fine now.'

He stood up and pulled on his pack.

'Wait, where are you going?' Adam grabbed his arm. Mike just looked at him.

'Why are you leaving? Please, I want to thank you. You may have just saved my dad's life.'

'He saved himself,' Mike said. 'I have to go.'

He turned and hurried off down the path as the sound of the helicopter became very loud. Mike didn't use the switchbacks, but scrambled down through the rocks and gorse, dropping a thousand feet in no more than a few minutes. By the time the paramedics got to George Guild, Mike was nowhere to be seen.

*

Cal was working on an armed robbery in a Morrison's supermarket when Roslyn came up to his desk. He was getting nowhere with the robbery, and suspected it might be an inside job.

'Sir? I've got something on the Dole case.'

'Show me,' he said, pushing the file to one side to look at later.

Roslyn took the seat opposite Cal and pulled out a folder.

'I've been on to the GRO and got a birth certificate for Michael Noone.'

She pushed it across the table and Cal picked it up.

'GRO? What the hell's that?'

'General Register Office. You put in your details and they send you what you ask for.'

Cal read: Michael Noone, born Bermondsey 1973, father unknown. Mike had been born on the 12th of February. He glanced up. Roslyn had another certificate in her hand.

'I searched for other births in the area around the same time and came up with this one.'

Cal read across the page: Michael Aloysius Dole, born Bermondsey 12th April 1971. Parents Vincent Alan Dole and Bernadette Dole. Vincent's job was listed as a bricklayer. Cal remembered the details from Mike's army records.

He looked at the date again. The stolen birth certificate would have made Mike 18 in 1989, old enough to join the army. He glanced up. Roslyn had that look in her eye again, the glint that he recognised now.

'What else have you found?'

She grinned, and pushed forward another certificate. This one was a different colour, and the writing across the top referred to an entry in the register of deaths. Cal had expected this. Little Michael Aloysius had died on the 23rd April 1971, cause of death pneumonia. He was two weeks old. Cal smiled.

'I checked out the family,' Roslyn continued. 'The mother died in 2000, the father's inside for armed robbery. There were two surviving children, Brendan and Philip. Philip died in a gang fight in 1990. Brendan still lives in Bermondsey. He's clean.'

Cal sat back.

'Philip was into fraud in a big way, forged and stolen documents, small time robbery. He was 23 when he died.'

'What about the other brother?'

'Brendan? He's 37 now. Makes him one of Mike Noone's contemporaries.'

They shared a quiet smile. 'So our Mike asks his pal Brendan if his big brother can find him a new ID, and lo and behold, Brendan had one in his house all the time, his own brother.'

Roslyn nodded. 'Do you want to speak to Brendan?'

Cal laughed. 'What do you think?'

She pushed her file across the table. Cal glanced at all the details she had uncovered.

'How did you get hold of all this stuff so fast?'

Roslyn had a smug smile on her face. 'I spent some time last year tracing my family tree, and got to know one of the people at the records office. He was only too happy to help with a police enquiry.'

Cal grinned. 'Nice one. What did you do with the hair?'

'Sent it up to Glasgow. They promised to let me know once they've compared it to the evidence from the bones.'

'Good,' he said, standing up. 'But I think we both know what they'll find. I'm going to take a trip down to London-'

He stood up again and headed for the door, trying not to compare DC Roslyn to poor Rob, who was going to be really pissed off when he head that Cal had gone to London again, and still not taken him along.

*

Major James Peters sat at his desk, the open newspaper in front of him. Marian Warren had clearly enjoyed her fifteen minutes of fame. The two women had been back for over two weeks now, and he had thought the story would have disappeared. But no, Marian had things to say, and was determined to say them.

He sighed, looking out at the rain, imagining Mike hiding somewhere, alone, as he had always been. Peters had hoped that Mike's past wouldn't be dragged into the open, but it was too late for that now.

The fact that he had been a soldier was out there, and it was only a matter of time before they found out his regiment. That was why when the *Mercury* reporter had called him that morning, he had agreed to speak to him. The army called it damage limitation, but it was not only that. There was no one in Mike's corner. The man deserved better, no matter what he had done.

He turned the page, away from the Warren woman's simpering smile. The other woman, Tess, she had stood up, refused to speak to the papers. He knew from their brief meeting that she was the strong one, not this Marian, despite what she might claim. If not for Tess, Marian would still be up there on Toilichte, struggling to survive.

He flicked absently through the tabloid, still thinking about Mike, when another photograph caught his eye. It was a picture of two men, obviously father and son, both grinning. The father was in a hospital gown, but holding ski poles. Curious, James looked at the headline:

SHY HERO SAVES CLIMBER

A 57-year-old man today owes his life to a mystery climber after suffering a heart attack on a Scottish mountaintop.

George Guild collapsed at the summit of Suilven, a mountain in the Assynt region of the North-West Highlands yesterday, but is recovering in hospital thanks to a quick-thinking stranger.

George and his son Adam had trekked seven miles before undertaking the 700-metre climb, but once the summit was reached Mr Guild got into difficulties. An unidentified mountaineer recognised his symptoms immediately and insisted Adam call 999, before disappearing.

Mr Guild was transported to Inverness Royal Infirmary by rescue teams where his condition was stabilised but, according to hospital staff, it was thanks to the stranger's actions that he survived.

'The paramedics got to him just in time,' Dr Angus Flynn told the paper. 'He is a very lucky man.'

'I'd like to meet him again,' Mr Guild said. 'I want to thank him. He saved my life.'

Adam Guild added: 'The man told my dad not to panic. He seemed to know exactly what to do. He was very calm and controlled. I've no doubt that it's thanks to him that I still have my dad.'

If anyone knows the identity of the mystery Samaritan, please contact the Newsdesk.

James looked up. He could feel his heart racing, and he smiled to himself. How ironic it was that the story of Mike rescuing the climber should be in the same edition as Marian telling her sorry tale.

And it *was* Mike, he could feel it. He felt a sense of hope lift him. Despite everything, Mike had risked being found in order to help someone. He got up and called to his adjutant to find him a map of Scotland, then lifted the phone to make the arrangements. The police were hunting for Mike, but if he was in the wild, they wouldn't find him.

No one would, unless they knew him, and even then, it would be damn hard.

But there was no one else who could do it. He would have to do it himself.

THIRTY EIGHT

Tess sat on the floor of her bedroom, looking out at the stars. They were faint and brittle, and looked what they were: a million miles away. Nothing like the way they looked on Toilichte, or Tolly, as she had taken to calling the island. No, up there, the stars were bright enough to give the moon some serious competition, and they pulsed with energy and possibility.

She laced her fingers together behind her head, leaning back on her bed. Somewhere in the estate, a dog barked and a car door slammed, and the sound of traffic on the A47 was never far away.

She found she missed the silence most of all. Ironic really, as she had spent some days talking aloud to herself just to hear a voice. Of course the island had never really been silent. The sea was ever present in all its moods, the wind piped and moaned, and the cries of the sea birds had always provided company of a sort. Back here, there was no silence to be had at all, not even now, in the small hours of the night. There was always something, the inevitable noise of thousands of people crammed together in the same small area.

And there were many nights when she lay awake and listened. *Many* nights.

Tess was aware that the changes that had happened to her had taken place deep inside, so far inside that her conscious brain seemed to have no way of knowing what was going to come next. She searched hard for the girl that had been content in this poky box of a house, that had enjoyed selling cheap ornaments, that had dreamed foolish, romantic dreams of love and adventure. She thought about her parents, and Cal Fisher, and, of course, Mike.

She wiggled her bare toes, ignoring the itching as the wounds slowly healed. Mike. He had made her what she was, and she wondered what would happen when they met. She knew it was only a matter of time.

Would he see her as a strong woman now, and be repulsed by her?

Would he hate her for destroying the safety of his island? Would he want revenge? More to the point, did she?

She sighed. Maybe she should go and look for him. See how *he* was doing looking after himself. Maybe she could join him.

She chuckled to herself. No, she wouldn't join him, but she could live like him. Right now, Tess felt there were few things she couldn't do. When she analysed this, she put it down not to arrogance, but to the simple truth she had learned: that people were capable of far more than they believed they were. She rubbed her sore heels on the soft pink carpet, searching among the stars for constellations she could recognise. But they were too faint.

I don't belong here, she thought.

She had wandered round the city for days, trying to think of what she should do, what job she might take now, where she was going, and the only thing she was certain of was that it couldn't be here.

But if not here, where?

She glanced at her bedside cabinet, at the books she had bought, the wildlife guides, the maps.

This house must have some equity in it now. She could sell it and leave, head north, see where her legs carried her. Maybe she could get jobs here and there to fund her travels. And she still had some savings.

Let's face it, up till three months ago, she had never gone anywhere or done anything that needed a lot of money. She lived from day to boring day, paid the mortgage and the bills, and left her money waiting for a rainy day.

Well, sod that, she thought. It rained all the time. It was time to get wet.

*

Mike camped in the forest. It was an old wood, like the one on the island, birch and beech and hawthorn, rowan and hazel. Under the leaf canopy, his camp was barely visible, blending into the dark shades of green and grey. Since the incident on Suilven, he was keeping a low profile, but it had been almost a week, and he had not seen a human since.

Anyway, he had thought hard about it. It was unlikely they would think of him as the man on the hill. They would be expecting him to hide away, not climb mountains.

He leaned forward, stirring the can. The soup was made from the remains of a brace of wood pigeons with some herbs and wild garlic, and the delicious smell filled the twilit glade. He could hear the faint rustling of animals, the wind in the high branches, the gentle crackling of the fire, his own breathing. The soft sounds were peaceful and comforting. He was happy.

What bullshit!

The tic jumped in his neck, and he took a sharp breath.

'Leave me alone.'

The voice was slipping through more often all the time. He had tried ignoring it, but that just seemed to make it more insistent. It was still just a voice, and he was in control, but he had the feeling that it was getting stronger all the time, and it scared him.

What was he to do?

Go back and get rid of the woman. It's the only way.

'I said leave me alone.'

She can take all this away from you. Don't you want to be happy?

'I am happy.'

But for how long? They'll find the body. They'll work it out. They'll come for you.

'They won't find me.'

They will. And then what? They'll send you to therapy. Counselling. They'll make you talk. Make you remember.

He shivered.

You have to go back, get rid of her.

'She will have told them everything. It's too late to think like that. It's time to move on.'

You're scared, is that it?

Yes, he thought, yes I am. Scared of what happens to me sometimes, scared of losing control, of going down paths where there is no turning back, and the only thing waiting for me at the end is the cliff edge.

He pulled the twig holding his billy can off the cross branch and lowered it to the ground. He was no longer hungry, but he ate the soup anyway, then cleaned up and banked the fire for the night, leaning back against an old birch tree and closing his eyes.

Sleep was elusive, the forest noises now and then interspersed with frantic dreams of flashlights and radios coming through the trees. As light began to filter through the branches, he got up and packed his bag, broke up the remains of the fire and soaked it. When he was satisfied the fire was dead, he raked fallen leaves over the camp site and walked away, leaving nothing to show that anyone had spent the night there at all.

The days grew steadily warmer, but a squall of rain came in and stayed around, making the ground even boggier than usual, and the going hard. Each night Mike sat by his fire and decided where to go the next day. He had no need to be anywhere, no deadlines, no purpose, and so he made plans for himself. One day it would be a twenty mile hike to a certain spot, another it would be a trip to a lonely inland loch to fish. The land was spectacular, each mountain subtly different, each forest its own little world. His days were full and satisfying. Only the nights were bad, when the voice would remind him that all this could be gone soon, and urged him on to unspeakable violence.

But Mike was still in charge, and he soon found that the tireder he made himself during the day, the easier it was for him to drift into sleep undisturbed. And so his days grew ever tougher, and his body grew leaner and fitter. Now and then he would see people; walkers, or men fishing in little boats, but they never saw him, and he would drift gently into the landscape and disappear. The Suilven Samaritan never surfaced to take his accolade.

And so it might have continued indefinitely, if it hadn't been for the major.

THIRTY NINE

Cal called the number Roslyn had found for Brendan Dole. Dole worked in a factory, and Cal was prepared for the personnel officer to have to find the man on the shop floor, but he was surprised.

'HR, Dole speaking. How can I help?'

'Uh, Is this Brendan Dole?'

'It is.'

The voice was steady and confident. Cal smiled wryly. So much for his preconceptions.

'Mr Dole, I'm DS Fisher of Leicestershire constabulary. I'm investigating a case in which I believe you might be able to help me with information. Would you be willing to meet with me to discuss it?'

'Mr Fisher? What's this about? I haven't done anything-'

'It's not about you, Mr Dole. You're not a suspect.'

Dole sighed. 'I've never even been to Leicester.'

Cal chuckled. 'I can meet you this afternoon, if it's convenient?'

'Convenient?' Dole said, his voice lightening. 'So I don't have to speak to you?'

'Not if you don't want to. But it would really help me.'

'I don't see how. I don't keep company with bad lads, and I-'

'This is something from a few years ago,' Cal said hurriedly, afraid of losing the impetus. There was a long pause.

'Is this about my brother?'

Cal bit his lip. 'Indirectly. Mr Dole, I'm not trying to make trouble for you or your family. I'm just trying to piece a story together. Will you help me?'

Another long pause. Cal held his breath.

'Well. All right. Where will you be?'

'You name the time and place and I'll be there.'

Dole gave him the name of a pub in Shepherds Bush and Cal snapped the phone shut and started the engine. Another trip down to London, the car probably knew the way by itself now. He rolled onto the ring road and took the M1 turn. He should have told the boss where he was going, but he didn't want to stop and lose impetus. The phone rang again as he pulled into the outside lane.

'Fisher.'

'Cal, please don't hang up.'

Cal stepped hard on the brake, although there was no one in front of him. The car behind him screeched. He pulled into the middle lane and the car swept past, horn blaring.

'Cal?'

'What is it, Lynne?'

'I just want to talk to you.'

He sighed. 'What's the point?'

But all the same, the sound of her voice had brought back the familiar ache, happy memories that he knew were only fragments of what had not been a happy time.

'I'd like to meet you, just to talk.'

He stared out at the traffic, ignoring his thumping heart. This was a bad idea, opening old wounds, and yet he wanted to see her, he hadn't known how much until she had said it.

'Please?'

'I don't think so, Lynne.'

There was a long silence, and Cal felt his resolve crumbling. He was about to speak when she did.

'I see. You've found someone else.'

He thought of Tess. Comparing the two women was wrong, but he couldn't help it. Lynne was tall and blonde and had been full of laughter until the secrets had begun to eat her heart. Tess was dark and quiet and tough. No comparison.

'We *are* divorced,' he said heavily. 'Did you expect me to sit around the rest of my life moping?'

'No, of course not. I'm happy for you, really. I just wanted to explain things.'

'You already did.'

He bit his lip. It was a lie. The truth had come out, but he had never allowed her to explain. He had been too busy casting bitter recriminations. And what was there to explain anyway? She'd lied. If she had told the truth in the beginning, things might have been different, but not after three years of marriage.

It's not as if it was a tiny white lie, either.

'I'm sorry, Lynne.'

He clicked off the phone before he could change his mind. He tried to put the conversation in a box, one he could open later when he had time. Why was she contacting him now? He had to think about it. But not now.

Traffic was heavy as he took the North Circular. Cal was sure Dole had arranged to meet somewhere well away from his patch to avoid being seen with a copper, but he didn't care. He found a space to park in a street backing on to Queen's Park Rangers football ground, and walked round to the sad looking green.

The pub was on the corner, described as a 'sports bar', which at the moment meant it had a big TV showing American football to the three old age pensioners who were the only customers. Cal had a pint of

Ruddles and sat down at a scarred wooden table. Dole arrived ten minutes later, a tall, broad shouldered man with prematurely greying hair and sharp green eyes. He spotted Cal and nodded to him, ordering a whisky and soda and carrying it over.

'You'll be Detective Fisher.'

'Thanks for coming, Mr Dole.'

'So what's this about?'

Dole was busy taking off his coat and pushing his chair into the table, so Cal thought about how to play things and decided to get him off guard.

'Your brother Michael.'

Dole's eyes opened wide. '*My* brother? I don't have a brother called Michael.'

'You did.'

Dole sipped his whisky carefully.

'My brother was called Philip, and he was killed years ago.'

Cal nodded. 'I know. But before he died he was into all sorts, wasn't he? Petty theft, stolen documents, fraud, forgeries. Clever young man, I hear.'

Dole kept his face carefully blank, but Cal could see the fear in the green eyes. He held out his hands.

'I said on the phone. I'm not here to make trouble for you. I'm trying to find out what happened to someone your brother helped before he died.'

Dole looked into the depths of his whisky, swirling the amber fluid around. He thought for a long moment.

'This is off the record, right?'

'If you like. But Brendan, you know you haven't done anything wrong, and I have a feeling anything you tell me will be helping your old friend, not hurting him.'

Brendan looked round quickly. The lunchtime rush was over, and it was too early for the evening drinkers. Apart from the pensioners nursing halves of bitter, they had the place to themselves.

'How did you find out about him? What's he done?'

Cal rolled his glass between his palms. He was going to have to offer something up front.

'He left the army a troubled man. He got angry with his girlfriend and tried to hurt her, only she turned the tables on him.'

'Jesus!' Dole said, sitting back. He tossed the drink down his throat. 'What is it with women?'

Cal said nothing, but motioned to the barman for another whisky. While he got up to pay for it, he watched the expressions change on Dole's face, from anger to regret to sadness.

Here.'

'Thanks. There's stuff you're not telling me.'

'You probably know I can't. He's gone to ground and I need to find him. Believe me, though, I'm trying to help him. I feel sorry for him.'

'So do I, mate.'

'When did you last see him?'

'See him?' Dole's eyebrows rose incredulously. 'Twenty two years ago, when I was sixteen, that's when.'

'Not since then?'

He shook his head. 'It's not as if we could keep in touch.'

Cal sipped his bitter.

'Brendan, why don't you tell me the whole story?'

Brendan looked up at him, and Cal saw the anger flash there for a moment, but it quickly passed.

'Have you met Mike's mother?'

'Yes.'

'Well, then, you'll have a flavour of it. What it was like for him.

Where we all lived on the council estate, it was a big community, lots of Irish Catholics. Jessie made no secret of how she made her money, and it was well known that some of the so-called pillars of the church used her services. She was universally despised, and so was Mike by association.

He was a quiet, clever lad, kind of ordinary looking. He adored his baby sister, was always looking out for her, buying her things with money he stole from Jessie. And he was a good mate. Always helped me when I got stuck with maths or whatever, and once he piled in on my side when the local scumbags were beating me up for my dinner money.'

He gazed at the grubby window.

'So school was torture?' Cal prompted.

Brendan shrugged. 'Things weren't so bad when we were young, but as he got older, the taunts began to hit home. The big lads slagged him something rotten, asking if he was pimping for his mum yet, and how much she charged for his friends, things like that. But if any of them said a word against Sandy, that was it, he'd go nuts. He was as brave as a lion, he'd pile in no matter the odds.' He shook his head.

'What changed?'

Brendan looked up, his strange eyes dark. 'Sandy. She grew up. Mike did all he could to protect her, but he couldn't be there all of the time. Jessie was determined to make her daughter just like her dear old ma, and she succeeded. Mike was devastated. Said it was his job to protect her, and he couldn't. Sandy wouldn't let him.'

'You mean she was on the game too?'

222

Brendan nodded, not meeting his eyes. 'She was two years younger than us. It was tearing him up.'

Cal felt another stab hit him in the chest.

'Jessie was into everything: pills, booze, drugs. I reckon she knew she was losing her looks and needed Sandy to take over to keep the cash coming in. Anyway it all came to a head one night. Mike came round my house and we went out for a walk. He was in a state, shaking, sweating, near to tears. Eventually he told me Sandy had told him to leave her alone, she could take care of herself. It didn't strike me as anything new at the time, but for some reason it had messed him up badly. He wanted Phil to get him new papers so he could get away.'

Brendan finished the whisky and shouted to the barman for another. Cal noticed his hands were shaking. When the new drink was poured and paid for, Brendan ran a hand through his iron grey hair.

'I didn't want to get involved. Phil was into some really bad stuff. One of the local gangs had gotten organised and were stealing passports and driving licenses to pass to him. I don't know who he was selling to, but he always had wads of cash. I was afraid for myself as well as Mike.

Then Mike pulled out a bag. He'd stolen all sorts from Jessie, drugs, money, all sorts.' The hand ran through the hair again. 'He said he couldn't go back now. He had no choice. I had to help him. And he told me things – Jesus-'

He raised the glass to his lips, closing his eyes.

'Things that Jessie had done to him,' his voice was no more than a whisper. 'The reason he had tried so hard to protect his sister. He begged me to help him, so I did.'

Cal swallowed. 'He didn't need Phil to help him at all.'

'No. I went home and got our poor little Michael's papers and gave them to him. I made him keep the stolen stuff, what was I going to do with it? When my mam eventually found the papers had gone, she blamed Phil for it, not me. I never saw Mike again, though he sent me a postcard once, from Germany. 'Thanks', it said. Nothing else.'

Brendan finished the whisky and wiped his mouth. His eyes looked tired, as though he had spent the day with a huge burden, which probably wasn't too far from the truth. Cal motioned the barman and bought him another one.

'This was 1989,' Cal said softly.

Brendan nodded. 'May. I remember. We'd had a little memorial for Michael two weeks before. That's how I knew where to find his birth certificate. Mike passed for 18 easily. Anyone looking in his eyes would think he was 40. And he didn't even have to change his name.'

Brendan stared into the bottom of the glass, his face pinched and pale.

223

Cal nodded. That explained why Mike had not joined the army on his apparent 18th birthday. He didn't have Dole's papers until a month later. He reached over and quickly squeezed Brendan's arm.

'Thanks for telling me this, Brendan. I know it wasn't easy, and for what it's worth, I think you did the right thing.'

Brendan looked up, hope in his eyes which quickly began to fade.

'A copper, telling me I did something right? There's a first.' He chuckled, and Cal joined in.

'What happens now?'

Cal sighed. 'I have to find Mike. He needs help. People have been letting him down all his life, people he tried to help. If it comes to it, will you speak for him?'

'If it keeps him out of jail? Of course I will.'

Cal stood up and shook Dole's hand. 'Thanks again,' he said.

He headed out into the afternoon light and walked down Uxbridge Road to his car, his head full of conflicting emotions. Mike had let that woman die, but wasn't what had been done to him far worse? He had meant what he said to Brendan. His mother, sister, friends, the army, even the Albanian woman refugee. He had tried to help and they had all let him down. He should just leave the poor man up in the wilderness to live in peace, if that's what he wanted. No one deserved what Mike had been through.

But he had let the woman die. And Tess and Marian could have died too. They told Mike they could look after themselves and it drove him crazy.

Mike had a long life to live, full of other people who had no idea the devastating power those few words had over him. Cal couldn't leave him alone, the man was a smouldering fuse.

FORTY

James Peters drove his 4x4 south from Lochinver, along a road that shadowed the coast. In places, the narrow single track road was chiselled out of the granite hillside, winding precariously, with only a tiny stone wall to prevent a fatal drop into the sea. There was nowhere here to hide a vehicle, or a boat.

He pulled over into a passing place to let a car behind him pass, noticing absently that it had German number plates. Tourist season was well under way, despite the wet weather. On the other side of a wide bay the road turned inland, and he stopped in a passing place to check the map. In another mile the road would climb into the mountains. Although this was close to the mountain Mike had climbed, James had no feel for the area. He knew he was going the wrong way.

He turned at Inverkirkaig car park, hesitating. This was where the Guilds had parked before heading out to climb Suilven. But there was no point taking this road, Mike would be far from here now. James headed back the way he had come.

He took the north road towards Stoer point, and here the land was flatter and empty, with just a few isolated houses dotted around the bleak landscape. He checked the map again. This place looked more hopeful.

There was a tourist viewpoint up ahead, and after that the road rose into the hills. Past the village of Drumbeg, a spit of land extended into Eddrachillis Bay, and here he pulled into another passing place and got out.

Through his binoculars he could see the land falling away sharply to the sea, but he was more interested in a small lochan far below, with a faint vehicle track nearby. He waited until a string of cars went past on the road, then drove on slowly. He almost missed the top of the track altogether, and was too late to turn in. He had to drive on to the next passing place, where he parked the car illegally and walked back.

He had to admire Mike's perfect logic. The track was barely visible, just over a hump and in a place where the road took a sharp rise and twist at the same time. Anyone driving would have to change down a gear and turn the car hard. They wouldn't notice anything out of the side window, hell, he had almost missed it, and he'd been looking for it.

He crossed to the other side of the road and looked back, but Mike had done his work here as well. The black and white sharp turn marker had been ripped out of its mounting and pulled outward at an angle that shielded the track from view. It was a brilliant piece of subterfuge, and James felt a strange swell of pride. As a soldier, the man was a genius.

He crossed back and jogged down the track, which wound for a kilometer or so down to the loch. The ground here was boggy, and much of the track under water, but he could still make out faint tyre tracks. He tracked them back to a gate leading upwards, where there were several footprints in the mud. He knew none of these belonged to Mike. When he had reached the mainland, it had been dry for a long period. He would have left no trace.

Peters stopped and turned a full circle. He was certain this was where Mike had come ashore, and that this was his starting point. He hurried back up to the road, where he found another car parked in front of his, and a man peering in his window.

'Hello?'

'Ye canna park here. There's signs everywhere.'

James put on an apologetic face. 'I'm sorry.'

The old man's lips made a thin line. 'Aye well.' He spotted James's binoculars.

'Is it the sea eagles you're after? You'll see them better down near Oldany.'

'Really? Thanks, I'll try there.'

He got into the car, watching the old man limp back to his ancient Land Rover, muttering. James couldn't hear what he was saying, but was willing to bet it was something along the lines of 'Bloody Tourists.'

All right, so he was in Mike's footsteps now, or tyre treads, rather. Where would he go? He knew Mike would abandon the car, but thought he might also try and place it somewhere he could go back to, if he had to. Mike was a careful man.

He rejoined the main road, and travelled south. Up here, there were few roads, and Mike would want to avoid all of them. That meant heading inland. He reached Ledmore junction, and stopped the car in a parking spot.

Again he got out and turned 360 degrees. *Think like Mike*, he told himself. To the west, the mountains of Canisp and Suilven rose out of the broken, loch-filled landscape of Coigach. The Inverpolly estate was no more than twenty kilometres across, a stunningly beautiful place, enclosed by roads, and this time of year, full of tourists. To the east lay Ben More Assynt, a favourite of climbers.

South lay Glen Oykel and the hills of Rappach, none of them very famous or challenging, and from there to the south and east the hills of Easter Ross were vast and lonely.

And that's where James would have gone, if he had to. He got back in the car and took the Lairg road. By this time, Mike would have been driving for an hour at least. He would not know how far the authorities were behind him, and be anxious to find a place to drop off the car. James drove slowly. The landscape here was softer, farmland and woods, the shimmering river Oykel shadowing the road. He looked up at the surrounding hills, and saw a phone mast.

He stopped the car. That was it. How often did those things get checked? And probably by different workers all the time. A car parked there would be put down to tourists.

Bloody tourists. He grinned, crawling along the road until he found the track to the mast. A gate was closed across it, but not locked. James opened it and drove through, closing it behind him, then bumping up the rutted path to the top. Sure enough, there was another car there, and he got out and walked over to it. He looked at the tyres, saw they had the same treads he had seen near Eddrachillis. The interior was clean and sparse, no personal belongings in sight. It was locked.

He knew this was Mike's car. He could feel it.

Now was the hard part. He knew Mike had been on Suilven, which had to be more than ten miles from here, but that distance was nothing to a man like Mike. James knew that up here, Mike was a man without purpose, but that he would give himself direction. James's job was to second guess him, find his camp sites, work out his routine.

It would not be easy, but he had to do it. The consequences of his failure were worse than a simple case of bad press for the army. Mike's very life might depend on it.

FORTY ONE

Lake Pastures looked very different in the rain. With all the cheery garden chairs and tables put away and the striped awnings rolled back, the big garden was just a bare patch of green. There was no one about, and the closed in building looked like what it was: an institution. Cal jogged through the rain to the front door and pressed the bell. The door was always locked, and Cal was never sure if that was to keep intruders out or the inmates in. Maybe both. A buzzer sounded and he pushed the door. One of the staff was waiting for him.

'Why, Sergeant Fisher. We didn't expect you today, what with the weather.'

Cal looked at the woman and felt anger rushing up inside his chest. Did she think he wouldn't bother to come out in the rain to visit his mother? What if it rained on the day of her funeral, did she think he'd just stay home?

'Is something wrong?'

'No,' he said. 'Excuse me.'

He hurried along the empty corridor. As ever, it smelt of the distinctive air freshener they used. He had no idea what flower it was supposed to represent, if any. It was cloying and sweet and stronger than usual today, probably because all the windows were closed. Cal congratulated himself on being such a great detective as he knocked on his mother's door. He didn't expect an answer, and none came, so he opened it gently and looked in.

'Mum?'

She was sitting up on her bed, watching TV, and she turned quickly to look at him.

'Who are you? What are you doing here?'

Her voice got higher as she spoke, and she fumbled for the cable with the red alarm button on it.

'Easy, mum. It's me, Calum, your son.'

He was getting used to this now, but it still hurt. She looked at him, her blue eyes filled with fear and confusion. He pulled a chair out from the wall and sat on it.

'What are you watching?'

She glanced back at the TV. '*Murder, She Wrote,*' she said. 'That man there is Jessica's nephew. They think he killed his girlfriend. You know, Jessica has such a lot of nieces and nephews.'

'Does she?' Cal asked gently. 'Does she have any children?'

'Of course not. She's not married. Don't you watch it?'

Cal shook his head. When would he ever get to see daytime TV?

Maggie looked back at the screen, and Cal looked at her. She was very pale, her skin not much darker than her white hair. Her jaw was still square, her chin jutting forward to take on the world. Only the skin around it had slackened. The bone was still strong. In truth, physically Maggie was as strong as an ox. Mentally, however-

'I wish she'd get herself a man. She's not bad looking for an old woman, and there must be some likely men in America.'

Cal took another look at Angela Lansbury. His mother had about twenty years on her.

'What is it you want, anyway?'

Cal looked down to hide his smile.

'I just came to see you, maybe have a chat?'

'Why do you want to talk to me? What have I done to deserve this?'

Cal held his hands out. 'You're my mum.'

Her forehead wrinkled in a frown.

'I am not! I have a son, you know. He's a policeman. If you don't tell the truth, I'll have him arrest you.'

Cal said nothing, and Maggie turned back to the TV again. The credits were rolling.

'Now see what you've done. I've missed the end.'

'I'm sorry.'

She looked at Cal again, and he saw something change behind the blue eyes. She blinked and looked back at the screen.

'About time you came to see me.'

Cal hid a sigh.

'How have you been keeping, mum?'

'Fine. Not that you care. How many weeks has it been since you've been here, six?'

'Mum, I was here yesterday.'

'Don't you tell lies, boy!'

Cal met her eyes. 'Is everything all right here? Are you happy?'

She made a huffing sound and folded her arms. 'Too bad if I'm not. There's nothing I can do about it.'

'Mum, if you don't like it, we'll find somewhere else.'

Another huffing noise. She turned and stared at the TV.

'Mum?'

Maggie ignored him, watching the start of some cheap quiz show.

'Mum, talk to me.'

But she wouldn't turn around, and he could see that her eyes were brimming. Cal stood up and leaned awkwardly across the bed. He put his arms round her and squeezed gently.

'I love you, mum.'

For an instant, she laid her head on his shoulder and sighed. Then she sat up straight and shrugged him away.

'What are you doing here? You're an important man. Get back and catch some criminals.'

'Yes, mum.'

'I like this show. That young man has a nice smile.'

Cal turned to go.

'I'll see you tomorrow.'

But Maggie was engrossed in the TV, and didn't move as he slowly closed the door. He walked slowly along the hot, smelly corridor, feeling as if he'd had his heart put through a wringer. Outside it was still raining, and he was looking forward to the touch of it.

'Hello, sergeant. How are you?'

He looked round. The red headed matron was smiling at him. He just wanted to leave, but something in the woman's smile made him hesitate. He smiled back.

'Maggie told me you wouldn't come today. She said you were too busy. You know, she watches the news with the other residents, and anytime there's a report of some crime being solved, you get the credit.'

Cal chuckled.

'She does love you, very much.'

Cal felt something hot touching the back of his eyes. He looked away.

'Thanks, Annie,' he said. 'I'll see you tomorrow.'

He pressed the button to release the door and stepped out into the rain.

FORTY TWO

It was a new little Italian restaurant, quiet, but not empty. It was done out in a rustic style, bare floorboards and bright primary coloured walls hung with pictures of flowers. The kitchen area was open, so the customers could watch the chefs at work. Cal had been anxious that Tess might not like Italian, but she seemed perfectly happy.

'I hope they do big portions,' she said, resting her forearms on the table. 'I'm starving.'

Cal grinned. 'Let's order some garlic bread to start with.'

It had been almost a week since he had asked her out, and he had been afraid she wouldn't come, but here she was, wearing black jeans and a black v neck T shirt under a teal coloured shirt. The teal brought out the grey in her eyes. She was beautiful. Cal was wearing charcoal chinos and a cream cotton shirt woven in a tiny waffle pattern. He had bought the shirt specially.

'So what's been happening?' Tess brought him back to earth.

'Uh, well, not a lot.' He had thought long and hard about whether to tell her about Brendan Dole, and decided against it. He wanted tonight to be about the two of them. He didn't want Mike Dole butting in.

'You haven't found Mike, though I see it's all over the papers. Have you found out any more about his past?'

Well, so much for that theory, he thought.

'I've found out who he really is,' he said.

'Who he really is? What do you mean?'

And so he told her. He told it all, everything except the horrors Brendan couldn't bring himself to voice. Tess's face grew sadder as he talked.

'They're still hunting for him?' she asked. Cal nodded.

'He's in the wilderness. Cal, we should just leave him there. He deserves some peace.'

Cal sighed.

'We can't leave him up there, Tess. He murdered one woman, he tried to kill you.'

'He didn't. He just left me to fend for myself.'

'It amounts to the same thing.'

Tess pursed her lips in annoyance, and Cal felt his heart drop like a lead weight.

'What will happen to him?' She said

Cal thought about it. The truth was, the evidence against Dole was largely circumstantial.

Even if the dead woman was his sister, there was nothing to prove he took her to the island and left her there, which took the charge down to kidnapping. In any case, Cal was certain a psychologist would rule Mike unfit to stand trial.

'I really don't know,' he said.

'I won't press charges.'

He smiled, and after a few seconds she did too. Their pasta came and Tess ordered another bottle of wine. Cal had not even realised that they had drunk the first.

'This is great.'

Cal nodded, his mouth full of fettuccine. She laughed.

'My mother won't eat stringy pasta,' she said, holding up a forkful of spaghetti. 'She thinks it's undignified.'

'She's right.'

'I don't care.'

Cal sipped his wine. He didn't want Tess knowing what he knew about her mother. He wondered if Tess knew it herself.

'How's your mum?' She said.

'Oh, she's up and down. Physically, she's in great shape.'

Tess put her head on one side. 'Makes it harder, I bet.'

He nodded.

'She was such a strong person.'

'What about your dad?'

'He died when I was a kid.'

'I'm sorry. It must have been hard, growing up.'

Cal smiled. 'Mum was something else. All the local kids lived in fear of her. I think it's because of her that I joined the cops.'

Tess leaned forward, and Cal noticed that most of her food was gone.

'Did she want you to?'

'It's not as simple as that. I think the way I was brought up put me down that road. I remember one Saturday I was kicking a football about and I broke the window of next door's shed. All the family were out, and I could have got away Scot free, but I was eaten up with guilt, and ended up telling mum.'

Tess sipped her wine, watching him. Having her eyes on him felt good.

'She made me promise to go next door and apologise for what I'd done, and tell Mr Stein I'd pay for the window out of my pocket money. Well, I was terrified.'

'This Stein was a terror, I take it?'

Cal nodded. 'He had a vegetable patch, and I once saw his own son, Paul, riding his bike around it. He'd destroyed all the brussel sprouts, and old Stein slapped him so hard Paul fell off his bike. The family didn't come home till late that evening, way past my bedtime, and I lay awake all night thinking of that slap.'

He shivered, then laughed. 'Even now, it gives me the creeps.'

'So what happened?'

He took a deep breath. 'I went round in the morning and Stein opened the door, looking grim. My heart was pounding. I told him I had accidentally broken his shed window, and I'd pay for it with my pocket money. Then I waited for the hammer to fall. Stein raised his hand and I shut my eyes-'

He could still remember the feel of the gravel path beneath his feet, the smell of Stein's tobacco stained fingers.

'What did he do? Tell me?'

Cal let out a laugh. 'He put his hand on my shoulder and said, come on, Cal, let's go and see the damage.'

Tess laughed. 'So he was a softy really.'

Cal held out his hands. 'We went to the shed and he rooted about inside and came out with a pane of glass. Here, he said. This ought to do the job. If you'll help me fix the window, we'll call it quits.'

Tess sat back, grinning. A waitress arrived to take their empty plates and leave dessert menus. Tess continued looking at him, and Cal felt quite wonderful.

'We got the window repaired and he sent me home,' he continued. 'Mum stood up when I came in, and I must have looked a bit strange, because she came over to me and took me by the shoulders. When I told her what had happened, she sat down and folded her arms. Well, Calum, she said. And what have you learned today?'

He laughed softly at the memory.

'I told her I'd learned how to repair a window, and she laughed and laughed. Then she made me apple crumble for tea, which was my most favourite thing.'

'It pays to be honest,' Tess said.

Cal shrugged. 'It taught me that you have to take responsibility for your actions.'

Tess nodded. 'Do you think that's why the man, Mr Stein, came down hard on his son?'

Cal finished his wine.

'I thought about that for ages. I mean, I could understand if he didn't want to hit me, after all, mother would have gone ballistic, but I expected at least a tongue lashing.'

'But you apologised.'

'Yes. Paul was caught in the act, and even though he saw his dad coming, he carried on riding around. And, you know, I've seen that happen with criminals. They can't help themselves. They see the man coming with the big strap, but they just keep on chewing up the vegetables.'

Tess threw back her head and laughed. She clutched at her stomach and looked at him with delight in her eyes.

'Sergeant Fisher, you are quite the philosopher,' she gasped, still giggling.

And Cal felt as if his heart was getting bigger and bigger and in a few seconds would be too big for his chest and it would simply burst. This beautiful woman was laughing at his dumb story and looking at him as if he was the funniest man alive.

'It's good to hear you laughing,' he whispered.

Tess's smile stayed put. 'I haven't laughed too much in my life until now. I intend to do a lot more of it in future.'

'I'd like to help you with that.'

A shadow crossed her face. 'Cal-' she said.

He felt a moment of panic. 'What is it?'

The waitress arrived and hovered. They both looked at her.

'Would you like to order dessert?'

Cal reluctantly picked up the menu, watching Tess do the same.

Then she looked up at him, her grin restored. He looked down at the menu and saw that the first option was apple crumble. He laughed, and Tess laughed, and everything was all right again.

After the bill was paid, they walked out into the street. The rain had stopped, and the city roads were shiny and reflective. Passing cars swished through the puddles. They walked up through the empty market place to the old Corn Exchange, where Tess hesitated, glancing up at the statue outside.

'Who's that meant to be?' she asked.

'The Duke of Rutland,' Cal said. He chuckled. 'They say the statue's meant to portray him being drunk.'

Tess laughed. 'How appropriate then, having him outside the pub.'

Cal nodded, smiling. The city was full of little quirks like that. It was part of what he loved about it. He realised Tess was looking at him.

'Where do you live?' she asked.

'Westbridge Wharf.'

He looked round, getting his bearings. Tess lived a good way out of town. 'I think there's a taxi rank down by the Haymarket.'

'Really? You know, we could walk to the canal in ten minutes.'

Then he looked at her. She was watching him with a lopsided smile, her eyes bright with amusement. Cal re-ran the last few sentences. His heart began to beat faster.

'Um, would you like to-'

He stopped, unable to think of something that wasn't a cliché. Tess laughed, linking her arm in his.

'Let's go,' she said. Cal felt a grin coming to his lips that he couldn't erase. As they walked up past the Shires shopping centre to the edge of town, Cal could still not believe his luck.

You know, your mother told me you were a timid little thing.'

She chuckled. 'I was. You have no idea. I never wanted to do anything, go anywhere. I'd never been out of Leicester! I was worried about what people thought of me, whether they liked me or not. I was scared of insects and being ill and lightning and-' she sighed. 'Life in general, I suppose.'

They skirted the remains of a kebab left lying on the kerb. The pungent smell of chilli sauce followed them down the road.

'But you're nothing like that,' Cal said.

'Not now. I changed. The island changed me.'

Cal felt her hand squeeze his arm, and a delicious jolt of electricity shot through him. 'How? Do you know?'

She sighed, and paused, and her footsteps slowed.

'I killed a rabbit. I didn't want to, didn't actually mean to, not really, but there it was. I killed it, and then I had to cut it up and eat it, and after that-'

Another convulsive squeeze of his arm.

'I wasn't the same.'

Cal had never killed anything bigger that a wasp. He thought about how it must have felt. And he remembered all the soft toys on Tess's bed. How hard must that have been. His admiration for her slid up a notch.

'You survived,' he said. 'You did what you had to.'

She nodded. 'I discovered something. We can do all sorts of things we believe are impossible. Amazing things. We just talk ourselves out of them. There's stuff inside all of us, stuff we don't even know is there.'

She looked at him, and he felt a chill run through him. What is there inside me? He thought. Abruptly she smiled.

'I'm glad, really. I was pathetic. My mother was ashamed of me. I had no friends, no real life. Just Mike, and I was scared of him too.'

'But you had the strength to let him down.'

'Let him down,' she repeated. 'Yes, that's just what I did, isn't it.'

Cal's heart sank. Why were they talking about bloody Mike Dole again. He was like a ghost on their shoulder. They walked past the Jewry wall, downhill to the building overlooking the Grand Union Canal where Cal lived. Tess looked up.

'The cops must pay you well to afford a flat here.'

He shrugged. 'I bought it before the property boom.' Right after the divorce, he thought bitterly. Funny how that still hurt, after all this time.

He entered the security code and they took the lift to the top floor.

He felt a momentary flutter of panic, wondering about the state of his flat. After all, he had never dreamed he'd be bringing Tess back here tonight. But then he remembered that it was Thursday, the day Mrs Thomas came and cleaned for him. Relieved, he opened the door and Tess walked in.

'Well, you have a great view,' she said, walking to the window. Cal chuckled. It was a great view of houses and factories, not what you'd call spectacular. Tess found the edge of the glass door and pulled it. The smell of the night air came in, a mix of rain, petrol, and the swampy odour of the dark water below.

'Shame about the canal,' Cal said. Tess chuckled.

'Did you know that no other UK city is farther from the sea than poor old Leicester?'

Cal knew that, but didn't let on.

'I miss the sea,' she said, her voice wistful.

Cal remembered something he had read long ago. That if you look into the abyss, the abyss looks back. He wondered what Tess had seen.

He wondered if there was any hope for him.

Tess turned round and, smiling, put her hands on his chest. Cal felt his heart hammering, and wondered if she could feel it.

'You have to promise me something,' she said.

'Anything,' he agreed readily, his mouth suddenly dry.

'You are not allowed to follow me, steal my keys, or become obsessive. You are also not allowed to sulk. And, you can't sneak off before I wake up in the morning.'

Cal hesitated. Mike again. Tess spotted it, and seemed to understand, and she grabbed his shirt and pulled herself up close to his face. Cal reached down and kissed her, closing his eyes and letting his fingers push through her thick hair. The fetid smell of the canal water wafted up on the breeze and he hooked a leg round the door and slammed it. Her hands were on his back, the heat of them intense. Cal lifted her up, an idea that just came to him before he could think it through. He wasn't that strong.

But Tess didn't appear to weigh much, or was it just the adrenalin flooding his blood? He stopped thinking about it as he reached the bedroom and collapsed on the mattress.

Tess giggled, and he found himself laughing too, as she fumbled off his clothes and ran her fingers over his chest. He knew he had a packet of condoms in the bedside cabinet, and wondered how to broach that subject. He also wondered if she would notice him blowing the dust off them.

But in the end, everything seemed to go ahead pretty smoothly, without incident, so to speak, except that somewhere in the middle of it, while the primitive emotions had hold of him, he thought about Lynne.

Tess sensed the sudden change and pulled him close, and the unwelcome thought shattered like glass.

He woke up to find Tess's face close to him, watching him. She smiled.

'You look sweet when you're asleep.'

'Sweet?'

She grinned. 'Don't worry, I won't tell the other cops.'

'I should think not. How am I going to arrest the bad guys with that moniker, Sweet DS Fisher?'

She touched his face gently, making him shiver.

'What happened that the ladies missed you?'

The shiver turned cold. 'I'm divorced,' he said.

She inclined her head. 'What happened?'

'Uh, it just didn't work out.'

He could see from her eyes that she didn't believe him, but she didn't press it.

'Well, it's her loss,' she said, lying back. Cal looked at her lithe body and felt himself harden again. She looked at him.

'Would you ever leave Leicester?'

He shrugged. 'I've never thought about it.'

'You love being a policeman, don't you?'

He nodded.

Tess sighed. 'Cal, I have no idea what I'm going to do, but I know one thing. I can't stay here.'

The temperature in the room seemed to drop. Cal's hard-on disappeared.

'Why not?'

She sat up. The curtains were still open, and she looked out at the sky.

'There's nothing for me here.'

'I'm here.'

She took his hand, smiling. 'I'm not what you want. I'd only disappoint you.'

Cal frowned. 'What? Why do you think that?'

She looked at him, but didn't speak. His pulse began to race again.

'I keep thinking of my dad. Mother got what she wanted, but dad, he didn't. He got nothing.'

Cal remembered Sheila's story. Her job, her career ambitions, Roy's domestic ones. A dull ache started in his chest as he realised that he and Roy were not so different. And Tess, did this mean she didn't want a home, a family? Was she right about him?

'Tess-'

'Shh,' she said, lying back and putting her hands on his chest. 'No more talk.'

She reached down and gently took hold of him, and he responded gallantly, even though deep inside, something was sadly fading away.

FORTY THREE

Major Peters pulled his pack off and let it slide to the ground before sitting heavily on a fallen trunk. The trees here were mainly coniferous, and the heavy canopy made the forest floor very dark, although it did give some protection from the near constant rain.

He pulled off his hat and scratched at his short hair. It had been almost a week now, and still no sign of Mike. He had come across places where someone had camped, someone careful. All that he could find were traces of ash and slivers of burnt wood, but he felt certain that was Mike's work. Who else would be so considerate and cautious.

He wondered if he could be wrong. He had convinced himself that this was where Dole would come, this empty, wild place, where few people ever ventured. Now he was beginning to doubt himself.

That morning he had climbed a hill and witnessed a police search over at Elphin. He watched them gathering in a lay-by for their briefings before setting off awkwardly up towards Cul Mor. They had absolutely no chance of finding him, it was a waste of time. Even with the heat-seeking helicopter, they were looking in the wrong place. James felt a twinge of annoyance. Why couldn't they just leave the man alone anyway? What had he done that was so wrong?

He sighed. He had left people to die, that's what. He put his hat back on and looked around. Might as well make camp for the night, it would be dark soon. He swept the ground of the sharp smelling pine needles and got a fire going, set up his tarp and bivvy bag, and broke out his rations.

The fire cast long crazy shadows on the tree barks, and he smiled to himself, thinking about how good Mike had been, not just at survival, but at training others. He had heard the squaddies talking when they came back, amazed at his knowledge, his obvious love of being out there in the wild. He was skilled at killing animals instantly, and had never let them take anything they didn't need, a compassion that James was sure Mike still felt. It was only humans that conspired against him, that forced him to do things against his true nature.

He sighed.

Maybe I should just go home.

But he couldn't abandon Mike to the cops. It was only a matter of time before the helicopters checked this area, and even with all Mike's tricks and know-how, eventually they would catch him.

He pulled out his map. Apart from the crackling of the fire, there was not a sound in the wood, and the unfolding map sounded loud. Tomorrow he would move south into Glencalvie, try his luck there. He checked the contours, working out the mileage.

'Hello, Major.'

James dropped the map into the fire, where Mike quickly grabbed it.

He stared up at the man, heart pumping hard. Where the hell had he come from? He had not heard a sound. Mike crouched before him, smiling apologetically, and putting down a small bag.

'I thought you might like something to eat other that brown biscuits.'

He smiled, and James almost laughed. Brown biscuits were a joke in the army. No one ever ate them.

'I see you've forgotten none of your training.'

Mike wore a dark brown moleskin shirt over trousers a few shades lighter, making him almost invisible in the woods. He still had an army buzz cut, and he was lean and fit, but his skin was pale, his eyes hollow and dark with shadows. The last seven years had not been good ones.

'How long have you been tracking me?'

'Two days. I wasn't sure if you were alone.'

James nodded. He reached into the little bag and pulled out what looked like pigeon meat.

'Thanks. Want a brew?'

'Yes please.'

Mike sat cross-legged on the ground, watching while James made the tea.

'Why are you here, sir?'

Of course he knew this would come. And he knew what he had to tell him. The truth.

'They're looking for you, Mike. The police.'

'I've seen them.'

'They've got a helicopter.'

Mike shrugged. 'I move around. They tend not to go back over the same places.'

James nodded. 'But one day they'll find the right place.'

Mike shrugged again.

James poured the tea into his mug and handed it over. Mike sipped the liquid carefully.

'I can't go back with you, sir.'

James had expected this too.

'Do you remember what I taught you, before you left the mob?'

Mike looked up, eyes as wary as a fawn's. 'I do, sir. It's helped me.'

'You trusted me then.'

'I still trust you.'

'I can help you.'

Mike glanced round, and the major noticed a tick jumping in his cheek.

'No one can help me,' he said in a matter-of-fact voice. He winced, as if from a sudden pain, and the tic jumped again.

'I should never have let them discharge you. You belong in the Regiment. We could have helped you there.'

Mike sighed. 'It wasn't your fault, sir. We all obey orders.'

He looked down and James saw him grit his teeth. He muttered something that sounded like 'be quiet'. His shoulders and arms were rigid and stiff, but his hands were shaking. Peters felt a cold hand grip his heart. Mike was in a far worse state than he had guessed. He ate the pigeon, saying nothing, waiting for Mike to calm down, which he did, slowly. When Mike looked up again, his shoulders had relaxed, but his eyes stayed bleak.

'Will you let me help you?'

'Sir, there's nothing you can do.'

'I won't let them put you away.'

Mike smiled. 'You have always been kind to me. I appreciate it.'

'Come back with me tomorrow.'

But Mike just looked at him for a long time.

'It's wonderful up here,' he said eventually. 'The mountains are so beautiful, the lochs so still and peaceful. And there's no one for me to hurt. I'm happy here-' the tic jumped again, and he swallowed. 'As happy as I can be.'

Peters leaned forward. 'If you let me help you, you can come back here one day, when you're feeling okay again.'

Mike chuckled softly and shook his head. James knew he was losing it.

'I could order you to come with me.'

Mike carefully laid the mug on the forest floor.

'With respect, sir, I'm not in the army now,' he said. 'You can't give me orders any more.'

He got to his feet in one fluid movement.

'You should leave tomorrow, sir.'

James stood up. 'What about you?'

'I'll take my chances.'

He turned to go, and James reached out and grasped his arm. Mike looked down at his hand as if it were an interesting insect.

'Mike, remember back in the Gulf, after the explosion? Do you remember what you said to me?'

He could feel Mike's arm start to shake. It felt as if he was being shocked.

'You said: 'I promised I'd look out for them.''

Mike closed his eyes. James could almost taste his misery.

'But you kept that promise. You did look out for them, you were lucky not to be killed yourself. There was nothing else you could have done. Mike, It wasn't your fault.'

The shaking got more violent, and Mike tried to pull away, tears slipping out of his tightly shut eyes. His whole body was rigid as steel, his breathing out of control. James felt a cold hand on his heart. His words had brought all Mike's demons to the fore. He grabbed the man by the shoulders.

'Mike, breathe, breathe slowly. Take deep breaths. Come on.'

Mike snatched a breath. He was shaking so much it felt as if he were convulsing.

'Another, come on, Mike, another deep breath.'

Mike struggled to comply. James began to talk to him quietly.

'Another deep breath, feel your heart, feel how fast it's beating. Now you know what to do. Think of the calm place. Slow it down. Take it gently. Slow down that heart.'

He watched Mike take another breath, and another, but it took a very long time before his heart slowed. Eventually Mike opened his eyes, the shaking almost under control, but his breath still laboured.

'Sorry, Mike,' he said. 'I'm an ass.'

Mike's lips curved in a smile, but it never made it to his eyes, and James had the feeling that it never could.

'Sit down. Come on, I promise I'll never talk about that again.'

Mike sat reluctantly. James sat opposite him, keeping eye contact.

'I can teach you other things,' James said. 'Other ways of keeping control.'

Mike watched him.

'You said you trusted me. I need you to trust me now. You and I will walk out of here tomorrow, just the two of us. No one else. We'll go back to the barracks and figure it out from there.'

Mike said nothing.

'I'm the only one who knows what you're up against,' he said, trying to keep the urgency out of his voice. 'Only I know what you're feeling. We're soldiers, and soldiers stick together.'

Mike looked down at his hands. The shaking had almost gone. James noticed that he had long, delicate fingers, not like soldier's hands at all.

'Will you trust me?'

Mike looked up again, and slowly nodded. 'Yes, sir,' he whispered.

FORTY FOUR

It was a six mile hike back to the main road, and Peters stopped often to check his map. Although the major was no more than five years older than him, Mike could tell that these days he spent much of his time behind a desk. He wasn't flabby, but he wasn't sharp, either.

He looked ahead. He knew the lay of the land perfectly well, and could find the radio mast without need of a map, but he let the major do the work. He probably needed it.

Mike had returned to his camp last night and lain down in his bivvy bag, but he didn't sleep. He knew that he should simply get up and leave in the night, move south into the higher mountains. Peters was an expert tracker, even out of shape as he was. And he had trained Mike. If anyone could find him, Peters could. Yet in five days, he hadn't come close. The major was a man of his word, and Mike knew he wouldn't talk about their meeting.

Trouble was, he was a man of his word too.

He sighed. Peters looked sideways at him, a wry smile on his face.

'You humouring me, soldier?'

'Sir?'

The major folded the map and put it away. 'You know exactly where you're going, don't you.'

He knew all right. Straight to hell.

He tried not to think about how the major was going to keep control of the situation once they were back at the barracks. The police would want him. Tess, and the other woman – he couldn't remember her name now – they'd want him to pay for what he had done. And they were right.

He should pay. Even if it killed him.

But the major could make the nightmares vanish. Every time they came now, it was harder and harder to pull out of the terrible spiral of pain and fear. Last night, Peters' voice had driven the demons away.

Maybe he could help him, after all. Maybe there was hope.

They skirted the edge of a dense evergreen wood, and there before them they could see the mast. Peters stopped and looked around.

'You chose a good spot,' he said.

The mast stood in a small clearing cut into the hillside above the only road in the area, which curved along the course of the fast flowing river. Both road and river were surrounded by thick evergreen woods. It was not the sort of spot to attract many tourists.

'You guessed it, though, sir.'

Peters grinned. 'Yeah, but I didn't find you. Come on, if we put our foot down, we can be back at Colchester in time for supper. It's spag bol tonight.'

Mike smiled. Mess food was never anything to rush back for. They splashed through a brook and began to climb the small hill when suddenly Mike heard voices. He dropped to the ground.

'Wha- Mike? What is –'

Mike ignored him. He crawled forward on his stomach, pulling himself up through the heather and bracken until he could see the clearing. His head began to pound as he looked at the police van, the men grouped round the two cars. Seven officers, only one of them in uniform, talking and laughing amongst themselves. The tiny spark of hope that had lived for a time in his heart sputtered and died. He turned and looked at Peters, tasting bitter bile in his mouth.

'Mike, I swear, I didn't know these people would be here. I-'

'I trusted you.' Mike shook his head. Peters' eyes looked pained, and for an instant Mike thought he might be telling the truth. But the orange lightning was in the back of his eyes. He had to keep it back, keep control.

'Please, Mike, you must believe me.'

Mike began to slide back down the hill, Peters following. The major was calling to him, but he didn't hear the words. Something black and ugly was opening inside his heart.

He could hear shouting, and knew that they were coming for him. He began to run as hard as he could over the boggy ground, the police struggling after him. He slid into the stream and hauled himself up the other side, adrenalin lending strength to his legs.

'Stop! Dole, you're under arrest, give it up!'

A hand grabbed at his back pack, trying to pull him off balance. He turned, using his momentum to fire a punch at the young policeman's cheek. The man let out a harsh gasp as the blow struck, and dropped like a stone. Behind him, another copper tried to launch himself at Mike, but he saw through the move easily, shifting his weight at the last minute. The man's arms flailed as he fell into the stream, tripping up the officer close behind him.

As they tried to extricate themselves, Mike took off running, the harsh breathing of his pursuers driving him on. They were young men in their twenties, and Mike knew they would have been picked specially for the job. They were strong and could easily outrun him. He undid the chest band of his pack in readiness. Up ahead he could see a boggy pond, and he headed for it, skirting the edge.

They were no more than five feet behind him when he stopped dead, shrugged the pack off his shoulders and threw it at the two men in front.

One of them ducked away, but the other tried to grab for the pack. Underestimating its weight, he fell backwards into the pond, flailing about in the gloopy mud. His young companion looked at Mike, grinning. He was still sporting a face full of acne, but he moved forward with a confidence beyond his years.

Mike waited until he could read the blow about to be launched at him, then took a step forward. The young man was still pulling his hand back for the punch, and Mike reached up and grabbed his right arm, forcing it upwards. The policeman had been putting so much into the blow that with the minimum of effort Mike could twist him easily and push him into the middle of the pond, where he lost his balance and fell.

Mike looked up. The two police following behind had stopped and were watching him warily. These were men his own age, experienced, and not willing to commit themselves until they knew what they were up against.

Mike relaxed. Professionals. That meant the rules were different.

'Come on, mate, give it up,' one of them said. He had very pale blue eyes in a long sad face. The eyes looked kind.

'We're not going to hurt you,' the other said. He had a dodgy looking little moustache which looked like it took a lot of caring for. His eyes were not so gentle.

Mike breathed evenly through his nose, waiting for them to make their move. Behind them, the three younger men were regrouping. The sixth man was out cold, and the seventh, the one in uniform, clearly didn't want to get it dirty.

'Bastard tried to break my arm,' Mr Acne complained, fixing him with an evil look.

'Your own stupid fault, Walters,' Kind Eyes said. 'Come on, mate. Don't do this.'

Mike looked from one to the other. The older men looked wary and careful, the younger men angry and pumped with adrenalin.

'I don't want to hurt anyone,' Mike said.

'Fine. Let's go,' Moustache said. 'No one will get hurt.'

'I can't go with you,' Mike yelled. 'Don't you understand?'

He looked again at the faces, and saw that the older mens' eyes were resigned. It was a look he recognised. They didn't want to fight, but they would, because those were their orders. He relaxed his shoulders and slid his legs wider. He put his hands by his sides, then took a deep breath and became very still.

'For fuck's sake!' A young cop yelled. 'There's five of us and only one of him. What are we waiting for?'

Kind Eyes swallowed, keeping his eyes fixed on Mike's. Then he sighed.

'Michael Dole, you are under arrest for-'

Mike's right hand came up from his side like a blur, and hit Moustache bang on the nose. He felt the bone break under his hand, and Moustache's face erupted with blood. Kind Eyes stared in amazement, and so didn't see Mike's left hand until it was too late. Mike smashed him on the edge of his jaw, and he stumbled back, arms flailing. On solid ground he might have had a chance, but not in this swamp.

As he fell, the three younger men came forward in a rush, whooping and yelling, wasting energy. Mike didn't have to think about it. He turned easily, ducking out of the first one's wild swing. He crouched, punched the man hard in the solar plexus, then came up to hit the second on the chin with the top of his head.

The man called Walters threw his arms around him, still howling, and Mike slammed his knee into the young man's groin. As he fell, the second lad recovered enough to swing a punch, but Mike saw the fear in his eyes as he realised he was the last man standing. Mike grabbed his fist as he telegraphed his punch, hooking his right leg round the lad's legs.

He fell in a heap, clutching his hand, and Mike snatched up his pack, turned and ran hard down the hill, while Peters and the uniform stood and stared.

He dove into the woods, moving as fast as he could between the thick trunks. The conifers were dense and tightly packed, and the woods were almost as dark as night. He stumbled, bumping into trees until his eyes slowly adapted to the dark. Adrenalin made him calm and focused, and the smell of turpentine was strong in his nostrils as he breathed hard.

There were angry yells behind him, but he knew he would be hard to track in the gloom. Hauling his rucksack on to his shoulders, he reached into his pocket for his compass, turning north. The sounds behind him grew fainter, but he didn't slow.

After five minutes or so, light appeared at the edge of the woods, and he slid to a halt behind a thick cypress. Breathing through his nose, he looked out at the road, at the river and woods beyond. If this had been his patrol, he would have sent soldiers down here to prevent him crossing. But the police had not thought of it, or perhaps he had surprised the only party, and they didn't have enough men. In any case, it was their problem, not his.

He eased out from behind the tree, listening hard, before sprinting across the empty road, sliding down the steep embankment and launching into the river.

The water was deeper than he expected, rising up to his chest, and so cold that it drove the air from his lungs and left him gasping. He was powerless to resist as the current forced him downstream, thumping his legs into unseen, underwater rocks. His frozen fingers worked again at the chest strap of his backpack, ready to ditch the whole pack if he got into trouble. The river was littered with boulders, and the water channelled powerfully through the gaps, tossing him like driftwood. It was beginning to look very dangerous, when at last he spotted a stream emptying into the river from the left, and the current suddenly changed as the waters mixed.

He grabbed at the nearest boulder, stopping his onward rush. There was a confusion of fallen branches near the left bank, and he pulled his tired and frozen legs beneath him, bracing them against the rock and pushing off as hard as he could. He grabbed at the dead branches, as white and hard as bone, closing his numb fingers around them. Hauling himself awkwardly over them, he staggered to his feet and dove into the gloom of the surrounding trees, where he leaned thankfully against a thick bough, breath rasping, teeth chattering.

But there was no time to rest. He checked the compass again with shaking hands, his breathing beginning to slow as he took stock of the situation. First, he had to get out of his wet clothes. Second, they would be searching for him south of the river, but it wouldn't take them long to realise he had slipped past them. They would fetch a helicopter, and he couldn't hide from that. There was no point running into the hills, he had to think of something else.

He dropped to his knees and let the pack fall to the ground, where he snapped it open and unfastened the waterproof lining. Suddenly he heard a sound, and froze.

A car. He looked up, out of the trees. It was driving slowly, but when it came into view what he saw was not a police car, but a motor home with foreign number plates. A tourist.

He smiled. That was his best, perhaps his only chance. He pulled out his map and checked the route of the river. About a half a mile ahead, it crossed under the road.

He reached inside his pack and pulled out a pair of cargo trousers and a T shirt, pulling them on quickly. He added a baseball cap with the logo of Aston Villa FC, and buried his soaked clothes in the soft leaf mulch beneath the trees.

Pulling his pack on, he winced as the wet material chilled his back. Then he pasted what he hoped was a friendly smile on his face and broke into a run, the compass in his outstretched hand like a torch in the dark.

FORTY FIVE

Cal sat down heavily, pushing his hand through his hair. Absently he noticed that there appeared to be even less of it, lately.

'He did what?'

'Tried to stop them,' Cramond said, definite amusement in his voice. 'Wanted them to let him go.'

'What happened?'

'What do you think? They ignored him.'

'But Dole got away.'

'Aye, I'm afraid so. I'll say this for him, he's smart.'

Cal leaned back, looking out of the window. It was a sunny afternoon, a warm breeze moving the grey city trees. It had never occurred to him that Peters would try and find Dole himself.

'We still don't know how he did it. The helicopter could find no trace of him. It did disturb a courting couple in Glen Oykel, though.' Cramond laughed.

'Our best guess is that he hitched a lift. He had a back pack on, and would have passed for a regular hiker.'

Cal sighed. 'Where's the major now?'

'They sent him packing.'

Cal hung up the phone and stood up. He opened the door, but hesitated, unsure what to do next. Until Cramond had rung him with yesterday's news, he had been quietly thinking about Tess, a warm feeling filling him that had now vanished.

'Hey, Cal. What's happening?'

He looked up as Rob came towards him, a sheepish look on his face.

'Not a lot, Rob.'

'You want to maybe grab a coffee?'

Cal shook his head. 'Not right now, I need to-'

What? What did he need to do? He was gripped with a dark foreboding. While Mike was hiding in the wilderness, Cal had been able to forget that he was a murderer, an unstable, wildly dangerous man with good reason to hold a grudge. Now, he had been driven out, and could be anywhere.

He remembered what Tess had told him: *I have the feeling I'll see him before you do.*

'I need to go out,' he finished eventually.

'Anything I can help with?'

Cal shook his head, heading for his car and checking his watch. Almost three. Tess was taking her driving test today. She had promised to call him afterwards, but he couldn't wait. He tore down to Welford Road test centre and pulled in behind an empty driving school car. He was about to go into the test centre when a car came round the corner and he spotted Tess at the wheel. She pulled up, and as the examiner spoke to her, Cal resisted the urge to haul the door open and pull her out. She didn't look very happy, and with a surge of shame he realised he was hoping she'd failed; he couldn't protect her if she went driving around on her own. As the examiner got out of the car, Tess waved at a man coming out of the test centre towards her. The man climbed into the car and Tess gave him a quick hug. Cal's heart sank.

Tess looked out of the window and saw him, and he saw a mixture of surprise and –something else- was it apprehension? in her eyes. He walked up to the window.

'How'd you get on?' he asked, aiming for nonchalant.

'I passed,' she said, grinning. 'Cal, this is Alan Collins, my superb instructor.'

Collins smiled. 'Hello Cal. Tess did very well.'

Cal nodded. 'Listen, sorry, Tess, but can I drive you home? Something's come up.'

A cloud crossed her face.

'That's all right, Tess, I have to drive the car back anyway, it's the rule.' Collins winked at her. 'Off you go, and well done.'

Tess followed him back to his car clutching her test papers, and Cal could sense her mood.

'What's this all about, Cal?' she said, as he unlocked the doors.

Cal hesitated. 'Mike's on the move,' he said. 'Come on, get in.'

'What do you mean, 'on the move''

'Major Peters tried to talk him home, and it backfired. They had a helicopter looking for him, and he hitched a lift to get away.'

She folded her arms. 'So what?'

Cal frowned, wishing she'd just get in the car. ''What', is that he could be anywhere. He could be here, looking for you.'

She laughed. 'I don't think so.'

'You said it yourself, you thought you'd see him before me.'

'That was before we knew about him. Come on, Cal, Mike's the master survivor. I bet he hitched to another area and he's out in the wilds again. What does he have here to come back for?'

Cal resisted the urge to say: 'you.' Tess shook her head.

'You're not going to start coddling me, are you? I've had enough of that already.'

She opened the door and climbed in, and Cal heaved an irrational sigh of relief.

'We don't know what he'll do,' he said, turning to her. He longed to take her in his arms, feel her soft hair on his cheek. Tess looked hard into his eyes, and then she smiled and took his hand, making his heart leap.

'I think you need to let us protect you, just in case.'

She laughed. 'Oh, Cal, you want to put a big policeman outside my door? Don't be silly.'

'No, I mean it.'

'Well, make sure he's good looking,' she grinned.

Cal chuckled, despite himself.

'Oh, look,' he said, 'It's great about your test, and I'm sorry to spoil it.'

She giggled, reaching up to kiss him gently. 'Don't worry, you can make it up to me. Dinner at Gibson's will do, I think.'

He smiled. The uneasy feeling was still there, but perhaps she was right. Perhaps Mike had no intention of coming back. Nevertheless, when he got back to the station, the first thing he was going to do was phone Peters and get the truth.

*

Peters looked down at the site of the battle. Three of the young constables were sitting on a rocky outcrop, their faces sullen and angry.

The two older men were crouched round the officer who had been knocked out cold. Kind Eyes had his arm around the lad's shoulders. The major sighed. Mike was right, they couldn't understand. If he'd wanted to, he could have killed them all. Easily.

DCI Morrison cast him a sidelong glance, and shouted above the jack-hammer noise of the helicopter hovering above.

'You want to tell me what that was about, back there?'

Peters gritted his teeth, but said nothing. A thin drizzle had begin to fall, making the day feel very cold.

'I could have you for obstruction,' Morrison tried.

'Obstruction?' Peters turned angrily. 'I'll give you obstruction. If you lot had not been here, Dole would be in custody now.'

Morrison raised an eyebrow. Peters tried not to swallow.

'I'm not sure I believe you, major.'

They both glanced round as a junior officer hurried up. A livid bruise was already forming under his left eye.

'Sir, the helicopter can't find him. They've swept the whole area. The pilot wants to know if he should try across the other side of the road.'

Both men looked down the hill to the road, the river; fast and swollen with the recent rain.

'What do you think, major. Could he have got across?'

Peters hesitated. Morrison didn't.

'Send them across, Jones.'

'Yes sir.'

Peters tried to keep calm, despite the angry beating of his heart. This was all his fault. 'He's long gone,' he said. 'You're too late.'

'I doubt it. He can't hide from the thermal imager. And let's face it, after that little show, the lads'll be seriously motivated to find him. *Seriously* motivated.'

Peters just looked at the man until some of his confidence waned.

'You'd be surprised at what he can do.'

'Are you thinking of helping him, major, because if you are-'

'Helping him? That's what I was trying to do! You think he'd let me help him now? He thinks I betrayed him.'

Morrison shrugged, a wry little smile on his face.

'Well, isn't that what you were going to do? You just told me he'd be in custody now if you'd had your way.'

Peters looked back down at the river, remorse and fear churning inside him. Mike was hanging on to sanity by his fingernails, and he hoped and prayed that this last betrayal hadn't finally pushed him over.

*

In his dream, the unicorn galloped in slow motion across the glade, shafts of sunlight breaking through the spring leaves to gild its white mane and tail. Its horn was the colour of pebbles under clear water, and the razor sharp tip reflected the sunlight like a mirror. He longed to reach out and touch the beast, to feel the strength of the muscles under the warm skin, the velvet softness of the muzzle, to look into the dark and all-knowing eyes.

But he couldn't move. He was rooted to the ground as surely as the surrounding trees, and even now he could feel their roots and branches curling round his limbs, encasing him in a living prison. He tried to pull away, but his muscles had gone. He was helpless, and now as he watched, the unicorn turned towards him.

His heart began to pound as he realised it was coming his way. He laughed, delighted. He would get to touch it after all. The unicorn was so beautiful, so perfect. A shaft of light turned its mane into white water. He felt the earth tremble beneath its hooves as it came towards him, saw the great head suddenly lowered, the horn pointing straight at his heart, and his laugh turned into a scream.

Mike woke, gasping, in a dark place he didn't recognise. He sat up, taking deep breaths as he looked around him, trying to hold back the panic. At last he heard the sound of water lapping at the shore, and he lay back and sighed, pulling up a sprig of heather and smelling its sweet woody scent.

The unicorn. He had not thought about it for a long time. Not since…

He sat up again. He was lying beneath the scrubby trees surrounding a little ochre beach.

The last thing he remembered was sitting in the back of an ancient camper van, listening to the couple in the front singing *Daydream Believer* along with the radio. The eye-watering scent of marijuana was strong in his nostrils, making him feel dizzy. He remembered telling them to stop the car, the bewilderment on their faces as he hurried out, the man shouting 'You're welcome!' in a sarcastic voice. He had dropped off the road into a surrounding field and started walking.

As the memory returned to him, so did a deep sense of gloom. He didn't know exactly where he was, or where he was going. Even as this thought occurred to him, he knew he needed a sense of purpose, it was the only thing keeping him sane. He pulled out the compass, listening to the gentle sound of the loch as the light slowly left the sky.

He looked round. The landscape was softer here, greener. He knew he was far south of where he had escaped from the police…

The police. The fight. Fragments of the past wafted round him like cruel ghosts: the major, telling him he would help him, then delivering him to the cops; Marian, whom he had thought was shy and innocent, but who turned out to be exactly the opposite; and the girl, Tess, who had looked after herself.

Before that, everything had been fine. He couldn't really remember what it *had* been, but he was sure it had been all right. Why had she done that to him? He didn't deserve it. A flare of anger rose inside him, and somewhere deep in his heart he sensed approval.

You were all right until you met her. She brought them back, all the nightmares, the flashbacks. The closer you tried to get to her, the more she pushed you away, until the words came out and you knew the truth; that she only wanted to hurt you.

She deceived you, made you think she was soft and good when in fact she was hard and cruel. And now she'll destroy you. She'll make them find you and rip your head apart and expose the terrible truth of your heart to the world. You can't let that happen. You have to go back and confront her.

He shook his head. Sandy was his sister. She was dead. She couldn't talk to him.

Want a bet?

'I don't know what to do.'

He stood up and walked to the water's edge. The little waves lapped round his boots. Maybe he should just walk in. In a few feet the water would be deep. He could sink below it into the darkness, and all this pain would go away.

You know what you have to do

He shook his head again, and his cheek twitched.

'I don't even know who I am,' he whispered.

It's time you found out

FORTY SIX

Tess didn't know quite when the decision had been made. It had just come to her. She had known for weeks now that she was going to have to leave, but up till now it had just been a thought in her head, without any definite timescale or plan. Now she knew.

She pulled into the outside lane of the dual carriageway, pressing her foot to the ground and feeling the little car respond. The sensation of speed, and her absolute control over it was still new and exciting. Barely a day had passed since buying the Mini that she had not driven up the M1 just for the sheer hell of it. She should have done this long ago.

Long ago.

She could no longer remember what it had been like to be little timid Tess Hardy, drifting along like a jellyfish on the tideline of life.

She pulled off the A50 towards Glenfield, the car shuddering as she hurled it round a roundabout. She smiled, and patted the steering wheel as if it were a good pet.

Mother's house was at the end of the street opposite a recreation ground. The empty swings looked sad and forlorn as she pulled into the drive, with all the kids at school. The heat of the day was oppressive as she stepped out of the car and away from the air conditioning. There had been a hosepipe ban in effect for two weeks now, but Tess was not surprised to see that Sheila's Busy Lizzies looked perfectly healthy. Tess rang the bell and waited. She could see her mother approaching through the frosted glass of the door, and she saw her hesitate before opening it.

'Hello, darling. Forgotten your key?'

Tess smiled. 'Hi mum. Hey, it's polite to knock, rather than just barge in.'

Sheila smiled back, though her eyes were wary.

'How's the car going?'

'It's great.' Tess followed her into the kitchen where Sheila put the kettle on.

Tess sat at the scrubbed kitchen table, and reached for an apple from the bowl placed dead centre. She tossed it up a couple of times.

'I'm about to give it a real run-in.'

'What do you mean?'

Tess put the apple back in the bowl. Sheila's mouth narrowed into a thin line, but she didn't say anything. Tess sat back and put her hands behind her head.

'I'm going away.'

Sheila had just picked up the two coffee mugs from the worktop. She stopped, staring at her daughter.

'Going away where?'

Tess shrugged. 'Just away. I don't really know yet.'

Sheila walked carefully to the table and put the mugs down on two coasters. Tess could sense her turmoil.

'I see,' she said at last, sitting down. 'Are you sure you've thought this through?'

Tess picked up the mug and sipped the rich coffee. She knew it was expensive stuff, but she'd still have preferred a simple cup of tea. She nodded.

'Yes, I'm sure. There's just one favour I need to ask you, if you don't mind?'

'Of course not. What is it?'

Tess looked into Sheila's eyes. They looked frightened, and Tess felt as if a stone had been dropped in her heart. She reached out and took hold of Sheila's hands.

'Don't worry, mum,' she smiled. 'I'm fine. I'm going to be fine.'

Tears appeared in her mother's eyes.

'Oh Tess,' she said, 'I've been so worried about you.'

Tess squeezed her hands. 'There's no need,' she said quietly. 'I really am all right.'

Tess looked at her mother. Try as she might, she couldn't see a single feature they shared. They might as well be strangers. Tess had always known she had not been wanted, but this woman had still cared for her. And if her childhood had been miserable at times, all she had to do was think about poor Mike's, and that put it all into perspective.

A sudden warm feeling invaded her limbs. She was going away, and it was exciting and a little scary, and she had no idea when she would see Sheila again. She squeezed her hands again.

'I love you, mum,' she said.

The tears escaped down Sheila's cheeks, collecting her mascara on the way. Tess read the look in her eyes; sadness, regret. Before Sheila could speak, Tess pulled her chair closer and a soft little laugh escaped.

'I'm going to go north first,' she said.

Sheila found a tissue in the pocket of her cardigan and wiped at her eyes.

'What little I saw of Scotland was so beautiful, I want to take my time and travel round. I've bought maps, and sort of planned a route, but I probably won't stick to it.'

Sheila's smile looked relieved. 'Well, that sounds nice,' she sniffed. 'How long are you going for?'

'I don't know.'

She sat back.

'You see, once I've seen Scotland, I might want to stay there. Or I might want to go somewhere else. I've never been anywhere,' she laughed again, 'as you know.'

Sheila looked bewildered. 'But darling, what will you do for money?'

'I still have some savings after buying the car. And it's tourist season. I'll do little jobs here and there if I need to.'

Tess felt her pulse racing just at the thought of it. She could hardly wait.

'But you've got the mortgage to pay-'

Tess shook her head, grinning. 'That's where the favour comes in. I've sold the house.' She reached into her back pocket and pulled out a brown envelope.

'This is a Power of Attorney. It gives you authority to sign any papers the solicitor needs to finalise the sale.'

Sheila's mouth fell open and stayed there. 'You've sold your house? But, but you didn't tell me! And why?'

Tess laughed again. 'Because I don't like it. I don't know how I ever did. And I don't need it. I'm going away. I don't know where I'll end up.'

Sheila's brow furrowed, and Tess knew exactly what she was thinking. *Why, all these years I've tried to get my daughter to be more adventurous, and now she's gone way off the deep end.*

She stifled a laugh. 'Well? Will you help me?'

Sheila gave her a hard look. 'Are you sure this is what you want?'

'I've never been surer.'

Tess met her eyes until at last they dropped to the papers. True to form, Sheila read the entire document carefully before heaving a deep sigh. Without raising her eyes, she stood up and turned to the window.

'I'll miss you,' she said.

Tess stood up. An unexpected lump had appeared in her throat. She walked over and put her arms round Sheila, breathing in her familiar pungent perfume. Sheila turned and gave her a fierce hug.

'You promise me you'll be careful,' she said in a tight voice, 'and if there's anything you need, anything at all, you call me. You promise me now!'

Tess sighed, smiling. 'I promise, mum,' she said.

FORTY SEVEN

'This is Peters.'

'Why didn't you tell me you were going after Dole by yourself?'

While the major hesitated, Cal took a deep breath and tried to calm down. The story of Mike's attack on the police had been all over the newspapers. David Driscoll of the *Mercury* had managed to get hold of a photo of him as well.

'Sergeant, I don't answer to you.'

'You're subject to the law the same as everyone else,' Cal snapped.

'I've broken no laws.'

'You've driven him out of his hiding place. Who knows where the hell he is now?'

'Look, Fisher, I was trying to help the man. It's not my fault if the local force sent out a bunch of spotty new recruits to find him.'

Cal felt his hands forming fists. 'They wouldn't have found him unless you'd got to him first. Don't you know what this means?'

Peters sighed. 'No, and neither do you. Chances are Mike has taken off back into the wilds. Even with thermal imaging, they can't cover the whole of the highlands.'

Cal sat down, picking up his pen and pulling his notebook closer. For the first time in a long time he wished he had a cigarette.

'Chances are,' he said slowly, 'that he's already on his way here.'

'He's got no reason to go there.'

'Yes he has. Tess Hardy is here.'

Peters snorted. 'Detective, I wonder if you're being completely objective.'

Cal bit down on his fury. Had his attraction for the girl been so obvious? He took a deep breath.

'Tess herself thought he would come back for her,' he said at last. 'The man's lost the plot. Who knows what's going on in his head?'

He looked up. Rob was standing at the door, looking sheepish as usual.

'Six police officers tried to arrest Mike Dole,' Peters said in a cold voice. 'If he'd wanted to, he could have killed them all. Instead, he simply pushed them aside and escaped. No one was badly hurt. One of them even heard Mike say that he didn't want to hurt anyone. Does that sound like a man hell bent on revenge?'

Cal hesitated.

'Nevertheless, he could still be on his way here.'

'Look, if he is, he'll be picked up. His photo's all over the papers, thanks to you, no doubt.'

Cal was stung.

'That had nothing to do with us. We wanted his picture kept out of circulation.'

'Well it's too late now.'

He looked up. Rob had left. Absently he wondered what the problem was this time.

'Look, major, you spoke to him, didn't you? So what's the story?'

There was a long pause, during which Cal felt he was about to explode with anger.

'He's not well,' Peters said in a quiet voice.

'I reckon we knew that.'

'He needs help.'

'I'm not inclined to feel sympathetic. You just told me how dangerous he is.'

'He's only a danger to himself.'

'You think he might top himself?'

Peters took a sharp intake of breath, and Cal felt a pang of regret at his callous words.

'We need to find him.'

'Well, in case you hadn't noticed, there's a huge manhunt under way.'

There was a long silence. Cal listened to the burbles and hisses on the phone line. Something occurred to him.

'Are you going back up to look for him?'

'No,' the major said shortly.

'So you don't think he's up there after all.'

'With respect, sergeant,' Peters said angrily, 'I'm an army officer. We can't all please ourselves what we do with our time.'

Cal nodded to himself. 'All right, major, but I hope to God you're right.'

As soon as he put the phone down, Rob opened the door again, as if he had been listening outside.

'Hi, Cal,' he said. 'How's it going?'

Cal shrugged. 'What's up, Rob?'

Rob sat down heavily. He was back to looking haggard and world-weary. His hair was greasy, his suit crumpled. Cal spotted a dried-in coffee stain on his left sleeve.

'What's the matter, Rob,' he asked, trying not to appear impatient. Rob looked up, and Cal could see that he knew very well Cal was just being polite, that he didn't really want to know. A stab of guilt made him sit forward.

'Is Lisa-?'

Rob sighed. 'She's gone,' he said. 'Run off with her self-assertion tutor.'

Cal bit back an involuntary grin.

'She kept telling me the point of this self-assertion course was to make her more independent. Well, she's as independent as she can get now, I suppose.'

'What about the kids?'

'Her mother's looking after them right now. She's been great, actually. Thinks Lisa's lost her marbles.'

'She might be right.'

Rob nodded sadly.

'I'm sorry, mate,' Cal said. 'When did this happen?'

'About a week back. I'd have told you before, but-'

But I was being an arse, Cal realised. He had been so obsessed with the Hardy case, and then the Hardy *woman*, that he had failed to realise Rob's anger and frustration was a reaction to this bad news.

'You need some time off?'

Rob shook his head. 'God no, I'd just sit home and mope.'

'I'm sorry,' Cal said again.

Rob looked at him, then his eyes dropped to the wrinkled knees of his cheap suit.

'Well, the thing is, Cal, I've not been pulling my weight lately, and you were right to pull me up about it. I'm going to go all out to improve, but if you've had enough, I'll tell Jarvis I want a transfer.'

Cal felt the remorse wash over him. They'd been partners a long time, and Rob was a good man, maybe not the best detective in the world, but what he lacked in insight he'd always made up for with decency and hard work. Cal glanced down at his notebook where he had drawn a dark, empty cave.

'Not a chance, Rob,' he said, standing up. 'Can't break up the team, can we?'

He smiled, and saw the flood of relief cross his friend's face.

'Thanks, Cal. You won't regret it.'

'Let's get some coffee, eh?'

On the way to the coffee machine, Cal saw DC Roslyn walking towards him. A glance at Rob's face showed that his smile had vanished.

'Sir, there's someone to see you in waiting room 4,' she said, frowning at the black look on Rob Matlock's face.

'What is it now?' Cal sighed, walking past her to the waiting room door. He looked through the peephole and felt his legs turn to lead.

Lynne.

Five years ago when they had first met, she had looked like a teenager, all blonde ponytail and long rangy legs, a carefree smile curving her wide lips. He didn't understand why she hadn't been snapped up already, or why she seemed to be attracted to him. The answer to both questions would be answered in the following two years. But looking at her now, he was transported back to that morning in the town centre, when their eyes met and she smiled, and he was lost. She looked just the same.

He realised that the other detectives were looking at him, and Rob must have noticed his discomfort.

'Want me to get rid of her?' Rob said gruffly.

Cal smiled. 'Thanks, mate, I better handle it.'

He pushed through the door before he could change his mind.

She turned and stood in one fluid movement. She was smiling, but her eyes were uneasy and a little scared.

'Hello, Cal,' she said, and he felt the sun come out on his heart. His throat was suddenly dry, and he took a deep breath. He wouldn't, *couldn't* go down this road again, it was too painful.

'What do you want, Lynne?' His voice was rougher than he had intended, and he winced as her forehead furrowed and she sat down, looking away.

'I know I deserve that,' she murmured. 'I deserve worse that that.'

'So what, you're here for me to shout at you?'

He ran his fingers through his hair. Even less of it than ever now. He thought about what it would be like to be bald. It was better than thinking about his ex-wife.

'If you want,' she said. She sounded resigned.

Cal swallowed hard. Might as well get this over with.

He sat on the opposite side of the table and folded his arms. Classic defence posture. Then, realising what he was doing, he unfolded them and laid his hands flat on the table.

'You look well,' she said, not looking at him.

'No I don't,' he replied. 'I'm skinny, nearly bald and this face is like a road map.'

She looked up at that, and smiled, and Cal couldn't help but smile back.

'You look great,' he said.

She shrugged. 'You've still got a fantastic smile.'

Cal said nothing, waiting for her to continue, but she stayed silent.

'So, what is it? What do you want from me, Lynne?'

She swallowed. 'We had some good times, didn't we?'

Cal nodded. 'We did.' He tried not to smile again. The good times had been very, very good. But of course, the bad times had made up for it. She pushed a strand of her ash blonde hair behind her ear, a mannerism which brought a terrible ache to his heart.

Abruptly she pulled in a deep breath and sat up straight. She fixed him with her beautiful blue eyes and breathed out hard.

'You were right,' she said. 'I should have told you right at the start. Maybe we'd never have got together, maybe we could have worked round it, but I should have told you.'

Cal nodded, feeling as if someone was holding his heart in one hand like an orange, and tearing strips out of it with the other.

'There's no point in going over all this now-'

'Yes, there is. I want you to know that I've come to terms with it all. Three years ago I tried to make you shoulder some of the responsibility. That was wrong. I accept all the blame.'

Cal leaned forward. 'It doesn't matter.'

'Yes it does!'

She closed her hands into fists. Closed her eyes. Cal's mouth was bone dry.

'I thought that if I told you the truth, you wouldn't want me. But the longer it went on, the harder it was. And by then, I couldn't bear to lose you.'

A single tear fell down her right cheek. Cal stared at it, his blood pounding in his veins.

'So when you wanted us to have kids-'

She bit her lip. Cal reached forward and grabbed her hand. It was warm and soft, and felt good.

'You don't have to do this,' he whispered. 'It's ancient history.'

She said nothing, trying to hold back the tears. There was a cooler in the corner of the tiny room, and he fetched her a plastic cup of water. She took it from him, smiling sadly. Cal sat on the edge of the table.

'Are you with someone else now?'

She looked up, her face creased.

'Me? Are you joking? What man would want to be with me!'

Cal raised an eyebrow. 'Lynne you're a beautiful woman. Men must be crawling over each other to get to you.'

She stood up and walked over to the tiny window. There were bars on the outside.

'It tends to put them off when they find out I killed my own baby and now can't have children.'

Cal closed his eyes. The man peeling his heart had almost finished.

'You're too hard on yourself. You weren't responsible for the abortion.'

She whirled on him. 'It was *my* body, *my* baby. Blaming my parents won't wash.'

'You were, what, fifteen?'

'Doesn't matter,' she whispered, holding back sobs. 'Oh Cal, I should have told you at the beginning. I should have told you!'

She put her head in her hands, and Cal went to her and held her. Her hair smelled of apples. He rested his chin on the top of her head, letting her sob into his chest. He closed his eyes, his heart filling with the memory of warmer, brighter days, and he felt whole for the first time in a long time. Lynne leaned back and pushed away suddenly, leaving him feeling alone.

'I'm sorry,' she said, shaking her head.

'It's all right,' he said, holding his hands out. 'Lynne-'

'No, I shouldn't have come.'

She hurried to the door and grasped the handle.

'Why did you come?'

She hesitated, then looked round. Cal saw a world of sadness in her pale eyes.

'I just wanted to see you again, just once.'

She hauled open the door and ran out. Cal watched her jog awkwardly down the dark corridor towards the light of the outside door.

He wanted to stop her. He wanted to say a lot of things he should have said before, but instead he just stood there, watching her leave, and breathing in the faint scent of her hair.

*

Wevers Brinkerhoff's accountancy firm had always had good links with Scotland. They acted for some of the shipping companies ferrying goods across the North Sea between Rotterdam and Leith, and had recently opened an office in Edinburgh.

Wevers had hiked through the highlands as a student, and had fallen in love with the mountains. Tired of city life, he was angling hard for a transfer to the Scottish office, and as far as he could see the only thing holding him back was his limited grasp of English. He enrolled in a language class and persuaded his wife Anki to take their summer holiday in the highlands.

So when they saw the hitch-hiker, despite Ankie's protestations that he 'looked a bit rough', Wevers pulled over, eager to engage the man in conversation. The hiker climbed into the back seat of the car, pulling his rucksack in behind him.

'Thanks very much,' he said.

Wevers looked round, and his smile froze on his face when he saw the gun pointed at his forehead.

'Just drive,' the man said in a polite voice. 'South, please.'

FORTY EIGHT

Tess looked round her living room for the last time. She was leaving most of the furniture. A young couple had bought her house, and she had offered the contents to them for free. After all, she wasn't going to need them. She glanced down at the paint peeling on the windowsill. She never had got those new windows Sheila was always nagging her about. Her lips curved in a grin. That seemed like another lifetime.

Locking the door, she turned to the car. She was taking a couple of sports bags stuffed with clothes, some books and maps, and that was about it. Travelling light. Her heart was beating faster just at the thought of it. Even her dad had seemed excited.

They had met the night before at the Old White Swan pub in Newbold Verdon, a village west of the town. Her choice, this time. She had come right out with her plans, may as well get it over with. Roy looked at her, eyebrows raised, a curious little smile on his face.

'Well, good for you, girl,' he said.

Tess was amazed.

'I thought you'd be upset, try to talk me out of it.'

He shook his head. 'You're young. You should go for it. Besides, I know what you've been through. You can't just go back to the way things were.'

She felt as if her heart were about to explode with emotion. Looking into his eyes, she saw something there she recognised, some kindred feeling. Since he'd been off the booze, Roy had lost weight, but more importantly, he had regained a quiet pride. He was dressed tonight in blue-grey chinos and an expensive looking cream shirt. His hair was freshly cut, and his aftershave smelt clean and sharp. Tess had noticed the barmaid, a lady of a certain age, giving him the once over. She had no idea how much of his transformation was due to the shock of her kidnapping, or if that had even been a factor, but dad had turned himself around. She took his hand.

'I love you, dad. I'm going to miss you.'

Tears swept into his eyes. *Same old dad, underneath,* she thought, smiling. Roy blinked hard.

'I'll miss you too, Tess, you know I will. But I want you to be happy.'

He squeezed her hand.

'You know,' he murmured. 'Things don't always turn out the way you expect.'

She chuckled softly. Wasn't that the truth.

'But I think, if you're true to yourself, they'll work out. That's what I believe.'

True to yourself, Tess thought. She looked up. Roy was grinning.

'Pretentious or what?' he laughed. 'Well, are we going to eat?'

Tess was smiling as she got into the car. Her mobile rang, and she looked at the screen:

'Hello Cal,' she said.

'Tess. Everything all right?'

She smiled. 'Yes. I've not met any murderous rogues around Kirby.'

He chuckled quietly. 'Well, that's not to say they're not there.'

She laughed. 'Are you at the station?'

'Yes. Are we still on for lunch?'

'Sure'.

'I've got something I want to talk to you about,' he said, his voice suddenly flat.

'Really?' she said, 'that's odd. I've got something I need to talk to you about too.'

'What is it?'

'I'll tell you when I get there. Where do you want to go?'

'How about the *Lady Jane*? I hear the food's good.'

Tess stifled a sigh. Halfway to the town centre, when she was eager to get on her way. But she couldn't just go without saying goodbye.

'Okay. I'll see you there in an hour.'

She got into the car and drove away from her former home without a backward glance.

*

The petrol warning light had come on just before Leeds. Mike was impressed.

'This is a very economical car,' he said.

'It is the best in class for fuel using,' Wevers said proudly. 'It is best in class also for emissions. Very green.'

Mike nodded. The man called Wevers was not afraid. In fact, Mike was sure he was enjoying the trip. Not so his wife, who was very pale and still, apart from her eyes, which darted round like those of a trapped bird.

Wevers pulled into the slip road to the service station, and Mike saw her lean forward slightly, licking her dry lips, ready to scream or run.
'Don't be afraid, Anki,' he said. 'I'll be leaving you soon. You won't be hurt.'

She jumped as if shocked, but didn't look at him.

'Pull over, here,' Mike said, pointing to the general car park for the service area. At this time of night it was full of trucks. When the car stopped, he leaned forward.

'You will be all right?' Wevers said. All the way down he had kept up a constant stream of comments, which Mike had largely ignored. At first he had thought the man was nervous, until Wevers confessed he was learning English.

Picked the wrong man for a conversation, Mike thought.

'Thank you,' Mike said quietly. 'I am sorry to have spoiled your holiday.'

'No, no,' Wevers said, holding up his hands. 'It is – adventure, ja?'

Mike caught sight of Anki's face. She didn't seem to be feeling the same thrill. He hurried into the bushes surrounding the car park, waiting until the car drove away. He could hear a woman sobbing.

He hunched down in the dark, looking out at the truck stop. The summer wind was warm on his face and smelt of diesel and greasy chips.

He was almost at the end of things.

He reached into his rucksack for the appropriate map. It would be difficult now, there were over a hundred miles to cover. A long way, when you were being hunted. But it's not as if he hadn't been on similar exercises in the past. Not so far, maybe, but still, the logic was the same. Break it into stages. Keep sight of priorities.

Lighting his maglite, he applied a temporary tattoo to the left side of his neck. It was a spider's web, big, ugly, and memorable. He returned the baseball cap to the pack and pulled out a red bandana which he wrapped round his head. Then he pulled on a tie-dyed blue shirt over his T-shirt, and used superglue to attach a large gold stud to his left ear.

He crept along the line of bushes until he reached the staff service lane, the only other exit apart from the motorway. By the petrol pumps he could see the Dutchman's car, parked to one side. No police yet. A truck rumbled by, and he thought for a moment about hitching a lift, but no doubt he would be in the news by now. The truckers would be wary of hitchers.

He took the service road. It was no more than a country lane, and he checked map and compass again before taking off across the fields, the lights of the motorway easily sufficient for him to see his path.

This is the right thing to do, said the voice.

'I'm not sure,' he whispered, touching the heather in his pocket.

You will be. Trust me.

FORTY NINE

Tess parked in the mall roof car park. The *Lady Jane* was on the opposite corner from the Sunningdale mall, and was already busy with workers on their lunch hour. The double doors were open to the July sunshine, but she couldn't see Cal in there. She checked the time on her phone. Twenty to one, she was early. Not in the mood to stand at the bar alone, she walked across the busy road to the mall.

The usual muzak was playing, and the place smelled of the distinctive mixture of disinfectant, hamburgers, sweat and coffee that she had come to know so well. It made her heart sink to think about all the time she had spent here, being paid crap money for a crap job.

Wait a minute, old Mrs Dennis still owed her money. She remembered the awkward phone message and smiled. Well, every cloud, as they said. If she had to come back here, she might as well get something out of it. She headed for the escalator and rode to the top floor.

It looked sadder than ever. There were no shoppers up here at all.

Three of the shops were boarded up, and even the pound shop had a 'closing down' notice on the window. She headed for *City of Glass*, the window bright and enticing up here in the empty gloom, filled with reflective mirrors and shining ornaments. She glanced down and saw that there was a gap between the window frame and the glass. The glaziers had done a poor job, which probably reflected the amount miserable old Mrs Dennis would have paid them.

But everything was just the same as she had left it: there was the Doulton tea service, so expensive that no one visiting Sunningdale would ever buy it; the champagne flutes and rose bowls and animals made of coloured glass. There was the unicorn, the one Mike had loved, on its perch in the far corner, its strange horn pointed out at the passers-by as if in warning.

She looked inside, and only then realised that the shop was closed for lunch. She sighed. There was no way she was coming back up here after she met Cal. She'd have to forget her last pay packet. She took one last look at the unicorn and turned back for the escalator.

*

Mike had had a stroke of luck early that morning, as he walked along a country lane. A tatty white van had pulled up alongside him.

'Hey mate, need a lift?'

The man was wearing a lumberjack shirt with the sleeves rolled up to reveal tattoos covering both arms. He had a swarthy complexion and thick grey hair tied back in a pony tail. Mike caught him checking out his own makeshift tattoo, his worn clothes and bandana.

'Cheers mate.'

'Where you heading?'

'South.'

'I'm going down to Loughborough. I'll take you there.'

The man had kept up a cheery one-sided conversation on the journey, which Mike tried to tune out. He was an old hippy who made a living as a carpenter, and had definite views about everything. The country was in a state. The police were a disgrace. The tax system was all wrong. There were too many immigrants. Mike closed his eyes. His head was throbbing, and somewhere in the back of his mind another monologue was going on, one he was powerless to drown out.

'Everything all right?' the man had asked eventually. Mike just nodded.

'Well, here we are.'

He looked out. They were in a car park in the centre of a small town. The early sunlight gleamed on the roofs of the cars, and a few late commuters hurried to their offices.

'Where-?'

'Loughborough, mate.'

Mike looked round at the man, who was giving him a bemused look.

'You sure you're all right?'

Mike nodded, reaching for his kit bag.

'Leicester,' he said.

The driver's grin dropped off his face as he saw the gun. His eyes darted up to Mike's, confused, afraid.

'Leicester,' Mike said again.

The man crunched the van into gear, turning back to face the road.

'Leicester it is,' he said in a choked voice. 'Only, don't hurt me, mate.'

Mike heard the applause in his head. The tic jumped in his cheek.

Somewhere deep inside, someone was screaming, only no one was listening any more.

FIFTY

Cal was late. There'd been a development on the Morrisons robbery that morning, and he had forgotten the time. He had just reached New Parks when his phone rang.

'Fisher.'

'Cal, it's Rob. I've just been speaking to a DI from Leeds. They've got a foreign couple there who gave a lift to a man with a gun. He made them drive him south. Leeds is where he got out. I think it's our boy.'

Cal's heart skipped and his shoulders tensed up. So Mike was on his way here after all.

'Why Leeds?'

'The car ran out of petrol. I think maybe he didn't want to take the chance on getting caught filling it up.'

Cal nodded to himself. That made sense. 'When did he leave them?'

'Last night, around ten.'

Ten o'clock. Fifteen hours ago, and the idiots were just getting round to putting two and two together. Leeds was a hundred miles away. Mike could be here now, if he'd hijacked another car. There was a giant lump in Cal's throat.

'Check around. Find out if anyone has reported giving a lift to anyone strange.'

'No problem, Cal. Roslyn's already looking into it.'

'And tell Jarvis. We need to be on our toes, Rob.'

'Okay. Where are you?'

'On my way to see Tess Hardy.'

'Well, I hope you get there first.'

Cal ended the call, immediately calling Tess. A bleep sounded: no signal.

'Damn!' he yelled, pressing his foot to the floor. Tess would be there already, waiting for him. And so might Mike. He couldn't bear to think about what Mike would do to her if he found her first.

*

He wouldn't be needing his rucksack any more. Mike stood and looked at it for a long time. It was hard to leave his kit. He felt naked without it.

Get a move on! It's a bag, for God's sake!

Mike had left the van on the A47, and wandered into the Old Newtonians rugby ground. At this time of day the place was deserted, and he found an outside tap, washed, removed his tattoo and ear stud, and changed his clothes. Then he looked at himself in his scrap of mirror glass.

He still looked the same. Funny, that.

Now he ran a quick check to make sure he had the few things he would need. At last he lifted the bag into a large green dustbin behind the Chinese take away.

Without the weight on his shoulder, he should have felt light. Instead, he felt as if he had swapped the bag for a solid lead bar.

He never saw a soul as he walked through the village, everyone who lived here in suburbia was out at work or taking the kids to school. He turned into the cul-de-sac, silent and bare of cars as usual at this time of the day. He didn't remember coming here, his legs had just brought him without any thought processes going on at all. He stood in front of the little house and looked at the 'SOLD' sign.

She was gone.

There was no point knocking at the door, the place already looked abandoned. He wondered who had bought it, whether they would be happier there than Tess had been. Than he had been. He wondered if people really were happy, if such a thing as happiness actually existed, or if everyone was just pretending, fooling themselves. Maybe he was the only honest one. He looked down at the cracked grey paving slabs, the tic jumping in his cheek. She had gone, and how would he find her now?

Do I have to do everything!?

'Yes,' he whispered. 'I think perhaps you do.'

He walked back to the main street, and stood at the bus stop. He thought about that dark loch, the one he had stepped into. He should have done what he thought of back then, and walked right in, let the water take him. It was too late now, he was too far away; in distance, and in spirit.

His chest felt hollow and empty. There wasn't much of him left.

He looked up as a bus arrived, the doors opening. His fingers reached into one of the pockets of his jacket and pulled out some loose change. His legs moved him up the steps towards the driver.

'Where to, mate?'

Someone spoke. It didn't sound like him, and he didn't feel his mouth move, but it must have been him. Who else could it have been?

'Sunningdale,' he said.

FIFTY ONE

Cal spotted Tess's Mini in the mall car park. Like a typical copper, he had memorised her number plate. He walked through the parked cars and down to the street where the pub was now so busy that people were sitting on the outside benches. Trucks and buses were thundering past just a few feet away from their plates of salad and quiche, but no one seemed to be bothered.

He couldn't find Tess, and walked back out. Maybe she was late. Maybe she didn't like the pub. Maybe she had changed her mind.

Maybe Mike had found her first.

Cal stood on the pavement as life went on around him, and tried to ignore the pounding of his heart. He dialled Tess's phone again, but there was still no signal. He looked over at the mall, remembering that the last time he had been at Tess's shop, he had been unable to phone out. Could she be in there? He crossed the road and was going through the automatic doors when his phone rang and he grabbed it.

'Fisher.'

'Sir, it's Roslyn. Jim Burdock's just taken a statement from a Mr Lovell who was forced to drive an armed man to Leicester this morning.'

Cal swallowed. 'How long ago?'

'About an hour and a half. The man's only just come in to report it. But it doesn't sound like our man. Lovell says the man had a tattoo on his neck and looked like a gypsy.'

Cal thought fast. What else might Mike have had in that big kit bag? A disguise?

'It's him,' he said. 'Where did he drop him?'

'On the A47 at Leicester Forest East.'

Just before Kirby Muxloe, Cal thought, *where Tess lives.* He felt a flutter of panic in his stomach.

'Roslyn, get someone round to Tess Hardy's house quick.'

'I've already sent someone, sir. The house is empty.'

Cal looked around at the busy mall. Had Mike already got her? Or if he turned up at her house to find her out, what would he do? Would he wait for her, or come here.

He'd come here. Cal was sure of it. He hurried along past the shops, trying to still the fear in his chest.

Calm down, he told himself. Maybe Tess was just late too. Maybe she's over at the pub waiting for you. He stopped and turned round, heading for the exit, and that was when at last his phone rang and he looked down to see Tess's number.

Tess stood outside the pub and pulled out her phone. Where had Cal got to? If he was going to be late, he always called.

But then, she'd been up at the shop, hadn't she, and everyone knew that phones could never catch a signal up there. She shook her head, calling up his number and wondering what it was he wanted to talk to her about. A chill ran through her as she considered it. She hoped he wasn't hoping for something serious between them. It wasn't that she didn't like him. She did, a lot. But now was not the time. She pressed 'send', waiting for him to answer. The streets were busy with shoppers, workers grabbing a quick lunch. Absently she scanned the faces.

And there, twenty feet away on the pavement, stood Mike Dole.

A massive rock thudded into her chest. He looked much the same, a bit thinner, but with the same empty eyes, his face as impassive as a statue. She could hear the blood pounding in her ears. She was standing here like a rabbit in the headlights. Like a rabbit in a snare.

Tess let out an angry breath she didn't realise she'd been holding and ran into the road. Brakes squealed. Drivers yelled and swore. A motorcycle swerved on to the pavement, making pedestrians scatter, screaming. One car didn't brake in time, and the wing hit her a glancing blow on the thigh. Tess went down in a hot surge of pain, but got straight back up and ran on.

She didn't look back. There was no need. She ran along the crowded pavement, breath coming in ragged gasps. Arms pushed at her angrily as she barged through pedestrians. Where the hell was Cal? Where could she go? The mall was in front of her. Full of people. She would find someone in there to help her. She hurtled through the automatic doors, sending a basket full of discount socks flying. The shopkeeper yelled at her, and she glanced back.

Mike was coming through the doors. He was reaching into his jacket.

She let out an involuntary gasp and ran into a Superdrug store. The shop had aisles set at right angles to the doors, and she groaned. She'd never lose him in here, all he had to do was wait her out. 'Call police!' she shouted breathlessly as she ran past the cashiers, glancing round again.

'What's going on?' An elderly man walked towards her, his face angry. He had a large hairy mole on his cheek, and was clutching a basket with shampoo and shaving foam in it. Funny how suddenly everything seemed so clear.

'A man's chasing me. Get out of the way,' she said, hearing the panic in her voice. It made her even angrier.

'Let's see about that!' the old chap said, but Tess pushed past him towards the feminine hygiene section. Anxiously she scanned the shelves.

There was nothing she could even use as a weapon: she doubted a super sized tampon was going to be much of a threat. She crouched down and glanced round the corner, hanging on to the shelf to help propel her backwards if need be.

There was no one there. It was a clear path to the door, but the aisle was broken halfway down, so it wasn't too hard to work out where Mike would be.

'What the devil are you doing!'

She stood up. The old fellow was standing in the aisle. Someone was holding his arm and he was pulling back against his assailant. Tess pushed off from the shelves, sending sanitary towels and feminine wipes flying. She ran for the door, brushing past the old man, seeing Mike's still impassive face watching her pass. He didn't even break into a run.

Christ, I'm in trouble, she thought, blasting into the mall. *Where the hell is Cal?*

She reached the ornamental flower beds, dipping down behind the sad looking begonias and fag-end riddled soil, clutching the edge of the concrete tub with shaking fingers. Mike came out of the shop like the Terminator, walking towards her as if he knew exactly where she was.

'Shit,' she said, turning and running again. She heard his footsteps running after her, and tears rushed into her eyes. 'Oh shit, shit, shit!' she cried, heading for the kid's shop. She deliberately upturned all the small toy baskets outside, hearing people shouting.

'Bloody hooligans!'

'Hey you! Get back here and clean this up!'

Three salesmen had come out of Dixon's to see what was going on.

They were all in their early twenties, and gave her a bemused look.

'Call police!' she yelled at them as she ran past, her vision blurring. 'Please!'

The man from the mobile phone shop was older and smarter. He looked past her, and she saw his face harden.

'Run, love,' he said. 'I'll deal with this one.'

'No!' she gasped, but the word was barely audible in her ragged breath, and the man ignored her. She heard a shout and a thump, and looked back to see the man lying on the ground, the Dixon's lads hurrying to his rescue. Mike was still coming. She turned and climbed the escalator steps, tripping over the top one and flying into a flower stall.

'Are you all right?' the woman asked, as Tess got to her feet among the smitten Chrysanthemums. She ran on, past the jeans shop and the chocolate shop, up towards the dark end of the mall. The place where no one ever came. The home of *City of Glass.*

She did not want to be here. There was no one to help her. She doubled back, past the balcony, sliding into New Look and heading for the tills.

'Is there another way out?' she yelled, breath coming in painful gasps. The two cashiers stared at her, then looked at each other.

'Is there another way out!' she screamed.

The first girl jumped. 'No,' she said, pointing back the way she had come. 'Just that way.'

Tess growled, heading for a rack filled with underwear, and crouched behind it. The whole rack shook as she held on to it, and she quickly let it go, dropping her hands to the floor to steady her. She could tell Mike had come into the shop by the frightened looks on the girls' faces. She watched their gazes follow him down the shop until she was sure he was behind her, then she made a dash for the door.

She heard screams behind her as Mike began to run too, and leaned against the balcony. A sob climbed up her throat and exploded from her mouth. It was too far down to drop, she'd break every bone. Down below, she could see the shopkeepers milling around in confusion, some looking up at her. She had to get back down there, somehow, but as she took a step towards the escalator, Mike came out of the shop and looked at her. It was as if he had some kind of homing device. She was never going to get away. Cal had been right all along.

She looked behind. There was nothing back there but the closed down units and her old shop. There was nothing else for it. She turned and ran.

FIFTY TWO

Cal looked down at Tess's number and sighed with relief.

'Hi Tess.'

There was no reply. All he could hear was the sound of brakes squealing and people yelling. His heart jumped into his throat. She'd had some kind of accident. He shouted into the phone. 'Tess, where are you? Are you all right?'

No reply.

He ran out of the mall doors, looking round. Traffic seemed to be moving normally, where was she?

He looked over towards the pub and hurried to the crossing, impatiently waiting for the lights to change before running over and stopping outside the doors. Tess was nowhere to be seen. He looked round, his eyes falling on the diners at the street benches.

'Excuse me,' he said. The two thirty something women looked up at him warily until he pulled out his police ID, when their expressions relaxed.

'Have you seen anything unusual here recently? Like an accident?'

'Nearly,' the blonde woman said, with a lift of her eyebrow. 'Some woman ran right across the street in front of the traffic.'

Cal stood very still. Tess was all right. She wasn't here, so she had got up and walked away. She was all right.

'What happened?'

The woman shrugged. 'She just took off running.'

'No,' the red-haired woman said, looking thoughtful. 'She saw someone. She was looking at someone and then she just ran. She looked scared.'

Cal felt a lead weight in his stomach.

'Who? Did you see who she was looking at?'

'A man. He ran after her.'

'Where did she go?'

The women looked at each other, hesitant.

Cal slammed both hands flat on the bench. 'Where! Think!'

The blonde woman gave him the eyebrow again, this time accompanied by a cold stare.

'Towards the mall, I think,' her friend said.

Cal turned and looked at the mall. His heart pounding. He raised the phone to his ear. They were still connected, but there was nothing to hear but background noises.

'Tess!' he yelled.

A pause, and then: 'Cal? Cal?'

'I'm here, Tess, where are you.'

'The mall,' her whispered words were ragged and terrified. 'Mike's here.'

'Hang on,' he said. 'I'm just across the street. I'm coming.'

He ran to the edge of the road, and holding his ID out, ran across, stopping the traffic only slightly more effectively than Tess had managed.

Inside the mall, people were milling around, and a very young PC was taking a statement from three men in Dixon's suits. Cal was squeezing past them when he heard a scream followed by the sound of glass shattering.

'Come with me!' he shouted, running for the escalator.

FIFTY THREE

Tess had backed up as far as the closed-down units. There was nowhere else to run. Before her, the corridor between the shops and balcony was no more than five feet wide. Too narrow. Unless she could somehow get past him, she was sunk. Mike walked towards her, silent and calm despite the chase. The left side of his face was bright in the reflection of the glass shop. His right side was in darkness.

'What are you doing here, Mike? What do you want?'

She heard the wavering fear in her voice and winced.

'Just to talk,' he said.

'Talk,' she said, closing her fists round her shaking fingers. 'Did you talk to Sandy?'

His head jerked back as if struck. She saw his eyes glittering.

'How does she know!' he shouted.

Tess breathed hard, trying to stay calm. What- what had that meant?

'Get rid of her! Take care of it!'

Mike stood rigid as death, his head canted back at a strange angle.

His teeth were clamped together, his eyes filled with a terrible, painful light. He looked like an animal in a trap; desperately hurt, but still waiting for the hunter, for one final chance to attack and escape.

'She takes care of herself,' he hissed from between his gritted teeth.

Tess saw his left hand shake as he reached into his pocket. He was going to kill her. This was her last chance. She pushed off the wall and ran.

He moved fast, snapping out his right arm like a bar, and Tess ran straight into it. In desperation, she lashed out with her fist, sobbing, landing a lucky punch on his neck which made him splutter.

His right arm closed round her shoulder, pulling her towards him, and she bit down hard on the flesh of his thumb. Mike grunted, but didn't let go. He took a step back to avoid her flailing legs, widening his stance to keep his balance. She pulled hard to get away, but he held her fast.

He's just holding me, she realised. *Holding me until I stop struggling, then I'm finished!*

The knowledge injected adrenalin into her tired legs. 'No!' she screamed, kicking back. Her blows landed this time, and he grunted again, moving backwards and lifting her off the ground. She put her chin down on her chest and launched a backward blow with the top of her head. It hit him on the chin and he gasped, stepping back.

She felt her feet touch the ground again, and dug her elbow into his stomach, lashing out with another head lunge. His arm was still round her chest like an iron bar, making it hard to breathe.

She dug her elbow in again, vision blurring with tears and lack of air, but he didn't let her go.

Her strength was failing, and she realised he would never let her go, not until it was too late. Tess used the last of her ragged breath in a despairing animal scream.

The sound echoed round the empty floor long after she had sagged, gasping for air, and Tess suddenly realised that it was coming from somewhere else.

Someone else was screaming. Someone in the shop. Mike turned to see who was there. He tripped over her feet, and suddenly they were falling.

'Oh no!' she cried, but the words were no more than gasps.

Mike's right shoulder was the first thing to hit the window. The glass exploded, carrying them both into the shop front in a hail of gleaming crystal shards. Tess landed first, savage little stabs of pain bursting in her back, though Mike's arm saved her from the worst of the impact. Mike landed on top of her, knocking the last of the wind out of her. She looked up, gasping, in time to see three long shards of glass, gleaming super-white in the hot lights, hanging from the top of the ruined window like stalactites.

Time slowed down and they hung there, swaying gently, for long, silent seconds. Then they fell.

Mike's head jerked back. His body stiffened, and he pulled his arm straight, bracing it on the glass strewn ground. He never made a sound.

His eyes flickered open, and at last, Tess saw something there in the cold blue, something she thought she recognised. It looked like relief.

He pushed himself off her.

'You're safe now,' he whispered.

Tess got to her knees, breathing hard, hissing in pain as broken glass cut through her jeans. She could hear someone crying behind her.

'Get an ambulance. Quickly!' she shouted. Mike was on his side looking at her, his face streaming with blood from hundreds of tiny cuts.

The long shards of glass protruded from his collar bone, waist and thigh, and a growing pool of blood engulfed the ruin of broken ornaments. The neck wound was worst, and blood was quickly turning his white T shirt crimson. Tess shuffled forward and put her hand on his shoulder to try and stem the flow.

'Just wanted to talk,' he murmured, still looking at her. His eyes were gentle now, as if another presence had taken over the cold shell she had known as Mike. A boulder of guilt rested on her shoulders.

'Sorry,' he whispered.

'No,' she said, leaning close. 'I'm the one who should be sorry.'

He had hit the glass first, protecting her. His eyes were sad and resigned, as if he knew he was dying, and there was nothing else for it. She felt her heart in her throat, and hot tears standing in her eyes.

'Mike,' she pressed her hand on his collar bone until he grunted, blinking.

'Don't give up. You mustn't die.'

His eyes were hooded now. He had lost too much blood, and was losing consciousness. Tess felt her throat constrict. She looked up and saw Cal standing there, his arms by his side, a helpless look on his face.

Tess felt as if she was drowning in sadness.

She looked up at the wreckage of the window, and saw that one last stand remained, the revolving dais with the little unicorn at the top.

She thought about how hard it must have been for Mike, living with the horrors of his past, his mistaken belief that he had failed all those he loved.

And she thought about the island, how hard it had been to survive, how it had changed her. The wilderness had crept into her heart, but it had always been part of his.

She picked up the unicorn. Mike's eyes followed her hand as she brought it close to his face.

'I have a job for you,' she said.

He blinked, focussing hard on the little object, his eyes reflected in the glass.

'I need you to look after this for me, Mike. Will you do that?'

His eyes shifted from the unicorn to hers, and she thought she could see a flicker of something there, something that might just be hope. She placed the ornament gently into his open hand. She remembered he had been afraid of crushing it. Now it took all his strength to close his fingers around it.

But close them he did. He nodded, his head lolling, and she put her arm around him, letting his head rest on her shoulder. She looked up at Cal, crouched in the window, his face stricken with sadness. Behind him, two paramedics in green uniforms pushed through the gathered crowd and began to work on Mike.

As they lifted him on to the stretcher, something fell out of his pocket. Cal bent and picked it up. It was a tiny sprig of heather.

Tess sighed.

'Tess, you're badly cut, you need to go to hospital.'

She shrugged, getting to her feet amongst a scraping of shattered glass. She didn't feel hurt, just bone tired and empty.

'He saved me,' she murmured.

'No,' Cal said. 'You saved him.'

She shook her head slowly, looking at the wreckage as the paramedics carried Mike out, his hand still closed round the glass unicorn. She sensed Cal's eyes on her.

'What happens if he breaks it?' he murmured.

She thought about the words that had driven them both to where they now stood.

'He won't,' she said. 'He won't.'

FIFTY FOUR

'Well, that was a colossal fuckup!'

Rob winced, folding his arms and leaning against the back wall. Jarvis rested one buttock on the edge of Cal's desk, rubbing his fingers together.

'I've had the press on the phone all morning, enjoying a good laugh at our expense.'

The DI ran a hand through his hair, dislodging a small avalanche of dandruff. Roslyn made a face.

'This Hardy girl, she not only rescues Dole's next victim, but manages to chuck the man through a plate glass window when he comes after her. And THEN she saves his life. They're making her out to be some kind of hero. Christ, what the hell were we doing all that time?'

He shot Rob a scathing look, and the sergeant looked away hurriedly.

'Maybe I should give her your job, eh?'

Cal sighed.

'Sorry, sir, we were slow off the mark.'

Jarvis stared at him, his face flushed, eyes glittering with anger.

'But, sir!' Rosyln protested. Cal gave her a warning look, but she ignored him. 'What else could we have done? We'd never have got a warrant based purely on a suspicion, and after the second kidnapping, it was down to the Scottish force to find him.'

Jarvis stood up, still rubbing the fingers of his left hand together. He stared at Roslyn for a long moment, but she met his eyes, unflinching.

Nodding, his lips moved in a grim smile.

'Just make sure the next case you handle doesn't leave us looking like bloody idiots.'

Jarvis slammed the door behind him, making the glass panel rattle ominously. The three officers breathed a collective sigh.

'That's so unfair,' Rob whined, slumping in his chair. 'He's forgotten all about the protection racket we broke up last month.'

Cal took a deep breath. 'No, he's right.'

He looked up. Roslyn had one eyebrow raised.

'What did we actually do, apart from uncover the story of a man's life? He's right.'

Roslyn was chewing on her lip.

'And he didn't come after her,' she added, apropos of nothing.

'What?' Rob said, pursing his lips. It was clear he still had not forgiven the young DC her eagerness.

'Mike Dole. He didn't come back for revenge, did he?'

Cal shook his head. 'Some part of him did, I think, but deep down, no. It wasn't revenge he was looking for, it was redemption.'

Ron just stared at him as if he had gone mad, and seeing his expression, Roslyn looked down to hide her grin.

'Well, it beats me,' Rob stood up, stretching.

'So,' Cal said, standing up himself. 'In order to get back into the DI's good books, a bit of hard graft is called for. Rob, you and Emma take the Morrisons robbery. I want to see some results by this evening. Meantime, I'll look at the antique shop job, see what stones I can turn over.'

'Yes, sir,' Roslyn said, a strange little smile on her face.

'What?' Cal said, heading for the coffee machine.

She shook her head, her brow creased.

'Tess Hardy, she's quite a character, isn't she? I mean, she started off completely ineffectual, and ended up pretty much saving the day.'

Cal smiled, ignoring the tugging ache in his heart. Tess was gone, and he was pretty sure she wasn't coming back. It was time to move on.

'She told me that she believes everyone is capable of amazing things,' he said. 'That we talk ourselves out of greatness.'

'Speak for yourself,' Rob said, and Roslyn threw back her head and laughed

FIFTY FIVE

Eight weeks later

Tess had just sat down, mug of tea in hand, when her mobile rang. She looked at the display.

'Hello, Cal,' she said.

'Tess! Glad I caught you. Is this a good time?'

'Yeah, sure,' she said, smiling. 'How are things?'

'Not too bad,' he said. 'Thought you might like an update on the Dole case?'

She sat forward. 'What's happened?'

'Major Peters has happened, that's what. Marian Warren has dropped all charges against Mike. No doubt Peters had a quiet word with her father, and since you won't press charges, that only leaves the dead woman. Forensics have failed to turn up anything linking Mike to the body, and cause of death is still uncertain.'

Tess thought for a moment. 'But what about the pattern, taking people to the island and leaving them. Don't they think that's how she must have got there?'

'Yeah, but it's circumstantial. They can't prove he took her there. The police turned it over to the CPS, and they say there's not enough to go on.'

'What about blowing up the island, his kit bag full of who knows what?'

Cal chuckled. 'He was smart, he dumped the lot. When he turned up at the shopping mall, he had nothing on him. We still haven't found that kit bag.'

'No gun?'

'Nothing but some loose change and a pocket full of heather.'

Tess sighed.

'Anyway, like I said, Major Peters stepped in and produced army medical reports proving Mike is not fit to stand trial even if evidence came forward. He's got him into some specialist army hospital. Peters is going to be supervising his care directly.'

Tess smiled. 'Looking after him,' she murmured. The sun came out from behind a cloud, as if in approval. 'I'm glad.'

'So am I. The bloke deserves a break, even if he did nearly kill you. Twice.'

Tess laughed, turning it into a stretch. The fresh salt air felt good filling her lungs.

'He's going to heal all right?'

'Seems so, even though he took the brunt of the glass. He was lucky the paramedics were quick.'

'It was Mrs Dennis's fault really.'

'Mrs Who?'

'Dennis. She owns the shop. Vandals shattered the window months ago and she obviously had it replaced with cheap glass.'

And she still hasn't paid me, Tess mused.

There was a long silence.

'So. Where are you?'

Tess looked out at the stunning sunset.

'I'm not quite sure,' she said, 'but it's very beautiful.'

'You coming back any time soon?'

'I don't know.'

'Are you all right? I mean-'

He hesitated, and Tess smiled.

'Are you happy?'

Tess thought about it as the warm wind rolled in to gently lift her hair. The sun lit up the grey and orange clouds from beneath, the dark islands just silhouettes against the shining light, and she glanced down at her half-finished painting.

It was crude and amateurish, but beyond her lack of expertise she could see the hint of what she had been hoping to achieve. With a little practise, she'd get better. And she had plenty of time for practise.

She glanced back at the foot of the mountain, where her tiny tent was a barely visible speck. She threw another log on the fire, as a seabird wheeled high above, her only companion.

Tess had discovered that *alone* and *lonely* were two totally different things, and neither of them were half as bad as they sounded.

'Yes,' she said. 'Yes I'm happy. I really am.'

*

The leaves of the Beech trees were turning yellow as Cal turned down the driveway of Lake Pastures, and through the trunks he could see a quiet game of boules being played on the lush grass. Hearing the engine, an elderly man turned from where he was resting his back against the "no ball games" sign, recognised him, and winked. Cal grinned, driving round the bend in the trees to the white building beyond.

'Are you sure about this?' Lynne said.

Cal stopped the car and turned to her. There were dark shadows under her blue eyes, and he saw a hollow beside her mouth where she was biting the inside of her cheek. He took hold of her hand and gave it a gentle squeeze.

'I'm certain,' he said, smiling. Her fingers closed round his, sending a warm flutter into his heart.

'She might hate me,' Lynne's eyes dropped, and now she was biting her lip.

Cal sighed. It was a fifty-fifty bet that his mother wouldn't even remember Lynne.

'Let's just see how it goes, hmm?' He said, 'Come on, let's go.'

The doors of the rest home were open wide to let in the warm autumn air, the strains of Glen Miller wafting out into the garden. Annie Flowers was posting something on a notice board when she noticed Cal's shadow, and she turned to him with her usual smile.

'Hello, Cal. Nice to see you.'

She smiled over at Lynne, who could only manage a stiff grimace before looking away.

'This is my friend Lynne Thorne,' Cal said, taking Lynne's hand.

Annie's eyes flickered down briefly, before her smile widened.

'I'm very pleased to meet you,' she said. 'I was beginning to despair of you, Cal.'

Cal was surprised to find his face flushing, something Annie seemed to find highly amusing.

'Come along, Maggie's out in the garden doing her sewing, I'll take you over.'

'Cal, I-' Annie walked ahead, and Lynne stalled, her mouth open, teeth gritted.

'It'll be all right,' he murmured. 'Trust me.'

She swallowed, and Cal tugged her gently forward.

The truth was, he had no idea how his mother would react. This had seemed like such a good idea a few days ago, but now? Maggie could be pretty volatile when she wanted to, and Lynne was a nervous wreck. He had only just convinced her that he was serious about rekindling their relationship. Maybe he was moving too soon.

He sighed, feeling his heart step up a pace as he caught sight of mother, sitting in a wicker chair, peering down at a circular wooden frame. The sun gleamed on the fine gold thread in her hand.

'Maggie? Cal's here,' Annie said in a cheerful voice. 'I'll leave you to it.'

Well, here we go, Cal thought, taking a deep breath and crouching before his mother.

'Hi mum, how are you doing?'

Maggie glanced up at him. 'I'm busy, young man. Go away. You've got the wrong person.'

Even though this was a regular occurrence, it still stuck a knife in Cal's heart.

Ah well, he thought, *today, it might be a boon.*

'What are you making?'

Maggie thrust her jaw out. She held the sewing at arms length and appraised it critically.

'It's not up to much.'

He looked down at the pattern of swallows swooping above a summer cornfield.

'Cross stitch takes both skill and patience,' Lynne said quietly, sitting on the step. 'I think it's very good.'

Maggie looked up, squinting in the bright sunlight and holding a hand up to shield her eyes. As she did, Cal held his breath. He had noticed the subtle change in his mother's eyes that he now knew heralded the return of her recalcitrant memory.

'You remember Lynne, don't you, mum?'

The two women locked eyes for a moment, and then Maggie turned back to her sewing.

'I remember,' she said.

Cal hesitated. 'I thought perhaps you -'

'Saw you on the telly,' Maggie interrupted, 'Talking about that man, the soldier who kidnapped the women.'

Cal took a surprised breath, and Maggie grinned.

'Think I don't follow what's happening in the outside world? Of course I do, 'specially when my son's involved.'

She tucked the needle into the cloth and dropped the frame in her lap.

'I'm so proud of you,' she said, her eyes on her sewing, her voice gruff.

Cal felt a rush of tears to the back of his eyes. He took hold of his mother's hands and squeezed them, a giant lump in his throat.

'Now off you go,' Maggie said, pulling her hands away and looking out to the garden. 'It'll be teatime soon, and it's dominoes tonight. I'm too busy to be bothered with you.'

'All right, mum,' Cal said, standing up. 'I'll be over to see you at the weekend.'

Maggie waved a pale hand at him. 'You don't have to keep coming over here. I'm sure you've got better things to do.'

She stared hard at Lynne, until the younger woman swallowed and looked away. Cal reached down and took her hand.

'We'll be back to see you on Saturday,' he said firmly, 'whether you like it or not.'

Maggie said nothing, but as they walked away he saw her lips quiver in an almost-smile.

'Well, that went pretty well,' Cal said, smiling, as they reached the car.

Lynne looked down.

'What's wrong?'

She shook her head. 'I can't believe you're doing this, giving me another chance like this.'

'Giving *us* another chance,' Cal said. He touched his fingers to her chin, making her look up at him. 'And this time, we'll be okay.'

He kissed her gently, feeling her lips curve under his. She opened her eyes and smiled.

'Do you think she really remembered me?'

Cal looked into his ex-wife's eyes, and thought about his answer.

Should he tell her yes; of course Maggie remembered her, remembered all the pain she had caused her son, or should he tell her no; Maggie had no idea, they were starting afresh, with no preconceived ideas.

Then he remembered that it was secrets and lies that had torn them apart in the first place.

'I really don't know,' he said.

'I guess we'll just have to wait and see.'

Afterword

Mike woke up to crisp, clean sheets, bare painted walls and the comforting smell of terrible army food. He relaxed his tense muscles and winced at the sudden pain. The recent memories hovered dangerously on the edge of recognition, and he shied from them, searching round the room for a diversion. The door opened suddenly, and three men came in.

One of them was holding a football, and they all had grins on their faces. Although dressed in jeans and casual shirts, they carried themselves like disciplined men. Squaddies, like him. The man with the football came up to his bed.

'Hello, Mike,' he said, smiling. 'I'm Gerry. This is Tim and Roddy.'

'Where is this? What barracks?'

Roddy smiled. He was about as wide as he was tall, with a definite five o'clock shadow creeping up his thick neck.

'This is Audley Court,' he said in a quiet voice. 'We hail from all regiments here. I was with the Blues and Royals.'

'Welsh Guards,' Tim said.

Mike tried to sit up, but Roddy pushed him back down. 'I know you're anxious to play football, but you're not quite ready for a game yet.'

Mike looked from one face to the next. The men were all around his own age, hard, fit men. And although they were smiling, their eyes were filled with dark places.

'Why am I here? Is this a prison?'

Tim shook his head, his smile gone. 'We're all here for the same reason. To get better.'

Mike felt a fist take hold of his heart. Sweat broke out on his brow as the realisation dawned. He was in a military hospital. He tried to sit up again and a shaft of pain bolted through his chest.

'Take it easy, mate,' Gerry said. 'It's all right here. It's not like the places you've been through before.'

Mike swallowed. 'How do you know what-'

'We've all been through it,' Tim interrupted. 'Useless doctors and dumb experiments. Authorities that don't give a shit. 'Pull yourself together' and 'let's talk it all through'. Bollocks. It's not like that here.'

'We're all squaddies here,' Roddy said. 'What was your regiment?'

Mike looked down. 'The Paras.'

Gerry let out a hoot. 'One more for my team,' he grinned. 'What battalion?'

Mike licked dry lips. '2 Para.'

'Well, well, and I bet you knew that old bastard Stobbo Robinson, eh? Nastiest sergeant in the whole mob. You were in the Gulf, weren't you? And Kosovo, I bet.'

The savage orange light began to dance behind Mike's eyes. He had hoped it would all be over, but it wasn't.

It would never be over.

He looked down. His hands were shaking.

'Hey, it's all right, mate. You don't need to talk about it.'

He swallowed again. 'I don't?'

Tim put a hand on his good shoulder and squeezed.

'You don't, boyo,' he said, smiling. 'Not here.'

'We all know, Roddy said. 'We all understand.'

Mike looked round the faces. The three men looked at each other, then at him, and they grinned.

'Can you smell that? Gerry said. 'It's supposed to be shepherd's pie, but it smells like it's made with fucking dog meat.'

'Nothing wrong with dog meat, in its place,' Roddy said.

Tim laughed. 'Don't think you'll escape in here,' he said. 'They'll bring you some and make you eat it. The fucking brew's terrible as well.'

Mike felt a pang of hot emotion so intense it felt like a solid lump in his chest. He clenched his fists and blinked hard.

'We'll be back later, to see if you've survived,' Gerry said. The three men turned, keeping their eyes carefully lowered to keep from embarrassing him.

Mike waited until they had gone before talking a deep breath through his nose and letting it out slowly through his mouth. He looked across at the window, where the afternoon sun was about to set over a stand of small trees. He caught sight of a reflection over to his left, and looked round.

The little unicorn sat on the bedside table. It was as bright and cheerful as summer, perfectly shaped and gleaming like a promise. It had a horn the colour of clear water running over pebbles. Mike's hands shook at the thought of touching something so fragile, of it belonging to him, being in his charge.

He dare not touch it.

But perhaps, someday, he might.

I hope I'll be forgiven for taking a few liberties with the places described in the book. Most of them are real, but some have been augmented...

Residents of Leicester will of course be aware that the Sunningdale Mall, the *Lady Jane* pub and *City of Glass* are figments of my imagination. Leicester has a perfectly good shopping centre called *the Shires*, which (as far as I know) doesn't have a dark side...

The island known as Toilichte (Gaelic for 'happy') does not exist either, but it would be nice if it did.

visit Jeanette's website at:
www.jeanettemccarthy.co.uk